Praise for *New York* ... MICHELLE SAGARA and The Chronicles of Elantra series

"No one provides an emotional payoff
like Michelle Sagara. Combine that with a
fast-paced police procedural, deadly magics, five very
different races and a wickedly dry sense of humor—
well, it doesn't get any better than this."
—Bestselling author Tanya Huff on
The Chronicles of Elantra series

"Intense, fast-paced, intriguing, compelling
and hard to put down…unforgettable."
—*In the Library Reviews* on *Cast in Shadow*

"Readers will embrace this compelling,
strong-willed heroine with her often sarcastic voice."
—*Publishers Weekly* on *Cast in Courtlight*

"The impressively detailed setting
and the book's spirited heroine are sure to
charm romance readers as well as fantasy fans
who like some mystery with their magic."
—*Publishers Weekly* on *Cast in Secret*

"Along with the exquisitely detailed worldbuilding,
Sagara's character development is mesmerizing. She
expertly breathes life into a stubborn yet evolving
heroine. A true master of her craft!"
—*RT Book Reviews* (4 ½ stars) on *Cast in Fury*

"With prose that is elegantly descriptive, Sagara
answers some longstanding questions and adds another
layer of mystery. Each visit to this amazing world, with
its richness of place and character, is one to relish."
—*RT Book Reviews* (4 ½ stars) on *Cast in Silence*.

The Chronicles of Elantra
by
Michelle Sagara

MICHELLE SAGARA

CAST IN FURY

LUNA™
www.LUNA-Books.com

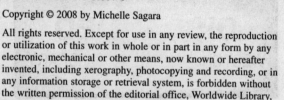

Recycling programs for this product may not exist in your area.

CAST IN FURY

ISBN-13: 978-0-373-80337-8

www.LUNA-Books.com

Printed in U.S.A.

Author's Note

One of the best things about writing a series is that you don't have to cram everything interesting into just one story. One of the worst things about writing a series is that you write about the same characters all of the time, and you run the risk of boring your readers by covering the same ground way too often. Authors live in fear of this because, obviously, if an idea can sustain a novel for hundreds of pages, *we* don't find it boring.

When I started writing about Elantra, I wanted the world to be as open as possible, with a lot of unexplored nooks and crannies. I wanted each book to be more or less self-contained (and the jury's still out on the success of that one), and I wanted room in which the characters—and their universe—could grow. *Cast in Shadow* introduced the races that live in the city itself without going into too much detail. *Cast in Courtlight* then went to the Barrani. *Cast in Secret* took a turn into the Tha'alani Quarter, but while the *story* was finished, some of the events had some unintended effects on the attitude of the rest of the city.

And because I can keep writing about Kaylin and the Hawks, I can also continue to address some of the issues that arose in *Shadow*, although I think of *Fury* as the Leontine book. I'm having a lot of fun exploring Kaylin's world as she herself learns more about it, and I hope that comes through on the page.

For Daniel, Ross, Jamie and Liam

CAST IN
FURY

CHAPTER 1

Private Kaylin Neya was on time for work and the world hadn't ended.

A few people's lives, on the other hand, were in question. The amount of sarcasm Clint could put into shocked silence wasn't illegal. Yet. But Kaylin had to grudgingly admit, as she glared her way past his lowered halberd and into the Halls of Law, the wings he extended were a nice touch.

The Aerie was almost empty, but it usually was at this time of day; the halls themselves were suspiciously quiet. Then again, maybe the Swords were actually earning their pay instead of milling around the halls looking smug. Even on her bleariest mornings, Kaylin couldn't have missed the tension and worry that seemed to permeate the city streets recently, and keeping the peace, such as it was in a crowded city, was *their* job. For a change. The day was already looking brighter. She glanced up as a shadow passed her, and saw a lone

Aerian traversing the space high above; he wasn't practicing maneuvers, and his wings were extended for a steady glide. She still envied the Aerians their wings, a little.

She felt a smidgen of sympathy for the Swords but didn't let it show. Much. It wasn't often that the entire city had almost created a new sea coast by the simple expedient of being under most of the surrounding water. She was certain that stories and rumors about the larger-than-Imperial-edict tidal wave that had almost destroyed the harbor—for a start—had already been making the rounds, and growing bigger, if that was even possible, with each telling.

She was waved through—without sarcasm—when she approached the guards that separated the Hawks' quarters from those of the Wolves or the Swords. The halls were vacant, and even the duty roster seemed to have gathered no darts.

"Oh, come on, guys," she said, when the entire office stopped as she entered and approached Marcus's desk. "I'm not *always* late. Don't you have anything better to do?"

"Have you checked the duty roster, dear?" Caitlin asked, from the safety of her desk. Not that she was ever in any danger; if the office had a collective mother, it was Caitlin.

"Oh. No." She turned and, at Marcus's bark of a command, turned back. Marcus's growl was low, and it was short. He must be tired. And a tired Leontine was generally best kept happy by little displays of obedience. Or big ones.

The paperwork on his desk hadn't really diminished

but also, to Kaylin's admittedly inexpert eye, hadn't grown; the emergency that had pulled a number of his Hawks out of their normal routine had been resolved; there was no Festival for almost another year. She couldn't quite see what would put him in a mood, but the fact that he was in one was obvious—having facial fur that bristled when you were ticked off was a dead giveaway. Having fangs that were almost as long as her fingers—the exposed parts of the fangs, at any rate— was another.

She came to stand a safe distance from the side of his desk, and waited. She even waited quietly.

Her reward? He lifted a stack of paper off his desk and dumped it in her hands. "This," he said curtly, "is your problem."

She looked down at what she had assumed were reports—or worse. The paperwork required of the office was, by all accounts, more arcane than any of the magic it also required. To punctuate this, the window very sweetly told the entire office what the hour was.

Kaylin really hated the window. There was money riding on how long it would take someone to accidentally break it, and money riding on who would have the accident. There weren't many rules that governed office bets, but one of them was that you couldn't place money on yourself. Which was fair but, in Kaylin's case, prevented her from winning much.

"Well? Are you going to stand there all day?"

Kaylin looked down at the first sheet in the stack— and it was a large stack. "No, sir."

"Good. Take note of the roster—your rounds have been changed."

"Since when? I checked it last night."

"Since then, obviously."

She caught Caitlin's frantic gestures out of the corner of her eye, and nodded. She considered going to the roster by way of Caitlin's desk, but since they were in opposite directions and Marcus could watch you while his back was turned, she decided to actually go to the roster instead.

Her shoulders did a severe downturn when she saw what had been written beside her name. Even Severn's name, at the same location, didn't bring much cheer. The Imperial Palace?

"Don't make that face," Teela said, in her left ear.

Barrani could walk in perfect silence, but it took work, and Teela was usually too damn lazy. Kaylin's little start did not, however, cause her to drop the bundle of paper. Given Marcus's mood, that was good.

"What's eating Marcus?"

Teela shrugged, long black hair rising and falling like a perfect curtain. Kaylin tried not to resent the fact that the Barrani weren't governed by any Hawk regulations when it came to anything they wore. Regulations were, after all, supposed to be practical and as far as Kaylin could tell, Barrani hair never tangled, never got caught in anything, and never got in the way.

And they were gorgeous and lived forever. If it weren't for the fact that they adored politics—preferably with blood and death—they'd be insufferable.

"He's Ironjaw," Teela said. "But he's been in that mood since late last night." Her tone of voice made it clear that it was serious enough that Kaylin should change the subject *now,* and Kaylin had known Teela for so many years it wasn't possible to misinterpret.

"Figures. Save a city, get sent to the Imperial Palace."

"It's more impressive than being sent to the docks or the Commons."

"More people to offend."

"True, and some of them are significant." Teela smiled. In all, it wasn't a happy expression. "Have you even taken a look at what you're holding?"

"I just got it, Teela."

"You might want to read it over," the Hawk replied. "Severn's waiting in the West room. And so is the Dragon."

The Dragon was generally known by the rank and file as Lord Sanabalis. One of Four Dragon Lords that comprised the Dragon contingent of the Imperial Court, he was also a member of the Imperial Order of Mages. He had graciously come out of teaching retirement to take on one pupil, that pupil being Kaylin herself. She tried to remember to be grateful, and usually succeeded when she wasn't actively staring at a candle wick in a vain attempt to get it to catch fire.

Which, come to think, was most of the time.

But she knew her lesson schedule more or less by heart now, and none of those lessons started at the beginning of her day. Given her nocturnal activities, and the desire of the Hawks not to annoy the mages, Marcus had forbidden any lesson that started before lunch. It gave her a decent chance of not missing any.

So Sanabalis wasn't here to teach her anything new about candles. She pushed the door open—it was open, so she didn't have to go through her daily ritual of teeth-grinding while waiting for the doorward to magically identify her—and saw that Severn and Sanabalis were seated across the room's only table, talking quietly.

They stopped when they saw her, and she slid between the door and its frame, dropping the stack of paper on the tabletop.

"Marcus is in a mood," she told Severn.

"It's better than yours."

"I'm not in a—" She stopped. "You mean better than mine will be?"

"Pretty much. Take a seat. Lord Sanabalis is here to inform us of our duties, and to escort us to the man we'll be aiding."

When Severn spoke Barrani, it was generally a bad sign. Lord Sanabalis, on the other hand, almost always spoke in Barrani.

"We don't have to talk to the Emperor, do we?" she said, sinking into the chair slowly. It was rock hard and weighed more than she did.

"No," Lord Sanabalis replied. "Unless something goes gravely, gravely wrong, the Emperor has more important duties to attend."

"Does this mean there's no lesson today?"

"There will be, as you say, no lesson for the course of your duties at the Palace."

"Well, that's something. Who are we investigating?" Severn hesitated.

"Investigating?" Sanabalis replied, raising a brow. "I rather think, if you were sent to investigate someone, the last place the Hawks would agree to second you would be the Imperial Palace. As you *should* know, the

Imperial Guards deal with any difficulties that arise in the Palace. And they do not arise."

"Yes, Sanabalis." She hesitated. "What are we doing there, then? We're not exactly guard material—"

One of his silver brows rose into his thinning hairline.

Fair enough; if the Imperial Guard would be offended at outside investigators, they would probably completely lose it at outside *guards*. "So we're not there as investigators, we're not there as guards. Are we there as Hawks?"

"In a manner of speaking."

She grimaced. "That usually means no."

"You are Hawks or you could not be seconded in this fashion. You are not, however, there as representatives of the Law."

The old bastard looked like he was enjoying himself. Exactly how he conveyed this, Kaylin wasn't quite certain—his expression was neutral enough, and his voice was smooth as glass.

"So what are we there as?"

"As Cultural Resources," he replied smoothly.

"As what?"

"Cultural Resources."

"I heard you. What exactly does that mean?"

"Ah. Have you taken a moment to peruse the documents you placed upon the table?"

"No."

"I'd advise you to do so. We are not expected at the Palace until after lunch. I felt, given the unpredictability of your schedule, that this was wisest."

"But—"

"Many of the questions you are no doubt impatient to ask will be answered by even the briefest of perusals."

She wondered if he were a betting man, or Dragon. But given Dragons in general, she doubted it.

"If it eases your mind, Private Neya, Sergeant Kassan *is* required to pay you for the time you spend seconded to the Palace. He also," he continued, lifting a hand to stop her from speaking, "expects you to report in each morning.

"For some reason, he is concerned about the assignment. I can't imagine why."

"Act One, Scene One." Kaylin looked at Severn. *"Act One, Scene One?"*

"It's a play," Severn said, shrugging slightly. The left corner of his mouth was turned up in something that hinted at amusement. "You're familiar with plays?"

Kaylin snorted. She read the description of stage materials—mostly the painted facades of buildings and bushes, in different sizes. And, she thought, in odd colors. "Poynter's road?"

Severn nodded. "It's—"

"I know where it is—but the buildings don't look anything *like* that on Poynter's."

"Kaylin—"

"No, Corporal Handred, allow her to speak freely. It will, in theory, get it out of her system."

"You want me to read a play?"

"Not exactly. The play itself is not complete, or not complete to our satisfaction. The author's name might be familiar to you." He raised one brow.

"Richard Rennick." She looked at Severn. "Should we know him?"

"He's the Imperial Playwright," Severn told her quietly. "The position is held by one Playwright every five years. There's usually a competition of some sort—a series of different plays staged for the Emperor. He apparently won, three years ago."

Lord Sanabalis said, "The Emperor feels that human arts should be encouraged. Don't look at me like that, Kaylin. Dragons seldom have an interest in drama."

"Who's the judge of this contest?"

"The Emperor."

"So the winner is the person who appeals most to someone who doesn't even like plays?"

"Something very like that," he replied.

"And you want us to…work with this Rennick?"

"Yes."

"Why?"

"Perhaps you should read more than three pages."

She grimaced. "Sanabalis—"

"Lord Sanabalis," Severn corrected her.

"Lord Sanabalis, then. What on earth do I know about plays?"

"Clearly nothing." He frowned. "However, it is not for your expertise in the dramatic arts that you have been seconded."

"Go on."

"It is for your expertise—such as it is—on the Tha'alani."

It was Kaylin's turn to frown, but some of the exasperation left her then. "I'm not an expert," she told him quietly.

"No. But the Tha'alani seconded to the Court would possibly be even less comfortable in an advisory role."

"If they can't—" She stopped. "Why has the Emperor commissioned a play about the Tha'alani?"

Lord Sanabalis didn't answer. But she met his eyes; they were their usual placid gold. His lower membranes, however, were up.

"It's because of—of the water, isn't it?"

"The tidal wave."

"That one."

"Yes. I am not aware of how much you saw, or how much you read about after the fact—but the Tha'alani, led by their castelord, left their Quarter in larger numbers than the city has ever seen. They walked to the docks, and they spread out along the port and the seawall. When the waters began to shift—and it was dramatic, Kaylin, even to one who has seen as much as I have—"

"You weren't there," she told him, but the words were soft. "You were with us."

"I accessed records when I returned to the Palace." He was now using his teacher tone of voice.

And I didn't, Kaylin supplied. She glanced at Severn, who nodded very slightly. She cleared her throat. It was still hard for her to think about the Tha'alaan, and the Tha'alani *were* the Tha'alaan in some ways. "They hoped to save the city, if the waters rose."

"Yes. But I invite you to think about appearances, Kaylin."

"The wave didn't hit the city."

"No. It did not. The Oracles, however, were not widely bandied about. For many people—for almost all of them—the first warning of danger was the sight of the water itself, rising. The storm before it signified nothing, to them—it was merely weather."

She nodded slowly.

"From their point of view—from what they could *see*—the Tha'alani went to the waters, and the waters rose."

She closed her eyes.

"You understand our difficulty."

She did.

"You yourself feared the Tha'alani. You do not do so now," he added. "But you must understand the fear that people have."

She nodded quietly.

"The Emperor understands it as well. He cannot, of course, explain the whole of what happened—and given the sparsity of reports generated by your office in the wake of events, I am not entirely certain he could explain it even if that was his desire. I am not, however, here to lecture you on the quality of your paperwork. I believe it best that some things remain uncommitted to paper.

"I, however, was fully debriefed. What I know, he now knows. He will not expose The Keeper, and no mention of the young Tha'alani man will leave the Court for that reason. Nor will the young Tha'alani man face the Emperor's Justice, for that reason."

The fact that the Emperor couldn't reach him probably had something to do with it, in Kaylin's opinion. She managed to keep this to herself. Instead, she returned to the matter at hand. "So this Richard Rennick wrote a…play. About the Tha'alani."

"He wrote a play about the Tha'alani's attempt to save the city, yes."

"But all of it's garbage. Because we're not allowed to tell the truth."

"*Garbage* is an unfortunate choice of word. Lose it," he added, condescending to speak Elantran. He must have been serious. There were whole days where he affected complete ignorance of the language which most of the city actually spoke.

She picked up the sheaf of dog-eared pages. "Have you even read this?"

"I have. It is not, I believe, the current version, if that's of any consequence."

"What do you mean?"

"Where we could prevail upon the Tha'alani at Court, we did. The effect that this had upon the playwright was…unfortunate."

"What happened?"

"Ybelline and her companions were given a copy of the play. They read it with some concern."

"I bet."

"They returned the play to Mr. Rennick. Luckily Lord Tiamaris was at hand; he intercepted their corrections."

"This would be lucky because?"

"They understand the Emperor's concerns. Believe that they feel them even more strongly than the Emperor does. They are not…however…" His hesitation spoke volumes.

Kaylin almost winced. When the silence became awkward, she sighed and looked at Severn.

Severn nodded.

"They don't *know* how to lie," she said quietly. "And this...all of it...it must seem like one big lie to them."

She'd managed to nudge Sanabalis's brows toward his receding hairline, which had to count for something. On the other hand, the fact that his surprise was more due to her comprehension than their inability probably counted for something too.

"If the truth is supposed to ease people's fear, Ybelline could learn to live with that. But in her world, lies don't ease fear. So I imagine what she handed back to Rennick—or what she tried to hand him—was pretty much all of the truth she thought it safe to put out there."

"Indeed."

"And the Emperor's version of safe to put out there isn't the same."

"Again, astute. We may yet make progress in your life as a student."

"I think it would be easier than this. What did Rennick say?"

Sanabalis did wince, at that. "I think it best to ignore that. Suffice it to say that he did not feel his efforts to be adequately appreciated. Ybelline, however, did understand the difficulty, and if you must find a person to blame for your current assignment—"

"I won't blame her."

"—she suggested you. And Corporal Handred. She said she was confident that you would work in the interests of her people, but with a better understanding of the intended audience for the play itself."

"Meaning my people."

Sanabalis nodded. "Which reminds me of another matter Ybelline also mentioned. The Swords have stationed a small force adjacent to the Tha'alani Quarter," he added, in a more subdued tone. "And before you ask, Kaylin, yes, it was entirely necessary.

"Ybelline has asked for your aid in the Quarter."

"For *my* aid? What the hell happened?"

"However," he added, lifting a hand in the universal *I'm not finished, so shut up* gesture, "you are to visit the Quarter *after* you report for duty."

On the off chance that Kaylin decided to reverse the order, Sanabalis chose to accompany her to the Palace. This wasn't the first time he'd done this, and to be fair, if he'd gone ahead, she would have gone to the Imperial Palace by whichever convoluted route took her to the Tha'alani Quarter *first.* But as she had to stop by the Quartermaster to get kitted out in appropriate dress uniform—and as the Quartermaster was still a touch angry, which wasn't exactly the right word for his state (the right words couldn't be used in polite company of any race, all of the Hawks being multilingual when it came to swearing)—she actually appreciated Sanabalis's suspicion, because if the Quartermaster was willing to make her wait or suffer, he was not willing to piss off a Dragon Lord.

He was, however, unfailingly polite and friendly when talking to Severn. Severn did not lose expensive dresses.

She took the uniform from Severn's hands and headed to the lockers, where she added a much cleaner—and longer—surcoat to the clothing she generally wore. If she were a Sword, she'd also get a thin chain hauberk that was shiny and clean, because those looked good;

Hawks didn't generally have them as part of their uniform, dress or no, although most of the human Hawks did own one.

She had managed to lose her daggers—where lose in this case meant that something magical had transformed them into part of a very elaborate yet somehow very skimpy dress—and had bought a single replacement. The other dagger was coming out of her pay.

But it wasn't coming out of her hide, for which she should probably be grateful.

Severn straightened her surcoat. It had the usual embroidered Hawk, dead center, but the golden thread and the beading was so perfectly clean it almost hurt to look at the flight feathers. To this, Kaylin added a small, beadwork patch.

"I don't think it's necessary," Severn told her. But he didn't tell her to take it off, probably because he knew she wouldn't. The beads survived anything. Which was more, she thought glumly, than could be said about the rest of the clothing she owned.

She took the time to clean her boots.

Severn caught her arm and said, "There's nothing to be nervous about."

She winced. "That obvious?"

"You don't generally care about your boots, no."

"I just—Marcus *hates* it when I go to the Palace. I swear he sits by his damn mirror waiting to hear that I've been thrown in the dungeons or eaten or something."

They started to walk down the hall, and Sanabalis took the lead.

"You aren't reporting directly to the Emperor,"

Severn replied. "So it's unlikely that anyone you offend will have you eaten."

"You're sure?"

"Unless the Emperor's decided that you really are a threat to his Empire, in which case he could dispense with the petty part of you actually annoying some high-ranking official, and go straight to the eating. He's an Emperor. He doesn't have to worry about the niceties of the Law."

She squared her shoulders. Smiled at Severn. "I know I'm going to have to learn how to do this—how to talk with people who've never even approached the banks of the Ablayne. But I'm not good at lying. I'm not good at talking."

"You talk all the time," he said, with just the hint of a smile. He was already moving out of the way before she hit him.

"I talk to people who know more or less what I know, and who don't bloody care if I say things nicely or not. I hate the idea that my career is riding on my ability to be someone else's idea of polite."

"I would dislike it as well," Sanabalis said, with a hint of the same smile Severn had offered. "But if it's of comfort, Kaylin, you will not feel this way in twenty years."

She bit her tongue. Hard.

And he nodded in approval.

This was going to be a long assignment.

On the way to the Palace, she read as much of the play as she could. She'd seen some street theater in her time, but her entire familiarity with plays put on for an audience involved a lot of loud children and the Foundling Halls' small stage. Marrin, the Leontine who guarded and raised the orphans in said Hall, had put aside one of the large rooms in the former manor for just that purpose. For most of the year it stood empty, but during Festival season, and at odd intervals throughout the year, the cloths were dragged off the various bits and pieces of furniture—and the paintings and candelabras—and the room was opened to the visiting actors.

Kaylin had been there for almost all of the plays that occurred at any time other than Festival; Marrin often called her in to help supervise. She didn't always *get* the play—and some of the stories, which were clearly meant to be familiar to small children before they watched the play, were a mystery to her—but the men and women in their funny hats and wigs and makeup were universally friendly and warm. The kids loved plays; they would watch in near silence—near being as much as anyone sane could hope for—and laugh or scream at all the right lines.

Kaylin seriously hoped that this play wasn't meant for those children, because they would have been bored *to tears.* And bored children were a special hell of their own.

As near as she could tell, Mr. Rennick had decided that a budding romance between two Tha'alani teens was a good idea—for reasons that made no sense to Kaylin. Having seen evidence of the Tha'alani concept of romance, Kaylin had no doubt at all that this would be first on the list of things that Ybelline had attempted to correct. Second on that list would be the disapproving parents. Third on that list would be the couple attempting to sneak off somewhere together so they could be alone.

She stopped herself from dumping the play out the window, and only partly because the Swords on the streets were in a bad enough mood they might stop even an Imperial Carriage and attempt to hand someone a ticket for littering.

"Does this *ever* get to the point?"

"Hmm?"

"I mean, does he even get to the docks and the damn tidal wave?"

"Well, yes—but the love story is meant to convey to the audience that the Tha'alani are as human as we are. And misunderstood love occurs in all species."

"It does?"

"Well, in Mr. Rennick's mind, yes. But I would say that he is not entirely wrong."

"Oh. What does a Dragon romance look like?" she asked.

Sanabalis snorted. Kaylin swore she saw a small plume of fire erupt just above his beard. Which seemed to constitute his answer on that front, and Kaylin couldn't offhand recall mention of a female Dragon at court. She was certain they must exist somewhere.

She wondered, briefly, what a Barrani romance looked like, and decided she probably wouldn't be able to tell the difference between that and one of their assassination attempts. Instead, she said, "Look, the Tha'alani *are* like the rest of us. Sort of. But this whole romance— it's just wrong. I think Ybelline would find the…the possessiveness, the sense of—"

"Ownership?"

"Don't mock me, Sanabalis. What I'm trying to say is that they don't experience love that way."

"Which is not, in fact, what you did say."

"Fine. The point is, they don't. They don't have the disapproving parents thing, and they definitely don't sneak off for privacy."

"Ah. Well, then, how would you structure a play in which it was utterly essential that the audience empathize with the Tha'alani?"

"Honestly?"

"Honestly."

"I'd write about the years in which they were tortured like criminals because they wouldn't serve the Emperor by reading *other people's minds for him.* Because they couldn't, without going insane, and driving everyone they knew and loved insane in the process."

Sanabalis's eyes shaded to orange. In Dragon eyes, this meant irritation. Red was anger, and in general, if you saw red Dragon eyes, it was probably the *last* thing you would ever see.

"Kaylin," Severn said.

"It would work," she told him, an edge to the words. "People could sympathize with that."

"I believe it would cast the Emperor in an unflattering light."

She said nothing. Loudly. But it didn't last. "I'm sorry, Sanabalis."

"Generally one apologizes for behavior one means to curb," he replied stiffly. But his eyes shaded back to burnished gold.

"It worked for me," she told him quietly. "Knowing that—knowing what they suffered—it changed the way

I felt about them. Look—I understand why people are afraid of the Tha'alani. I know why *I* was. It never occurred to me that they wanted to be left alone. That they never ever wanted to read *our* minds. And the experiments conducted on the Tha'alani—it changed the way I felt about them. Forever."

He nodded. "You understand, however, why that information could not be part of a public entertainment."

She nodded slowly. "It's just that it would work, that's all." She looked at Severn. "Did you *ever* fear them?"

"Yes. But my understanding of the Tha'alani was different."

She had the grace to say, "You *wanted* to understand them."

"Yes."

"I wanted to hide from them."

He nodded again. "It's natural. Kaylin, I'm five years older than you are. Five years ago—"

"It's not your age," she said, swatting the words away. Willing to be this truthful. "It's *you.*"

"Perhaps. But I have often found understanding my enemies gives me an edge when confronting them." He paused and then added, "The first Tha'alani I met was Ybelline herself."

"You met her *first?*"

"I was under consideration for the Shadows," he told her. "Ybelline could read everything of note, and still remain detached. There are very few others who could. She was summoned. And it is very, very hard to fear Ybelline."

Kaylin smiled at this. It was a small smile, but it acknowledged the truth: it was hard to fear her. Even though she could ferret all truth, all secrets, from a human mind. Because in spite of it, one had the sense that Ybelline could know everything and like you *anyway.*

Maybe that was something they could work with.

CHAPTER 2

Kaylin's first impression of Richard Rennick could be summed up in two words: Oh, god.

She wasn't fussy about *which* god, either. She was pretty sure she couldn't name half of the ones that figured in official religions, and of the half she could name, the spelling or accents would be off. One of the things that living in the fiefs taught you was that it didn't particularly matter which god you prayed to—none of them listened, anyway.

Rennick looked like an Arcanist might look if he had been kept from sleep for a week, and kept from the other amenities that came with sleep—like, say, shaving utensils—for at least as long, if not longer. His hair made her hair look tidy. It wasn't long, but it couldn't be called short either, and it seemed to fray every which way the light caught it. He didn't have a beard, and he didn't have much of a chin, either. It was buried beneath what might, in a few long weeks, be a beard—but messier.

His clothing, on the other hand, was very expensive and had it been on any other person, would have gone past the border of ostentatious; on him it looked lived in. She thought he might be forty. Or thirty. It was hard to tell.

What wasn't hard to tell: he was having a bad day. And he wasn't averse to sharing.

He didn't have manners, either. When Sanabalis entered the room, he looked up from his desk—well, from the very, very long dining table at which he was seated—and grunted in annoyance.

The table itself was what one would expect in the Palace—it was dark, large, obviously well oiled. But the surface was covered in bits and pieces of paper, some of it crumpled in balls that had obviously been thrown some distance. Not all of those were on the table; the carpets had their fair share too.

"Mr. Rennick," Lord Sanabalis said, bowing. "Forgive me for intruding."

Another grunt. Sanabalis didn't even blink an eye.

"I would like to introduce you to Corporal Handred and Private Neya. These are the people Ybelline Rabon'alani spoke of when we last discussed the importance of your work."

He looked up at that, and managed to lose some slouch. "I hope you last longer than my previous assistants."

"You had other assistants for this?"

"Oh, not for this project. In general, the office of Official Imperial Playwright comes with assistants." The sneer that he put in the words managed to remain off his face. Barely. "They won't, however, allow me to hire my *own* assistants, and the ones they've sent me must have been dredged from the bottom of the filing pool."

Kaylin gave Sanabalis what she hoped was a smile. She moved her lips in the right direction.

"We don't intend to interfere in any way," she began.

"Oh, *please.* Take a number and stand in line. If you somehow—by some small miracle—manage not to interfere, you'll be the only people in this godsforsaken Palace who haven't tried to *tell me how to do my job.*"

Sanabalis offered Kaylin a smile that was at least as genuine as hers had been.

On the other hand, if the Emperor hadn't eaten Rennick, things obviously weren't as formal as all that, and Kaylin felt a surprisingly strong relief; she was almost happy to have met him. Or would have been, if it were all in the past.

"This is *not* like filing," he added, clearly warming up. He even vacated his seat and shoved his hands into pockets that lined the seams of his robes. "This is not an exact bloody science. Do you have any *idea* what they've asked of me?"

She had a fairly good idea, but said, "No."

Something in her tone caused his eyes to narrow and Severn's foot to stray slightly closer to hers. But she offered what she hoped was a sympathetic grimace; it was all she was up for.

"No, you probably don't. But I'll tell you."

Of this, no one could be in any doubt.

"They want me to write a play that makes the Tha'alani *human.*"

There was certainly a sneer in his expression now, and Kaylin had to actively work to keep her hands from becoming fists. *You've said worse,* she told herself. *You've said a lot worse.*

Yes, she added, *but he's never going to go through what you did to change your bloody mind.* Because she was used to arguing with herself, she then thought, *And we're going to have to do what experience won't. Oh, god.*

"I am willing to face a challenge," he added. "Even one as difficult as this—but the Tha'alani themselves don't seem to understand the purpose of the play I did write. They said it wasn't *true.* I told them I wanted a bigger truth. It wasn't *real,* but truth isn't always arrived at by the *real.*"

"I can see how that would confuse them," she offered.

"And now they've sent *you.* Have you ever even seen one of my plays?"

"I haven't seen a play that wasn't written for children," she replied.

This didn't seem to surprise him. He seemed to expect it.

Severn, however, said, "I have."

"Oh, really?" A voice shouldn't have legally been able to contain that much sarcasm. And, Kaylin thought, a person shouldn't be subject to as much sarcasm as this twice in a single day. "Which one?"

"Winter," Severn replied.

Rennick opened his mouth, but for the moment, he seemed to have run out of words. His eyes widened, his jaw closed, and his lips turned up in a genuine smile. Thirty, Kaylin thought. Or maybe even younger. "That was my second play—I wrote it before I won the seat."

He paused, and then his eyes narrowed. "Where did you see it?"

"It was staged in the Forum," Severn replied, without missing a beat. "Constance Dargo directed it. I believe the actress who played the role of Lament was—"

"Trudy."

"Gertrude Ellen."

"That would be Trudy." His eyes, however, had lost some of their suspicion. "She could be *such* a bitch. But she made a number of good points about some of the dialogue."

"The dialogue was changed?"

"Good god, yes. Dialogue on the page is always stiffer than spoken dialogue—you can't get a real sense of what it sounds like until actors put it through its paces. The first staging of any play defines the play. What did you think of it?"

"I thought it very interesting, especially given where it played, and when. It was also unusual in that it didn't feature a relationship as its central motivation."

"Starving people seldom have the time to worry about social niceties."

Severn glanced at Kaylin.

"But you might be the *first* person sent me who's actually familiar with my work," Rennick said, picking up the reins where he had dropped them.

"And as one such person, I have no intention of guiding your work. You know it. I don't."

"And let me tell you—you don't... Oh."

"But the Emperor's dictates are clear," Severn continued, into the very welcome silence. "*Winter* was a work that reached out to people who had everything and reminded them, for a moment, of the fate of the rest of the city. You were chosen to write this for a reason."

"I was chosen because they don't have to pay me *more*."

At that, Kaylin did chuckle. Rennick actually looked in her direction, but the hostility had ebbed. Slightly. As far as Rennick seemed to be concerned, Dragons didn't exist, and he didn't bother to glance at Sanabalis.

Kaylin did. The Dragon's eyes were a placid gold. Clearly, he had met Rennick before, and for some reason, he had decided not to kill him then.

"Look," Rennick added, running his hands through his hair as if he would like to pull it all out by its roots, "*Winter* wasn't *meant* to be a message. It wasn't meant to tell the audience anything about the state of the poor or the starving. I loved Lament—I wanted to tell her story in a way that would move people. Talia Korvick was the first Lament—I'll grant that Trudy did a better job, but Trudy wouldn't touch my unknown little play for its first staging."

The idea that Rennick cared about moving anyone in a way that didn't mean *out of my sight* surprised Kaylin. Almost as much as the fact that he would admit it.

"You achieved that—but you also made people think about what her life entailed, and how her life might have been different."

"Yes—but that was *incidental*. I don't know how to make people *think* differently. And the Emperor appears to want me to…to educate people. With characters that are in no way my own creations. It's dishonest," he added.

Given that he told lies for a living, this struck Kaylin as funny. Sanabalis, however, stepped on her foot.

"Lament wasn't a real person but you made her real. The Tha'alani are real in the same way that the rest of us are—and Lament was human." Severn frowned slightly, his thinking expression. "Have you been out in the streets since the storm?"

Rennick frowned. "Not far, no."

"People are afraid. Frightened people are often ugly people. The Tha'alani—"

"From all reports, they tried to kill us."

Kaylin didn't care at that moment if Sanabalis stepped on her foot and broke it. "By standing *in* the way of the tidal wave? They would have been the first people hit by the damn thing!"

Rennick actually looked at her, possibly for the first time. After a moment, he said, "There is that."

"Look, I don't know what you've heard, and I don't bloody care—they tried to *save* the city. And if this is what they get for trying to save it, they should have just let it drown."

"And you know this how?"

"I was there—" She shut her mouth. Loudly. "I'm the cultural expert," she told him instead.

"You were there?"

"She was not," Sanabalis said, speaking in his deep rumble. "But she is a friend of the Tha'alani, and as much as anyone who was not born Tha'alani can, she now understands them. Mr. Rennick, I am aware that you find the current assignment somewhat stressful—"

"The Imperial Playwright writes *his own* work," Rennick snapped. "This is—this is political propaganda."

"But what you write, and what you stage—provided any of the directors available meet your rather strict criteria—will influence the city for decades to come. It is *necessary* work, even if you find it distasteful."

"In other words," Kaylin added sweetly, "the Emperor doesn't care what you think."

Severn glanced at Kaylin, and his expression cleared. Whatever he had been balancing in the back of his mind had settled into a decision. "With your leave, Lord Sanabalis, we have duties elsewhere."

"What?" Rennick glared at Severn. "You definitely haven't outlasted the previous assistants."

"Our presence has been requested by the castelord of the Tha'alani," he continued, ignoring Rennick—which might, to Kaylin's mind, be the best policy. "And if you think it would be of help to you, you may accompany us."

Hard to believe that only a few weeks ago, Kaylin would have skirted this Quarter of the town as if it had the plague. Fear made things big; her mental map of the Tha'alani district had been a huge, gray shadow that would, luck willing, remain completely in the dark.

Now, it seemed small. It had one large gate, and way too few guards—usually one—between it and the rest of the city. The only people who left the Quarter for much of anything were the Tha'alani seconded to the Imperial Service—and like many, many people in Elantra, they hated their jobs. Of course they *did* their jobs to prevent the Emperor from turning their race into small piles of ash, but they didn't make this a big public complaint.

And they still liked the Hawks. Kaylin privately

thought that was crazy—in their situation, she wouldn't have.

Lord Sanabalis had arranged for a carriage, but he had not chosen to accompany them to the Quarter. This was probably for the best, as a Dragon wandering the streets could make anyone who noticed him nervous. On the other hand, people were *already* nervous, and if they wanted to take it out on something, Kaylin privately had a preference for something that could fight back, although she conceded that this was a fief definition of the word "fight."

Rennick was silent for the most part, which came as a bit of a shock. He stuck his head out the window once or twice when something caught his eye, and he frequently stuck his arm out as if writing on air, but Severn said nothing; clearly Rennick was not of a station where babysitting was considered part of their duties.

But he pulled both arm and head into the carriage when they at last began the drive up Poynter's road, because even Rennick could tell that the bodies on this particular street were on the wrong side of "tense." They were like little murders waiting to happen.

"Don't they have anything better to do?" she muttered to Severn.

He said nothing.

It was Rennick who said, "Probably not. They don't want the Tha'alani to leave the Quarter, and they're making sure that they don't. Hey! That man has a crossbow!"

Kaylin had seen it. The fact that it was still in his hands implied that the Swords had far more work than they should have, and it troubled her. But not enough that she wanted to stop the carriage, get down and start a fight.

Because it would be a fight, and it would probably get messy.

"They're frightened," she said, surprising herself.

"Funny how frightened people can be damn scary," Rennick replied. But he looked thoughtful, not worried.

"How many?" Kaylin asked Severn.

"A hundred and fifty, maybe. Some of them are in the upper windows along the street. I imagine that the Tha'alani who serve the Emperor are being heavily escorted."

"Or given a vacation."

He nodded.

"Has there been any official word about the incident?" Rennick asked quietly.

Kaylin shrugged.

"You *don't know?*"

"Right up until one of those idiots fires his crossbow or swings his—is that a pickax?" Severn nodded. "Swings his ax," she continued, "it's not Hawk business. It's Sword, and the Swords are here."

And they were. Kaylin had thought they'd send twenty men out; she was wrong by almost an order of magnitude. She thought there were maybe two hundred in total—no wonder the Halls of Law were so damn quiet.

But while they lined the street, they hadn't built an official barricade, they *did* meet the carriage in the road, well away from the gatehouse, and they *did* tell the driver to step down. They also opened the doors, and Kaylin made sure she tumbled out first.

"Private Neya?" said the man who had delivered the curt instructions. He was older than Kaylin by about fifteen years, and the day seemed to have added about a hundred new wrinkles, and a layer of gray to his skin, but she recognized him. "Max— Uh, Sergeant," she added, as he looked pointedly over her shoulder. "Sergeant Voone. You're out here?"

Max wasn't retired, exactly, but he spent a lot of his time behind a desk. He appeared to like it a great deal more than Marcus—but a corpse would have given that impression as well. And Max looked *tired*.

"Most of us are, as you put it, out here. I know why we're here—what are you doing in a fancy box?"

"Oh. Uh, we were sent here."

"By?"

"Lord Sanabalis."

He whistled. "To do what?"

"Not to step all over your toes, relax."

His chuckle was entirely mirthless. "We'll relax when these people remember they have jobs and family."

"I'm thinking they remember the family part," Kaylin replied. "People go crazy when they think they're protecting their own."

"Tell me about it. No, strike that. Don't."

"When did it get this bad?"

"There was an incident two days ago."

"Incident?"

"It was messy," he replied, his voice entirely neutral. "The Swordlord made it clear that there will be no more incidents. The Emperor was not impressed."

She winced. It wasn't often that she felt sympathy for the Swords. But while she resented the easy life the

Swords generally called work, she liked them better than the people with the crossbows down the street.

"You know they're armed?" she asked casually.

"We are *well aware* that they're armed. And no, thank you, we don't require help in disarming them. They're waiting for an invitation. Let them wait. At that distance."

She looked at Severn as Severn exited the carriage. Rennick tumbled out after him. "Sergeant Voone," Severn said, before the sergeant could speak, "Richard Rennick. He's the Imperial Playwright."

"This is not a good time for sightseeing," the Sword said to Rennick.

Rennick looked him up and down, and then shrugged. "It wasn't my idea." But he was subdued, now. He lifted a hand to his face, rubbing the scruff on his chin.

"You can call the Hawks out," Kaylin continued. "At least the Aerians—"

"We've got Aerians here. They're not currently in the air," he added. And then he gave her an odd look. "The Hawks have their own difficulties to worry about. I was sorry to hear the news."

"What news?"

His whole expression shuttered, not that it was ever all that open.

"Voone, what news? What's happened?"

"You came from the Halls?"

"The Halls don't usually have access to Imperial Carriages. What happened?"

"No one died," he replied, and his tone of voice added *yet*. "But you might want to check in at the office before you head home."

She wanted to push him for more, but Severn shook his head slightly. "Ybelline."

There was no Tha'alani guard at the guardhouse. That position was taken up by a dozen Swords. They wore chain, and they carried unsheathed swords. You'd have to be crazy to rush the gatehouse.

Kaylin approached it quietly and answered the questions the Swords asked; they were all perfunctory. Voone escorted them to the squad and left them there, after mentioning her name loudly enough to wake the dead. She noted all of this and tried to squelch her own fear. Severn was right, of course. They'd come here for Ybelline. But the sympathies of Voone made her nervous.

The Swords hadn't entered the Quarter; they were met by Tha'alani guards. Four men in armor. Their stalks swiveled toward her as she entered.

She saw that they, too, bore unsheathed swords, and it made her…angry. Those weapons just looked *wrong* in Tha'alani hands; she wondered if they even knew how to use them.

But using them wasn't an issue. They bowed to her, almost as one man. "Ybelline is waiting for you," one told her quietly.

"At her house?"

"Not at her domicile. Demett will take you to her." The man so identified stepped away from his companions.

"Where is she?"

"At the longhouse" was his reply—spoken in the stiff and exact cadence that Tha'alani who were unused to speech used. He obviously expected her to know what the longhouse was, and she didn't bother to correct him.

She followed him, and it took her a moment to realize why the streets here felt so *wrong*—they were empty. Usually walking down a Tha'alani street was like walking in the Foundling Hall—it was a gauntlet of little attention-seeking children, with their open curiosity and their utter lack of decorum.

She didn't care for the change. Hell, even the plants were drooping. Rennick walked between Severn and her, and made certain that there was always at least one body between him and the nearest Tha'alani. He wasn't overly obvious about it, but it rankled. Even when Kaylin had been terrified of the Tha'alani, she wouldn't have tried to hide. One, it wouldn't have done much good and two—well, two, she didn't casually throw strangers to fates she herself feared.

It was not going to be easy working with Rennick. She spared him a glance every so often, which was more than any of the Tha'alani did. They hadn't even questioned his presence. It would have been convenient if they had. He'd be on the other side of the gates, where he'd be marginally less annoying.

The guards walked past the latticework of open—and utterly empty—fountains; past the blush of bright pink, deep red and shocking blue flower beds that bordered them; past the neat little circular domes that reminded Kaylin of nothing so much as hills. And if those homes were hills, they were approaching a small fortress that nestled among them. It was two stories tall, and the beams that supported the clay face were almost as wide as she was, and certainly taller. It was larger by far than the building in which Ybelline, the castelord—a word that didn't suit her at all—chose to live. It was almost imposing.

It was also bloody crowded.

It boasted normal doors—rectangular doors, not the strange ones that adorned most of the Tha'alani homes; these doors weren't meant to blend with the structure. They stood out. And they were pulled wide and pegged open. Which, given the number of people on the other side of them, made sense—closed doors would have made breathing anything but stale air and sweat almost impossible. As it was, it was dicey.

"This is the longhouse," Kaylin said.

Demett nodded.

"Demett," she said, as he turned, "what is the long-house used for?"

His face went that shade of expressionless that actually meant he was talking—but only to the Tha'alaan: to the minds of his people, and the memories of the dead. She waited for it to pass, as if it were a cloud; it took a while.

"Wait for Ybelline," he told her quietly.

Ybelline came through the crowd slowly. You could see where she might be moving because her movement caused the other Tha'alani to move, like a human wave composed entirely of bodies. The building was packed. Kaylin thought there might be six or seven hundred people just beyond the open doors, more if the children so absent from the streets were also there.

But Ybelline did not come alone; the movement of the crowd, the slow outward push, wouldn't have been necessary to allow just one person through. The people spilled out into the streets, beyond Kaylin and Severn. Rennick's shoulders curled in, and he brought his hands up once or twice, as if to fend off any contact.

The Tha'alani in turn avoided him.

They would. They knew fear when they saw it, especially Rennick's fear—and his fear was poison to them. They tried just as hard as he did to avoid any contact, but Kaylin had to admit they were more polite about it.

Ybelline appeared at last, between the shoulders of about sixteen tightly grouped men and women. She wore robes, an earth-brown with green edges; her hair was arranged both artlessly and perfectly above her slender neck. Her eyes were the honey-brown of that hair, but they were ringed with gray circles. She looked exhausted.

Exhaustion did not stop her from opening her arms, stepping forward and hugging Kaylin. And nothing in the world would have stopped Kaylin from returning that hug. Nothing.

"Tell me," she whispered, her lips beside Ybelline's ear. She knew she should have introduced Rennick, but it had been Severn's idea to drag him here, and he was therefore, for the moment, Severn's problem.

The slender stalks, which were the most obvious racial trait of all the Tha'alani, brushed strands of Kaylin's hair from her forehead, and then settled gently against skin. They were so delicate, the touch so light, they could hardly be felt at all.

But Ybelline could be—and more, she could be clearly heard. Could clearly *hear*. With this much contact, she could, if she wanted to, peruse every memory

Kaylin had, including ones she wasn't aware of herself. All the hidden things could be revealed, every bad or stupid or humiliating thing Kaylin had ever done.

And Kaylin, knowing this, didn't care.

But she wasn't prepared for Ybelline's voice when it came. It was raw and, at first, there were no words—just the sense of things that might have become words with enough distance and effort. With too much distance and effort.

But she saw what Ybelline meant her to see in the brief glimpse of steel and blood and the bodies of the fallen, all interposed, all flashing over and over again in quick succession in front of Kaylin's eyes. Except that her eyes were closed.

Help me. Just that, two words.

Kaylin rolled up her sleeves and, without even looking at her wrist, pressed the gems on the bracer in the sequence that would open it: white, blue, white, blue, red, red, red. She dropped it on the ground as if it were garbage—but she could. If she'd tossed it on a garbage heap, it would find its way back to her. She'd only tried that once. Maybe twice.

This was magic's cage. And without it, she was free to do whatever she could. For this reason it was technically against orders to remove it.

Her hands were tingling. "Ybelline," she said, and then, *Ybelline.*

Ybelline, you have to let go of me.

The Tha'alani castelord did as Kaylin bid; she let go, withdrew her arms, her stalks. With them went the wild taste of fear—Ybelline's fear. She kept it from the Tha'alaan, and therefore from her people, but she was *exhausted.* And Kaylin understood the exhaustion; it was hard for any Tha'alani to live alone, on the inside of their thoughts, the way humans did.

The way humans *needed* to.

The Tha'alani who had followed Ybelline out of the longhouse had come bearing stretchers. Four stretchers. Four men. They might once have worn armor—had, Kaylin thought, remembering the brief flash of images that had emerged from her contact with Ybelline.

But they weren't dead. They weren't dead yet.

"Put them down," Kaylin said, easing her voice into the command that came naturally when she was on the beat. There were no children here; she had time to notice their absence, to be grateful for it. No more.

The crowd stepped back. The bodies lay on stretchers. Someone had dressed wounds, had cleaned burns—burns!—had done what they could to preserve life. Freed of the constraints that the ancient bracer placed on her magic, Kaylin knelt between two of these stretchers and touched two foreheads with her right and left palms. She was gentle, although she didn't have to be—the men here were in no danger of regaining consciousness anytime soon. They had that gray-white pallor that spoke of loss of blood. She was surprised that they hadn't succumbed to the wounds they had taken. Many of those wounds weren't clean cuts; they had been caused by people who weren't used to handling weapons.

Kaylin grimaced. "Severn?"

She saw his shadow. Knew he was listening.

"Get water," she told him. "I'll need it."

"There are four men—"

"I can *do* this. Just—water. Food."

His shadow was still for a moment, but he was silent. Everything they said or did now—every single thing—would be watched by *all* of the Tha'alani, no matter where they were, no matter how young or how old, how strong or how weak. All of the Tha'alani who watched would see, and what they saw would become part of the Tha'alaan, the living memory of the entire race; Tha'alani children four hundred years from now could search the Tha'alaan and see the events of this day through the eyes of these witnesses.

And for once in her life, Kaylin was determined to make a good impression.

Severn knew; he wasn't an idiot. He knew that humans—her kind, and his—had done this damage. He knew how important it was to the city that humans be seen to *undo* it. She didn't even hear him go.

It was hard.

It was harder than destroying walls that were solid stone, harder than killing a man. Healing always was. It was harder than saving infants who were trapped in a womb; harder, even, than holding their mothers when shock and loss of blood threatened their lives.

Harder than saving a child in the Foundling Hall.

But she had done all of that.

She felt the shape of their bodies and the beat—erratic and labored—of their hearts. She heard their thoughts, not as thoughts, but as memories, almost inseparable from her own. She felt their injuries, the broken bones, the old scars from—falling out of a tree? She even snorted. These weren't men who got caught out in bar brawls.

They weren't men who were accustomed to war of any kind.

She could save them. She could see where infection had taken its toll, eating into flesh and muscle. Two men. If she wanted them to live, she couldn't use any more power than was absolutely necessary. No miracles, not yet. No obvious miracles.

But the subtle ones were the only ones that counted.

The bones that would knit on their own, she left; the ones that wouldn't mend properly, she fixed. She tried not to *see* what had caused the breaks, but gave up quickly. That took too much effort, too much energy.

When she lifted her hands from their faces, she felt the touch of their stalks, clinging briefly to her skin. She told them to sleep.

She heard Ybelline's voice. Felt Severn's hands under her arms, shoring her up as she stood and wobbled. She didn't brush him off, didn't try. She let him carry some of her weight as she approached the last two men, their stretchers like pale bruises on the ground.

She felt grass beneath her knees as she crushed it, folding too quickly to the ground. Righting herself, which really meant letting Severn pick her up, she reached out to touch them.

Shuddered.

They didn't *wear* helmets. And the most obvious weapon they had—in the eyes of humans, of anyone outside—were their stalks. One man's were broken. Just…broken. There were no bones in the stalks themselves—but even muscle and tendon could be crushed out of shape, smeared against a skull that was also fractured badly. Bones don't hurt. The stalks—there were nerves there, so many nerves.

Gritting her teeth, she said, "Ybelline—I think this is going to hurt him. I think he'll—"

Ybelline knelt in her shadow, knowing which of the two Kaylin meant. She reached out, caught the man's bruised hands (two fingers broken), and held them fast. Leaning, she bent over his face, and her own stalks, whole, unbruised, reached out to stroke the sides of his face, his cheeks, his jaw. "Do it," she said softly.

Kaylin nodded.

Here, too, she reached out with her power, with the power that had come the day the marks had appeared on her arms and legs. Words burned on the inside of her thighs, where no one could see them. They burned up and down the length of her arms, and flared on the back of her neck.

She didn't care.

It's very important that no one know of this, Marcus said, in memory. *It's important that you do not reveal your power to anyone. Do you understand, Kaylin?*

Get stuffed, she told him.

He fell silent, memory closing its windows. What she had actually said? More polite, longer, a promise of secrecy.

It didn't matter. Nothing mattered, now, but this: healing those horribly damaged stalks.

The man woke when she'd knit bone and brain into something like its former shape; she had known he would. He screamed, once, when she started on his stalks. The scream cut out in the middle, and silence eradicated its echoes.

* * *

The last man shouldn't have been alive. He had taken a single clean wound to one side of the heart, and he had bled so much. Kaylin felt magic in him, around him, when she touched his chest. She let it be, and concentrated, though it was much, much harder now.

But it didn't matter, for he was the last. The three would live, and the fourth—damn it—he'd live too. She felt her lips cracking as she spoke. Her hands were shaking too much to keep steady; she didn't even bother to try.

Just this one, she thought. Just this one, and I'll be good. I'll be good for months. I'll be good for-bloody-ever. Just this.

"She's awake," someone said. A young someone. Either that or a very skinny midget with a very high voice. Kaylin winced and managed to lift an eyelid. She regretted it almost instantly. There was just too much damn *light*.

"She's speaking!" the child said. He said it *loudly*.

Kaylin opened her eyes—both of them—and winced again, lifting her hands to her face. Getting up was almost out of the question.

"You're awake, aren't you?" The child spoke slowly, his Elantran deliberate.

"I'm awake," she answered. She could see his eyes—they were brown, and they were wide. His stalks were flapping in the nonexistent breeze.

"I'm supposed to tell Ybelline you're awake. When you're awake."

"She must trust you a lot," Kaylin managed.

The child—boy? Girl?—beamed. "I'm going to grow up to be castelord!"

"It's a very hard job," Kaylin replied, wanting him to take his smile and play somewhere else. Feeling bad about it, too. There wasn't much you could feel that couldn't be made worse by a solid dose of guilt.

"It's an *Important* job."

"That too. Are my friends still here?"

"Yes!"

"Good. Um, where am I?"

"In the home of Ybelline Rabon'alani," Severn said, his voice drifting in from an archway that she could barely see. "It's…more crowded than it was the last time we were here."

"I'd noticed." She tried to sit up. Gave up halfway through.

"I brought water, and food. Ybelline had you carried here when you collapsed." He glanced at the child as he made his way to Kaylin. "I would have waited," he said, "but Rennick wished to speak with Ybelline—and her advisors, as he calls them—and I thought it best to… translate. She asked Ellis to watch over you."

"Ellis?"

Severn glanced pointedly at the back—well, top, really—of the child's head. "He joined us when we were on the way here, and there wasn't much that could be done to convince him it wasn't safe. You're known here," he added, with a slight smile. "And Ybelline knew you were concerned about the absence of the children."

Kaylin did not nod. It would have hurt too much. But she did manage a feeble smile. "Where did the—the others go?"

"The Tha'alani guards that were injured are in the longhouse. Two of them are awake, two of them are sleeping. None of them are now in danger. The Tha'alani doctors are quite surprised."

She winced. "It's not as if they'll tell anyone."

"It's not the Tha'alani that I'm worried about."

"Then who? Oh. Rennick."

"Ellis, come and hold this waterskin for Kaylin. You can feed her anything she'll eat," he added. He bent down quickly and kissed her forehead. "Well done, Kaylin," he said softly. "I don't want to leave Rennick alone."

She was stupid; she nodded.

"Oh, and Ellis? She'll tell you she's ready to get up and walk around long before she's actually ready to get up and walk around."

Ellis looked a bit doubtful, and the waterskin shook in his hands. It looked huge in contrast, like some headless, stuffed toy. "How will I know when it's okay?"

"When she's finished eating *all* the food and drinking *all* the water."

Severn gave Kaylin the sweetest of smiles.

What she wanted to give him would not endear her to the future would-be castelord, and she tried very hard to remember this.

CHAPTER 3

Kaylin wanted to sleep for a day. Sadly, she wanted that day to be now, and would also have liked it to be longer by forty-eight hours than the average day. Ellis didn't talk a lot; the effort of making Elantran words was obviously not trivial. But, mindful of Severn's dictate, he encouraged her to eat and drink.

He must have either had younger siblings or spent time in the Tha'alaan watching other people's children, because his form of coaching left something to be desired. The cooing, Kaylin admitted to herself, might be cute—and even hilariously funny—on another day.

Like, say, a day in which she didn't feel like she'd been on the losing end of a bar brawl with the occupants of an entire tavern. But the food did help, as did the effort of keeping the ill humor out of the words she was speaking to a child. She did not, however, offer to let him touch her forehead with his stalks. If he wanted

to be castelord, he was going to damn well have to learn
how to talk the hard way.

And explaining the words that she was thinking to a
young child of any race—never mind a young child with
an entire Quarter's worth of parents and grandparents
in attendance courtesy of the racial gift of mindspeak-
ing—was not on her list of things to do on any day.

When she had finished eating and drinking everything—and Ellis had shaken the waterskin up and down
just to make certain—Ellis tried to help her to her feet.
She was certain that her knees would recover from the
way she had to fall in order not to crush him.

But even at her crankiest—and this was pretty much
the nadir—she found something about his solemnity
touching. She stumbled beside him as he led her to Ybelline because, even if she couldn't read minds, it didn't
take mind-reading to know that he considered this babysitting of a Real Adult a task of honor and importance,
and she didn't want to take it away from him.

She was entirely unprepared for Ybelline, because
Ybelline met her on one side of the arch that Ellis, talking
to her as if she were a sick puppy, was urging her toward.
Ybelline's hair was down—literally—in a honey-gold
cascade that obscured her shoulders. Her eyes were the
same color, the same almost gold, almost brown. The
light that came in—far too brightly—from the open windows and half-walls seemed to have stopped there for
the sheer pleasure of illuminating the castelord of the
Tha'alani.

The Tha'alani woman, who wasn't classically beautiful—if there was such a thing—was radiant anyway.

She had changed into a simple, cream gown that fell from her shoulders to her ankles unimpeded. All of this, Kaylin took in at a glance—and even if she'd wanted to see more, she wouldn't have been able to, because Ybelline Rabon'alani crossed the distance, ignoring Ellis's loud warnings, and enfolded Kaylin Neya, scruffy and severely under-rested Hawk, in her arms.

It felt like home, to Kaylin. She let her forehead lean against the taller woman's shoulder, and she wanted to stand that way forever. But that wasn't why she'd come, and she knew that Severn and Rennick were waiting somewhere. She hoped that Rennick hadn't offended anyone. Anyone else.

"He's been remarkably quiet," Ybelline replied, speaking with the ease of long practice.

"That's probably bad."

Ybelline was silent for a moment, and when she spoke, her tone was guarded. "Possibly bad for you."

"For me? Why?"

"He was at the longhouse. I would have refused him entry into the Quarter, but I was…distracted."

"You had every right to be. The others—"

"They'll live. They're well." Her voice was soft, and soothing.

"Good. I wanted—"

"You had to be the one to help them. Kravel was beyond us," Ybelline added. "Even had we been able to heal him in other ways, he would have been lost to the Tha'alaan. But they have seen, and they have understood. Not all of your kind are insane. Not all of them are so maddened by fear that they must, in turn, be feared."

"They'll forget," Kaylin said.

"They are not human, Kaylin. They will not forget."

"And if they do, you'll remind them?"

Ybelline shook her head, and her hair brushed Kaylin's face as she lifted it. "No. You are not Tha'alani. But you have touched the Tha'alaan. What you understand might change in time—but they will remember you because they desire it. Not one of them wishes to fear the whole of a race. To fear even the ones who injured them is burden enough.

"And it is my fault and my responsibility. I have worked among your kind for most of my adult life, and I didn't think before I left the Quarter. I didn't think about how it would look to people who have so little knowledge. I should have realized—"

"You were trying to save a city. You had a lot on your mind."

The smile on Ybelline's face was wry, but the panic was gone. "Have you had a chance to speak at length with Richard Rennick?"

A number of answers came and went. Kaylin said simply, "Not at length." It was about as polite as she could be, given everything.

"Then you understand what he has been ordered to do?"

"More or less."

"Can you please explain it to me? No, not the reasoning behind that—believe that given the events of this past week, I understand the reasons perfectly. I don't, however, understand exactly why this task was given to Rennick. I do not understand how what he produces—which by Imperial mandate must be untrue—will serve the goal of educating the…public, as Mr. Rennick calls people."

Had this been a normal day, Kaylin's head would have hurt. And since misery loves company, she said, "Maybe we should answer this question while Rennick is actually there."

All in all, not her brightest suggestion.

She was escorted—having been parted from Ellis with gods only knew what difficulty—by Ybelline into the main hall whose chief decoration was a large table, with simple chairs, and the occasional flower in a bowl or a vase to add any color that wasn't provided by faces.

Rennick in particular was an odd shade of gray. He was separated from the rest of the Tha'alani by Severn, and if the seating arrangement was accidental, Kaylin would have eaten her hat. Or her hairpin, given she didn't own a hat. There were only five other Tha'alani in the room, all in robes very similar to Ybelline's, which, given the heat and the humidity of the season, made sense.

Sense and clothing seldom went together, in Kaylin's experience, and she didn't recall seeing robes like this the last couple of times she'd braved the Quarter, so she assumed they were some sort of formal dress. Whether or not this assumption was right, the dress seemed to be accepted wear for both the three men and the two women. The colors of the dress were basically the same—a creamy gold that was almost white. The shoulders had different embroidery at the height of the seam, which might—although she doubted it, given the Tha'alani—be some sort of symbol for their rank.

Rennick rose when she entered the room. He was quiet, but not for lack of trying; if she'd seen a better imitation of a fish out of water, she couldn't offhand recall it.

"At ease," she told him. When this comment appeared to make no sense to him—and given Severn's expression, it wouldn't—she said, "Sit down."

He sat. "Are you sure you shouldn't be the one sitting?"

"I slept."

"For three hours," he added.

She could have told him that three hours after a day like this was a catnap, but didn't. "I think we have the worst of the difficulties facing the Quarter from the inside in hand," she told him instead. "The difficulties facing the Quarter from the other side of the guardhouse, not so much. You've been talking to the Tha'alani for the last three hours—what have they told you?"

"Nothing."

She looked across to Severn. He shrugged. "Rennick thought it was relevant to ask them everything they knew about you," he replied.

"Oh. They don't know much."

"She called you here to help, and they don't know much?" He didn't trouble to keep the scorn from his voice, but on the other hand, no scorn would probably be no voice, for Rennick.

"They don't know much they want to share at any rate," she told him. "And I'm not your job. They are. You saw the casualties," she added.

He nodded, wincing slightly. "They're all going to survive. One of the men got up and walked away."

"He was probably less injured than he looked."

"Private Neya?"

"Yes?"

"Learn to lie better. Or don't bother. Bad lies insult the intelligence of the listener, and I believe that you don't want to insult me."

This wasn't exactly true, but Kaylin was too tired to start a fruitless argument, which was generally when she started them. "Humans almost killed those men," she told him, meeting and holding his gaze. "Humans saved them. We're done with that now. Move on."

"And where, exactly, would you like me to move?"

"To the part where you stop humans from wanting to kill any of the Tha'alani ever again. We brought you here because we thought you'd see a bit more of what the Tha'alani are like. Today wasn't their usual day, so that's a wash. But none of them want to hurt you and they certainly don't want to read your mind.

"They just want to be left alone. They tried to save the city, and we're going to make sure that people understand that."

One of the Tha'alani men in the room stood. "It is to address this concern that we are here," he said, in stilted Elantran. He didn't bow to her, which was good. "But there is some concern."

"We're here to address those concerns," she said, wearing her best Hawk's face although her head really was throbbing. "Humans have…stories. Those stories aren't like the Tha'alaan," she added softly. "They're not real stories. People don't experience them as memories, and they certainly don't live them the way some people can live old memories in the Tha'alaan."

"These stories, are they true?"

Kaylin looked to Severn for help. As a rule, she didn't ask for rescue, having learned early that it was pointless. But when it came to people, Severn was just better. He always had been.

Ybelline, however, lifted a hand. "Scoros," she said, "sit. The stories that she speaks of are not true in the sense that our stories are true. They change with time, they change with the teller of the tale."

He frowned.

"Scoros," Ybelline added to Kaylin, "is a teacher. He teaches the Tha'alanari, and he is respected. He understands what they will face."

Kaylin nodded.

"It is however very seldom that my kin are exposed to your stories, and some explanation will be required."

Severn shrugged again. "You were always better at creating stories than I was," he told her.

"But not better at lying."

"No. This however is yours."

She pressed her palms into her closed eyes for a minute. Then she nodded.

"Understand," she said, addressing all of the Tha'alani present, "that humans don't have the Tha'alaan. We don't have access to perfect memories. I can't remember clearly what I was doing eight years ago—but if you wanted to, you could. I can construct what I was probably doing eight years ago. And if it was utterly necessary, I could ask Ybelline to actually sort through my memories and tell me what I was doing—but without the help of the Tha'alani, if my twelve-year-old self wasn't doing something in easy reach of Records, there's no way for me to be certain."

Scoros nodded; clearly this was nothing new to him.

"This is especially true of people who have had no sleep for a few years."

Scoros frowned and Ybelline said, "She is not being literal."

His frown deepened slightly, and then eased. Ybelline was speaking Elantran for their benefit, but, clearly, was speaking in other ways as well.

"The oldest of our stories are probably religious stories," Kaylin continued. "Stories about the gods."

"These are the ones you remember?"

"Me? Not exactly. When I say oldest, I mean, the oldest ones that anyone knows about." She winced and gave up. "The earliest stories we're told, we're told as children, usually by our parents, sometimes by our friends. Children don't always have enough experience to understand very, very complicated things, and stories are a way of explaining the world to them."

"But they're not true."

"Well, not exactly."

"We do not understand what you are explaining, then."

Scoros looked at Ybelline. Ybelline looked at Kaylin. Kaylin looked at the tabletop.

And Rennick stood up with a disgusted snort.

"Rennick, sit down," Kaylin told him.

Rennick didn't appear to hear her. Given the color he was turning, it might not have been an act.

"Castelord," he said, managing somehow to be polite and icy at the same time. "Do you have no art, here?"

She frowned. "Art?"

"Paintings. Sculptures. Tapestries. Art."

"We have," Scoros answered. His voice had dropped a few degrees as well.

"If what I've heard today is true, the Tha'alani have perfect memory. Anything, at any time, that any of you have experienced, you can recall. True?"

"Rennick—"

"No, Private. If I am to do my job, as you so quaintly call it, I need to understand what I'm working with, or working against. You aren't even asking the right questions."

"Rennick—"

"Kaylin, no," Severn said, his quiet voice still audible over the echoes of Rennick's much louder tirade. "He's right. My apologies for the interruption, Mr. Rennick. Please continue."

"Is it true?"

Scoros was silent for a moment. Kaylin imagined that he was trying to figure out what Rennick's game was. She could sympathize. "It is as you say," Scoros said.

"What is the purpose of your art?"

"Pardon?"

"Why do you make it? The sculptures? The paintings? The tapestries?"

"What does this have to do with your stories?"

"Everything."

"I am not an artist," Scoros replied. "But I will attempt to answer. We create these things because they are beautiful."

"Beautiful? More beautiful than life? More beautiful than what's real?"

Scoros's silence was longer and quieter. When he spoke again, the chill in the words was gone. "Yes. And no. They are not the same." The tail end of what might have been a question colored the last word.

"But you could find beautiful things, surely, in the— what did you call it? The Tha'alaan?"

"Yes. That is what it is called."

"Can you?"

"Yes. But it is not a simple matter of demanding beauty and having it surrendered to us. We are not the same person. No two of us think exactly the same way, although to the deaf—"

"Scoros," Ybelline said softly.

"To the humans," Scoros corrected himself. "To your kin, we might seem thus. We do not have the range of… differences. Even so, some memories will strike different Tha'alani as beautiful but not all."

"Yes, well. You can find beauty, but you choose to create it instead?"

"Some of my kin do so, yes."

"Imagine, for a moment, what it is like to be my kin."

"Rennick—"

Scoros, however, stood. The two men faced each other across the length of the table. Severn kicked Kaylin under the same table, motioning for silence.

"He doesn't understand what they've suffered," she hissed.

"Then allow Scoros to make that clear, if that is their wish."

Scoros's antennae were weaving frantically in the air, and Ybelline's were doing a similar dance. But watching the two, Kaylin could see the differences in their gestures, these antennae that had seemed so much like a threat. Ybelline's movements were graceful and exact, as if each rise and fall of stalk was perfectly timed and deliberate. Scoros's looked like whips.

Two conversations. Two arguments.

Scoros turned to Rennick. "I spend little time imagining anything else," he told the playwright. Ice was gone; fire was present. He was angry. "My job—my duty—is to prepare our young for life in your world. And it is a life that they are not suited to live. They do not lie, they do not fear, they do not hoard. Nor do they steal or kill.

"Imagine what it is like to be you? What is it, exactly, that you do that allows you to come here and speak thus to us? You create these—these lies—and you spread them. And you are proud of this. Do you think we want to serve—"

"Scoros." If Kaylin had ever wondered whether or not Ybelline's kindness was based in strength, she had her answer. There was steel there.

"What do you value?" Scoros snapped, retreating from the previous sentence as if it were death. "Gold. Precious gems. Fine cloth—things. How do you reassure yourself of your own worth? By soliciting the admiration of people who value only that much. You spoke of love, in your travesty of—of—disinformation. What do you know about love? Your love is little better than base greed and insecurity! You want the regard of your peers, but you allow none to be peers. You want impossible, stupid things.

"You kill each other, rape each other, steal from each other—how are you to speak our truths? How are you to decide what beauty means?"

"Because it doesn't matter what it means to you, or your kin. It only matters what it means to mine." Rennick folded his arms across his chest. He appeared to be entirely unfazed by the fury that he had provoked. Kaylin, head pounding, couldn't say the same. "I don't demand that you like us. I don't care if you respect us." He shrugged. "You wouldn't be the first race to look down on us, you certainly won't be the last.

"And you interrupted me," he added quietly.

Scoros's eyes rounded. He was actually shocked.

"So, clearly you've thought about some of what it means to be us. Let me direct your thoughts to other aspects. You speak of fear—how do you recognize it if you don't feel it yourself?"

"A fair question, Scoros," Ybelline said pointedly. "Please answer it."

"We understand fear," he replied stiffly. "Nothing that lives is without fear. We fear for our sick, when the doctors have done all they can. We fear for our children. We fear—"

"Do you fear death?"

"No. Pain, perhaps, but not death."

"Do you fear to be forgotten?"

"We will never be forgotten, while even one of us lives."

Rennick lifted a hand. "And the rest?"

"The rest?"

"Greed. What you call human love. You don't feel it?"

"We've all felt greed," was the equally stiff reply. "We were all children once."

"And love?"

"We do not mean the same thing by that word."

"Very well. Speak of your meaning, mine is no longer an issue here."

Scoros's antennae waved again in the air, and Ybelline's snapped back.

Grudging every word, and speaking in the stilted way of Tha'alani who are using language they are not familiar with, Scoros said. "It is joy, to us."

"And what do you love?"

"My people. Our children," he added. "Their lives. Our parents. Our siblings. Our...husbands, if we have them, or our wives, if we have them."

"Plural?"

"No one person can be all things to all people. Some have tried, and some try—but it is youthful, and experience teaches much."

"I...see." Rennick was silent for a moment, gathering his thoughts. Kaylin highly doubted that he would stay that way, but she was fascinated in spite of herself. She was also grateful, because if there was a diplomatic incident today, it wouldn't be her fault.

"Imagine lives without that love," Rennick finally said. It was not what she expected. "Without the certainty of kin. We create art, and not all of it is beautiful to all people—but you have said that this is true of your kin as well.

"We don't have perfect memory. We don't have any faith that we'll be remembered when we're dead, and yes, I know it makes no sense, but we do care. When we talk of making our mark on the world, we simply mean we want to be remembered. Remembered fondly," he added.

"Because we don't have perfect memory, and we also lack the Tha'alaan, we have no way of truly understanding each other's lives. We don't even understand our own parents or the decisions they made." This last sentence was accompanied by a twisted, bitter smile that spoke of experience. "What we want, we sometimes can't explain to ourselves, let alone others. But some of us try anyway, and the best way to do that, for many of us, is with words.

"My art," he said, "if you can call it that, is just such an attempt. People will take the words you've read—my people—and they will speak them in front of an audience, and they'll speak them as if they were their own words. They'll lend the words emotion, strength, that you can't see."

"But they'll be lies."

"Yes. And no. They will be like your paintings, or like your sculptures—they will be true, in some fashion. They will evoke something that the reality itself can't evoke as cleanly or as easily. We don't consider them lies, just a different way at getting at a truth that might be too big—or too small—to be seen.

"People are busy. They know their own problems and their own fears and they have no easy way of letting everyone else know what they are. And if I'm being truthful—which you seem to prize—most of us simply don't care what other people's fears are. Ours take up too much of our time. But when someone watches one of my plays, they leave those problems behind. They signal, by being in the audience, that they're willing to be lifted out of their own lives, and concerns.

"It's only for a few hours, but for those few hours,

they're watching and they're listening to things that they would never otherwise think about." He sat down, then, heavily. "I admit that the situation here is more complicated than I thought. There are many things I don't understand," he said, and he turned a thoughtful look upon Kaylin. "But I understand better what did not work in the play that I originally conceived."

"Why would you say this? You said you don't care about my kin," said Scoros.

"I don't care if they hate me," he replied mildly. "It would hardly be the first time someone has. But…I do care about the city. I don't want it torn apart by riots. I don't want to see your people burned out of their homes.

"I can do this. Private Neya and Corporal Handred seem to have some understanding of your people, and they've been assigned to work with me. I don't ask you to trust me. But the Emperor does, and in the end, we all live at his whim."

Or die by it. Kaylin bit her tongue, hard, to keep the words on the right side of her lips. She thought Rennick had finished, but he surprised her. There seemed to be no end to his words.

"I admit that when I was handed this task, I did not consider it carefully enough. I considered it…political propaganda. Something useful for the Emperor, and of no consequence to the rest of us. Because of that, I could take…shortcuts. I could tell the easy story, pull the cheap strings. I was wrong, and I apologize for my ignorance. And I thank the Hawks for bringing me to your Quarter, because I understand better what's at stake.

"I also understand that you are forbidden to speak of what actually happened…but I imagine, now, that what

Private Neya believes is true. You did what you could to save the city. It's not something I would have dared," he added, "given public fear and sentiment. I would have holed up in my rooms in the Palace. I did, in fact, do just that.

"But from those rooms, I can now enter the fight in a different way. I will think about the Tha'alaan, and the tidal wave, and the fact that you walked out to meet it." He turned toward the door, and then looked at Kaylin and Severn, both still seated. "Private? Corporal?"

Kaylin rose with effort. She bowed stiffly to the Tha'alani, and nodded once to Ybelline. But she lingered in the room as Severn and Rennick left it, and found that the wait was rewarded.

The Tha'alani, as one, seemed to shrink, their shoulders losing the unnatural stiffness of anger, their jaws unclenching. Their antennae were weaving in a riot of motion, beneath strands of hair that had curled with the city's damn humidity.

"We thank you, as well," Ybelline told Kaylin.

Scoros rose. "For saving our kin," he said, "we offer no thanks—they are your kin as well, Kaylin Neya. You are the only one of your kind to be welcome in the Tha'alaan—and it holds some small part of your memories."

She paled. "I tried—"

"Yes. You tried. And much was withheld, and we are grateful for that absence as well. But what you could not withhold, all can see. And believe," he added, with a slight smile, "that all did see. They know you are not of the Tha'alani, and that you cannot again touch the Tha'alaan—but those moments were enough. They know you, and they will not fear you.

"But…your companion is both infuriating and surprising, and I think…I think perhaps we will trust him. And it is for that, that we offer our thanks."

Kaylin nodded slowly. "I don't like him much," she replied at length, "but he surprised me as well. And as he can't be bothered to be polite when his life depends on it—trust me, I've seen him with Dragons—he probably wasn't lying about his concern. Or his apology."

"You must join them. We have the Swords at our gates, and I do not think we will risk our own again until things are calmer."

"Swords are better. They know how to calm a crowd." She didn't say anything about the most drastic of crowd-calming methods. She knew, as they all did, that the human mob outside was vastly less likely to attack the Swords.

The carriage was waiting for them. The Swords had ensured that. They had also ensured that all of the wheels and fine gilding were still intact, although the Imperial Crest probably had a lot to do with the fact; not even the most drunken and wayward of idiots thought his life worth defacing an Imperial Crest. It wasn't a mistake you could repeat.

"Please drive us to the Halls of Law," Severn told the coachman.

"You're not coming back to the Palace?"

"Not for the remainder of the day." Day wasn't quite the right word for the shade of pinkish purple the sky had gone. "We will report to you in the morning."

"In the morning?" Rennick said.

"Yes."

"When in the morning?" The playwright now looked uncomfortable.

"We report for duty, fully kitted out, at eight."

"In the morning?"

Severn nodded, his expression deliberately bland.

"Well, you can report," Rennick said. "But bring some cards, or whatever it is you do when you're not doing anything else—I'm a bear at that time of the day."

"A bear?" Kaylin asked, inserting herself into the conversation.

"A figure of speech. Mornings make me grouchy."

"We didn't arrive in the morning today," she told him.

"Exactly. And your point is?"

"It probably speaks for itself." She tried to imagine Rennick in a more foul temper, and gave up quickly. There were some things it was better not to know.

"I will be sleeping at that ungodly hour. I think you should see about arranging some sort of shift work."

She imagined the face full of fur that was an angry Leontine. You did not mess up Marcus's schedule without a pressing reason to do so—end of all life as we know it being one.

"I'll see what I can do," she murmured, staring out the carriage window as the city rolled past.

Severn shook her awake when they arrived. The front doors were manned by Aerians. Clint was still on duty, which was unusual, given the hour. She took a few minutes to find her feet, and tried not to imagine her bed.

They made their way to the front doors, and Kaylin

stopped as Clint lowered his halberd. "Aren't you off duty?" she asked.

"I pulled in a favor."

"You pulled in a favor."

"Yes."

"So you could stay later, guarding a door that no one ever attacks, with a halberd that hasn't seen real use in more than a decade."

"Less than a year," he replied. "But yes, I take your point. We were in the fiefs at the time."

"Point returned. But why exactly did you pull in a favor to work a double shift when you're on duty in the morning? Clint?" She didn't like the expression on his face. At all. "I've had a long day," she said, running her hands over eyes that felt like they were full of sand. "So I'm a bit slow."

"Be quicker," he told her, without smiling. "I thought you would come back a bit earlier. I knew you'd be back before tomorrow."

"This—what's happened, Clint?" She pulled a memory out of her exhaustion: a Sword offering her his sympathies. It seemed like he'd said it weeks ago.

"You won't like it," he said, leaving her in no doubt whatsoever that this was an understatement. "But it doesn't matter whether or not you like it, do you understand?"

"Yes."

"I'm serious, Kaylin. You get away with a lot when you're dealing with Marcus, because he's seen how much you've changed in seven years. He saw you at thirteen. He watched you struggle to become the Hawk that you are now. Part of him still thinks of you as if you're thirteen years old, and that's not likely to change."

"And so?"

"Kaylin, please understand that this is important. All jokes about your punctuality aside, Marcus accepts you as you are. Not all of the older Hawks feel the same way, and not all of them have been won over."

She stared at him dumbly and was surprised when he handed his polearm to the other guard, and caught her shoulders in both hands. His wings were high; he was worried. "I'm very fond of you," he said, his gaze an un-blinking shade of gray that was unlike any color she'd seen. "But I took my oaths, and I'm sworn to uphold them. I also need to eat, and feed my family."

"Clint—what are you talking about? Why are you saying this?"

"Because the people you will now be dealing with will not be Old Ironjaw. And if you don't deal carefully, you won't be a Private. It's as simple as that."

"W-what happened?"

"There was an incident," he continued carefully. "In-volving the Leontine Quarter."

"What happened, Clint?"

"We're not entirely certain. Teela and Tain are trying to ferret out information, but any information we get is going to come to us when we're off the payroll. Under-stand?"

She nodded, although she didn't.

"Marcus has been stood down. He's been relieved of duty."

"On what grounds?"

"Kaylin—we don't know what happened. But the case has been referred to the Caste Courts, not ours."

"What case?"

"Someone died."

"Pardon?"

"A Leontine from a prominent clan died. He was killed by another Leontine. That much, we do know."

"How?"

"The death didn't occur in the Leontine Quarter. However, none of the witnesses were harmed, and remanding all investigations involving that death to the Caste Courts is well within the dictates of the Law."

"But—"

"Marcus was present at the scene of the crime."

"What do you mean, present?"

Clint closed his eyes for a moment. When he opened them, they were clear, and his face had hardened into lines that Kaylin hated to see there. "He is currently in the custody of the Caste Court, awaiting a trial on murder charges."

For once, Kaylin had no words to offer. A million questions, yes, but they were jammed up in the tightness of her throat.

"Corporal Handred?"

"Here."

"You've been instructed to report for duty to the acting Sergeant."

"The acting Sergeant? Clint!"

The Aerian to his left was an older man that Kaylin recognized. There wasn't an Aerian on the force that she didn't know by name, because there wasn't an Aerian on the force who hadn't been begged, pleaded with and cajoled by a much younger Kaylin. They could fly— they could carry her with them.

"Breen?"

Breen had clearly decided to let Clint absorb all the heat of this particular conversation, but his dusky skin, pale brown to Clint's deep, warm darkness, looked a little on the green side.

"To whom am I to report?" Severn asked.

The hesitation was almost too much to bear. But when Clint finally spoke, it was worse.

"Sergeant Mallory."

CHAPTER 4

Severn did not take Kaylin with him when he went to report for duty to the new acting Sergeant. He did not, in fact, report for duty immediately; instead, he grabbed her by the elbow and dragged her from the steps atop which the two Aerians stood. It took her about two minutes to realize that the dragging had a purpose: he was taking her home.

And she was exhausted enough to let him.

"I know what you're thinking, Kaylin. Don't."

"What am I thinking?"

"That you should have been there."

She winced. But she'd always been obvious to Severn.

"What you *were* doing affects an entire race. What we'll be doing when we're not dealing with the ugly fears of a mob will affect a much, much smaller group of people."

"The Hawks."

He nodded quietly.

"Why did he ask for you?" She couldn't bring herself to actually say Mallory's name out loud.

"I don't know. I've met the man once."

"You ran interference for me when we went to Missing Persons."

Severn nodded. "But given his feelings about you—and he was quite clear on those—I imagine that he won't find my role as a Hawk much more to his liking."

"He probably doesn't know where you're from."

"Then he hasn't done his homework."

"Doesn't seem likely."

"No, it doesn't. I imagine that Mallory knows quite a bit about the Hawks at this point." He stopped. She stared at the street, and he pushed her gently up the few steps to her own apartment door. She'd gotten a new key, and it worked, but it took her three tries to get the damn thing into the lock.

"You're tired," he told her, when she cursed in Leontine. "Tired and Mallory are not going to be a pretty combination. Sleep it off. But understand that when you walk into the office in the morning, the rules will be different and everything will change. You wanted to be a Hawk," he added. "Be one. Tomorrow."

"I want to talk to the Hawklord."

"Do that tomorrow as well." He paused, and then added, "We couldn't have talked to the Hawklord without speaking to Mallory first. I imagine he's guarding the tower. Kaylin, he's made it clear from the start, if I understand things correctly, that you should never have been a Hawk. Nothing would give him more pleasure than correcting an obvious error in judgment. But if he is a vindictive man—and I don't discount it—he also appears to play *by the rules.*

"Don't give him the satisfaction. Do nothing that he can use as an excuse. He'll have his own worries," Severn said.

"What worries?"

"His disdain for Marcus was widely known, and Marcus was popular."

"Is."

"Is what?"

"*Is* popular." She began to stumble up the narrow stairs to her rooms. "Don't talk about him as if he's dead."

"Is popular," he said, gentling his voice as he followed her. "Most of the department knows how Mallory regards the Hawks under Marcus, and if Mallory is to succeed, he can't afford to further alienate them. But if you give him an excuse, he'll use it."

She opened the door to a darkening room, the shutters wired into a safe—and closed—position. She might not have cared much for Rennick, but she shared his view about morning. And still got her butt out of bed on most days.

"I'll be good," she told him in the darkness.

"Tomorrow."

She nodded again and walked across the room, stepping around the piles of debris that littered it. She removed the stick that held her stubborn hair in place, and sank, fully clothed, into bed.

"Sleep," he told her. Just that.

She wanted more. She wanted him to tell her that the bad dream would vanish in the sunlight, that she would wake up and the city would be sane, and Marcus would be chewing his lower lip and creating new gouges on his desktop while he moved offending paperwork out of the way.

But she'd grown up in the fiefs, after all, and she knew that what she wanted and what she got had nothing, in the end, in common. She didn't cry.

But she came close when he kissed her forehead and brushed the lids of her closed eyes with his fingertips.

She woke up to a loud, insistent knocking at her door. Daylight had wedged its unwelcome way through the shutters. She had to remember to get them fixed. Say, by putting a block of stone in their place.

She checked her mirror before she made her way to the door, still wearing the rumpled clothing from the day before. She paused. Someone had messaged her. Someone had tried to get her attention, but they hadn't tried for very long. She didn't want to check, besides which, the pounding at the door wasn't stopping anytime soon. She bypassed the mirror, because if the *first* thing she saw this morning was the afterimage of Mallory's unwelcome face, she'd break the damn thing, and the mirror was the most expensive thing she owned. She wouldn't have bothered with the expense—gods knew she never had money—but her duties at the midwives guild pretty much made it a necessity.

Severn was standing in the door frame when she opened the door. He handed her a basket. "Breakfast," he told her. "Eat."

"What time is it?"

"Not so late that you don't have time to eat." It wasn't

precisely an answer. She lifted the basket top, and the smell of fresh bread became the only thing in the room. That and her growling stomach. "Hey," she said, as she sat on the bedside and motioned Severn toward the chair. "Is this enchanted?"

"The bread?"

Her frown would have killed lesser men. "Very funny. The basket."

"Yes."

She nodded. "I didn't smell the bread at all until I opened it."

"It keeps the rodents at bay. More or less."

"Where'd you get it done?"

"Evanton's."

"He'd like it. It's practical."

"I think he thought it perhaps too practical. But he took the money." He paused and then added, "It keeps the food fresher, as well. It won't last forever," he said, "but it lasts longer. Which, given the insane hours you generally keep, also seemed practical."

"Wait—it's for me?"

"It's for you."

She hesitated, and then nodded. "Thanks. Did you talk to Mallory?"

"Last night."

"The Hawklord?"

"No. I'll say this for Mallory, that paperwork is going to get done before the week's out."

"Ha. I've seen that pile—most of it was there when I got inducted."

"Betting?"

"Sure. We can pool in the office."

"Actually, we can't."

Silence. It didn't last longer than it took to finish swallowing something that could have been chewed longer, judging by the way it lodged in the back of her throat. "We can't *bet?*" To a fiefling, it was like being told *don't breathe.*

"It's not in keeping with the formal tone he feels is professional in office environs. He is looking forward to correcting the laxity."

Kaylin's bread now resembled clay. Her stomach was kind enough to stop growling, so her throat could pick up the sound.

"Change your clothing," he added. "And you may have to get your hair cut."

"What?"

"I think you heard me."

"My hair?"

"It's not regulation length."

"Neither is Teela's!"

"I believe he intends for *all* of the Hawks to sport regulation cuts."

If she hadn't swallowed the mouthful, she would have probably sprayed it across the room. "He thinks he can make the *Barrani* cut their hair?"

"He hopes to make his mark on the office," Severn replied, a perfectly serious expression smoothing out the lines of his face. "I think he believes it will speak well of his tenure if he can be seen to have effected changes that Marcus could not."

"Marcus never tried."

"No. But there are no Barrani in Missing Persons. There are no Leontines. There are no Aerians."

"So what you're saying is you think he failed Racial Integration classes as well."

"Pretty much. Oh, I imagine he passed them—some people can pass a test without ever looking at the content."

"The Aerians pretty much go by regs. I keep my hair out of the way."

"I don't think that will be a convincing argument. Stay clear of it if he brings it up."

"What does that mean?"

"Say yes, and ignore him for a day or two. Your yes will pale beside the very Barrani No he's likely to get from twelve of his Hawks. He's not a fool. I imagine that the dictate will be quietly set aside as insignificant given the flaws that he obviously sees in the present office bureaucracy. By which I mean reports and paperwork. He will feel the need to impress upon his superiors the qualities that he can bring to the job, particularly if those qualities are ones which his predecessor lacked."

She nodded, and finished eating. Then she picked up what was hopefully a clean shirt, and began to change. It was going to be a *long* day.

"Kaylin?"

"Hmm?"

"Someone mirrored you."

"Oh, right. I didn't want to look in case it was Mallory. Who was it?"

"I don't know."

"Well *look*."

He was silent for a moment, after which he said, "Your mirror isn't keyed?"

"Hells no—that costs money."

"Kaylin—the Hawks would pay to have it done. Some of our investigations would not be helped if anyone could listen in on more sensitive discussions."

"Look, if someone's listening in on *my* life, they've got no bloody life of their own, and they're welcome to be as bored as they like. Usually it's just Marcus screaming about the time, anyway."

She could tell by the set of his lips that the conversation was not finished. He did, however, touch the mirror and ask for a replay.

The mirror hummed a moment, and then went flat.

"You said this wasn't keyed."

"It's not."

"It's not playing."

"Crap. If it's broken, I'll—I'll—" She shoved a stick into the bun she had made of her hair, and stomped over to the mirror. What she did *not* need right now was anything she couldn't afford. A new mirror being her chief concern.

"Mirror," she said, in the tone of voice she usually reserved for choice Leontine words. "Replay."

The mirror shimmered, the neutral matte of its sleeping surface slowly breaking to reveal a face. A Leontine face.

"The mirror's not keyed," Kaylin said, her voice losing heat as she struggled with her very inadequate memory. The woman was familiar. Not one of Marcus's wives—she knew all of them on sight, having been to their home dozens of times before she was allowed to join the Hawks.

"No," Severn said thoughtfully. "But the message is. I can wait in the hall if you want the privacy."

"Don't bother. It'll save me the hassle of repeating what it says. I know her," Kaylin said suddenly. "I saw her when I went to the Quarter for the midwives. Her name was Arlan. But it was supposed to be—"

"Kaylin Neya," the woman said, her voice so hushed Kaylin wasn't surprised when the image in the mirror turned and looked over its shoulder furtively. "You came. You helped birth my son, Roshan Kaylarr. He has need of your aid, and there is no one else I can ask. I humbly beseech you, return to him." She looked over her shoulder again. "I cannot speak freely. But come again this evening at the same hour you arrived in my den on your first visit. Come alone, if it is possible. Bring only people you can trust, if it is not. I must go." She faced the mirror fully and said a phrase in Leontine before the mirror blanked.

Severn looked at her. "What did she say?"

"You don't know?"

"I didn't understand all of the Leontine, no."

"But you *always* understand more than I do."

He raised a brow.

"She said her throat was in my claws."

"That's what it sounded like. What does it mean?"

"She's begging. More than begging. She's promising that she'll do anything—anything *at all*—that I ask of her in return for this favor. No, it's more than that— she's saying that if I don't do this, she faces a fate worse than death. Yes, it's a little over the top. They don't use it much." She closed her eyes. "Her son was the only cub in her litter, and he barely survived the birthing. If something's gone wrong with him—"

"She would have called you *now,* not at some unspecified hour."

"That's what I'm thinking," Kaylin replied, rearranging her hair thoughtfully. "I'm also thinking that it can't be entirely coincidence that something's wrong in the Quarter at this time. I went in to help with the baby—Leontines don't usually call in the human midwives, but...it was an odd birth. None of her wives were present and she was alone. The entire place was empty. I left the midwives behind because it was the Leontine Quarter, and they allowed it—barely."

"She looks—and I admit I'm not an expert in Leontine physiology—young. Maybe she has no wives yet."

"Maybe. And maybe she got my name from Marcus the first time I visited, and maybe she can tell us something about what's happening to him."

"Careful, Kaylin. You don't want to start an intercourt incident."

"I never want to start an incident," she replied, opening the door. "Then again, I never want to stand in the rain getting soaked either. Some things are just beyond my control."

As if in reply to this, he reached into his pouch and pulled out the heavy, golden bracer that she wore when she wasn't with the midwives. Or, more accurately, when she wasn't being called upon to use the strange magic that came with the marks on her arms, legs and back.

"That's why you came?" she asked, taking the bracer and clamping it firmly shut around her wrist.

"That," he replied, "and to make sure you get to work on time."

* * *

Clint was on duty. If she had the timing right, he'd flown to the Southern Stretch, slept and flown back, without much else in between. He didn't look surprised to see her and, given she had been on time two days in a row, this said something. It wasn't a good something, but it was something. He let them both in without a word, although he returned Severn's nod as they passed.

Her first stop was the Quartermaster. Given the silent war they'd been waging for the past several weeks—over a stupid dress, no less—she expected bad news. She had no doubt at all that the acting Sergeant had asked for a general inventory of items, and the various Hawks those items currently resided with. Kaylin's minor problem was that she'd lost one hauberk, one surcoat and two daggers. If she had lost them in the line of Official duty—which did happen in some of the messier take-downs—that was considered an expense for the Departmental Budget; if she'd lost them—as she had—to work that *must* remain unofficial, she was going to be out the money.

Or out the door.

Begging was something she'd done in her time, but it didn't come naturally now. Nor did letting down her guard. She had, however, decided to take Severn at his word. She needed to play nice, to be official.

The Quartermaster was clearly in the middle of the inventory that she guessed he'd been asked to take. He took about five minutes to look up, a sure sign that he'd seen her coming.

He surprised her. "I see you've managed to hold on to the surcoat for a day. Color me surprised." He bent below the counter and came up with two daggers, in reg sheaths, in his hand. "Put them on. Don't lose them."

She was almost speechless.

"I don't like your attitude," he told her. "I never have."

She nodded. The fact that she felt the same about him was not something the conversation needed at the moment. It seemed to be—miraculously—going well on its own.

"But you've earned your rank, such as it is. And you've got keen sight. Maybe in ten years, experience will grind the edges off you. Maybe it won't. But if you want to get yourself cashiered, it'll have to be for a better reason than losing armor and weapons while saving the City. I've marked the loss as in the line of duty. If he asks, lie." He paused and added, "If you repeat that, I'll have a sudden change of heart. Is that understood, Private?"

"Yes, sir."

"Good. Go away. I'm busy."

"Yes, sir." She made it about four steps from the desk when he said, quietly, "Good luck, girl."

Severn said, much more quietly, "If nothing good comes of Mallory, at least you've made peace with the Quartermaster. *Try* to make it last."

Even before they made it to the heart of the office, Kaylin noted one change: the duty roster. It had been rewritten on a pristine roll of paper, in a fastidiously tidy hand, and the only holes in it were the ones beneath the pins. She saw that she was still marked for Imperial Palace duty, as was Severn. If she'd hated the idea when she'd first seen it, she was grateful for it now—it meant time away from the office.

To one side of the roster, in an equally neat hand, was a smaller piece of paper. On it, under a prominent heading that said Code of Conduct, were a bunch of lines with numbers beside it. Usually, this was exactly the type of document the Hawks ignored, if they noted it at all. Kaylin, aware of how much she would have to change in order to remain a Hawk, grimaced and read.

1. All official documentation is to be written in Court Barrani.
2. For investigations in process: All reports are to be tendered no more than forty-eight hours after the relevant investigation takes place.
3. For arrests: All reports are to be tendered no more than twenty-four hours after the relevant arrest takes place.
4. There will be no betting or drinking on the premises. There will be no betting or drinking while on duty anywhere.
5. The Official City languages are not to be used to promulgate obscenities.
6. Before beginning your rounds, you will clock in. There are no exceptions to this rule. When finished, you will clock out.
7. Regulation dress and grooming is mandatory while on duty.

Kaylin said nothing while she read. She said nothing after she finished, taking a moment to school her expression. When she was certain she looked calm, she turned to face the rest of the office. The first thing she should have noticed was Marcus's absence. But the first thing she did notice was that Caitlin was missing. At the desk beside the mirror from which most general office business was done, an older man sat. He was trim and fit in build, with a very well-groomed beard; his hair had grayed enough to be salt-and-pepper, but not enough to be white.

She hesitated for a moment, and managed to stop herself from running up to the desk and demanding to know where Caitlin was. But it was hard. Had Severn not been at her side, it might well have been impossible.

The rest of the office seemed to have taken the change in stride, if you didn't notice the silence that hovered above a group of people famed for their gossip and chatter. One or two of them met her eyes in silence.

"Who is he?" she asked Severn, her voice a muted whisper.

"Caitlin's replacement. Sergeant Mallory wished to work with a man who's accustomed to him. It comes with the job," he added, before she could speak. "His name is Kevan Smithson."

"He worked in Missing Persons?"

"For eight years. Before that, he was part of the office pool here. Let's get this over with," he said, and began to walk toward the desk that Mallory now occupied.

She'd burn in hell before she called it his desk.

"Corporal Handred," Sergeant Mallory said, looking up from his paperwork. Kaylin was barely willing to give him this: it was half the size of the stack she'd last seen, and it was a good deal more tidy. "Private Neya."

He rose as he said her name. She stood at attention. She wasn't particularly good at standing at attention on most days, but on most days, it wasn't demanded.

He didn't, however, seem to notice. "You are both on call at the Imperial Palace."

"Sir," Severn replied.

"I have attempted to ascertain the duration of your work at the Palace, but the Imperial Court could not be precise." He turned, then, to look at Kaylin. "You are *not* the Hawk I would have chosen for that duty," he said, reaching behind him to pick up a folder. There was no immediately visible writing on it, but Kaylin had a pretty good idea of what it contained. "And I have spoken with the Hawklord about this matter. Apparently, you were specifically requested."

"Sir," she said, hoping she sounded as curt—and as correct—as Severn.

"You will report to the office before you leave for the Palace while you have duties there."

"Sir."

"And you will tender a report of your activities to Mr. Smithson at the end of each day."

"It's neither an investigation nor an arrest," she told him.

"Yes. I'm aware of that. But given the delicate nature of relations with the Palace, and given the probability that I will be called upon to explain your behavior while there, I require a report.

"Ah, and I wish you to lift your right arm."

She did as he ordered.

He walked over to her and rolled up her sleeve. The golden surface of the bracer caught the ambient light, reflecting it perfectly. "I will also require you to show proof of your compliance with the Hawklord's orders when you report.

"You are aware, perhaps, that the former Sergeant and I did not see eye to eye on many things. I have spent some time perusing your file," he said, lifting and waving it as if it were a red flag and Kaylin were a bull, "and while I better understand some of his decisions with regards to your behavior, I feel that he placed too much emphasis on your possible import.

"I will be watching you, Private Neya. Do *one* thing to embarrass this department, and you will no longer be part of it. Is that understood?"

"Sir."

"Yes or no, Private."

"Yes, sir."

"Good. I'm glad we understand each other. Dismissed."

Kaylin took a breath and walked away from his desk.

"Private! That is not the way to the carriage yards."

She turned on heel. "No, sir. I'm reporting to the Hawklord."

"No, Private, you are not. I report to the Hawklord. You report to *me*. Is that clear?"

She was almost speechless. Having to walk past Mallory—and be interrogated by him—was one thing. Being told that all communication between the Hawklord and herself was forbidden was another. Her hands slid up to her hips.

Severn stepped on her foot. She met his gaze and saw the warning in it.

Was about to ignore it entirely when Severn said, "If you're cashiered, you can't help Marcus."

"Sir," she said, in a slightly strangled tone of voice.

"Good. Do not be late for your assignment." He went back to the desk that, damn it all, he shouldn't be behind, and took the chair. "I look forward to your report this evening."

"Kaylin, I don't think this is a good idea," Severn told her quietly. "There's every chance that Mallory will keep an eye on you for the first couple of weeks."

Kaylin said nothing. Instead of making her way to the carriage yards, she had made her way to the Aerie. In it, high above her head, and just below the vaulted ceilings, the Aerians were flying. She knew most of them by name. Certainly all of them on sight.

"I know what I'm doing," she told him, each word a little bolt of fury.

"I know what you intend to do as well," he replied. "I just don't think it's wise."

"I'm not asking you to come."

"No. You are not, however, on your way to the Palace."

"Rennick won't even be *awake*."

"True."

"So there's no point in going there now."

"Less true," Severn said.

"You didn't tell Mallory that we're not required until well past lunch?"

"No. I thought we might make use of the time."

"I am."

"In less obvious disregard of your superior officer's orders."

She made her way to the middle of the Aerie and waited. In about five minutes, three of the flying Aerians began to circle lower, and eventually they landed. Two of them were Hawks; one was a Wolf. The Wolf nodded carefully at Severn, who returned the nod.

"If the change of leadership doesn't suit you, Corporal Handred, the Wolves are waiting."

"It's an internal matter," Severn replied, with care. "But I'll remember what you've said."

The two Hawks watched Severn for a moment, weighing him. Severn had been a Hawk for a couple of months—at most—and most of his duties didn't bring him in contact with the Aerians. Most of Kaylin's didn't, either, but that hadn't always been the case, and with the Aerians, history counted for something.

"Kaylin," one of the two said. He was a younger man, Severn's age, and his skin was the same deep brown that Clint's was.

"Perenne," she replied. "Will you come outside with me for a second?"

He said something suggestive, and she smacked his chest with her open palm. "Very funny. I'm serious."

"If I can be excused from my drill practice, yes." He turned to the older Hawk.

"It's heading to break anyway. Do *not* do anything stupid." That said, the older Hawk launched himself into the air.

Perenne was not as stocky as the older Hawks, and he was taller. He had arrived on the force some five years past and, while technically he'd been a Hawk for longer than Kaylin, was well aware that she'd been dogging the feathers of members more senior for years.

"You want me to what?" he said, when she told him what she needed him to do.

"Just fly up to the top of the tower and dangle me over the window."

"Kaylin—"

"Perenne, I need to talk to the Hawklord, and Mallory's standing guard in front of the usual door."

"Meaning he ordered you not to talk to him."

"Not exactly."

"What, exactly, did he say?"

"I can't remember."

"Corporal Handred?"

"He told her that she is not required to report to the Hawklord—that's his duty."

"In exactly those words?"

"More or less."

Perenne grimaced. "I *like* this job," he said. "I'd like to keep it for a while."

"You don't have to do anything else," she replied. "I just—I need to talk to the Hawklord, and I'll be in the dumps for insubordination if I ignore Mallory to his face."

"You'll be in the cells for insubordination if you ignore him behind his back," Perenne replied reasonably. But he opened his arms, and his wings went from their light, airy fold behind his back to a full tip-to-tip stretch.

"Don't expect much," he said, as he caught her in

his arms and adjusted for her weight. "Mallory was appointed with the Hawklord's approval."

"The man's an arrogant prick."

"True. But he's not a homicidal one."

"Marcus isn't homicidal."

"Much. Look, I know there's some history with Mallory, but the Hawklord trusts him enough to let him run and staff Missing Persons."

The ground receded.

"Perenne, he's going to insist that the Barrani cut their hair."

Perenne winced. "I didn't say he was sane. But let him. He won't last long if he does."

"I couldn't talk him out of it if I tried."

The dome that enclosed the Hawklord's tower grew larger as they approached it from above. It was closed. Kaylin swore.

"Look, just—dangle me above it while I knock."

"Knock?"

"Kick."

"Better. Have you put on weight?"

"Very funny."

The Hawklord could be called many things. Stupid was not one of them. Almost before Kaylin had finished kicking the dome—and it was actually easier said than done if she didn't want Perenne to drop her—the dome itself began to slide open, eight parts receding into the stone of the tower's upper walls. Perenne took the open dome as an invitation to relieve himself of his burden, and very gently set her down, his wings beating slowly.

He landed behind her and snapped the Hawklord a

salute. The Hawklord nodded at Perenne. "Circle the dome," he told the Aerian. "Private Neya has no other way of leaving, but I assume she thought this out beforehand." His white wings were folded at his back, and his hands were at his sides.

But his eyes were ringed and dark, and he looked tired. He waited in silence for Perenne's ascent, and then turned his regard on Kaylin. "I believe you were told not to report to me."

"I'm not."

"Ah. And what, exactly, are you doing?"

"I want *you* to report to *me*."

"I see." He turned and walked toward the mirror that graced the tower. "You refer to Marcus Kassan."

"What happened? Why is he—"

"I don't know, Kaylin. I know that he is currently in the custody of the Caste Courts. The Leontine Caste Court. More than that I have not been able to ascertain. But his arrest is within the purview of the Caste Courts, and unless Marcus demands a public hearing or a public trial in the Imperial Courts, it is not our concern."

"You can't believe he—"

"It doesn't matter what I believe. It doesn't matter what you believe. The Caste Courts have the right to convene in this fashion. If we decide to disrupt Caste law, we risk too much. The city can't cope with two Caste difficulties." He paused and then said, "You visited Ybelline Rabon'alani."

"Yes. At her request. And she's not going to file an incident report."

"Good. And you found her well?"

"No."

"And your duties at the Imperial Palace?"

"I'm not allowed to report to you," she reminded him.

"Sergeant Mallory would not consider something this informal to be a report," the Hawklord replied.

She started to argue, and stopped herself because it was true.

"Acting Sergeant Mallory," she said instead.

"As you say."

"Why in the hells did you choose him? Why not promote someone from the department? He's handled Missing Persons reports for the last gods know how many years—he's not—"

The Hawklord lifted a hand. "Do not question my judgment in this. And before you embarrass yourself by asking, Sergeant Mallory does not have any information he can use against me. He was put forward as the most senior candidate who could fill the position on no notice."

"By who?"

"It's not your concern, Kaylin."

"He's never liked the fact that I'm a Hawk."

"No."

"He'll do whatever he can to get rid of me."

"He'll allow you to do whatever you can to give him the excuse, yes. A year ago, that would have taken a day, two at the outside. I expect that it will now take him much longer. Especially given the nature of your duties at the Palace."

"Where's Caitlin?"

"Caitlin—and she has a rank, Private, but as this is entirely informal, I will allow you to forget it—has chosen to take a leave of absence. Her duties under

Marcus Kassan did not leave her much free time, and she is, in fact, owed several weeks of back pay, and several more weeks of time off. She is utilizing both at the moment."

"But when they run out?"

"She is still a Hawk in good standing. If her position is not vacant when she chooses to return, another position will be found for her. She has also received at least two offers of employment from the Swords."

Kaylin watched his reflection in the mirror, waiting for it to dim as he accessed Records. She waited for at least five minutes before she realized he had no intention of accessing Records at this time.

He just didn't want to look at her.

It was surprising how much this stung.

"Access to the Tower during Sergeant Mallory's stay will be restricted," the Hawklord told her. "If there is an emergency, those restrictions do not apply—but do not create an emergency."

"But—"

He turned away from the mirror, then, "I am aware of the schedule Richard Rennick chooses to keep," he said, his voice sharp and low. "I am aware of the hours you are expected to serve. You have half a day of paid time in which to play cards. Corporal Handred is also blessed with the same abundance of time. *Use it,* Kaylin. There is nothing that Marcus will tell me. I haven't eaten at his table. I haven't been given the hospitality of his hearth. I haven't been adopted by his Pridlea. You've spoken to his wives before—speak to them now, if they'll talk.

"I trust you," he said, his voice still low and intense. "I trust you to use your training as a Hawk. As a groundhawk, when you're focused, you have very few equals. Go where I cannot go. Discover what I cannot discover. Survive Mallory's dislike. It is not beyond your skills." He looked as if he would say more, but he stopped for a moment. "Marcus is the only Leontine on my force at the moment. His loss will be a blow to the city, even if the Hawks see only their own difficulties. You have five days."

"Five days?"

"The trial is set for five days hence."

"Five *days?* We couldn't get something like this to trial in less than five *weeks!*"

But the Hawklord lifted his head and uttered a series of high, clicking whistles. It wasn't Aerian, exactly; it was the Aerian version of a shout.

Perenne began his descent.

"I regret the necessity of putting you in this situation. But it *is* necessary, Kaylin. Do what you do best."

"What is it I do best?"

He offered her a weary but genuine smile. "Get involved in everyone else's business, whether or not they request it. My mirror has been keyed for your use and the key sequence is your voice. *Attempt* to exercise caution when you contact me. Now go. Mallory will be here in less than fifteen minutes."

"Why?"

"He follows a schedule for his reports."

She nodded. Bit back the words that she wanted to say. Lifted her arms to catch Perenne as he landed.

"Well?" Severn asked. He was waiting for her by the entrance to the carriage yard.

"Bad."

"How bad?"

"Not so bad that we can't do something. Yet."

"Tell me."

She waited for the carriage to roll out of the carriage house. "I'll tell you when we're en route."

"To?"

"The Leontine Quarter."

He nodded as if he had expected no less.

CHAPTER 5

"Given Rennick's general regard for authority—and I must admit to being impressed—we have some leeway in our timing." Severn glanced out the window, but it was a measured glance; he was, she knew, following the streets, cataloguing the buildings. She wondered if he was constantly fleshing out a map of the city on the inside of his head. Nevertheless, watching or not, he was still with her, as his next words proved. "But while timing with regards to Rennick isn't a major issue, our presence or absence will be. You don't care for Rennick—he is, however, important."

"He's not an idiot," she said, grudging the admission. "But I don't get him. I don't understand why he writes this stuff for people when he clearly doesn't like them much."

Severn shrugged. "It's art," he said, as if that explained anything. Maybe it did. "Where does Marcus live?"

"In the middle of the damn Quarter."

"And we're approaching it?"

"It's not like the Tha'alani enclave. There's no gate. But it's kind of hard to miss it—the streets are pretty much always crowded. They don't seem to have a market in the strict sense of the word."

Severn nodded.

"You already know all of this."

"I've learned some of it," he replied. "But I've seldom had cause to travel in the Leontine Quarter, and the Leontines are not known for their hospitality."

"Really?"

"Really. Leontines don't make people worry in the same way the Tha'alani do—in the end, we all have things we'd rather no one else know about. They make people worry in the same way that giant, man-eating animals do."

"Where, by people, you mean humans."

"I mean anything that can be killed and eaten."

"The Barrani don't seem to mind them."

"How would you know? The Barrani affect nonchalance when it comes to bloody dragons."

"True." The day Teela said "I'm afraid" was probably the day the world ended—because if Teela weren't certain it was going to end, she wouldn't bother with something as dangerous as vulnerability. She'd expose herself only if she was certain no one else could ever use it against her.

"Do they frighten you?"

"No."

"Why not?"

"I've seen what men can do," he replied carefully.

"There's not much a wild animal can do that would be worse. Or messier."

"Well, I think you'll like the Pridlea."

"I think you're right. *If* I'm not told to wait outside in the street."

"Why on earth would you have to wait outside in the street?"

He raised an eyebrow and said, "Are you in a betting mood?"

Kaylin left instructions with the carriage driver, and Severn left different instructions about ten seconds later. The driver seemed to take this in stride, which is to say, he did his level best not to look too amused at her expense. You had to like that in a driver.

She approached the door. Door, at this time of year, was not exactly the right word to describe the heavy, colored curtains that shut out the sounds of the street. During the humid season that any port city suffers, these were the only doors that the Pridlea either desired or needed. After all, it wasn't as if someone was just going to walk in off the street.

The colors—predominantly a yellow gold—were embroidered into the fabric, which also seemed to boast a profusion of textures. Kaylin had seldom come to the Pridlea when she was on duty, and she stopped a moment to study the heavy, hanging rug. Gold was nubbled in knots around a central patch of color that seemed, to her eye, to be furrier, somehow. She bent forward, and said, "Hey, I think they used Leontine *hair* in this."

"We did," she heard a familiar voice say. It was the voice of all Leontines when they chose to speak

Elantran, and it implied a growl that wasn't actually present. "The hanging contains the fur of every Leontine of age in Marcus's clan. The fur of his sons are here," she added, as she stepped out of the building—which was a squat, clay rectangle that seemed to go on forever at her back. There were windows in the front of the building, but in the back, very few. As a child, Kaylin had referred to it as Marcus's cave. Marcus, batting her playfully—but still painfully—on the side of the head had called it *Kayala's* cave.

"The ones that don't live here?"

"There are no sons here, no. And yes, when they reached the age of majority, they offered some of their throat fur for this purpose, and we accepted it." She let her hand fall away from the hanging, and hugged Kaylin suddenly and without warning.

Kaylin, however, didn't need a warning; she knew what to expect, and if Leontine claws and teeth were sharper and harder than some of the crappier Imperial steel she'd seen, their fur was softer than *anything*. She returned the hug at least as ferociously as she received it, and heard the throat-sound of an older Leontine's purr just above her ear.

"You look good enough to eat," Kayala told her, as she stepped back. "We thought you might visit. But I'm afraid the house is not in order." She looked as if she were about to say more, but stopped and slowly turned just her head to look at Severn. "You may go now," she told him. "We will watch over Kaylin while she is with our Pridlea. She is as kin."

Severn glanced at Kaylin.

"He's not here as my escort," Kaylin said. She could

see the Leontine eyes begin to shade to an unfortunate shade of copper—something they had in common with the dragons. She also had no idea why.

"Kaylin has not made racial differences a study," Severn told Kayala, speaking both formally and softly. He didn't move at all as he spoke to the Leontine Matriarch. He didn't gesture or change the position of his head. "She came here to see you the minute she could—but she didn't stop to think."

"Ah. Well. *Thinking,*" Kayala said, inflecting the word with distaste.

Severn didn't nod. Instead, he said, "Because she didn't, she has *no* idea why you will not, in fact, allow me to cross the boundaries of your home."

Well, the orange was gone. But if you knew Leontine faces well enough, you could easily see the shocked rise of eyebrows in that furry, feline face.

"She probably also doesn't understand," Severn continued, "why you had to accompany Marcus when he visited her after she was injured in the fiefs. Nor does she fully appreciate how unusual Marcus—and by extension, his Pridlea—is."

"Unusual?" Kayala said, as if tasting the word.

"He means it as a compliment," Kaylin said quickly. "And I do—he's the only Leontine on the force for a reason."

"Yes. He can coexist in an office that has, among its many members, other males."

"They're mostly human," Kayala offered.

"So is Severn," Kaylin told her.

"If Corporal Handred chose to visit us in the human Quarter, we would of course grant him the hospitality of the Pridlea. He has, however, come to the Pridlea, and in the Leontine Quarter, social rules must be observed." She sniffed, a very catlike sound of disdain. "Although why one would consider them *male,* I have never fully understood."

Kaylin winced.

Severn, however, did not. "He can *also* coexist in an office that has, among its members, many females. And his wives accept this." He moved something other than his mouth for the first time, and bowed.

"They are not our kind," Kayala said, but the edge had gone out of her words. "They are human, or—what do you call the long ears that are hard to kill?"

"Barrani."

"Barrani. And bird-men. They are not of the Pride. We are not threatened by them. They cannot trespass upon our home."

"Wait," Kaylin said. "What if there were other Leontine men?"

"There won't be."

"But if there were?"

She was silent. Kayala's silences usually meant death. Quite literally.

"And other Leontine women?"

The silence was almost profound. Kaylin had once asked Marcus why he was the only Leontine on the force, and Marcus had growled an answer: *There's only room for one. If you want another one, talk to the Swords or the Wolves.* She had thought he was joking at the time.

"What about me?"

"Ah, you. You are his kitling, the one he can't lose through growth or time. You are not of the Pride," she added, but she ruffled Kaylin's hair—which had long since come loose from its binding—with affection as she said the words. "He brought you home," she added, "and we saw you—hairless, furless, like our young."

"But Severn's—"

"Corporal Handred is *not* like you, Kaylin. But he understands and accepts his role here." There was no question in the words. "Come," she said, and growled.

Severn bowed again. "I will wait for Kaylin in the carriage."

"Good. It is not a good time to be in the Quarter without escort."

"Kayala, I can take care of myself."

"Of course you can," was the smooth reply. "We can all hunt and kill. But the trick to living in a city that is so crowded and so dangerous is to avoid having to kill."

Marcus had four other wives—five in total. Each of his wives had their own room, or rooms, and each of them had their own growls. They had different ways of showing submission, and of expressing rage. Kayala could do either without consequence, but if Kayala was the eldest, she was a far cry from old.

Then again, Marrin at the Foundling Hall was old, and you didn't cross her.

Tessa was next in line, and her fur was a slate-gray that was almost black. Her whiskers were dark, and her fur was shorter than the fur of the rest of her Pridlea. She was fastidious while eating and grooming, and of the five wives, Kaylin thought her the most dangerous. But for all that, she was often the friendliest as well, and little human foibles didn't bother her.

She didn't, however, react well to the sight of blood, and Kaylin did her best not to bleed around her.

Graylin—a very unimaginative name—had been the runt of her litter, and her parents, convinced she wouldn't survive her childhood years, had been less than attentive. Kayala said that Graylin was almost feral when this mistake in judgment was acknowledged. If Tessa was the most fastidious—by a whisker—Graylin was the *least,* by a whole lot more. She had been civilized to the point where she could eat in a large group and not go nuts about food distribution—but she seldom left the Pridlea. She had the softest voice, the softest purr, and the most tangled fur.

Reesa was golden in color, just like Marcus or Kayala, and she looked younger. Her eyes were large for Leontine eyes, and she seldom blinked, which some people found discomforting. Reesa thought this was funny, and after a while, Kaylin had to agree. Like, say, a year of visiting at mealtimes.

And Sarabe, the youngest of Marcus's wives, was also a russet-colored Leontine—a color that was considered unusual, although Kaylin had met one other, at least, that bore the same red fur. Only the face, the hands and the feet were fringed in the more traditional gold. Sarabe liked to sing. Singing Leontines were a bit more than Kaylin could handle for hours at a time.

She wasn't singing now. None of them were even speaking. They sat curled up on each other in what looked like the end result of a football tackle, and didn't bother to get up when Kayala escorted Kaylin into the common room. In the common room—which had a Leontine name that Kaylin had never had much luck pronouncing, to the gleeful amusement of Reesa—dinner was served, and matters of concern to the Pridlea were discussed. Marcus, oddly enough, was seldom invited to the common room. He came for meals, and for discussions about his children, and he left as quickly as he could. Kaylin, loving this room at thirteen, had never understood why.

But if the common room was not his room, it was clear that his absence marked it, and not for the better.

Sarabe jumped up. "The kits will want to see you," she said. Kaylin, watching bodies roll to either side at the sudden lurch of Leontine momentum, smiled. She'd been on the inside of these pile-ons as a child, and she had been allowed to play with Sarabe's kits if she asked politely. Where "asked politely" meant speak in Leontine. Sarabe was the most…human of the Leontines. She was also a good deal younger than Kayala or Marcus.

"The kits will have to wait," Kayala replied.

The kits were triplets—this was fairly common for Leontines—and they were all girls. None of them had Sarabe's coloring; two were gray, and one was a pale brown. Sarabe had noted this lack with satisfaction, and Kaylin had never asked why; she understood that Sarabe was a bit self-conscious.

"Easy for you to say, Kayala. You won't have to deal with their cries of outrage."

"I can, if you prefer."

Reesa laughed. It was a grim laugh. She rolled to her feet next. "Kitling," she said to Kaylin.

Kaylin nodded. "I suppose you were expecting me."

"I was expecting you last night," Reesa replied

gravely, her gaze unblinking gold as her eyes met Kaylin's and held them.

Kaylin winced. "We were up in the Tha'alani Quarter. I had to heal," she added. "The crowd there is ugly. And there are more Swords gathered in one spot than you see anywhere, even Festival."

Reesa hissed. It was the Leontine version of a whistle. Well, this hiss, at any rate.

"And I had to force Perenne to carry me up to the damn dome to talk with the Hawklord," she added. "Mallory's in charge of the office."

This drew a round of a different type of hiss from all of the wives, even Kayala. "You will have to keep us apprised of the situation in the office," the Matriarch said. Kaylin didn't like the word "Matriarch," but it was, Marcus assured her, the *right* Elantran word for his wife.

"I'll trade," Kaylin replied, tensing slightly.

Kayala became still. "Trade?" she said.

"Keep me apprised of the situation in the Quarter. The Hawklord said that Marcus goes on trial in the Caste Court in five bloody days."

"It is true."

"Can you agree to this?"

"No. There is no trade among kin," Kayala replied.

Kaylin said nothing for a long while. "Not a trade," she finally managed. "I'll tell you what's happening in the office anyway—Marcus clearly did."

Kayala nodded. "We will tell you what we can. Sarabe, start."

Sarabe looked away.

"Why Sarabe?" Kaylin asked Kayala.

"Because it is Sarabe's tale, to start. And if we have all become a part of it, it is still hers."

Sarabe looked at her hands. She sat still, looking at them, until Reesa put an arm around her shoulders, flexing her claws with unvoiced worry. Worried Leontines could often appear, to the non-furred, the same as angry Leontines. When Sarabe spoke at last, it was to Kaylin.

"Kitling," she said softly, "you have met my sister."

Kaylin was confused. And, being Kaylin, showed it. "Your sister?"

Sarabe nodded. "Not long ago, you visited her. You helped her deliver her cub."

Kaylin's eyes widened. "Is that where she got my name?"

Sarabe nodded gravely. "It was much discussed in the Pridlea, but Marcus insisted."

"Was that bad?"

Silence.

"I've come as a midwife to other Leontines before."

"Yes."

"Sarabe, I'm sorry, but I don't understand." She paused, and then said, "But your sister mirrored me. She wants to talk to me."

Kayala's growl was instant, a low thrum of sound more felt than heard.

"Kayala, she's allowed to contact me. I licked her baby clean at birth."

"Why?"

"She asked," Kaylin replied with a shrug. "I knew it was an honor, so I did it."

All of Marcus's wives now looked at each other in

turn. The silence—a silence that was very unusual in the Pridlea—was heavy. "We told him," Kayala said at last. "Sarabe—"

Sarabe said nothing.

"Guys, look—Marcus needs help. And to help him, I need to know what's going on."

"You will likely know more than we know by the time you have finished speaking with my sister," Sarabe said at last. "But I will say what I can. You've noticed my fur color?"

Kaylin nodded. "I like it," she offered.

"I don't. And my sister does not. It marks us, and we are forbidden sons because of it."

"Forbidden…sons."

"Yes."

A thought—an unwelcome thought—occurred to Kaylin. "You can choose the sex of your cubs?"

"No. We cannot. We merely have the duty to see that if sons are born, they do not survive. Don't look at me like that, Kaylin. You don't understand our history. You don't understand what the color of our fur *means*."

"No. But I'm listening."

"In times past," Sarabe continued, "we would have been drowned at birth. My sister and I. But our mother was young, and foolish, and the old ways are not as strong in this city as they are among our other tribes. My mother's husband—that is your word, yes?—was old and also foolish, and he had lost many wives to birthings. He desired cubs, and when we were born, he approached the Elders, and he petitioned for our lives. He understood that he could not hide us. He could not dye our fur, and expect us to survive in the world without the blessing of his Elders. He was a friend of Marcus, his mentor. He was unusual in many ways for a Leontine, and if Marcus is unusual, my father is often blamed." She shot a side glance at Kayala, who nodded.

"Because we were girls, and at the urging of many of the more liberal of our kind, he was granted his petition and we were allowed to grow. There was no certainty that we would survive to adulthood—many who are otherwise unmarked do not. But we were not seen as a threat. Indeed, it was thought that none would take us to wife, and we would find no Pridlea, and have no children, of our own.

"It is in our children that our greatest threat lies," Sarabe added.

"You *have* children."

"I was blessed with three daughters," Sarabe said. "I do not know what Marcus would have done had one of my cubs been a son."

"He would have drowned him," Kayala said firmly. "And if not he, then one of us."

Kaylin couldn't believe her ears. She asked Kayala a question in her high, broken Leontine, and Kayala reached out and ruffled her hair. "We are a dangerous people," the Matriarch told Kaylin, "and our ways are harsh. But better the death of the son than the death of the race."

"You're talking about *babies,*" Kaylin said, finding no easy way to express her outrage in Leontine. Which, given that Leontine was her language of choice for cursing, said something.

"You may have noticed that babies do not stay young," Kayala replied. "Reesa, stop that—we just replaced that table." Reesa obligingly pulled her claws out of the wooden surface. Kaylin had always wondered what Leontines outside of the city used for scratching posts—or dinner tables—but she wasn't certain at this moment she wanted to know. "Babies grow. And the sons who are born to those who bear the witch-fur grow into something wild and dangerous."

"I've practically lived with Marcus for eight years. He doesn't move a piece of paper without telling you all about it. As far as I can tell this is true of *all* Leontine men. Hells, he might ask you first on a good day. You're saying—"

"Marcus is a kit," said Tessa firmly. It was full of affectionate amusement. "He understands that the Pridlea is his in name only, and he doesn't meddle." The warmth of the smile left her face, leaving fangs in its wake. "Not all men are as smart, and not all men are as…what is your word? Casual?"

"Laid-back, maybe."

"Laid-back. Doesn't that mean dead?"

Probably, to a Leontine. "It means relaxed."

"Ah! Yes, that is the word. Relaxed. Not all men are as relaxed or as sensible as ours."

"Marcus desires our happiness," Kayala said gently. "He always did. He learned, as he grew whiskers, that our happiness and his were entwined—but he wanted our happiness first. You must have noticed the way he takes you into his own shadow, Kaylin? He wants what is best for you."

"Getting yourself thrown into a Caste jail while vultures rule the Hawks is *not* what is best for me. And it doesn't make me happy either."

Graylin hissed.

Kaylin lifted a hand, palm up, in immediate surrender. "I'm sorry," she told them all quietly. "I don't know where that came from."

Kayala batted the side of Kaylin's head. It hurt. It did not, however, send her flying, which told Kaylin it was meant affectionately. "You are like us, when you worry," she said. "We understand."

"He always notices the strangers," Sarabe continued, her voice so soft it was hard to hear. "He always notices the outcasts or the misfits. He speaks unkindly, but while he bares fangs and exposes claws, he stands between us and those who mean us harm. Many of his brothers think he is—what is the word, Kayala?"

"I don't think Kaylin needs to hear the word," Kayala replied sharply. Which probably meant it was, in Kaylin's line of work, a *useful* word. She held her peace, however.

"They think he is weak," Sarabe continued, choosing a less colorful, and entirely Elantran, substitute. "Because he doesn't fight unless he needs to. But if he is cornered, he can kill. We've seen it, and we know."

"If you're cornered, you can *all* kill."

"Yes, but Marcus doesn't choose to hunt for sport. He is gentle."

Tell that to the Quartermaster, Kaylin thought, remembering the carved surfaces of far too many desks.

"Let me continue, then. My sister and I were allowed to live. We were allowed to grow, and we were allowed to request the rites of majority. All of this was considered safe, for us, although many of the more conservative Leontines resented it. They made our lives harder," she added, baring fangs.

"Sarabe," Graylin told her, "if you begin to catalogue all wrongs done you, we will be here all night, with Kaylin no wiser."

Sarabe smacked Graylin, who rolled with the blow. "He is *much* kinder than his wives.

"But…we were allowed to live normal lives because it was understood that we would never progress beyond the Pridlea, we would have no Pridlea, and no husbands of our own."

"But…"

"Yes. I have my Pridlea. But it was understood that I would not, when I was born."

"How did that happen?"

"Kaylin," Kayala said. "Ask her another time."

"Sorry."

"No, it is a good question," Sarabe said, reassuring her, but also following Kayala's unspoken command. "And I will answer it—briefly—because it's relevant." She dared a glance at Kayala, whose lips had thinned, making her teeth much more prominent. The first time she'd seen this, Kaylin had been terrified; now it was just so much bickering. The Leontines could deal damage, yes, but they were also built to take more of it.

Kayala however considered what had been said, and nodded briskly.

"Marcus took me in when my father died." She smiled. "His Pridlea was very, very different from my mother's—it was a bit shocking, at first. But…it wasn't so fearful. My parents always worried for us.

They always watched over us, they always looked at the future with uncertainty. I'm sure it aged them both.

"Marcus did worry about me, but not in the same way. After three days, he treated me like—"

"Like one of his wives," Graylin said, with a rare smile.

"Which means," Reesa added, "that he did what she said, more or less, when she said it. I don't think he noticed it himself, but the rest of us did. There was a bit of a fuss maybe three months in," she added, the smile growing sharper. "Some people felt that Marcus's interest in Sarabe was—what is your word? Obscene?"

"I don't think that's the right word," Kaylin replied.

"Actually, Kaylin, it *is* the right word," Kayala told her. "They thought it was twisted, and wrong. A small group of the older Leontines—by which I mean those who conform to the Elders, because some of them were young enough to damn well know better—came to see us."

Kaylin thought about this for a couple of minutes. "Wait, they came to see you here?"

"Yes."

"And they were all women?"

"Ah, you understand. No, in fact. None of them were women."

"But you wouldn't even let Severn in—"

"Not with his genitalia intact, no."

Kaylin blushed, and Graylin frowned. "Why are you doing that?" she asked softly.

"Well—it's—"

"You've said much, much ruder things at our table."

"No I haven't!" Kayala retorted.

"Yes, you have. You've said—"

"Graylin." Kayala lifted a hand. "Very often, when one curses in a different tongue, it doesn't feel or sound the same as cursing in one's own. And Kaylin's colorful phrases all mean the same thing. She's tired, hungry or angry. And this is why it's hard to tell you anything. There are always interruptions."

"But—"

"Yes. It was wrong, and it was dangerous. We could not, of course, allow them into the Pridlea."

"Wait—is that where Reesa's scar comes from?"

"Yes," Reesa said, with an entirely self-satisfied grin.

And she had thought it odd when Severn had become so completely *still*. She hated that she could feel so bewildered about people she'd seen for so much of her life. "So they went away?"

"They went away. However, they claimed that Sarabe was being ill-treated in our Pridlea, and they demanded that she leave with them."

"They said that with straight faces?"

"Bleeding faces, more or less," Reesa replied. "But if you mean were they serious? Yes." She shook her head. "We realized at that point that we had come to a crossroad. So we talked among ourselves, and then we informed Marcus of our decision."

"Which was?"

"He could make Sarabe his wife," was the prompt reply.

"Or what?"

"There was no or." Reesa grimaced. "Marcus wanted to anyway," she told Kaylin. "He'd wanted to for at least two of the three months—believe that we could smell it. But he felt that Sarabe, with no Pridlea to barter for her, was not in a position of strength—he feared to take advantage of her situation. Sometimes he thinks too much."

"And Sarabe was okay with this."

Sarabe smiled. "I was overjoyed," she said, and she looked it, just remembering. "I loved the Pridlea already, and I was terrified of the day I would have to leave it. I didn't expect it," she said, "but I wanted it. I wanted to stay with these women. I wanted to help build a home for that man."

Kaylin gave her a few minutes before she asked the obvious question, the one that would chase the memory away and leave shadows and fear. But she was here to ask that question, or ones like it. "What happened to your sister?"

The quiet was subdued and, yes, shadowed by a different kind of memory. "Understand that with the death of my father, the Pridlea lost its focus," was her reply. "He had only two wives, the others had either abandoned him or died.

"But he had friends, some of them powerful, or we would never have lived beyond our birthing. My mother was gray," she added, "and it was not known until we were born that she carried the taint.

"When my mother died, my father had only one wife, a younger wife. When my father died, she was alone. But she was not without choices. *We* were. She could join another Pridlea, or she could seek shelter with her sisters in theirs—but she could do neither with both of us.

"Marcus offered to help her, and she acceded. She

allowed me to come to live here, while she attempted to find better arrangements."

"Which she knew she could never find on her own."

"I believe that was the way she thought. My sister, however, did not choose to accept Marcus's invitation. She was excited," Sarabe added, "because she thought she could find a Pridlea of her own."

"With who?"

Sarabe was silent.

Kayala was also silent. It wasn't the same type of silence, but clearly, Kayala was waiting for Sarabe to break it.

"A friend of my father's. He did not, of course, visit— that is a human custom and it is an odd one to us—but there are public places in which we meet our father's friends. It is often the same place in which we might meet our future husbands or wives."

"He approached my aunt and offered her a home for both my sister and I."

"But you came here."

"Marcus asked first," she said, perhaps a bit too quickly. "But…I had met both men, and I had also met Kayala and Reesa and Tessa. Graylin doesn't leave the house much. I liked his wives," she added.

"And this friend you don't name had wives you didn't like?"

"He had no wives."

The idea of an adult male Leontine with no wives momentarily deprived Kaylin of speech. Luckily, she was good at recovering from that particular setback. "He had *no* wives?"

"He was not lucky," she repeated with great care.

"And he had lost two wives. He did not originally come from the city, but he was known here, among those who drift in from the outlands. He is respected," she added, again with care. "And I would tell you his name, but I do not think you would recognize it."

"Fine. So, nameless male friend with *no* wives asks your aunt out of the goodness of his heart if you would like to live with him. Your sister says yes. You say no."

She nodded. "I tried to change her mind," she added. "We argued. It was a bitter argument. In *this* Pridlea, they argue *all* the time, but…even though they argue, they still know they're on the same side. They still have many of the same goals.

"My sister and I never argued. We knew, growing up, that we had only each other. So when it came time to make the choice, it was…bitter."

"How bitter? Not speaking to each other bitter?"

"She would not speak to *me*," was the slightly more heated reply. "But I had everything, here. They treated me like one of their own. I was happy. I was afraid of the happiness," she added. "Because sometimes you lose things, and it's best not to want them too badly if you don't also want the pain. But it's hard to be afraid in this house."

"Say that to Marcus," Kaylin replied with a grin.

"I will. When this problem is sorted out, I will," she said firmly. "I wanted her to have what I had. She wanted me to have what she had."

"So she went to live with this man, but not as a wife."

"No."

"And she was pregnant how?"

There was a shocked silence.

CHAPTER 6

"**A**nd you blush at what Kayala says?" Graylin's brows, already of a color with her fur, seemed to have disappeared entirely.

"Did I just say something no one else knew about?"

"No," Kayala said, her voice as warm as winter rain. "We knew. Of course we knew. But…you do not understand her position. She has never formally been taken or accepted as wife. She has no Pridlea and she cannot begin to form one without that recognition. Even if everyone knew—and very, very few do—she would be shunned by mothers such as *I,* because to send your daughters into a house with no *Mrryn* is to send them into chaos."

"Mrryn?"

Reesa laughed at Kaylin's pronunciation, and Tessa chuckled, clucking. Given their reaction, Kaylin wondered what she'd actually said, because she was pretty certain it wasn't what she'd tried to repeat.

"Matriarch," Kayala supplied in Elantran. "I don't like the word—my wives are *not* my daughters—but I think it is as close as you Elantrans come to understanding my role." By Elantran, she clearly meant human, but Kaylin didn't bother to quibble.

"When the men are young, they fight, they want sex, but they care only for their own opinions of each other, and in the wrong mood, they pee on everything.

"But when they are more mature, they come to understand the value of a home, and of cubs. They understand that we are not interested, in the end, in the opinion of their male friends—or in any male opinion that is not their own. And they *choose* to leave the world of men when they choose a wife. There are rituals that are still performed in older tribes, in which the men must prove their worth. Some do not survive it. Some do not complete the rituals because they are not yet ready to do so.

"But those that prove worthy make a home, and they give it to us because they must trust us. We build it for ourselves and for our husband. What happens beyond the hanging is private, and I am sure that Pridlea differ widely. But the men are willing at that point to confine their behavior. They turn away from their youth. It is a statement of intent, Kaylin. It is a public statement."

"But you don't even allow other men to visit—how public can that be?"

"Never mind. That is a long discussion, for later. I'll let Sarabe handle it, because she'll certainly have to explain it to her daughters soon enough. I merely mention it because—"

"This mystery male didn't make that statement."

"No."

"And you think he's still grandstanding or peeing on fountains."

Kayala grimaced. "Marcus told me to watch my tongue around you, kitling. It seems he knows you well. Of all the words to fasten onto, you choose those ones."

Graylin said, "Not all of our men marry. And no, the ones who do not choose a Pridlea do *not,* as you say, pee on fountains. Or in them. Or anything like it. But… it is not a world for a kit. It is not the world for one who *wants* a Pridlea. Do you understand?"

"So wait, there are women who don't want one?"

"Yes."

"And they don't have one."

"No."

"But—"

"Some are like your Marrin. They build family, rather than bear it. Marrin could not be wife to anyone, ever. She will not give up her adopted cubs, and she will not trust other Leontines with them. I think she's wise," Kayala added, "and I like her a great deal. But she has chosen a different life."

"She doesn't kill men on sight, no."

"She doesn't have to. Her kits are human, and they must live a human life; she makes certain they live well while they are with her, and she makes certain they are doing well when they are not. They are her only concern. She has no room for any other."

"What about the other women?"

"Some of them live alone, in isolation, as many of the unmarried men do. It is…not an easy life. But some prefer it. Not all Pridleas are gentle—not all are sane. Some women have tried marriage and found that they felt trapped by it, suffocated by it. A good Pridlea is a blessing. A bad Pridlea is worse than none at all. And there is no way to determine which is which before you enter it.

"You may, in time, meet women who are not married. I do not think Marcus will expose you to his friends, but I am not certain. You're human," she added, as if this weren't obvious, "and their instinctive reaction to you is not the same as it would be to us."

"I don't want to know."

"No, kitling, you don't. But we are relying on you. We speak to other wives, of course, but we cannot depend on them to travel or to talk to other men. When you do—if you do—take Corporal Handred with you."

"The one you wouldn't let in here with his balls."

Kayala hissed. "I *will* watch my tongue around you, kitling. Or injure you. I haven't decided which. Yes, *that* Corporal Handred. He would die for you. But he would also kill for you. He will not hesitate if he sees the need. Marcus will not be able to protect you here, for obvious reasons."

"I don't need a lot of protection."

Reesa laughed. It was a lovely, growly sound. "None of us *needs* protection on our own, Kaylin. It's not because you're fangless that Kayala says this to you. But there are situations in which it is better to be surrounded by your kin."

"He's not my—"

"The Hawks are all your kin. We do not feel weak when we say we need the Pridlea. Do not feel weak when we say you need no less."

Kaylin nodded. "I'll try," she said. "Old habits. But Sarabe, your sister?"

"She became pregnant. It was only then that she spoke to me." Sarabe looked at the table, where several sets of claws were making new marks. Not that it was easy to tell, there were so many old ones. "I was shocked. But I was not entirely surprised." She hesitated for another moment. "She begged me to tell no one, and I agreed."

"You told everyone here."

"Oh, that—that doesn't count. She could no more ask me to keep secrets from my wives or husband than she could ask me not to breathe. She knew I would speak to them."

Kaylin thought for a moment. She chose her words as carefully as she could. "Sarabe, you and your sister were born—"

"Yes."

"I mean—"

"I understand what you mean. When I became pregnant, I was taken to the Elders, and the pregnancy was registered. There was some argument about it at the time. So many angry men," she added. "But Marcus took the oath, and convinced the others that if his litter contained any boys, he would kill them and bring the Elders the body."

"Oh." The idea of Marcus killing was nothing new; the idea of Marcus killing a *baby* was, and Kaylin didn't like it. At all. She struggled to keep her voice even. "She didn't do that."

"No. She didn't. It would have been difficult for her

to do so, given the circumstances—but even in these circumstances, it is required by our laws."

"She had her baby in secret."

"Yes."

"But she had a boy, Sarabe."

The silence was utter and profound. It robbed the room of color and movement.

"Did Marcus know this?" Kayala asked at last, breaking the silence.

Kaylin started to say yes and stopped. "I don't know."

"He didn't explain any of this to you."

"Well, no."

She uttered a single Leontine word, which Kaylin thought was *men*. "What exactly did he say?"

"He didn't say anything. I wasn't even certain he knew—I received the call from the midwives guild, and I went to the house in the Quarter. I helped a small Leontine woman named Arlan deliver a single live cub. I licked birth fluids off its eyelids, and I left." She held out her hands, palm up. "I didn't know, Kayala."

"Arlan is not her name," Sarabe said. "Maybe you are thinking of the wrong—"

"She had your coloring."

Silence.

"Was the birth difficult?" Kayala asked softly.

"Yes. I'm not sure why."

Sarabe made an almost subvocal sound, pushed herself away from the table and walked out of the room. Kaylin started to follow, and Tessa grabbed her arm. "Leave her," she said quietly. "She needs time."

"Marcus must have known," Kayala said. "He must have."

"I honestly don't remember—Marcus considers off-duty time my own problem, and he never asks. Well, unless I'm hungover and he's trying to make a point, in which case he doesn't care what he *says,* he only cares that he says it loudly."

"How was the mother?"

"She was…odd. But she said the child was very important."

"Oh, he is. He will be."

"From the sounds of it, it doesn't look as if he'll survive." Even saying it made her tighten up. And Kayala noticed. Nothing happened under this roof that she didn't know about. Kaylin let the silence continue until she couldn't stand it anymore. "How does Marcus fit into this?"

"Marcus went to see her on Sarabe's behalf."

"Recently?" Kaylin continued.

"Very recently."

"Kayala—the Leontine who was killed—"

"He was one of the Elders," she replied.

"His name?"

"Does it matter?"

"I can't exactly ask questions if I don't know at least that much."

"Gorran."

"He was married?"

Both of her brows rose. "Of course! You can't be an Elder without being married. If our ways are lax in the city, they are *not* that lax."

"Got it."

"Did Marcus kill him?"

Kayala turned away.

"Kayala?"

"It was not murder," she said at last. "Of that, I'm certain."

"But you're not certain he didn't kill him."

"There were witnesses, Kaylin. Many witnesses."

"Yes, but the death didn't occur in the Leontine Quarter, and to non-Leontines, you all look the same. Well, if your fur is the same color."

"Some of them were Leontines."

Kaylin frowned. "Say that again?"

"Some of the witnesses were Leontines."

"So…we have not one, but two, Leontines outside of the Quarter—the murderer and the victim—and then we have *other* Leontines to bear witness? Kayala, Leontines almost never leave the Quarter."

"This one did."

"Did Marcus know him?"

There was a pause. "I cannot say for certain if the Leontine he killed was the Leontine he went to meet—but yes, he knew Gorran. They were friends of long standing."

"He agreed to meet a Leontine outside of the Quarter."

Kayala nodded. "It was unusual."

"I bet. And the Leontine died, and Marcus—apparently—killed him. Can I speak with Marcus?"

They looked at each other again.

"Is that a no?"

"Marcus must agree to meet with you," Kayala replied.

"None of you have seen him."

"No."

"Spoken with him?"

"How?"

"Mirror."

"Ah. No."

"Let me guess. Caste jails don't have mirrors."

"No."

"Was he injured?"

Kayala finally hissed. It was a brief, angry sound. Kaylin immediately lifted her chin, exposing her throat.

The hiss died. "Kaylin, kitling," Kayala said wearily. "It is tiring for me to explain so much. You are part of my Pridlea, but you are not Leontine, and you do not understand our customs."

"But I need to," Kaylin said. And then she paused for a moment. "Kayala, if there are tribes of your people who exist outside of the city, why are your people *here?*

"I understand why the Tha'alani are here," she added. "They're just as isolated as you are, but they seem to… suit life in a city. The Barrani and the humans wander the whole city at will, and they get into whatever trouble they get into—the Aerians fly it, and they come to market from time to time. They also interact with some of the other races, in the human Quarter."

"The humans don't really *have* a quarter," Tessa answered, when Kayala did not. "They get into *everything.*"

"You could say the same about rats."

"I have."

Kaylin grimaced. "Thank you."

"Kitling—"

Kaylin lifted a hand. "I'm going to talk to Severn," she told them all. "Since my guess would be he'll have to ask for access to Marcus as no one will listen to me."

"They may listen," Graylin said quietly. "They may just kill you out of hand, or try to take you home." Her expression hadn't changed at all; if she was joking, she gave no sign of humor.

"They could try."

"Kitling," Kayala said, also lifting a furred hand, "we make no jokes here."

"Neither do I. If they tried, you can damn well bet it wouldn't be a case for the Caste Courts."

"Only if you survived."

"Do you doubt it? Marcus trained me, Kayala—do you really doubt it?"

At that, Kayala let out a small burst of sound—a truncated chuckle. "I understand why he loves you," she said.

It shouldn't have mattered, but it did. "How did Marcus receive the message to visit this—this friend?"

"By mirror."

"Here?"

"No. At the office."

"At the office."

Kayala nodded.

"I wish you'd told me this while I was also at the office."

"Why?"

"We can sometimes track mirror messages," she replied. "We can tell where they originated, and if they're keyed—which I highly doubt—we'll know who sent them. If they're not keyed, we'll still have a good idea where they started. If they're rerouted, it'll be a bit harder, but that will tell us something, too."

"What will it tell you?"

"That whoever wanted to talk to Marcus didn't want to be immediately traceable. That he was taking precautions to remain hidden. Most people hide for a reason," she said. "I still have a couple of hours before I have to be on duty. I'll see what I can find out. Can I mirror?"

Kayala nodded. "The mirror is keyed."

"To Marcus?"

"To all of us, yes. But I believe it is keyed to accept your messages as well. Marcus always worried."

Severn was waiting and the carriage was waiting and the horses looked as if waiting was something they did only on the outer edge of panic; horses and Leontines were not the *best* combination, and there were a lot of Leontines. The driver looked decidedly relieved to see her. She waved at him as she opened the carriage door and wedged herself through the small entrance.

Severn's arms were folded across his chest; he appeared to be napping. But he opened his eyes as she sat down. "Well?"

"Do you even know where the Caste Court building is?"

He nodded.

"Can we go there?"

"We can go anywhere," he replied quietly. "However, we have no jurisdiction in the Caste Courts."

"The Emperor made the laws, right?"

Severn shifted his weight toward the window of his carriage door, and he slid out of it with a good deal more grace than Kaylin had used going through a much larger opening. She heard his voice, and his instructions, before he returned to her.

"Yes, the Emperor created the laws."

"So he created the Caste Court system."

"Yes."

"So in theory it's sort of Imperial."

"Theory and reality seldom have so little in common. The Caste Courts take a form and observe customs that are not Imperial Court customs. I am not certain you would recognize them as the same entity. The Caste Court is *not* the Imperial Court writ small—each Court is different. The human Caste Court, which is almost never used, is functionally similar to the Imperial one. The Tha'alani Caste Court exists entirely in theory—there are no jails, and no separate building, although matters that might concern a separate Tha'alani law are conducted in the longhouse. I do not believe the Barrani Caste Court exists outside of the High Halls."

Kaylin, who was certain she'd been taught this before, and at greater length, nodded. "I always hated the Caste Court system," she told him.

"You would. But it serves a purpose."

"Which would be?"

"It allows each race to deal with the elements of its populace that it doesn't wish to be held up as an example—a bad one—of racial behavior. It also allowed the laws and customs of each people to be respected, to have weight. People let go of old laws slowly, if at all. I imagine the Barrani will have a Caste Court for at least as long as their race exists."

"I never understood why the Barrani were part of the Empire, either."

"Given the Barrani-Dragon wars, I admit it's a mystery to me—but it could have something to do with the location of the Empire's capital. They can't move the High Halls and, for reasons you are familiar with, they cannot abandon them. But they are not uneasy in the city."

"No."

"What do you think the Leontine Caste Court will look like?"

"I don't know. I've seldom been inside Leontine buildings, and before you ask, they have very few restaurants and very few bars."

"But not none."

"Not none, no. But they are not simply human establishments with fur—there are significant differences. And no, you don't want to know what they are."

She nodded. She didn't.

To call anything a court when it existed as a flat, open space and a lot of stand-alone cages was not in any Elantran vocabulary. Kaylin's vocabulary, already quite extensive, got a workout after she found her voice. The "court," as it was called, appeared to be a series of descending concentric circles—large, arena-size circles—which ended in one flat circle on the ground well below where she now stood. The circles were smooth; Kaylin imagined that people actually sat in them, side by side, looking down.

Most of the cages were empty. One of them was not. She began to make a beeline for the one that wasn't, and halfway down—when she'd reached the third of five circles—she was stopped by two Leontine men. One of the Leontines was golden, the most common color, the other a dusty gray.

As a rule, Leontines didn't wear armor. As a rule, when it was warm, they didn't wear much. Marcus, a Hawk, wore regulation uniform when he was in the office. He wore robes when he was at home—at least when Kaylin visited. These men obviously didn't see the need for either. They did wear loincloths; they did wear bracers. They wore belts, across which hung small pouches and—of all things—truncheons.

Marcus was not required to carry a sword in service to the Hawks. His weapons were a bit more natural.

Severn was a few steps behind Kaylin, but he caught up quickly. He put a hand on Kaylin's arm, which was probably a good thing, because her hand was resting on the pommel of a dagger. She hadn't had the chance to go and get it enchanted in Elani street yet, but silence wasn't required here.

But Severn came to stand by her side; he wanted—by the direction he attempted to push her in—to stand in front of her. She wasn't biting. In a manner of speaking. Neither were the Leontines—yet.

"Stay out of this," he told her. She started to speak, and he moved, his kick—aimed at a region that would have been considered unsporting in a practice bout—signaling an end to conversation.

She stood her ground, although it was difficult. One on one against Leontine claws was considered poor odds for a human. Two on one would be considered astronomically worse. But Kayala's words had made it clear that women didn't interfere in the affairs of men—which affairs, apparently, involved a lot of fighting for dominant space. She understood what Severn was doing. She even understood why it was necessary.

Neither of the guards raised an alarm; neither shouted for help. Their breathing, short and sharp as they moved to counter Severn, was quiet. It wasn't feral; they weren't enraged.

They didn't even seem to be surprised, although the first kick had landed pretty much exactly where Severn had intended to place it.

But they didn't unsheathe their claws; they pulled their truncheons. Severn had not drawn a weapon either. He was *fast,* she'd give him that. Fast, and much stronger than he looked when compared to the Leontine bulk. The Leontines were steady on their feet, much like the cats that were their namesake. They jumped to either side of Severn, and he rolled through them, continuing the motion down to the next circle, the second above the cages. Which was smart; they'd already leaped to intercept him. They missed.

He didn't.

None of his blows were fatal; none of them were slight. He favored kicks, for reach, and he could snap them, pulling back, keeping his body in motion so that no part of him could be easily grabbed. They tried. One Leontine leaped a little too close, and Severn pivoted sideways, avoiding, by the sudden appearance of an un-expected profile, the collision with a much heavier body. The Leontine missed and fell.

Two minutes, three minutes, four minutes—Kaylin

was counting seconds. Severn couldn't keep this up forever. Two against one? You went for broke as fast as you could; you tried to even the odds.

He wasn't quite doing that. The golden-furred Leontine that he'd kicked was definitely slower, but not so slow that it was an advantage for Severn, given the presence of the gray one.

She forced herself to be silent when the second cat clipped Severn's jaw, sending him out of his stance. She forced herself to be still, which was harder. Her hand itched, hovering above the dagger she wore. She couldn't fight the Leontines without drawing the dagger. She didn't have the mass to play this game, and the game she had the skill for involved attrition through blood loss, hopefully none of it hers.

Severn took a blow to the ribs, and managed to avoid a second one—how, she wasn't certain. He caught the gray Leontine in the knee, kicked him in the chest as he faltered. In all this, he said nothing, and they said nothing; the only noise was impact.

Six minutes, she thought. Too long.

And then someone *did* roar, and she turned in an instant at the sound of the voice, the hair on the back of her neck rising.

The two Leontines froze almost instantly, and Severn himself took a single step back before he put up his hands.

From the arena floor, from a chair nestled within the cages, a white-furred Leontine strode out toward them.

He glanced at the two guards and nodded. Then he turned his gaze on Severn, and his eyes were the most remarkable color for a Leontine—they were blue. Kaylin had never seen blue Leontine eyes before, and she wondered what they meant.

Humans were the only race whose eyes did not reflect their moods. They had words for that, and their skin tones changed, but the eyes only shifted color when the light shifted in strength or focus.

As he approached them, the two Leontines lifted their chins, exposing their throats slightly. It was, Kaylin thought, a gesture of respect, but not of subservience. The white Leontine nodded and they fell back. He approached Severn.

Severn stood his ground.

"You are armed," the Leontine said, his Elantran distinctly more growly than Marcus's. "But you did not draw weapons."

"No."

"Why?"

"I was introducing myself, no more."

The large Leontine hissed—amused, Kaylin thought. "You understand some of our ways, human."

Severn said quietly, "I served the Emperor as a Wolf for many years, before I donned the Hawk."

The blue eyes narrowed. "You have been given no leave to hunt here."

"No leave is required to hunt in the Empire. The Wolves operate under the jurisdiction of Imperial Writ."

"And if I say permission is required here?"

"You will say it when the skies darken and the Emperor lands," Severn replied.

Again the hiss, and again Kaylin thought it a chuckle. The face fur that surrounded those shocking blue eyes was flat.

"It is said there are no fools called upon to hunt in the Empire," the Leontine replied. "I have yet to see an exception to this rule. I am Adar."

"I am Severn."

"And your rank?"

"Corporal. Which you recognize."

A third chuckle. "Indeed. It is a good introduction. You lasted far longer than the previous human who came to Court."

"He was not a Wolf."

"No. He was not a man." He shrugged, and turned his gaze upon Kaylin. "And you, you also bear the Hawk."

"Private Neya," she said stiffly.

"Adar," he replied, "of the Claw."

She knew Severn well enough to notice the very slight tightening of his expression, but she couldn't quite tell what had caused it. He said nothing else.

"You are the denwarden, here?"

"I am. There is no other."

"And you are, by Imperial Law, the castelord?" Kaylin knew Severn asked the last question for her benefit.

Adar nodded quietly. "I am that, in Elantran."

"I have come to speak with Marcus."

The Leontine nodded. "If he will speak with you, you have earned that right. But if you are familiar with some of our ways, you are not familiar with all of them—you brought your female with you."

"She is not mine," he replied. "She is a Hawk, in her own right, as you no doubt noticed."

"The Hawks are Marcus's dominion in the city."

"They are."

"And you both serve Marcus."

"We serve the Empire, as Marcus is also sworn to do," Severn told Adar.

"Very well. Follow."

The cage was about two inches taller than Marcus at full height, if that. Kaylin knew this because he was, in fact, standing as they approached, his arms folded across his bare chest, his equally bare legs planted slightly apart. His eyes were gold tinged with orange, and his golden fur was flat and dull. He looked exhausted.

"Marcus Kassan," Adar said quietly, "these two have come to speak with you. Will you allow it?"

"I will."

"I will leave you, then, to discuss whatever matters you wish to discuss. I will not lock the cage behind your visitors."

Marcus nodded, as if this were perfectly natural. He waited until the white Leontine had retreated, and then stood there, looking at Kaylin and Severn, his fingers flexing.

"I spoke with Kayala before I came," Kaylin told him.

"I see."

"Marcus—what happened?"

"I met a friend outside of the Quarter at his request. The request was privately keyed," he added, "and arrived at my office before lunch yesterday."

"He died."

"Yes."

"How?"

"I killed him."

CHAPTER 7

Right up until that moment, Kaylin had been hoping that he would proclaim his innocence. That he would tell her it had all been a mistake. That he would tell her he'd been anywhere else in the city. Disappointment and shock kept her quiet for another minute before she rallied.

"Marcus—why? What did he do?"

At that, the Leontine seemed to deflate. "Kaylin—"

"No, don't Kaylin me. Mallory is in charge of the office. He's the acting sergeant while you're away. And damn it, you'd better be coming back."

"Kitling, it has nothing to do with you. Or with the Hawks. It is a private affair."

"I know about Sarabe's sister."

He was silent for a moment. "You would," he said at last, and heavily. "Her sister called you."

"Yes."

"Kaylin, if I ask, as a favor, that you leave this alone, will it do any good at all?"

"No." She paused. "Maybe. If I understood why—" She paused again. "It's the child, isn't it? Your nephew?"

He turned his head away, but not before she could see the change in the color of his eyes. Gold was tinged with something that might be blue on fire.

"Sergeant Kassan." Severn spoke for the first time, his hands at his sides.

"I am not your Sergeant."

"As you wish. Kaylin is present," he added, "and she dislikes the rules of authority if they deprive her of her family."

Kaylin had no argument to offer; it was true. He was the only Sergeant the Hawks had, and the only one they wanted.

"For Kaylin's sake, then," Marcus said, his voice on the edge of a wild growl. "Take her out of the Quarter. Keep her out of the Quarter."

Severn lifted a brow. "I could only make the attempt once, and if I succeeded, she would return to the Quarter without me."

The growl deepened, and Kaylin saw claws flexing in their furbeds. She'd seen them before, but there was no desk on which to dull their edge. She wanted to be careful on a bone-deep, visceral level. "Kaylin doesn't understand the tribe," Marcus told Severn. "And that is my fault and my failing. I saw, in her, an orphan cub. Not a boy, not a girl—a human. I wanted to give her some sense of family, of the Pridlea that she had never had."

"She wanted that," Severn said quietly. "But like all humans, she isn't good at letting go."

"No," Marcus said. "She is not, at that. You have some experience with it."

"I do."

Marcus growled and straightened out to his full height; the cage hit the fur on his head, flattening it. "How did your first day at the Imperial Palace go?" he asked Kaylin.

"It was interesting."

"Ah. And interesting means?"

"We're babysitting an Imperial Playwright so he can fabricate a story that will make humans in Elantra feel safe around the Tha'alani."

Marcus nodded. "A worthy endeavor."

"The man is an ass."

"Agreed."

"And he—wait, what do you mean agreed?"

"I had the privilege of making his acquaintance."

"And you sent me there *anyway?*"

"He doesn't appear to love rules, and he appears to have survived this dislike intact. I felt you would be safe there. I don't think it's possible to offend him."

"Wrong."

"I don't think it's possible to offend him and be thrown in jail—or worse—for the offense."

"Oh."

"However he seems to have offended you—and he is likewise not in jail. What happened?"

She hesitated.

"Kaylin. *Private.*"

"We took him to the Tha'alani Quarter."

Surprise and shock were difficult to distinguish when plastered across Leontine facial fur. "You took Richard Rennick to the *Tha'alani Quarter?*"

"He'd written this pile of crap, Marcus. It was just… crap. Everything about it was wrong. We thought it would be better if he could see the Tha'alani for himself. If he could talk to them. And Ybelline sent a message to Sanabalis—Lord Sanabalis," she added, seeing the slightly orange tinge to his golden eyes. "She wanted to see me."

"You took a man that makes *you* look tactful to the Tha'alani Quarter."

Put like that, it didn't seem like such a good idea. "More or less."

"And there were no riots."

"Actually, there were."

Marcus covered his eyes with one of his hands. The other was strangling the air around his body. "Do continue."

"But they happened before we arrived. Honest."

The hand fell slowly.

"The Swords were there in force. I think they pulled out more people than they do for Festival Season. They were standing between the Tha'alani Quarter and the civilians who just happened to have found crossbows and other pointy weapons."

"Casualties?"

"Four Tha'alani were injured. I don't think any of the humans were hurt, more's the pity."

"The injuries?"

She hesitated.

"They were not life-threatening," Severn interjected.

The Leontine sighed and his hand stopped twisting in the air. "The city is balanced on a thin edge," he said. "The work that Rennick is undertaking is considered necessary. For humans—who comprise most of the Elantran population."

"I know," Kaylin replied. "Rennick did talk with the Tha'alani, and with Ybelline. It started out badly, got worse, and then got better. I'm not sure how the last part worked, so don't ask."

"Good. If that's all?"

She knew a dismissal when she heard it, but before she could automatically retreat, she said, "Marcus, that's *not* why we came. You are going to have to answer at least a couple of questions or Kayala will rip out my throat."

At that, he did smile. It was a toothy grin, but all Leontine grins were and, as far as it went, it was genuine.

"Why did you kill your friend?"

"He was trying to kill me," the Leontine replied.

"Did you happen to *mention* any of this to the guy outside?"

"Which one?"

"The white one."

"No."

"Marcus—why?"

"The man I killed—to use the Elantran word—was a friend. The son of my father's closest friend. We were not raised in the same Pridlea, of course, but we might as well have been. I trusted him," he added. "And if it came down to it, I would still trust him."

"You just said he tried to kill you."

"Yes."

"And you were expecting that?"

"No. Had I known, I'm not sure what I would have done."

"Stayed away?"

His eyes were golden, but the gold was pale and tired. "No, Kaylin, I don't think I could have stayed away. But the only possible help I could have taken with me was you."

"What?"

"It would have been a long shot," he replied. "But there is literally no one else I would give this information to outside of the Quarter."

"What could I have done?"

"Kaylin—*I don't know.*"

"Then why me?"

Severn said, quietly, "You think magery was involved somehow."

"You really were a Wolf, boy," Marcus replied. "But you see keenly. I'm glad I took you on—you were wasted on the Wolves. Yes, I think some sort of magery was involved."

"Marcus—why won't you take this to the Imperial Courts? Why won't you come to the Hawks?"

"Because it doesn't concern them," he replied. "My friend was clearly not himself."

"Then *tell them that.* Tell them that you killed in self-defense."

"Against what?"

"Against someone who was enspelled against his will."

"Kaylin—"

"They're going to put you on trial in the Quarter in five days."

"Yes."

"And you're going to let them."

"Kaylin, there is more to this than you understand."

"Then explain it. *Explain it.* Make me understand. You don't know who your enemy was? An Imperial Mage could probably tell you if he looked at the corpse for, oh, half a second. I've never heard of magic that works quite like this—but if it can make someone do something they'd never do otherwise, it's probably pretty damn powerful. Mages leave a signature."

"And I thought you failed magical theory."

"I did. It came up later."

He shook his head. "Your teachers would strangle you slowly if they heard you now."

"And I'd let them, Marcus. I'd let them if they could answer the questions you won't answer. I don't think they're going to find you innocent," she said.

"No."

"But you're not guilty of murder."

He said nothing for a while.

She took a step toward him and ran into Severn's arm, which was raised so quickly she didn't have time to stop gracefully. Or at all, really.

"Marcus," he said, "who is Adar?"

"Adar? He is the judge, the jury, and possibly the executioner. You would call him the castelord," Marcus replied.

"Yes. But how was he chosen to be castelord?" Someone else couldn't have asked that question in Severn's neutral tone. At least not if that someone was Kaylin.

But Severn asked it as if it were the most reasonable question in the world, and concerned something as trivial as the weather at the same time. She was going to have to learn that.

Later.

"He is the son of the son, descended in an unbroken line, from the father of our tribe."

"The father of your tribe? The first Leontine?"

Marcus said, "The first of our tribe, yes."

Severn was quiet for a moment, but it was a thoughtful quiet. "In human lands, we grant seniority by birth. The elder children are more senior. This doesn't happen with Leontines."

"No."

"And Adar's brothers?"

"He has none."

"None?"

"None."

"And his father's brothers?"

"There were none."

"His sons?"

"One."

Severn nodded as if this made sense. It didn't to Kaylin. "He therefore has the authority to make a judgment."

Marcus nodded.

"And you will abide by it."

"I will probably die by it."

"I don't think he can kill you."

Marcus laughed. "He can kill," he said quietly. "When necessary, he can kill. He tests. It is the way of the fathers."

"Marcus, this has something to do with the cub, doesn't it? The one I helped birth?" Kaylin interrupted Severn to ask.

Marcus said nothing. Loudly.

Severn came to his rescue. "We have an appointment in less than hour," he told Kaylin.

"What?"

"Richard Rennick. And before you open your mouth, remember why his work is necessary."

"Marcus—"

"He's right, kitling. Go. I have no doubt that I'll see you again."

She wanted to hit him. Or hug him. Or something in between. She stood staring at him, stripped of his uniform and his rank and his office, and she almost couldn't make sense of it.

Severn caught her by the hand and pulled her out of the cage. She didn't resist.

For once there was silence. Kaylin needed time to digest the information she'd been given, and time to think about the information she hadn't. Severn watched her, waiting for her to break the silence. She didn't. The roads were bumpy, and the carriage, not fitted by Imperial cartwrights, was uncomfortable—but complaining wouldn't have helped; complaining about life's little miseries was one of the few conversational luxuries people were allowed, and at the moment, Kaylin couldn't put herself behind complaint.

The streets of the city passed by the carriage windows, people dodging out of the way well before the horses got close. They were coming to and from the market, business as usual clearly marking their faces. She saw no crossbows, no angry, frightened crowds—but the ride didn't take them past the Tha'alani Quarter, and she had no doubt the Swords were still there.

If there was some petty rivalry between the three towers that comprised the Halls of Law—and there was—it only scratched the surface; she knew that if the Swords had taken matters in hand, they were in damn good hands. Better, she thought, with a rueful grimace, than they would have been in hers. People made her angry. Stupid people made her very angry. She wasn't so patient with frightened, either, if it resulted in mobs.

But people were *always* frightened. They were afraid of the Barrani—with good cause, especially in the fief of Nightshade. They were afraid of the Leontines. They were afraid of the Arcanists and the Imperial Mages. They were afraid of the Emperor. It didn't really end, fear. The best you could hope for was cautious fear. The kind that made people politer because it might save their lives.

The worst you could dream of was the fear that now stalked the Tha'alani.

The sad thing was, she *understood* where the crossbows had come from. When she was terrified, she wanted to *do* something. It had taken her years of training to understand that she could use that desperate frenzy to do something *useful*.

Years, damn it. She wasn't going to throw them away.

"Severn?"

"Hmm?"

"When Marcus said Adar had no brothers, did he mean what I think he meant?"

"I don't know. What do you think he meant?"

"When there's already a healthy son, they kill the others."

"Yes."

"How did *you* know?"

"I didn't, until I spoke with Marcus. He understands you, Kaylin. In some ways, he understands you better than I do—in some ways, not even close. But he knows how you feel about children. About those you consider weaker than yourself.

"If he told you, it wouldn't have changed *anything* except your opinion. And in his present condition, he doesn't actually want, or need, that opinion. And I'm not entirely certain he doesn't share your opinion. The Leontines, for the most part, don't live in cities. These ones do, and the city will have its influence.

"Marcus is the only Leontine who has ever served as an officer of the Halls. He's not the only one to be seconded to Imperial Service, but the others were temporary, and no, before you ask, I don't think it's relevant.

"Marcus therefore is a bit of a rebel. A misfit. He governs the Hawks, he oversees investigations into murders and other crimes. Most of the perpetrators are not Leontine so he's had a long time to get used to the way the city functions." Severn glanced out the window, his words muted by the breeze of movement.

"Watching humans, investigating Arcanists, commanding Barrani—he's had to observe some of a culture that isn't his own. I don't think that he considers the child of Sarabe's sister to *be* a threat—it's a fangless cub, a litter of one. I do think he feels responsible in some way for Sarabe's sister. She is his wife's only surviving kin, and he offered to take her into his Pridlea and protect her.

"I do not think he would have killed her son—but I'm not completely certain. Nor am I entirely certain that Sarabe's sister told Sarabe that the child was, in fact, a son. From what you've said, there's a good chance she didn't."

"And I shouldn't have said anything."

"I didn't say that."

"But he's a baby—"

"Yes. But I didn't say that. If, as you suspect, the baby is somehow part of this investigation, we need to understand what the baby means to the Leontines—because the Leontines have chosen to keep Marcus's trial in Caste Court.

"And likewise, with cultural custom, if the Leontines in question don't ask for Imperial help—it doesn't matter. They can kill all of their children, quickly or slowly, and it *doesn't break the law*. You need to remember that, because if you attempt to stop them, and it goes wrong, you'll be breaking the Emperor's law."

"If I survive."

Severn nodded. "You're good at that," he added. "You always have been."

"I've always had help."

"Having help, accepting it—that's a skill as well. Understand that the Leontines don't value life in the same way that we do. On the plains, in the wastes, it doesn't matter. And for a city like ours to exist, it can't matter too much."

"If Sarabe's sister were to ask for intervention—"

"Yes," he said quietly. "That would change everything. For good or ill, it would change everything."

Kaylin nodded quietly. She only had to get through the day, write a damn report, and then—then she would speak with Sarabe's sister.

Richard Rennick's idea of awake was pretty much the same as Kaylin's idea of awake. He came to the door to his huge rooms in a bathrobe that looked like cats had used it for a scratching post. If he had servants—and this was the Palace, so he must—they'd obviously had the good sense to flee; he wasn't in what could even charitably be described as a good mood. He also hadn't shaved, and whatever he'd eaten for breakfast—if he had, as he claimed, been awake for half an hour—was liquid.

"You two took your time," he said curtly, throwing the doors open.

Severn took it as an invitation, and quietly entered the room. As if dealing with half-dressed lunatics was just business as usual.

Kaylin said "good morning" in a voice that matched Rennick's for friendly enthusiasm, and followed Severn in.

The large table in the dining room—which didn't look as if it were ever *used* for dining—was covered in paper. It looked exactly like Marcus's desk would look if the Leontine's desk took up five times the space, and the ever-present piles of hated paperwork had had a chance to topple and spill.

Rennick, clearly not a man for pleasantries at any time of the day, got down to business. "You said the

Tha'alani were trying to *talk* to the tidal wave, didn't you?"

Kaylin couldn't remember saying any such thing, but nodded anyway. She probably had.

"In an attempt to convince it not to drown the city?"

She nodded again.

"And was there any objective evidence that the water could hear whatever it was they had to say? Do *not* stand there trying to come up with something pleasant and mindless to say—I have bureaucrats all over the damn palace who'll do that just fine. They're also getting paid for it, I might add, and you're not."

She almost laughed. Yes, he was angry, and yes, he looked as if he could murder morning, but still. "Yes and no."

"Oh, *that* was helpful." He tossed whatever he'd been scribbling on onto one of the gentle inclines that formed hillocks on the wood's surface.

"They don't speak in words," she offered. "And they can't speak to the elements as if they were people."

"But they can speak to the elements?"

Shaky ground, Kaylin. She grimaced. "That's the yes and no. I'd say yes, but it's not that simple—and the yes in this case isn't likely to make people feel *less* threatened by the Tha'alani."

"They're not famed for their ability to read the mind of every muddy puddle in the city, no," Rennick said. "Look, yesterday gave me something I can work with. I can work with it *now*," he added. "People might become mobs, but in crowds, they also fear a mob. I can use what we saw yesterday." He continued, in a completely different tone of voice, "What did you do, in the Quarter?"

If she hadn't been so damn upset about Marcus, this would have been the question she was dreading. Almost self-consciously, she touched her wrist. The bracer was there. "I'd rather not say."

"Why don't I tell you what I saw?"

Since she knew she couldn't stop him anyway, she shrugged. "Why don't you?"

"I saw four men—Tha'alani, but still men—who might as well be dead. They were carried out of a very smelly, very dark and very crowded building on stretchers. They were brought to *you,* Private."

She waited.

"You touched them. When you collapsed, they were pretty much whole. Two of them could walk away. One of them looked—before you touched him—like he was missing *half his bloody skull.*" He sat back in his chair, tipping it up onto its hind legs. It was too much to hope that it would fall over and take him with it. "It looked very much like you'd healed them. I'm aware that there *are* healers in the Empire. I think there are two or three—they don't advertise, for obvious reasons. I think they are all also seconded to the Imperial Service."

"I serve the Emperor," she replied woodenly.

"You serve the Hawks," he shot back.

"Who enforce *Imperial* law, in case it escaped your attention."

"Pedant."

Severn lifted his fingers to his temples. "If the two of you are completely finished," he said quietly.

They both turned to look at him.

"We have matters here that demand attention. What Kaylin did, or did not do, are not those matters."

"They might be," Rennick replied.

"Leave Kaylin out of your story," Severn said, stepping toward the playwright. He walked quietly and slowly.

"She's obviously part of it, or she wouldn't be here."

"She's here because she has a better understanding of the Tha'alani than you currently have," Severn replied. He stopped walking six inches short of Rennick and looked down. Rennick remained seated.

"Severn—" Kaylin began.

"She is not part of your play," Severn continued.

Rennick's bluster gave way to a voice that was as cold and precise as Severn's. "She is not part of my mandate," he said. "But what she did in the Quarter yesterday—"

"She did nothing in the Quarter yesterday."

"She saved four bloody lives!"

"I think you will find, if you choose to submit a story that contains that information, that it will be summarily rejected. I believe that all versions of your play must, in fact, meet Imperial approval in this particular case."

"And you speak for her now? I hadn't noticed she lacked the ability to speak for herself."

Severn was about two seconds from grabbing Rennick by the throat. Kaylin could see it clearly in the lines of his shoulders and his back. She couldn't see his face, and she was almost glad of it.

But Rennick could, and he didn't seem to be entirely impressed. For the first time, she wondered who Rennick was, and where he'd come from. "Rennick," she said softly, "don't push him."

Rennick shrugged. "Fine. But events like those have story built into them."

"Events like those aren't supposed to happen without direct Imperial permission," Kaylin replied. "And there's an armload of paperwork waiting."

"You won't file it."

"Probably not," she agreed. "But it's trouble for me, and as this isn't supposed to be about me, I'd rather give it a miss."

"All right. But answer a few questions."

"If I can." She watched the slow easing of tension in Severn's shoulders.

"You saved their lives?"

"Yes."

"And Ybelline Rabon'alani summoned you to the Quarter, and waited with the dying, because she expected you'd be able to do so?"

"More or less."

"My sources say you used to loathe the Tha'alani. What changed?"

"I got to know them," she replied, with just the hint of a grimace. "And I believe that in getting to know them, I became better acquainted with my own failings."

He picked up a pen. "What about them caused you to let go of your fear?" The pen's shadow was sharp as it rested against a perfect, pristine page.

She frowned. "They're...they're innocent. Not naive, not stupid—but...there's just something about them. They don't lie," she continued after a pause. "They don't steal. They don't—as far as we know—beat each other, either. They don't want to touch our minds or hear our thoughts—they find them dark and frightening. And with reason," she said. "They want to be left alone."

"And you learned this in one visit?"

She nodded. "They like children," she added.

"All of them?"

"I imagine they'd like any child—"

"I mean the Tha'alani. Do they all like children?"

She nodded.

"And you're fond of them yourself, and they realize this."

She nodded again. He was now writing, his hands steady, his letters loopy but in a perfect line, anyway.

"We don't really have anything they want," she finally said. "They don't want our secrets, they don't want our power. They don't want our jobs or our lives."

"So you stopped hating them because you realized we were totally insignificant to them?"

"I didn't say that." She hesitated and then tried again. For someone who was good with words, she wasn't, sometimes. "They don't take," she told him softly, thinking about Ybelline. "They can't take without giving. Anything I give them, I get back."

"Example?"

He really sounded like a teacher at this particular moment.

"Friendship. Warmth. Intangible things. I took the foundlings there," she added, watching his hand move, pen just an extension of his fingers. "Where I grew up, giving wasn't the norm. We bartered, and worse, when we were desperate and we could get away with it."

She looked up at Severn then. "But there were always exceptions, even there. People who couldn't take without giving something in return, and people who could just give. I didn't think about it a lot as a child." She walked over to Severn's side and touched his arm lightly.

He looked down at her, and she almost had to turn away. But she didn't. "I think the Tha'alani are like— like a family. But they're like a family that will welcome you no matter who you are, as long as you're not afraid of who you are. They're—I don't know. Like the family I would build, if I could just make one up out of whole cloth."

She let go of Severn's arm, then, and spread her hands out, palms up. "I don't think I can explain it better than that."

"That was good enough," he replied. "You're saying they don't expect you to be anything other than what we all are, in the end—flawed, twisted, and ultimately alone." The edge was gone from his voice, and he looked younger. "My mother used to say that we don't always get what we deserve."

"Smart woman," Severn said, the tension also gone from his body, his hands and his voice. "Sometimes we get less and make do—we expect less. Sometimes we get more and we fumble."

Rennick nodded. "What made you two go into police work, anyway?"

"That's a long, boring story," Kaylin said quietly. She forced herself not to say it too quickly, but it was difficult. "Maybe when you've finished this play, I'll buy you a drink and tell you."

"I seldom find people stories boring," Rennick replied. "But I like drinking, so I'll take you up on the offer. Corporal?"

"It seemed like a good idea at the time."

"No drink for you," Rennick replied. But he smiled,

and again, with no edge to harden the expression, he looked younger.

"So…what we have on our side are people who are afraid of the Tha'alani ability to expose all the dirty little secrets we're not proud of having. Am I wrong?"

"No. I'd say you're dead right."

"And on their side, people who don't have dirty little secrets because they can't."

She nodded. "It's not that they're perfect," she added. "It's just that they don't—they don't have these ideas of other people as perfect people. They expect people to get angry or frustrated. They expect people to be, well, people. I don't think they understand our fears," she added. "But it makes them crazy, to try to live in our lives. They've never had to live in isolation." She didn't mention the exceptions. It wasn't important now.

"I've been thinking about that since yesterday," he said.

"You mean when you weren't sleeping?"

"I didn't go to sleep until dawn. If the two of you could stop just standing there and pull up chairs or something, I'd find this a lot less awkward."

Kaylin didn't need to be told twice. Usually, she didn't need to be told once, but Rennick's temper was still a bit of an unknown and she couldn't afford to offend him enough for an incident report—not when Mallory would be the one reading it. At least with Marcus, you could be certain he wouldn't get around to reading it until the middle of next month, by which point there would be more pressing things to deal with.

"Anyway," Rennick said, when Severn also took a seat, "I've been thinking of what it would be like to grow up without privacy. Without the desire for privacy. What do we need privacy for, after all? It's the place where we can *relax.*

"And I've thought about what you said about the Tha'alani version of love or marriage. I don't understand the marriage part, either, but I'm trying to look into it on the side. I suppose if you're certain you're loved, love isn't the same obsession. You didn't ask them about sex, did you?"

Kaylin felt herself coloring, which annoyed her. Sadly, it wasn't the annoyance that caused the flush. "Why would I ask them something like that?"

"They don't have privacy," Rennick said, "so it wouldn't strike them as unusual in the same way it would strike you. Or me."

She nodded because it was true they didn't. And wouldn't. "I'm still me," she told him firmly. "And there are some questions I probably don't want the answers to—so I don't ask them."

"Fair enough. But…our story cycles—the things that we can create with—are often defined by our concepts of love. Or duty. Or honor. I understand that the Tha'alani aren't motivated by the same interpretations—"

"Duty would move them," she said.

"Ah. That's something to note. But as you've pointed out, I won't be putting this play on *for* the Tha'alani. And our people need something that makes them *feel.* They can think about things as well, that's always a bonus. But if we're too esoteric, we won't reach people. Not the way we need to." He ran his hand—the one with the pen in it—through his hair, and Kaylin winced, waiting for him to poke his own eye out.

"I considered—and tossed out—any attempt at inter-racial romance. I'm not sure I could believe in it enough to make it work."

"You need to believe in it?"

"While I'm working, yes. I do. Does that strike you as odd?"

Kaylin had to be benched in order to write anything longer than "gone for lunch." On the other hand, Kaylin wasn't the Imperial Playwright, and it wasn't her job; she was willing to believe that someone *else* would be happy doing it. For a value of happy that Rennick wasn't clearly demonstrating at the moment. "If you can base your play on the facts—even if they're embellished—you *could* stage this for the Tha'alani. I'm not sure they have plays," she said. "I don't visit the Quarter that often. But I know they're curious."

"They were outraged."

"They don't understand the lies we need to tell our-selves," she said softly. "And they know that there's so much misunderstanding, they can't see how lies would change that. That's not their fault. I don't think it's our fault either. It's just the big difference."

"Wait."

"What?"

"Did you say you took foundlings to the Quarter?"

She nodded.

"When?"

"A week or two ago. They *wanted* to go."

"To the Tha'alani Quarter."

"They don't know that much about the Tha'alani, and

they'd just met one. She was the same age as the younger kids, and she wanted to show them where she lived."

"Until I went to the Quarter, with yourself and the Corporal—who I note has been utterly silent—I'd never seen a Tha'alani child before."

"They don't leave the Quarter."

"How, then, did these foundlings—and I assume there's a story behind them as well, and look at me not asking—meet one?"

"It's not public knowledge," she said, hesitating, "but an Arcanist under the Wolves edict kidnapped a young Tha'alani girl. We were given the case, and we found her. She was…traumatized, and I made the mistake of mentioning my kids—my children—while trying to calm her down. She insisted on meeting them." She smiled at that. "She didn't even think it odd that they weren't actually mine—they were mine in a way that's familiar to *her*." She started to add more, but her stomach interrupted her.

"What was that noise?"

"Hunger," Severn said, speaking for the first time since he'd taken his seat. "Kaylin's stomach speaks volumes, and once it starts, it doesn't stop until it's fed."

"You haven't eaten?"

"What do you think?"

"Good point." He shoved a particularly large pile of paper to one side, and pulled a bell off the tabletop. It was a shiny, small bell, but it had gold around its lip, and its handle was a dark wood that gleamed. He rang it.

Something that small shouldn't have made that much

noise. "I haven't eaten either," he told Kaylin. "And as we'll be here until well past the normal dinner hour, we might as well eat now."

CHAPTER 8

In spite of the fact that memories of Marcus kept returning to her, the food did not taste like sawdust. It was *good*. She hadn't expected to like it—it smelled funny, and the meat—real meat—was covered in the type of sauce you'd expect merchants to use to hide the fact the meat had soured. But it was good, and she ate more than Rennick or Severn combined. There was enough food to feed an entire office of Hawks, so there was no danger of making anyone else go hungry.

Rennick didn't have much of a sense of protocol or manners; he ate beside his papers, pen in hand. He also instructed the servants to just leave the food. They were clearly used to this and did as asked without comment. "I'm going to miss the food here when I get replaced," he told them. "And the cleaning up, which I don't have to do myself."

"The work?"

"Not so much. I'll be doing the same work. Well, if you don't include this particular assignment."

"It's probably the one that will affect the most people."

"Only because it has to." He paused, and then said, "I owe you. I thought it was pointless propaganda when I was given the task. Now—now it has more meaning to me." He laughed. "Before, I was certain it wasn't worthy of me. Now I'm not sure *I'm* worthy of the task. But it's better to be uncertain, I think."

Kaylin privately thought he was crazy, and he must have seen this on her face, because he laughed.

"If we don't challenge ourselves, we get stuck in a rut. We do the same things over and over, until they're all faded echoes of the first thing we did. This will certainly be different," he said. "But I think I see how we can start it. And possibly where we have to end it."

"The tidal wave?"

He nodded. "By the time we've reached the end of the play, the tidal wave has to be addressed and explained."

He talked during the meal. And listened. To her surprise, he was actually good at listening. He asked odd questions, a lot of them about children. But he paused when Severn interrupted him.

"Mr. Rennick," he said softly, "Kaylin is not central to this story."

"No, of course not."

"You've had her talk about almost nothing else."

"Pardon?"

"Her childhood—and if she's being circumspect, she's still told you more than she thinks. What she thinks of children. Tha'alani children. Her work with the midwives. Her work with the Foundling Hall."

"Yes?"

"Why are you interested in them?"

Rennick's expression was one of open confusion. "Because they're interesting," he replied mildly. "Is there some reason they shouldn't be?"

"No. But they're not relevant."

"You never know what's going to be relevant," Rennick replied. "I don't care much for people as people—as a faceless mass, or a political one. But I find their stories interesting, and I actually know very few people who do volunteer work at the midwives guild or the Foundling Hall. In the former case, most of the people I know would faint at a birthing. I hear they're quite messy.

"And in the second? I've done one or two plays at the Foundling Hall during Festival Season—"

"A playwright of your stature?"

"This may come as a surprise to you," Rennick said, "but I actually enjoy those plays. The audience *wants* to believe everything they see. They don't just watch, they become as involved as you let them become. They're humanity writ small, and many of them haven't learned how to hide, how to pretend to know things they don't know, how to doubt the things they want to believe in.

"On the other hand," he said, looking to Kaylin, "I wouldn't expect to *survive* any work I did there that wasn't a few hours in duration at most—that Leontine in charge of the kids? She's got a nasty temper."

Kaylin opened her mouth to disagree and shut it. He was right. Marrin had a temper. "She does," she agreed. "But she doesn't turn it on the children. Yes, she nags them. Yes, she growls at them—but her fangs are never exposed when she does it. Her claws never leave her pads. I've seen her rake trails in the stair-rails when she's frustrated," she said, "but she has *never* turned that anger upon the orphans.

"She wants them to be as safe as she can make them. She wants them to do well in the world they'll have to live in. Of course she worries. She's—she's their mother."

"So you know something about Leontines, then?"

Kaylin nodded. Normally she would have smiled, but the word *Leontine* and the name *Marcus* were twinned in her mind, and at the moment, Marcus was in danger. Hard to smile about that.

"You know the Tha'alani Castelord well enough that she called you in an emergency, and you understand Leontines well enough to work with Marrin." He shook his head and, glancing sidelong at Severn, said, "Of course it's interesting to me. You appear to be known to Lord Sanabalis. Do you count the Barrani among your friends?"

"We have Barrani in the Hawks," she replied. "Friend is one of those words they consider 'quaint' and 'human.' But if push came to shove, then yes, I'd consider them friends. I wouldn't let them drive a carriage if my life depended on it, though."

"I've met Barrani at Court," Rennick told her. "I can't stand them. Arrogant, perfect bastards, the lot of them."

"Pretty much."

"And you work with them?"

"I'm working with you," she replied.

He laughed at that. He laughed openly and loudly,

setting his pen down so he wouldn't impale his own leg. "Your point," he said, when the laugh had died down to a chuckle. "You're right, of course. If it comes to that, the Barrani can't stand me either. In the most civil and correct way possible."

"That would be the Barrani," Kaylin said, smiling in spite of herself.

"All right, the two of you throw dice or play cards or something. I need to block out a few scenes and run them past you."

The sky was a shade of pink purple that meant it was getting late. Kaylin had taken the opportunity to grab a few pieces of Rennick's paper, and instead of throwing dice—which she would have vastly preferred—had begun to itemize the day's official duties. Severn did the same, and Kaylin managed not to complain. Much.

"Write it in High Barrani," Severn suggested.

"Why?"

"It's Mallory's mandated language."

She started to snap something sarcastic, remembered who the report was going to and crumpled up the first sheet of paper. It had a lot of company.

When she was mostly finished, Rennick waved them over. "You two might as well go home," he said. "This is going to be a long night, and if you're reading for me, the only thing that will make you snore is the crap I'm writing at the moment."

Sergeant Mallory, true to his word, was still in the office when Kaylin and Severn finally reached the Halls of Law. It had been a damn long day, and seeing Mallory at Marcus's desk, while Marcus was living in a bloody cage, was hard. Harder than it should have been, given she was expecting it.

"You're late," Mallory said, when he was certain she would hear him. He did not like to raise his voice; Kaylin was almost at the desk when he spoke.

"We're keeping Mr. Rennick's hours," she said briskly. "At the request of the Dragon Court."

"Yes, yes." He held out a hand and looked slightly surprised when she took three folded sheets out of her breast pocket and placed them in his open palm. He opened the folded papers, clapped the desk light on, and began to read. The desk light was new. Marcus didn't stay late to read paperwork.

It took him more than fifteen minutes to read the report; he actually picked up a pencil and corrected a few words. Kaylin managed to keep her hands at her sides and, although it was harder, also kept her mouth closed.

"Very well," Mallory said. "Corporal Handred?"

Severn's paper was much more neatly folded, and his handwriting was impeccable. He handed his report to Mallory, and Mallory set it aside without opening it. "The day went well?" he asked, speaking to Severn. Only to Severn.

"Given the nature of Mr. Rennick's assignment, as well as one could expect."

"I note that no report has been tendered for the previous day's work."

"An oversight," Severn replied smoothly.

"Correct it."

"Sir."

"This is an important assignment," Mallory continued. "If you had not been requested specifically, I would have replaced you. Relations with the Imperial Court must be handled with care and diplomacy. Private Neya," he added dourly, "appears to have failed many of the classes involving etiquette." He glanced at a very modest pile of paperwork. "In fact, she appears to have failed most of the classes she was required to enroll in as a prerequisite for joining the Hawks."

Kaylin did not like where this was going. And given it was Mallory, it wasn't likely to change course. Severn gave her one sharp glance and then turned his attention to Mallory—or to a point just beyond his left shoulder.

"As Private Neya's academic record has been referred to by Lord Sanabalis, among others, I believe it is time to correct this deficiency in her education. Private Neya?" Mallory said.

"Sir."

"You will be re-enrolled in the courses you failed. You will pass them. If you were not considered necessary in your current assignment, I would suspend you—with pay, of course—until you achieved sufficient understanding to satisfy your teachers." He looked at her. "You will commence classes when the current assignment is at an end. Do I make myself clear?"

"Sir."

"Good." He sat back in his chair. "Dismissed."

The walk back to her apartment would have been quiet and somber had Severn gone to his own apartments. As it was, it was very, very vocal—and also multilingual.

"Just to be clear, I don't need an escort."

"Not here, no. But, just to be clearer, you *do* require some escort in the Leontine Quarter, and I believe you said you had an appointment there."

She frowned. Looked at the night sky. The sun had long since set, and not even the dark hue of purple twilight now interrupted the reign of moons. "Not for another couple of hours," she told him.

"I can go home and come back, or we can wait together. Up to you."

She shrugged. "Might as well wait," she said glumly. "Although I want to point out that I *did* go to the Quarter without the benefit of a male escort the last time I went to see this woman."

"If you're right—and your instincts have always been good—the child is somehow involved. What you could get away with before the baby was born is probably very different from what you can get away with now. Think. If there's trouble, someone may well be waiting for you."

He was right, and she knew it.

"But if I take you, you'll have to wait in the streets again."

"I wouldn't be absolutely certain of that. From what you told me, there is no Pridlea. If there is no Pridlea, no offense can be taken."

She nodded slowly.

"What are you thinking, Kaylin?"

"I'm thinking about what you just said."

"Ah. And?"

"I'm wondering if part of the reason there's no Pridlea is exactly that—there are other males involved somehow, and they need a place to meet."

He raised a brow. "Interesting thought."

"Interesting good or interesting bad?"

"Interesting in that it hadn't occurred to me."

"I'll take that as a 'good,'" Kaylin said.

He smiled.

"I don't suppose you'd care to wear my uniform and sit behind a school desk?"

He laughed at that. "You expected this from Mallory, didn't you?"

"No."

"Really?"

"I wasn't thinking about Mallory at all."

"Except in the usual colorful way."

"Except that way, yes—but I can find a hundred reasons to swear in any language—I don't need him for that. At least he didn't pull me from the Palace."

"He couldn't. I would be very surprised if he hadn't already tried. But Rennick's work will probably take a few weeks, and Marcus has five days. Don't worry about classes."

"I wasn't. I don't swear like that when I'm *worried.*"

"Fine. Don't get enraged at the idea."

She snorted. Shoved her hands into her pouch and pulled out the very old-fashioned key. Cursed liberally until she managed, in the moonlight, to fit it into the lock. "Come on upstairs," she told him, as the door creaked open. "There's no food, though."

"Imagine my shock."

She laughed in spite of herself, feeling at ease with Severn. Everything else had been turned upside down—but he was what he'd always been. She'd hated him for it for almost half her life. She could honestly say she loved him for it now.

He took the time to dress a little more carefully. Which is to say, he unwound the chain of his only weapon. It looked like a very, very heavy belt—one that happened to have daggers at either end.

It wasn't.

"Where did you get that anyway?" Kaylin asked.

"It was a gift."

"For what?"

"From the Wolves."

"Which means you can't say," she said.

"Pretty much. It's not usually the first question people ask me about the weapon."

"What do they normally ask?"

"'Where did you learn how to use that?'" Severn responded dryly.

"Fair enough. But you're not going to answer that one either."

"No. You're a Hawk—if I answer that question you'll be able to figure out the rest if you're nosy enough." He finished, straightened out his shirt. He'd taken off his surcoat, and carefully spread it flat across the unmade bed. He didn't remove his hauberk, but Kaylin didn't expect him to. Chain slowed claws, and if it came to a fight, anything that slowed Leontine claws was a good thing. "Are you ready?"

She nodded. She hadn't taken nearly as much care as Severn had, but she'd almost dressed for midwife work. Looking at his armor, she grimaced—hers was in desperate need of cleaning, and if the nights were cooler at this time of year, they were still too damn humid.

"Why are you smiling?" Severn asked.

"Just remembering the first chain mail I ever owned. Well, that I was given by the Quartermaster. I was so damn excited, so unbearably proud of it—I tried to sleep in it the first night. I didn't want to wake up and have it all be a dream."

He laughed, but the laughter trailed into a soft smile. "You really love this life, don't you?"

"It's better than begging or stealing," she said with a shrug. But something in his gaze forced her to add, "Yes. I love it. It's not perfect. It's not what I daydreamed about when I was a child in the fiefs. But I made it, Severn. I *made* it happen. I worked damn hard for it."

As she spoke, she gathered up cloths and bandages and shoved them messily into her pack. "It was home. Even with the Barrani, and a Leontine for a superior, it was home. Damn Marcus anyway."

"You forgot the unguents."

"They don't do anything useful anyway. The herbs do—when they're fresh enough—but I remembered those."

"Why carry the unguents at all?"

"It makes nervous parents-to-be feel better if they think we're doing something. And since they're usually out of their minds to begin with, any little thing helps. It's almost like a ceremony," she added. "We even boil water."

"I believe you boil water in case you require it to clean—"

"Don't go there." She tied the leather straps as tightly as she could. "I'm squeamish. I'm also ready."

"Have you thought about what you're going to ask?"

"Not really. I have about a hundred questions, but I'm not sure what a good opener is. I'll let her lead the discussion."

He nodded and opened the door. When she walked through it, he closed it behind them both and locked up.

They'd had no locks in the fiefs.

The Leontine Quarter was not like the Tha'alani Quarter. There were no walls, no gatehouse and no visible guards—but then again, they weren't really needed. People—even drunk people in the dead of night—paid a lot of attention to where they were throwing up in this part of town. The buildings should have given it away, but at the edge of the Leontine Quarter, they didn't. The buildings there were old and in some disrepair, and the aged often took up residence, the furry version of squatters. The Leontines had come to the city sometime after its founding, and after the fires. They had been granted dispensation to live in the city itself by the Eternal Emperor. If the other residents had something to say, they kept it to themselves, because no matter *how* stupid they were, ticking off a dragon was a step further down the intellect rung than anyone breathing could go. At least if they wanted to keep on breathing.

The buildings in the Quarter proper looked different, and if you happened to get lost, those squat, clay rectangles were a clear indication that getting lost anywhere else was a good idea. People had a visceral fear of large things with fangs and fur. There was no vandalism in the Quarter—at least that the Law heard about. There were no interracial incidents. There just weren't many humans.

There were always exceptions to any rule, however, and as usual, it was the merchants who made them. Merchants would cross the boundaries with their wagons, their loud voices, their portable stalls. They sold meat, of course—although there were Leontine butchers, from all accounts—but they also sold carpets, cloth, baubles and spices. Salt was very popular, and Leontines didn't produce it. They did however barter for it.

Kaylin had never been certain what they bartered, because she usually had just enough coin in hand to feed her for the next meal or two. Figuring out how other people spent money—if it wasn't shoved under her nose—was part of the day's business that she left to others.

There were, however, no merchants here today. At this time of night, there wasn't much in the way of foot traffic. Kaylin wasn't the world's best navigator unless she planned the route out in advance, and that planning reminded her of things in life she had no desire to remember. Severn, on the other hand, knew the city better than he knew the back of his hand.

In fact, watching him covertly as they entered the Quarter—and it was, of course, Severn who pointed out the almost invisible boundary—she thought he might know it better. After all, how often did people really look at the backs of their own hands? She didn't. She couldn't really remember, in this night made of streets and her own worry, what the backs of her hands looked like.

She could remember his, though. And she watched him walk these streets as if every square inch of the city was known to him. Not—quite—as if he owned it, but he was at home here. Wherever here was. He carried home with him.

Or maybe he didn't need a home.

Kaylin did. Hers was with the Hawks, and at the Foundling Hall, and in the rush and crazy bustle of the midwives guild. Marcus had given her so much of her life, losing him was like starting over. She wasn't good at that. She also had no desire at all to begin again anywhere else.

She sighed. She could only watch Severn for so long; the streets demanded some part of her attention. The Leontines didn't navigate by street name, which made finding anything they described almost an arcane art. But she'd managed to find the home the first time she'd come—at a very fast jog—to the Quarter, and she remembered where she was going. More or less.

"I don't know a lot about the Leontine Quarter," Severn said quietly, as she slowed. "I've only been here a handful of times, and it was tense each time. They are not very unlike the Tha'alani."

"People aren't afraid of them in the same way, and it makes more sense to be afraid of people who seem to look like you. In this day and age, people aren't afraid of being eaten, but they are *always* afraid of being caught out."

He nodded. "That house?"

She nodded in turn. It was very similar to Kayala's home on the exterior. In the dark, Kaylin would have said they looked the same.

But in *this* dark, there were differences.

"What was her name?"

"I don't know."

"You didn't ask?"

"Yes, I did. She said her name was Arlan. Sarabe, however, says that isn't her name, and of the two, I'm inclined to trust Sarabe." She shrugged. "It was just a name. She could have called herself 'dog-eater' for all I cared. I was here to help deliver a baby. The birth—it shouldn't have been hard, but it was. I wasn't sure why. She didn't have small hips, and there was only one cub. But I don't know Leontine physiology all that well—and if you do, don't share. She was exhausted and weak. I assumed it was because of the labor.

"I didn't think I'd see her again. I've delivered a lot of babies to women I've never met before or since. It's not my job to ask them questions, it's only my job to save their lives."

Severn nodded again. "Fair enough."

"Do you want to wait for me here?"

"If it's required, yes. But I'd like to test that first." He looked at her again. "There were no men here when you came?"

"To a Leontine birthing? None at all. They like living."

He chuckled at that.

"Not that she could or would have hurt anyone, but that's by no means always the case. Especially not to listen to Marcus." The smile that had crossed her lips faded into a momentary grimace of pain.

Kaylin approached the hanging that separated inside from outside at this time of year. This time, like last time, the night had obscured the colors of the fur that were woven into it; she had literally no idea what it looked like. The last time she'd been here, she hadn't cared.

There was a brass bell to one side of it, and she touched its still rim nervously. The last thing she wanted to do at this time of night was ring it. But she had a feeling she wouldn't have to.

Nor was she wrong. As she stood in front of it, weighing her options, the hangings moved. A familiar face peered out from behind the curtain, eyes shining faintly in the light of the twin moons. Here, the streets were moonlit or dark; the magestones that lit the rest of the city were absent. If the Leontines were taxed—and until this moment it hadn't occurred to Kaylin to wonder—that money did *not* go toward brightly lit nightscapes. Then again, the Leontines had exceptional night vision. Came with the fur and fangs, as Marcus—damn it—would say.

But this time, Kaylin knew the color of the Leontine fur was both distinctive and dangerous—for her.

"I'm here," she told the woman softly.

"Alone?"

"No."

Silence. It was awkward, but it didn't last. "You were to come alone—"

"At the moment," Severn said, keeping a respectful distance—which in the case of a Leontine was entirely too far away, "I don't consider it safe for her. Do you?" He also walked toward the hanging, from which the woman had failed to emerge.

She cringed and seemed to grow...smaller. "You heard," she said to Kaylin.

"I practically live with your sister's husband," Kaylin replied. There was no birthing emergency to hush her voice or lend her the strength to be gentle. "There's no way I wouldn't have found out."

"Come in," the woman said, after another pause. "Both of you. We can't talk here."

Pointing out that the streets were empty didn't seem to be required. Kaylin nodded and stepped through the curtain that divided the world into inside and outside.

CHAPTER 9

Kaylin stepped into the hall and Severn followed her; the Leontine woman said nothing as he entered. Kaylin barely noticed. What she noticed, instead, was the lack of light. Moonlight didn't breach walls, and there were no lamps. She took a hesitant step forward, and then another, but there was no way her eyes were going to acclimatize here.

It hadn't been this dark the last time she'd visited. She frowned. "I came through a different door last time," she said, letting the last couple of words rise in question.

No answer.

"Severn—"

Metal against metal, in the darkness; Severn considered it dangerous enough to draw his blade. Kaylin turned suddenly to the side, flattening herself against the wall in one easy pivot. Her hands fell to her daggers, and they left their sheaths, scraping scabbard as the blades cleared them. She swore; she *had* to get to Elani street to get these damn things enchanted.

"Back out," Severn said softly.

The hair on the back of Kaylin's neck did the sudden stand to attention that spoke of magic. Or paperwork, on the wrong day.

"I don't think that's an option," she said, equally quietly. The words seemed loud in the darkness.

But not louder than breathing—or growling.

"Blink," Severn told her tersely.

She did. When he used that tone of voice, there was no room for question or argument.

She heard something clatter against the ground and there was, some ten feet away, the sudden glow of mage-light. He'd thrown it. He'd known enough to bring something with him.

Standing above that light, shoulders bunched and ready, was the largest cat Kaylin had ever seen. It wasn't a Leontine—it was an animal. But it was black and sleek and huge; it had a mane that trailed off into shadows. The fangs that hung out of its mouth were at least as long as Leontine fangs, and she guessed the claws she couldn't see as clearly weren't much less deadly.

It was the only thing she could see—the woman who had invited her in was nowhere in sight. "Nice kitty," she said softly.

"Nice kitty?"

It leaped.

There was magic in the room. It was, like all magic, sharp and unpleasant. Leaping, tensing, bringing daggers to bear, she could feel it. But she could feel the rumble of the great cat's growl more clearly and she did *not* want to get in its way.

It had other plans.

Kaylin had time to wonder why it was the Tha'alani that were so feared before claws sheared their way through the thigh-side of her pants as if it were sodden cheesecloth. The pain was sharp and clean; it wasn't just the leather that had been sliced open. The damn thing moved so *fast.*

She rolled to her feet; the cut was bleeding, but claws hadn't severed muscle; nothing was stopping Kaylin from moving. She didn't move as fast as the cat, and if she had come alone, that would have been fatal.

But Severn was there, and if claws could slice through flesh, so could blades—and he'd drawn his; she could hear the singing of chains tightening and dangling as the blade flew.

She could hear the roar of the cat as it turned, could see its shadows, diffuse and huge, cast by the single source of light in the room. Its shoulders bunched, muscles hardening as it tensed to leap.

Kaylin threw a dagger.

The flash of metal caught light and was extinguished by those muscles, the darkness of that fur; the hilt disappeared as the cat spun to face her. Severn's blade came down in the distance, and the cat snarled in fury, turning again.

And it struck Kaylin, as the cat turned, that it was clumsy, for all that it was fast; that it didn't understand exactly what it was doing.

She knew, then. Or thought she knew. She drew away from the wall, standing in the light, and slowly sheathed her remaining dagger. Then she held out her hands, palms out, a universal gesture.

Severn's expression was hidden; the light granted that much. "Kaylin—"

The cat snarled.

Turned.

"We didn't come here to hurt the baby," Kaylin said quietly. The words were firm and cool; Marcus—had he been here and not in some cage in the center of the quarter—would have recognized his training. He might not have appreciated the use to which she put it.

"I birthed your son," she continued, as the cat hunched its shoulders. "I licked his lids clean. I did *not* come here to kill a baby."

"But they will," a new voice said, as the darkness opened again, and spit out a tall Leontine that Kaylin didn't recognize. "They've seen you now. They have no choice."

"No!" Kaylin shouted, as the cat tensed to leap. Its eyes were golden, she thought, and wide, although that could have been the reflection of too little light in the darkness. "I claim the right of kin, sister to Sarabe. I claim the right of Pridlea."

The Leontine stranger had cat's eyes, but they narrowed in a very human way. "Impossible," he said flatly.

"You are no part of the birthing," Kaylin told him, just as flatly. "You weren't there. You didn't witness."

"There *is* no Pridlea."

"But there is," Severn said, standing, blades in hand. All this time, he had said nothing, done nothing. He did not sheathe his weapons, but maybe it wasn't important—he was male, after all.

"Upon the open plains," Severn said softly, "and in the forests, there were Pridlea. The children, the mothers. The fathers were inconsequential. The children were everything.

"And she remembers," he added softly. "How could she not? She is what they were."

The cat turned its head toward him, acknowledging him for the first time.

"It was the Pridlea that kept the children safe from their fathers. It was the Pridlea that protected the birthing mothers. The Pridlea that licked fur clean, offering warmth and food and life.

"If she cannot claim that right," he added, glancing briefly at Kaylin, "*no one* can. And if she claims it, neither you nor I can gainsay it, except by killing them all."

"The child," the Leontine said coldly, "is *mine.*"

The black cat hesitated for another moment, its head now swiveling in three directions. And then it seemed to shrug, and it padded slowly and gracefully across the room to where Kaylin stood.

It sniffed the air around her, and Kaylin stood very, very still. Then it nudged Kaylin's wounded thigh, and a great, rough tongue darted out from between massive jaws and began to lick it clean. Kaylin winced. She would have liked to say it tickled, but sandpaper was probably softer.

"The right of Pridlea," Kaylin said softly, and lifted her head.

"You have no such right here."

"But I have. And she's accepted it."

The Leontine roared. Severn pivoted toward him, both blades out. It would not be a clean fight. But Severn wasn't fighting to make a point here; he'd fight to survive. Kaylin didn't like the odds.

"Marai," the Leontine said curtly. "Come."

The cat stayed where it was. Kaylin knelt, slowly, until her lips were as close to the great twitching ears as she could safely put them. She was keenly aware that her throat, though it was not bared, was a lot more exposed than she would like it to be.

"Go," she whispered to the cat. "Marai," she added, lifting the name that had been spoken so imperiously and making it almost a plea. "Go and get our son. We'll stall."

Marai growled softly.

Kaylin added, "Please."

The cat suddenly bolted into the darkness behind the Leontine male. He turned, his claws extended toward her exposed back, and Severn was there in an instant, parrying.

Kaylin felt her hair stand on end as the Leontine leaped back, away from those blades. "Severn!"

He wasn't there.

Fire was.

Gods curse him, he was a *mage*. And the fire that had left his hands now burned through rug and wooden table, catching the edges of hangings across the wall. Smoke flared, greasy and black. Had it been a normal fire, it would have taken time to spread. Magical flame was under no such restriction.

But the fire itself? That was real. It couldn't be called back. Kaylin shouted a warning, but Severn was beyond it; his blades flew as he began to spin them in front of his chest. They moved fast, catching light until light was a transparent wall, traced by the moving blades, the winding chains.

She saw the Leontine clearly for a moment longer, and then he changed; she saw it through the black haze of smoke. He had been taller than Marcus, and it seemed that he crouched—but when he unfurled from that crouch, he was no longer what he had been. Gray furred, long fanged, he was a giant cat.

He leaped over the tongues of flame and past Severn—down the hall that had swallowed Marai.

Offering a single choice Aerian curse, Kaylin took a deep breath and ran through the spreading flames after him.

The snarling and the roaring that came out of the darkness in the corridor she traveled was louder than the slowly growing crackle of flame. If fires had conversation, this was it: heated, broken, ugly. The weapon she had sheathed came to hand as she drew it, counting seconds, measuring all lives in the rectangular home by those beats of time. In all, it was a lousy way to measure life.

She traced the noise of fighting back to one room, the hanging in the frame now rumpled awkwardly across the floor.

"Kaylin." Severn. At her back, as always. She didn't even turn at the sound of his voice. "We need to get out."

"That's not the only door," she replied, back against the wall, catfight growing louder inches away. "It's not the one I entered the first time."

"It's the one we know—"

"We need to get Marai and her cub out."

He said nothing else, but she felt him move past her in the hall. Her fingers caught his shoulder; more than that, she couldn't do without dropping or sheathing her blade. "Be careful—"

Fire erupted. A dragon's breath would have been just as hot, and just as contained—barely—by the rounded curve of archway that formed a Leontine door. They didn't bother with fiddly things like hinges.

Gods, her skin *ached*. Magic was so damn strong here, it was almost a taste in the air—sharper and harsher than the black smoke of burning wood and hair-rugs. She could see that Severn was standing; could see where the fire had almost hit him. But he hadn't dropped his blades or lifted his hands at the sudden appearance of angry, red-orange light.

He counted out three, and then he rolled along the floor into the room. Kaylin didn't bother with a count; she ran in after him. Could hear the angry roar of Leontine words, made harsh and animal—well, more animal—by the throats that contained them.

She could almost understand what was said. *Fool* was universal, delivered in that harsh and furious tone. His voice, she thought. She heard Marai's wordless reply, heard the desperation in it, heard, as well, the pain. He was larger than she was, and clearly more familiar with the form.

But familiar or no, he paused, his fangs leaving Marai's flesh wet and sticky; blood colored those teeth, and his eyes—his eyes were the color of flame. He leaped for Severn, and Severn suddenly pulled the chain between blade and hand taut.

The Quartermaster would be handing out a new tabard if Severn hadn't seen fit to leave his in Kaylin's apartment. Unfortunately, he was in short supply of rib cages. The fangs failed to reach Severn; the claws didn't. But they weren't Leontine claws; the weight of the beast caused Severn to stagger.

But only to stagger; he didn't go down.

Kaylin was there in a minute, her dagger making a clean strike at the cat's eyes. It leaped up and away before she could connect. She jumped in the opposite direction; without Severn's mass behind her, she had no chance of meeting any attack head-on. She didn't try.

"Marai!" she shouted. The Leontine woman—the large, black cat—stood shakily on its forepaws. "Get Roshan! Get the child out of here!" But Marai was dazed, slowed. In the darkness that was slowly becoming acrid, Kaylin couldn't see her injuries.

And right at this moment, she didn't care. She cursed once in Aerian and then forced her throat to accommodate the harsh, guttural growls of Leontine command. "Get our son!"

The words, butchered as they were by a merely human throat, reached Marai. She shook her head, growling softly, and turned. It was dark in the room.

Even the fire that erupted in the room's center didn't change that; it flashed against walls and ceilings and began to kindle in the things that would normally burn before it vanished.

Gods, she hated magic.

Severn shouted. Not a warning, and not quite a curse. "He's running!"

"He can!" she shouted back. "Let him go—we'll hunt

him later. We need to get Marai out of here. We need to get the baby!"

And he understood, reining the Wolf in, giving her the Severn she needed. She dropped her dagger into what she hoped was its sheath, stumbled over the corner of a snarled, old rug, and made her way to Marai.

Marai looked up, her head pressed against the fur of a sleeping cub. Just *how* it could be sleeping, she'd wonder later. Kaylin lifted the child from its bed, wrapping the furs around its body. "Out!" she shouted, in Leontine. Then, lowering her voice, forcing the fear from the syllables, she added, "Marai, you need to lead us out. Not the way we entered tonight. The other way."

Marai growled softly.

"I won't hurt him," Kaylin told the cat. "I won't let anyone else hurt him. But the fire will kill us if we don't leave. This wasn't much of a home to you," she added, speaking Elantran now because the smoke made it too hard to speak in Leontine. "Lead us out."

And Marai turned to where fire lapped the walls in the hall. She growled at Severn.

"He's mine," Kaylin told her. "The cub is mine. He'll protect us while he lives."

It was enough. Marai began to run. Her gait was awkward, slow. Wounds had taken whatever grace she had had when she had first appeared. But grace didn't count here. You couldn't fight fire with fangs or claws.

Or at all, really.

Sometimes you just had to run.

Halfway across the Quarter, Marai began to change. The moons were up; the sky was clear. If there were no magelights in this part of town, they weren't needed. The cat stopped walking and began to shudder. Kaylin saw it—almost felt it—and turned, babe in arms.

The cat fell forward, hissing; the hiss changed to mewling, a sound caught between pain and fear. It was not a happy sound, but given the transformation that Kaylin watched, it couldn't be. It *looked* wrong. The body lost form and cohesion; the paws grew narrower and longer, the claws in the footpads retracting as if they grudged the change. Shoulders that looked very like cat's shoulders began to flatten and widen across a back that was doing the same, and even the fur changed color, becoming russet-gray in the moons' light.

Kaylin looked away. Watching the face change was more than she could stomach. She whispered Elantran nonsense words to the sleeping babe instead, Kaylin's version of prayer.

The baby snorted and pawed at her face, his breath a whuffle of sensation and sound. It was not nearly loud enough to drown out the sounds of bones snapping into place, but it would do. The baby was clearly alive, and clearly healthy; not even Kaylin's anxiety could disguise that.

She turned when it was quiet again.

And discovered that transformations of this particular nature did not include clothing. Not that the Leontines wore a lot of it. She would have looked away for decency's sake, but she could see, now, where Marai had been injured. The wounds were deep, and they wept blood.

"Severn, the baby—"

"*No!*"

"Okay, not the baby. Can you hold him, Marai? I need to look at those wounds—"

"No. Hold him."

"Marai—"

The hiss of a desperate Leontine filled the empty streets.

Severn said, "Leave it, Kaylin. Go."

"But she—"

"She'll bleed to death in the streets first. *Go.*"

It wasn't hard to find Kayala's house. It was the only safe place Kaylin could think of that also happened to be close enough. It was much harder to leave Severn in the street.

"I'll be fine," he said softly. "And even now, it's not safe for me to go there."

"But—"

"Kaylin."

"What if he comes back?"

Severn shook his head. "He was injured and he used an enormous amount of magic, there. I don't think he'll be hunting us now."

She wanted to argue, and not just because that's what she did. She wanted to point out that were their positions reversed, he wouldn't leave her out in the streets of the Quarter. Wanted to, and didn't. Marai was still bleeding, and it was clear that she would not allow herself to be so much as touched in the streets.

Instead, Kaylin turned and began to walk down the path that led from the street to the only Leontine home she knew.

The only home, besides the office, that she had ever really known.

"You can't take him there," Marai said.

"If I can't take him there," Kaylin told the Leontine gently, "there is *no* safe place I can take him."

"They'll kill him." Marai's voice had slid up an octave. Leontine vocal registers shouldn't have allowed this. "They'll have to kill him." Her eyes were glassy. Round, now.

Kaylin said, quietly, "Over my dead body."

It was, again, enough. Marai drifted closer, stumbling on two legs, as if four were so natural now she would never be at home any other way.

Kaylin looked at the dull, dark brass of the bell. Shifting Roshan's weight, she lifted the clapper, but no peal broke the silence.

"We're awake," a familiar voice said. "And you made enough noise just now to make sure that anyone else who sleeps lightly for miles is *also* awake."

Kaylin turned to face Kayala, Marcus's first wife, and the mother of the Pridlea. "Kayala—"

Kayala didn't spare Kaylin another word or look. Her breath broke in a hiss as she stepped out into moonlight. "Marai," she said softly. "You're injured. Come."

"I can't. I—"

"My husband is not at home," Kayala replied quietly. "As you must know. It is safe."

"You don't—"

"It is safe," Kayala repeated, in the tone of voice she reserved for the very young. "Come. Your sister is worried."

Marai did not move.

But Kayala did, stepping to one side. Behind her, hidden until now by Kayala's larger body, stood Sarabe. She took one look at her sister and let out a low, loud cry. Stepping from the building, her arms wide, she caught her sister in an embrace that would have broken Kaylin's ribs. "Marai," she whispered. "Marai, what has happened? What has happened to you?"

Marai hesitated for just another minute, and then collapsed into her sister's arms.

Sarabe managed to bear her weight as they retreated from the open street, the unforgiving moonlight.

Kaylin knew the inside of the Pridlea by heart. She had often wondered where that expression—by heart—had come from, but she felt, now, that she understood. It wasn't that the details were memorized—she could memorize a crime scene down to rusty nails and scuffs on the walls. But there was water and hot milk on the table, spiced with cinnamon and ginger; there were paper lamps—so out of place in the Pridlea they had probably been given to Marcus as an office gift and he had dumped them here. More than that, there was Kayala and her wives.

Graylin was awake, and she carried thick blankets over both of her arms. They were, of all colors, a rosy pink, and it took Kaylin a full minute to realize that they were blankets she had bought for the Pridlea with her first pay. She'd liked the color, then—she couldn't imagine why. But if they had seen little use, they had obviously been valued by the four women who had been, in their own way, like fanged, furry mothers.

Sarabe sat with her arms around her sister. Marai

allowed Sarabe to look at her wounds—and to lick them clean. Kaylin, having seen the younger cubs tended to in just such a fashion, didn't even blink. It wasn't what *she* would have done, on the other hand. There was a silence around these two women that was definitive, and it lasted for a while.

When it was broken, it was broken by Kayala, and Kayala didn't speak to either of the sisters directly. Instead, she turned her wide, round eyes on Kaylin and the babe she carried.

"What happened?"

Kaylin, child tucked into her arms, hesitated. "I met with Marai, as planned."

"Alone?"

"No."

"You took your Severn with you?"

"He's not mine, and I didn't take him. He kind of insisted on going."

"And he is?"

"Outside somewhere."

Kayala nodded. "I approve of him," she told Kaylin, as if that settled something.

"Kayala—"

"And the child you carry? Marai's cub?"

Her arms tightened as Kayala approached. Kayala, of course, noticed. She didn't stop, but she noticed.

"His fur's not red," Kaylin said quietly. She couldn't bring herself to surrender the child. Couldn't have said why, but maybe that was because she didn't want to admit that she was afraid to trust Kayala. This child, she knew, was a child who should never have been born.

"It wouldn't have to be," Kayala replied. She glanced down at the sleeping face, and her expression softened.

"I don't think Marai was the only Leontine to bear a forbidden child."

"Oh?"

"The father," Kaylin replied.

Silence. But it was now a different silence, and it encompassed the watchful room. Even Sarabe and Marai now sat, breath held, waiting.

Kayala said, quietly, "What do you mean?"

"You said something yesterday. You called it—the color of the fur—witch-fur. I remembered it, but it all seemed like so much witch hunting to me, it seemed like a—a story that you tell children. But it wasn't just a story, was it? Kayala, the man that Marai was living with was a mage. Marcus once told me there was no such thing as a Leontine mage—but I *know* magic."

Kayala lifted both of her paws in front of her face, palms out, as if she needed protection from the words themselves. "A...mage?"

"I've met a few in my time. Trust me."

"Kaylin, why do you say—"

"Most Leontines don't throw great balls of fire around their home." She hesitated and then said, "Kayala—he changed. His shape. His form."

Kayala was silent again. The words seemed to strike her like blows; she weathered them, but they caused damage.

"But, Kayala, so did Marai."

"Impossible," Sarabe said. The other wives were standing or sitting in the corners of the dining room;

Sarabe had not let go of her sister, and they formed an isolated huddle of two in the quiet room.

Marai said nothing. But the look she gave Kaylin had no accusation in it, and it made no plea. Because it made none, Kaylin fell silent.

"Continue, kitling," Kayala said softly.

Still, Kaylin waited. Minutes passed; claws didn't so much as scratch the scarred table.

Marai said at last, "It's true."

Sarabe's arms tightened, and Kaylin remembered that in a different life, they had only had each other. They still did.

But Kayala made a lie of that, a quiet, cautious one; she approached them, and when she was close enough to touch, she crouched, bringing her face close to Marai's. "When?" she asked quietly. "When did you discover this?"

Marai shook her head.

"When you were young?"

"No. Only after."

"After."

"After *he* came. He said—" She turned her head, caught a glimpse of Sarabe and drew a long breath. "He said we were special, Sarabe and I. And that he was like us. He wanted Sarabe to live with us. He told me—he said it was important that we be together. But she wouldn't come. I thought he wouldn't take me," she said. "But he did. And he showed me—what I could do. He taught me how to become—become my other self.

"Sarabe could do it," Marai said. Her sister's hands tightened around her arms, but she offered no words.

"You could teach her this?" Kayala asked softly.

"No. But he could. He could do so many things," she said. She seemed to shrink in on herself. "I was happy. For a while. I was *happy*. He didn't despise me and he didn't pity me."

"Sarabe is neither despised nor pitied."

"But she couldn't *be* what we are. She could never be what we are, living here. Living with you."

Kayala nodded. "There are some things forbidden us."

"But *why?* Why are they forbidden? Is it so very evil to be able to run and hunt and see? Is it wrong to be able to do what others can't? It was envy, that's what he said. Envy and fear. You're all afraid of what we can do.

"And we *let* you fear us. We let you kill us," she added. "We live by your rules."

Sarabe let her sister talk; Kaylin would have stopped her. But Kayala seemed neither afraid nor offended. She let Marai talk, and she let Marai cry—and Marai did both, as if she were a child.

But after she had finished, Kayala said, "Why did you ask to meet with Kaylin?"

Marai froze.

"Kayala—" Kaylin began.

"No. She will answer the question. Kit, I smell your blood. We *all* can. If you tell me that she did not invite you to the home of the *man* she lives with in order to harm you, I will believe you."

"It's because—"

"But I will listen to your answer *when I ask you for it*. Until then, be silent."

Instinct made Kaylin's jaw snap shut.

"Good. Marai?"

Marai burrowed into Sarabe's arms. "She knew. About my son."

"She was not the only one."

"No."

"Marcus knew."

Silence. In that silence, a muted look of pain or horror slowly transforming her face, Sarabe disentangled herself from her sister. It was almost more than Kaylin could bear, and she held the child in her arms as closely as she could, as if he were a shield.

"Did you try to kill Kaylin, Marai?"

The silence was terrible. Kaylin broke it. "Yes."

There was anger in the Pridlea then, sudden and terrifying.

CHAPTER 10

"Why are you even asking the question when you already know the answer?" Kaylin's voice sounded thin to her own ears. Thin and angry, because she *was* angry.

Kayala rose and Kaylin took a step back. She stopped herself from taking a second one. When a Leontine was angry, fleeing was the *last* thing you wanted to do. If you wanted to survive.

"I wanted her answer," Kayala replied curtly.

"She's only giving you half of it, anyway. She wants to protect her son. Yes, she meant to—she meant to harm me. You know that. But I'm not angry about it. I don't see why you should be."

"You are my kit," was her cool growl of a reply.

"She stopped. She didn't kill me. She didn't even keep trying. I wouldn't have brought her here if—"

"You are Marcus's," Kayala said. "You would have. He would have. You have no common sense."

"No."

"Why do you think she stopped?"

Kaylin drew a deep, steadying breath. "Because I claimed the right of Pridlea. I promised to protect our child. And Kayala? I meant it. I will not let you harm this baby."

Kayala said nothing. She didn't even growl. But she looked at the sleeping cub for a long, long moment.

"He's a baby, Kayala. Whatever it is you're afraid of, he's just a baby."

"And his father?"

"It doesn't matter. She birthed him, I helped. I don't understand what this child means, but—"

"Do you understand what his father means?"

"No."

"Then maybe you should." Kayala turned to look down at Marai. Her voice gentled, which surprised Kaylin. "Be grateful that Kaylin is who she is. Our husband has had a hand in shaping what he found, and he would be proud of her. Frustrated by her, certainly, but proud of her. I will not harm your son," she added, "not tonight, and not unless it is necessary. But if it is necessary, you will know.

"I do not know what it is to grow as you grew. I cannot imagine the life you must have lived. For my part, I am grateful that you and your sister were allowed to live, for I love Sarabe dearly. But your—guardian is another story.

"He is a danger, Marai."

Marai swallowed and nodded. "He would have killed us all," she said. "All of us but his son. He wanted a son," she added.

"Why?" Kaylin asked. "Why a son? It would mean—"

She hesitated. "Marai, you couldn't have raised a son. Not among the Leontines."

"I don't *know*," Marai replied at last. "I don't know why. I know it was important to him. That's all."

"And what were you going to do?" Kaylin asked. "How were you going to live?" She held the baby carefully. "I don't understand what the child means to his father. If he had wanted to hide, wouldn't he have run?"

Marai shook her head. "He said we could leave. The three of us. We could find a home outside of the city. I could form a Pridlea of my own on the plains."

"But you didn't leave."

"No."

"What was he waiting for?"

She closed her eyes. "I don't know," she said. "But a week ago, maybe a little less, he left the Quarter for two days."

"After the baby was born."

She nodded.

"And was he different when he came back?"

"I thought so. But I was nervous. I was afraid."

"Marai, did he speak with Marcus at all?"

"I don't know. After the baby was born, I couldn't leave the house. I couldn't leave him," she added.

"You didn't trust his father."

The hesitation was marked, profound. But in the end, she nodded. "I couldn't. He wanted to take the baby with him—"

"When he was days old?" Kayala's voice rose at least an octave on the last word. It was the only thing musical about her.

She nodded. "He thought I was sleeping."

"I bet you didn't sleep much after that."

"No. I'm sorry," she added. "I didn't want to kill you. I thought I had no choice." She tried to stand and Sarabe caught her, pulling her back into the safety of calmer, steady arms.

"I'm fine with it," Kaylin said, meaning it. "But I'm not fine with Marcus."

"Marcus wasn't there."

"No, he wasn't. He's locked in a cage in the middle of fancy pit. And I'm willing to bet money—my own, even—that the crime he's accused of and your missing guardian are connected. Marai, I don't know your guardian. I don't judge him. I want to kill him, yes, but that's almost beside the point. He's a *mage*. Magic was used in the Quarter tonight, and we *need* to bring mages in to track it."

"Track it?"

"All magic leaves a…a signature. If it's a very weak magic, it's hard to tell what it is—but if it's a column of flame, any mage worth their working title will be able to tell you who cast the spell if they've seen the signature before. At the very least it will tell us whether or not he's performed other acts of magic that Imperial Mages know about. It would help me if I knew what he could do."

"You mean the magic?"

Kaylin nodded.

"I'm sorry, Kaylin. I don't know."

Marai didn't know very much, and Kaylin had to bite her tongue to stop herself from pointing this out.

"The form you saw—I knew of it. I know he can move quickly—much more quickly than I can—and that he can hide in the shadows. He can't be tracked by scent. But the fire wasn't something he showed *me*." There was more than a trace of bitterness in those words.

"Did he say anything at all about the baby?"

"Only that it was important. He knew I knew it had to be kept secret from other Leontines. He wasn't happy that I called you," she said. "But the birthing, the labor— I was afraid. I was afraid that it was wrong somehow. I—"

"You got my name from Marcus."

"Yes."

"In person?"

She nodded.

"You were pregnant—that much must have been obvious to Marcus."

She nodded again. "I meant to tell Marcus that the child died in birth, if it was a boy. If it was a girl, it wasn't significant. Sarabe has girls."

"But you didn't?"

She shook her head. "I didn't have the chance. Things happened here—" She waved one shaking hand in a half circle that encompassed the Pridlea, and possibly the Quarter.

"I don't think this—this mage—meant to raise the child," Kaylin said.

"What else could he have meant for it?" Kayala asked sharply. "Had he intended to kill the child, he would not have been in this danger."

Kaylin shrugged, but very, very carefully. An armful of baby made nonchalance difficult. "I don't know," she replied. "But if he'd just wanted a son, he could have left the city with Marai the day after he met her. It would be far, far safer out there than it is here."

"Out there, as you put it, her fur would mark her no matter where she traveled. And if the child was seen as hers, it would mark him as well."

"Why are mages so hated among the Leontines? Marcus told me once that there *weren't* any. He was proud of that, by the way—he hates Arcanists at least as much as I do. He's only barely more polite to the Imperial Mages than I am." Kaylin had the grace to wince at this.

Kayala was silent. They all were. At last Kayala said, "Bring your mages, if you must. It will be interesting to hear what they have to say."

"You're not going to tell me that this is not a matter for outsiders?"

"I would, if I thought you would listen."

"She's lying," Reesa said calmly, speaking in her soothing purr of a voice. "She would not tell you that if she thought you would heed her. We need our husband back," she added, as if this wasn't obvious. "And we would like him back in one piece, if at all possible."

"Reesa."

"However, there may be those among the Elders who will object to your visit."

Kaylin started to shrug again.

"The attempt on your life was an attempt on *your* life. If you choose to heed the words of the Elders—"

"Not in this lifetime."

"—then you will turn back. But as you are not Leontine, you are not beholden to our laws."

"That part, I understood."

Sarabe lifted her head. "If you are not careful," she said, her voice so soft it was almost human, "you will be forced to mention my sister's transformation. They will kill her."

Kaylin took a deep breath. "Explain why your children are so dangerous. If it's the magic—"

"It's the magic," Kayala said flatly. "But more. Our oldest stories warn us of the danger."

"You've been married to Marcus a long time, Kayala. You know he has to deal with mages."

She nodded. "But they are not Leontine. The Leontines have no mages."

"Not if they kill them at birth, no."

Kayala glanced at Sarabe, who shook her head firmly.

"It might be better if you leave us," the Matriarch said to Sarabe, when it became clear that a glance was not enough to encourage her departure.

"No."

Kayala lifted a brow. "Very well, then." She turned her back upon her youngest wife and her wife's sister. "You saw what he was."

"You mean the giant cat?"

She nodded. "And…Marai has that taint."

"Why exactly is it a taint?"

"You have stories, surely, of men who turn into wolves. Marcus has mentioned them."

Kaylin hesitated and then nodded. The past year had taught her that sneering at old stories wasn't always wise. "Werewolves."

"Yes."

"So you're saying he's the Leontine version of a were?"

"I'm saying that anything that can change its shape, that can become something entirely different, is a danger in *any* race. There is a...*wrongness* to this ability in those who are mortal."

"This has nothing to do with magic."

"Not directly, no. But..." She hesitated again. "This is a discussion for the Elders."

"I don't want to talk to the Elders unless I know enough to hold my own."

"That will probably be never," Reesa interjected.

"If you are very lucky, kitling, yes. Mortals are born living, they live, they die. It is the same with your race and mine."

"And the Tha'alani."

"Any mortal race. It is said that the Barrani and the Dragons require more to live. They are not born alive in a way that we understand it."

Kaylin, thinking of the High Halls and the High Court, nodded quietly.

"To your people we most resemble animals."

"No—"

"Kaylin."

"To some of them," Kaylin finished lamely.

"In our oldest stories, Kaylin, we *were* animals."

"But—"

"Does Marcus accept these constant interruptions?"

"More or less."

"Ah. Well then, it's a good thing I'm not a member of the Hawks."

"Yes, Kayala."

"Don't play meek, it doesn't suit you. In our oldest stories, *as I was saying,* we were animals. We were like the Wolves and the Hawks from which you take your name. And in our oldest stories, one of the Ancients found us, and he gave us his words, and lifted us unto two legs, and bade us speak, and dress and hunt like men." She used the Leontine word.

Kaylin nodded. It seemed safest.

"But the Ancients were capricious, and they fought— as we all do—among themselves, and when another came to us, offering gifts, we were too young to understand the cost. We welcomed him, and we welcomed his word and his touch, as we had welcomed his brother's.

"And this Ancient gave the gift of magic." She lifted a hand as Kaylin's mouth opened and waited until it snapped shut. "Good girl. We were beguiled by the change. But the change was visual, and the magic was accompanied by a wildness that we could not control. Those who were changed often reverted to the shape of an animal, but their power was tremendous, and they desired what animals desire.

"It nearly destroyed us. The Ancient who had given us life and intelligence returned, and saw what had happened. He purified those who could be purified. And he told us that the magic, in us, was dark and chaotic, that it could not reside in a mortal vessel without changing the vessel beyond recognition. He told us the signs, and he warned us that we would fail as a race if we did not guard against those who still bore the taint."

"But I don't understand. How can magic be evil? A sword isn't evil. It's just another tool."

"Yes, it is. But in whose hand?" She turned to look at Marai. Turned away. "You have seen the Ferals."

Kaylin nodded.

"You understand, as we do, that they are not truly alive."

She nodded again.

"Where they come from," Kayala continued, "is a mystery to you. But to my kind, it is known. They come from the shadows and the darkness and the chaos. They come to destroy life. And from those shadows and that chaos, power comes to the tainted. They hear the old voices, and they desire the old power."

Kaylin was very, very quiet. She looked down at the sleeping infant in her arms for a long moment, seeing no trace of hunting Ferals in his sleeping features. At last she said, "Those are just stories."

"Perhaps. But in our stories, and in the stories the Elders learn, there is more. The ability to change form, as if one's body were simple clothing, is dangerous."

Kaylin remembered the vast cavern beneath the High Halls, and the creatures it contained, their bodies fluid nightmares. She shuddered a moment, and then nodded.

"Magic was not meant for my kind. I do not know if it was meant for yours, but your people are not my problem. It is almost certain that Marai's guardian was tainted. How strongly, we cannot yet say," Kayala said.

Kaylin nodded again. "I need to talk to a few people," she told Kayala.

Marai looked up.

"Will you keep her safe?"

"Yes."

"And her son?"

"Yes, Kaylin. For now, the Pridlea will watch them both." She held out her arms, and after a long hesitation, Kaylin gave her the baby. "I admit that sleeping like this doesn't make him look dangerous. Or not more dangerous than any of our other children."

Severn was waiting when she left the house, if lounging against the side of a home in the dead of night could be called waiting. "You left the child?"

"Kayala promised she wouldn't kill him without warning me first."

She could sense the lift of his brow, but the sudden onset of night hid it from view, and by the time her eyes had acclimatized fully to the light of the twin moons, his expression was neutral. He began to walk and she fell into step beside him, just as if they were patrolling together.

"We go home?"

She nodded. "But I want to bring a mage to the Quarter to look at the house. And I want the body of the Leontine Marcus has been accused of murdering exhumed for the same purpose."

"Good luck with that. We can't compel the Leontines to cooperate."

"Yes, we can. The attack was made against us. We didn't come here as Hawks, we came here off duty. If we're involved it's a case for the Imperial Courts, not the damn Caste Courts."

"Careful, Kaylin."

"Trying to be. I know which mage I'm asking."

"Good luck with that, as well." The way he said the words was different, but she couldn't see his expression; he was watching the streets like their mutual namesake.

"Why?"

"All requisitions for mages seconded for our

investigations go through Mallory now. Given the regard in which he holds the Hawk, he would likely accede to your request—but what reason are you going to give him for our presence in the Leontine Quarter in the first place?"

Her colorful Leontine phrases would have shriveled the ears off any Leontine who happened to be awake and listening.

The morning, when it came, was barely a pink glow in the sky. On a normal day, she would have classified it as night, and gone back to sleep. Her body was sore and her muscles ached. She was certain she had a new collection of bruises, and the scratches she'd received from Marai weren't exactly paper cuts.

But there weren't going to be any normal mornings until Marcus was back in the office. She dragged herself out of bed. Severn was waiting.

"Don't you ever knock?"

"I tried. Six times."

"Oh." She grimaced. "More than that would probably wake up the crazy lady down the hall."

"That was my thought."

"Don't you *ever* get tired?"

"I'm tired now," he replied.

"Sleepy, then."

He shrugged. "Yes. I brought breakfast. We're required to check in at the office before we head to the Palace."

He watched her sort through her clothing. The regulation pants—the last set she had—had a very large hole in the thigh.

"Wear something else," he said with a short sigh. "I'll speak with the Quartermaster when we arrive. You have maybe twenty minutes to dress and eat. And please, do them in that order."

The Quartermaster, Kaylin thought, must love Severn. Either that or the Wolves had blackmail information hidden away somewhere. He took the pants that Severn handed him. They were neatly folded, but not even the folds could disguise the great, jagged tears from the previous night's work.

He glanced at them and looked at Severn. His lips thinned slightly. "Take a walk on the wrong side of town?"

"The right side of the river."

The Quartermaster nodded. He lifted a hand to forestall the usual whining and excuse-making—not that Severn would have done much of either—and turned to the door at his back. Opening it, he disappeared for less than five minutes, as if he had expected to replace at least this much gear. He handed Severn a neatly folded pile, and then went back to his records.

Severn took it and walked away.

"He looked like he expected that," Kaylin said.

"I imagine he did. Let's just report quickly and go."

She nodded. The guards at the door were men she only vaguely recognized, which caused her to grind her teeth. Given the acoustics in this utterly silent hall, she stopped after a very short time. She did not add obscenities to the silence, but that was harder.

The duty board was unoccupied when they approached it; the office was not. But the office, like the inner hall, was abnormally silent. She looked around the room once, and saw Mallory watching her.

"I'm happy to see you're capable of punctuality," he said. He said it quietly but, given the lack of any other noise, it carried a fair distance. "Perhaps the previous Sergeant didn't give you enough incentive."

"The Imperial Palace is all the incentive I need," she told him curtly.

"A good thing, then. We don't want anything to reflect poorly on the Hawks."

Sixteen different rejoinders rushed up to meet the closed wall of her teeth. They stayed on the right side of her mouth.

"I will see you when you deliver your report on the day's duties. Dismissed."

The carriage wheels, heavy Imperial work, probably added ruts to stone. Kaylin stared out the window in perfect silence.

"Kaylin."

The buildings went past; the people went past. Some stopped to stare at the carriage as it drove by. She might have been one of them, once.

"You did well, there."

"Did I? I wanted to hit him."

"You didn't."

"No. And I'm trying hard not to regret it. I hate what he's done to the Hawks," she said. "I hate it." She struggled to keep the whine out of her words.

"I think very few appreciate his presence."

"No. And none of them have hit him."

"Not to my knowledge. Are we going to the Palace?"

She nodded. "I need to speak to someone there."

"Good. A mage?"

"The only one I seem to have trouble offending."

Lord Sanabalis of the Dragon Court was waiting for them when they stepped out of a carriage surrounded by more livery than passengers. "I received your message," he said, nodding slightly to Severn.

Kaylin snapped a glance at Severn, and he shrugged.

"It was suitably vague," the Dragon added. "You are here to attend Mr. Rennick?"

"When he's ready to receive us." Severn's reply was tendered in perfect High Barrani.

"I see. It may be some time yet. Will you take refreshments with me?"

"If it will not keep you from your duties."

Sanabalis bowed. "My duties at the moment are similar to yours. Therefore, while we wait Mr. Rennick's pleasure, we might make use of the time."

If they started another round of polite phrases, Kaylin thought she'd scream. Sanabalis glanced at her, and his lips turned up in a smile that, on another face, would look suspiciously like a smirk. On his, she wasn't certain.

"Follow me," Sanabalis told them both.

He led them through the long, tall halls of a palace that seemed like a very opulent maze. Kaylin remembered the floors and the height of the ceilings from previous visits, but the geography of the building failed to imprint itself in her memories. Then again, with the exception of Richard Rennick's chambers, she had never come to the same set of rooms twice, and privately thought she could visit every day for a year, and never see the entire Palace.

But at last he paused in front of a set of forbiddingly perfect doors. They had no door wards, and by this lack, Kaylin assumed they were rooms used by important visitors. Still, if there were no obvious wards, she felt a tingle at the base of her neck that shouted *magic*. Since magic was, sadly, not that uncommon, she ignored it and crossed the threshold in Sanabalis's shadow. It wasn't that much of a shadow; the lights in the sconces were so high above the damn ground the Palace staff probably included a few Aerians whose sole duty it was to clean them. The room itself boasted ceilings that were not—quite—as tall as the outer halls. The windows that adorned the far wall were impressive; colored, beveled glass suggested the sun's rise, the sun's height and the sun's fall.

Beyond those panes, she could see the green of grass, and the flower beds that were no less a work of art than the windows themselves—and beyond those, beyond the gates, the only other building in the city that was, by Imperial dictate, allowed so much height: The Halls of Law.

"A reminder," Sanabalis said softly, discerning what had caught her attention. "If it is needed. Come. You look…underslept."

"I ate," she said. There was no point in lying about sleep.

"I haven't. Humor me."

She took the chair he pointed to and sat in it almost gratefully. It was soft enough to sleep in, but given the curved wood and arms that housed burgundy cushions, she was pretty sure it was almost impossible to move. Wood of a certain type, she had discovered, was bloody heavy.

"I believe you visited the Leontine Quarter last evening after you finished your official duties." He indicated a plate of sandwiches, and a pitcher of orange juice. He did not, however, touch either himself.

"I really *did* eat, Sanabalis."

"Humor me," he repeated. "It is, after all, free."

"Good point. Severn told you this?"

"Ah. No. But some information has crept into the Palace by less official routes. Corporal Handred did, however, imply that you had work for me."

"Ye-es."

"I'm retired."

"You teach me," she countered.

"A foible of age. And a desire not to offend the Imperial Mages more than strictly necessary. I am not terribly easy to offend," he added. "It takes both diligent research and effort, and you are famously lazy when it comes to either of these things."

"I don't *try* to offend."

"You don't try hard enough not to offend. And I would quibble with the truth of your statement."

"Unless I'm offended first."

"They started it?"

She winced. "Something like that."

"And they are old enough to know better. As are you." She ate for a few minutes in silence.

"Since I am retired, I cannot be employed."

"But the Hawks *pay* you to teach me!"

"That is a matter for the Imperial Order of Mages to decide. I am, however, open to things that amuse or challenge me. This means," he said, lifting a hand before she could speak, "that I'm willing to hear your offer."

"Offer?"

"If you have a job for a mage, there is generally a question of compensation which naturally arises."

"Sanabalis—"

"And which you could not, of course, afford in other circumstances. We have a few hours before Mr. Rennick is sentient."

"And you're going to spend them playing word games."

"It amuses me," Sanabalis said with a lazy smile. It was a genuine smile; he *was* amused. "I have little else that does at the moment, although on occasion Mr. Rennick does provide distraction. I admit that I miss our lessons."

She started to tell him she didn't, and stopped. It wasn't entirely true.

"Kaylin may have other lessons to occupy her time in the foreseeable future," Severn said. He had, of course, taken sandwiches and orange juice, and he had eaten the one and drunk the other as slowly as Sanabalis talked.

"Oh?"

"Sergeant Mallory feels her academic record speaks poorly of the Hawks, and he has instructed her to retake those courses she failed. She will be suspended with pay until she passes them, or until her teachers give up."

"I see." He drew his hands up into a steeple in front of his beard.

"I believe that the expense of training her in other

disciplines—yours, for instance—will not be seen as worthwhile until she proves herself adept at regular classroom work."

"The lessons she receives from me are not optional."

"No. I don't believe that Sergeant Mallory is apprised of all of the particulars of Kaylin's situation."

"Which implies his tenure is not intended to be indefinite."

"That's the hope," Kaylin interjected. "We need you to help."

"Ah. And how might I help?"

"In the Leontine Quarter last night, we met a mage."

He frowned. "Continue."

"He used a crapload of magic and burned down a house. He wanted us to be in it," she added.

"You weren't."

"We were."

"And you have not taken this to the Halls of Law."

"Um, no."

"I'm sure your reasons for this oversight are fascinating. You wish me to track this mage?"

"Not exactly."

"You wish to ascertain whether or not he's an Arcanist?"

"Oh, he's not."

"He is not a member of the Imperial Order."

"No."

"And you are certain of both these facts?"

"Yes."

"Good. Why?"

"He was Leontine."

* * *

She wasn't certain what she expected him to say or do, but his expression shifted in a second into something as open and welcoming as the Imperial Prisons.

And if she could let a little thing like that stop her, she would never have become a Hawk. She gave him time to answer, and when it became clear he wasn't going to, she continued.

"He used fire. Not a summoning—it was mage fire. That much magic has got to leave a signature."

"A signature is only relevant if it will tell us anything we do not already know."

"In and of itself, yes. But…the man that Marcus killed—the man he's accused of murdering, if the Leontines even have a word for it—was possibly enspelled. We need to visit both the burned-out house and the corpse of the murdered Leontine, and look for signatures. If the signatures match, we know who did it."

"And if there is no signature?"

She deflated slightly. "Marcus is not a murderer, or half the office would be names on headstones by now. He killed his friend in self-defense. I'm certain of it."

"There are many ways to motivate a man to kill," Sanabalis said evenly. "Magic is probably the least reliable, and it is certainly not the most commonly used."

"If Marcus trusted him, he was worth that trust. It had to be *something*."

"As you say." He let his hands fall to the rests of his chair, and levered himself out of it. Kaylin could have sworn she heard the wood creak. "I am intrigued by your tale. I will visit the ruins of the house. The body, however, may be more difficult. The case has not been remanded to the Imperial Court, and the jurisdiction of the Caste Court holds sway."

"We know," she said, shedding crumbs as she stood. "We'll work on that."

"Work with care," he replied. "I believe you've been forbidden any part in the investigation."

"It won't be the first time I've done a job that doesn't exist as far as official records are concerned."

His gaze was bright and piercing, his eyes a glow of golden orange. "That, Kaylin, I am well aware of. Have a care. The past can return to haunt you at unexpected moments."

Meeting his gaze, narrowing her eyes at the odd light in it, she wondered what he knew. And if it mattered.

CHAPTER 11

It was too much to hope that the streets would be as deserted as they had been the evening before. Too much, perhaps, to hope that they wouldn't be as crowded as the markets in the human Quarter. It was a slap in the face, however, to find the carriage halted simply because there was nowhere for the horses to *go*. The streets were packed.

The fact that they were packed this close to the wreckage implied a prurient interest she thought Leontines didn't have—or at least not the men.

In human streets, the regalia of the Imperial Service, plastered with such loving detail on the sides of the doors, the back of the carriage and the body of the man who drove it, would have pretty much cleared the crowd; if humans were curious, they weren't generally stupid, and no one really wanted to test the Emperor's patience. If it even could be tested; volunteers were in short supply.

The Leontines, however, simply failed to notice.

"Everybody loves an accident," Kaylin muttered as she reached for the door handle closest to her. "I'll go and see what's happening."

"Not you," Severn said, catching her wrist before she could open the door and elbow her way through the press of people.

"If someone tries to attack me here—"

"I'll go."

"I got that the first time. There won't *be* any danger. They probably can't even lift their damn arms!"

Sanabalis ended the budding argument. "I will leave the carriage," he told them both. "I will clear a path for the driver. You—both of you—will remain here." His eyes were a shade of orange. "Is that understood?"

Kaylin nodded. Severn nodded as well.

The Dragon Lord opened the door, which took longer than it should have, and stepped into the milling crowd.

"I wonder if they know he's a Dragon?" Kaylin asked, sticking her head out the window only after Sanabalis had cleared it.

"You should have been a lawyer," she heard Severn say behind her. "You understand the letter of the law perfectly, and you ignore the spirit when it suits you."

"And you don't?" she asked, without looking back.

"I understand when a Dragon is skirting the edge of anger," he replied. "You used to know how to be cautious."

"I'm not leaving the carriage. I just want to see—oh."

"Oh?"

"They know he's a Dragon."

* * *

The crowd that had been milling and talking—if Leontine growls ever sounded as casual as normal speech—turned in ones and twos to stare at Sanabalis. Silence spread like the ripples a stone makes in a still pond, destroying all but the most intent conversation. Even these faltered as voices that were raised to be heard over the din of hundreds of other voices grew unnaturally loud.

Sanabalis didn't take on his true form—which, by Imperial Edict, was strictly forbidden—but he didn't have to. He walked with an authority that even the adolescent males couldn't mimic if they tried. Kaylin snorted, watching them. She had no doubt they would, and that it might impress their male friends. She'd never quite gotten the hang of that dynamic.

"It's quieter," Kaylin said.

"Really?"

She considered surrendering her perch to smack Severn but decided against it; as a response to sarcasm, it set a bad precedent.

People moved for Sanabalis in a way they hadn't for his carriage. She would have to ask Kayala about that later, if she remembered. But even if they moved, even if they *wanted* to move, they were hampered by numbers—the crowd that surrounded the burned-out ruins of a Leontine home was just too thick. She watched Leontines back up into other Leontines, and watched as the crowd that couldn't actually see Sanabalis responded to this invasion of territorial space. This was how bar brawls started, and she'd seen a number of them; with

Teela and Tain for drinking partners, it was almost a matter of course.

But Sanabalis didn't seem to notice. He continued to walk, and the path that had been made for his passage didn't close at his back. They didn't seem afraid of him, not exactly.

"The carriage is not going to fit through that crowd," she told Severn.

"No. It would be hard to get the horses to trample Leontines."

She looked at the prominent fangs of the nearest of said Leontines and said, "Forget about the horses—you couldn't pay me enough to try."

He laughed. It was a soft sound, and it caught her attention where his almost-lecture had demanded as little of it as she could get away with. "You used to hate fighting," he said, when the laugh had died down to a faint smile. "Especially when I did it."

"I hated that I couldn't help you. I hated that I had to cower behind you. I hated not knowing how it would work out." She grimaced. "And *yes,* I hated the fighting. Satisfied?"

"Why did that change?"

"Did it?"

"Kaylin, you run *at* fights now, not from them."

"I was trained to fight, when the Hawks took me in. I'm actually good at it. Gods know I'm not much good at anything else."

"You never told me how you ended up with the Hawks."

"You never asked," she countered.

"I'm asking." He reached out and caught one of her

hands in both of his, leaning forward into the question, or perhaps into the hope of an answer. His hands were smooth and warm; the calluses that she knew were there couldn't be felt. It had been a long time since he had done this. She didn't withdraw her hand.

She wanted to tell him, then. She wanted to say it, have done with it. She took a deep breath, more because that's what you did than because she needed it. Words? They were always hard when you couldn't hide behind clever. "When I left Nightshade—"

They both turned at the sound of a Dragon's voice, and their heads almost collided as they tried to look out the window at the same time. They sat back and exchanged a rueful grimace.

"Yes," Kaylin said, "it's definitely Sanabalis's voice."

The words that Kaylin had been marshaling deserted her under the force of these new, foreign words. Sanabalis wasn't speaking Elantran.

Sanabalis wasn't speaking Dragon either, from what she could hear. She looked at Severn and Severn frowned slightly. It wasn't Dragon.

But the voice—the voice was a Dragon's voice. Sanabalis could speak Elantran like a native—well, like a native scholar at any rate. He simply despised it, and used it as infrequently as possible in any public venue. He had, however, condescended to teach half of the lessons they shared in Elantran—usually the half in which Kaylin's frustration was swamping her comprehension. Kaylin had heard the true depth and breadth of a Dragon's vocal range on only a handful of occasions, but it had never quite sounded like this. There was something about it that gave her goose bumps and caused the fine hair on the back of her neck and her arms to rise slightly.

"Do you recognize the language?" Severn asked her.

She shook her head. "No. I don't. It's not one of the official languages. It sounds almost like High Barrani, but it's wrong for that." She clenched her jaw a moment in frustration. "But, Severn—it sounds familiar to me. It sounds like something I *should* know. You?"

"It doesn't sound familiar to me at all." He waited a beat, and then said, "Is it magic?"

"If he's casting a spell, it's unlike any spell I've heard before. Most mages don't bother with words, and he's saying a lot of them. But…I think there's *some* kind of magic here. It's making my skin itch." Her eyes were drawn to the window, which might as well have been a wall for all she could see if she wasn't precariously balanced on its edge.

He looked down at her wrist. The bracer was there.

"Kaylin, look."

She followed his gaze. The bracer, gold and studded with what seemed to be precious gems, was flashing at her; the lights were going crazy.

She started to move, but Severn still held her hand. "He told us to remain here," he said quietly. It was the type of quiet that stone is.

"Severn—"

"We wait," he told her. "If he's speaking as a *Dragon*, we wait."

No rejoinder offered itself up for easy use. Something about Sanabalis's speech made her deeply uneasy, and the fact that she couldn't put her finger on *why* didn't help.

When he caught her hand again, she realized that she'd opened the door. She hadn't been aware of it. "Severn—I have to go outside. I have to see him."

"Kaylin—" He stopped speaking as she met his gaze. After a moment, he nodded. "We'll both go."

"The Leontines are not going to attack me, Severn. They're not even paying attention to the carriage and I—"

"It's not them I'm worried about."

She had to let it go. Severn wouldn't let her leave until she did. Gods, Sanabalis's *voice*. He wasn't singing; there was nothing musical about the cadence of his foreign words. But shorn of notes, the rise and fall of attenuated syllables, it *felt* like music to Kaylin. Like the essence of music, something that any song might strive to achieve, and fail, even if it failed gloriously.

It was what the Leontines now heard, as they stood still as statues in the crowded street. Kaylin knew it.

But she also knew that it wasn't what Severn heard. The bracer's gems continued to flash, although the heavy weave of her sleeves muted the light. She tugged them down for good measure, and then looked at her partner. "What do you hear?" she asked softly—so softly she was almost whispering. She hadn't intended that. But it seemed to her impossible to speak in any other way while Sanabalis was also speaking.

And Severn, Hawk as well, looked out at the crowd—seeing some faces in profile, but seeing mostly the broad and furry expanse of Leontine shoulders and backs—before looking back to her. "Not," he said slowly, "what you hear."

"Tell me."

"He's speaking a language I've never heard. For a Dragon, he's speaking softly, and no, before you ask, I'm not at liberty to talk about any other occasion I've heard Dragons speak. Suffice it to say it was louder. And infinitely less persuasive. What is he saying, Kaylin?"

"I told you—I don't recognize the language."

"No. But I would bet that the Leontines don't either, and they're listening as intently as you are. More, if that's even possible. What is he saying?"

Her first impulse was irritation, but it wasn't a Hawk's impulse. Sitting on it, she let her second impulse guide her. She listened to the voice—she couldn't help that—and tried to glean meaning from what she heard. She dissected syllables, holding some of them in memory even as she grasped for more. Nothing.

"Severn—"

"There are more Leontines coming," he told her. "I would guess that at least some of them are the Elders." Another pause. He said, "Don't move, Kaylin," and his arm released the elbow she hadn't realized he was holding.

The carriage barely creaked as he mounted it. His voice, different in every way from Sanabalis's, was nonetheless clear and sharp. "It's a group of four Leontines, all male. Fur is graying at the edges. Two are golden, one is entirely pale gray. The last—ah, you've met him. Adar. They're stopping," he told her. "They clearly hear whatever it is the other Leontines hear. They hear," he added, "what you hear."

"The driver?"

"I hear Lord Sanabalis," the driver replied calmly, as

if being spoken about in the third person was an every-day occurrence. "I don't know what he's saying, but if they don't respect the Imperial regalia—" and his voice made clear how little he thought of that "—they clearly respect a Dragon Lord."

He heard what Severn heard.

"Severn?"

"Coming," he replied, and leaped down.

"They don't hear what I hear, not the same way," she told him, as they began to thread their way through the crowd. It was a lot easier when none of the sharp bits attached to the Leontines were actually in motion.

"No?"

"They're standing still," she offered.

"Your point. Why do you need to see him?"

She shook her head. "I don't know."

"Fair enough. Neither do I."

They made their way through a section of street so crowded it made the landscape unrecognizable. But the burned-out building that formed an inverted dais for the Dragon Lord was unmistakable.

Dragons in their human forms were not formidably tall, and Sanabalis was probably the shortest of the five Kaylin had personally met. She couldn't see him until she cleared the living wall, and that took a little effort. Not as much as she had thought it would, when she was thinking about anything but his words.

And when she did clear the last of the Leontines, with Severn as her familiar—and yes, comforting—shadow, the words were the only thing she could think about.

Because she could see them.

* * *

They weren't like written words. They weren't like printed words. They weren't like the words in ancient, expensive texts that were so ornamented she couldn't even recognize them. They weren't, in any sense, like words at all—but they *were* the words he was speaking.

"What do you see, Kaylin?" Severn asked.

She shook her head. "Words," she said. And then, aware that she was telling him nothing at all of use, she added, "They don't look like words, Severn. If you saw them, I don't think you would think of them *as* words. They're like—light. No, not quite light—but it's the closest I can come."

"Light? Not fireworks."

"No—those wouldn't look or feel like words. Not magelights, either. They—look like…ghosts."

He waited.

"Like the ghosts of light. They're not quite here, they're not quite gone. They—they're moving, but…" She shrugged. "They don't look like our ghosts." She was aware that she was giving this particular Hawk a description as frustrating as any description ever given to some poor sod in Missing Persons.

"If you had seen them without hearing them, would you recognize them as words?"

She considered this carefully, and then nodded. "I think so. It's hard to separate them from Sanabalis. But I think so."

"Why?"

Since *I don't know* was not useful, she struggled to be of use, and only partly for Severn's sake. Some people loved a mystery. None of those people had ever been

Kaylin. She needed to know things, and she needed to understand what she knew.

When it was relevant.

At last she said, "I feel them." She took a breath and then continued. "I'm not even sure that what I'm seeing isn't part of that. They *feel* like words to me." And then she stopped. "They feel like words…"

"Not like Elantran words."

"Nothing like our words, no. We pick and choose. Our whole language is a patchwork quilt. Every word can be jumbled with other words, and we make sentences that we understand—but people hearing them will also understand them, and the understanding won't be the same. This is…"

He waited.

His whole life, the life that she had known, he'd been damn good at waiting. He'd told her once that he was so good at waiting because she was so bad at it, as if they were two halves of a whole.

Seven years, he had waited for her. And she had gone on in painful, furious ignorance.

"They're like…Barrani names," she whispered. "They don't look like them, but they have that solidity to them. Some sense of a meaning so complete that everyone who *could* understand them at all would understand the *same thing*. You couldn't lie in a language like that. Because it's what it is, not more, not less. I *didn't* understand the Barrani names when I touched them in the High Halls, but they didn't care."

"Words don't generally care," he told her. It might have been flippant, if said in any other tone. It wasn't.

"No. In one way, they're very much alike—I

understand neither, but I feel as if I should. As if I *could,* if I just tried harder. Worked at it."

"What is he saying, Kaylin?" Severn asked, again, in that serious tone.

This time, she could almost touch it. The meaning, not behind the words, but of the words themselves. Her body ached with it. Hurt with it. She realized, even as she thought that, that it wasn't her body—it was her *skin.* She reached for the arm that didn't sport a golden shackle, and fumbled with the buttons, unable to take her eyes off either Sanabalis or the moving, ethereal stream that seemed to surround him.

She pulled the sleeve up.

She heard the momentary gap in Severn's breathing, and managed to lift her arm so she could see it without moving her head. The marks were glowing a faint, luminescent blue, and it seemed to Kaylin that they were moving somehow, the swirls and strokes and dots coming apart and coalescing again.

Severn caught her hand and forced her arm down. Her sleeve, tugged by gravity and the weight of fabric not suited to the heat and humidity of Elantran summer, fell again. He buttoned it shut.

He had said nothing.

But Sanabalis *did.* He turned, his speech not faltering. His eyes were a color so close to glowing white that she took a step back; she had never seen a similar color in any of the races she'd met.

It was as if his single glance were a bridge that could be crossed. Without thought, she took a step forward, and then another. The third was interrupted by Severn, his arm around her shoulders heavy and at the same time almost otherworldly. "Kaylin," he whispered, his lips tickling the lobe of her ear.

She wanted to nod. She wanted to pay attention. Or to tell him that he was tickling her.

But she moved again anyway, drawn to Sanabalis.

Drawn, she realized, to what had been said, to what was being said now. And when the light moved, when the words, so ghostly and so strange, suddenly turned toward her, she thought she would never move again.

But she did.

Sanabalis continued to speak, but as he did, he lifted a hand. It looked…like his hand. But it looked, for a moment, like a Dragon's claws, like a Leontine's paws. It was both solid and changing, as if shape were as fluid as language.

And he clearly meant for her to take that hand.

She lifted her arm. It was the hand that Severn held, and there was a moment of awkwardness—of something stronger and more desperate—before he let go. Before he moved to her side, and gently engaged her other hand.

She was almost afraid to raise the hand he had surrendered; she was afraid to see in it what she now saw in Sanabalis. But she only knew one way of conquering fear, and that was to charge into it, blindly.

If charging could be this hesitant, it was what she did now. She placed her hand, palm down, across his. It looked like a child's hand in the hand of a large man.

Then Sanabalis continued to speak, and after a moment, she realized that he was once again at the center of the words and their odd, moving light. So was she. They drifted past her upturned face, swept across her cheeks, touched strands of her hair. She could feel them, moving around her. And across her skin.

She opened her mouth, and it opened to silence; she could feel her lips move, but nothing escaped them. Here, there was no need for *her* words. Her words, as she had said to Severn, were imperfect, flawed vessels that explained so little.

But she wanted them anyway: her words, her own voice.

Even when Sanabalis looked down at her again, with his pale, platinum irises, so much like the whites he almost seemed to *have* no eyes.

His hand was Dragon scale beneath hers; it was callused skin; it was hard, ebon claw—all and none of these things.

And hers? She thought it was just her hand. There was no hidden form waiting to leap out, no other self to call on.

No feathers, she thought. No flight feathers. No freedom from gravity: just Kaylin. But she hadn't always been just Kaylin. She had been Elianne, in the fief of Nightshade. And elsewhere.

She waited until Sanabalis was finished.

It seemed to take forever. It seemed over too quickly. Caught between these things, she was silent.

But when his voice stopped, the words stopped as well, melting in sunlight, in a morning in the streets of Elantra, as so much magic did—with the added bonus of there being no corpses.

"So," the Dragon Lord said, speaking in measured High Barrani again, his voice the voice of her teacher. "I believe I told you to *remain in the carriage.*"

"I tried," she said quietly, the more so because she realized how stupid it sounded.

"And you failed."

"I heard you," she told him. "I heard...the words. I—"

"She was moving before she realized she was moving," Severn said, as if he had not just interrupted her flail for a better excuse.

"So," Sanabalis said again, heavily. "What did you hear, Kaylin?"

"You. Speaking. I didn't recognize the language."

"No."

"But it sounded as if I *should*."

His brows drew together in a furrow that changed the lines of his face. "And what did you see?"

She shook her head. "Words," she said, aware of how lame that sounded. "But the Leontines—"

The Leontines had, at last, moved to make way for the Elders that Severn had caught a glimpse of, when perched at the height of a carriage she could clearly make out over the heads of the crowd. The horses were nervous, but they were Imperial horses all, and the driver kept them as still as one could expect.

Adar was at the head of the approaching delegation, his fur tinted ivory by sunlight. The golden Leontines stopped before they crossed the threshold of the ruin; the gray-furred Leontine stopped just within its boundaries. But Adar, white furred, blue eyes the color of sky, continued to walk. As if a Dragon Lord held no fear for him.

As if he owned the Quarter, which, technically, he couldn't. He was, however, the racial version of a castelord, and if the Leontines didn't live like the rest of the populace, she was fairly certain he understood the laws that overlapped.

She was surprised when he bowed.

"First Son," Sanabalis said gravely.

"We welcome you."

"It has been long indeed since I have walked among your children," Sanabalis replied, his voice still grave and level. "And I have missed their company."

"And we have missed yours, Eldest, and with greater cause. These two," Adar added, indicating Severn and Kaylin with a minimal movement of his head. "They are yours?"

"She is my student," the Dragon Lord replied. "And as is the case with so many of the young, she sees leashes and cages where there are none."

The Leontine made a sound that was kin to a chuckle—but with more growl and fang in it.

"And she came to our Quarter at your behest?"

"She came without my knowledge."

"Ah."

"Therefore no regrets for your treatment of her— whatever it was—should be offered. But had she not come, First Son, things would have gone ill."

Adar bowed his head. When he lifted it, he squared his shoulders. "I was not vigilant," he began.

Sanabalis lifted a hand. "Let us repair to your seat, and discuss what must be discussed there. There are too many ears in this crowd."

"You had but to ask, Eldest, and they would have cleared the streets at your command. But you told the oldest of our stories, and they listened."

"Yes," Sanabalis said, passing a hand over his eyes. "And it was long in the telling, and tiring. Forbid them this site," he added, "and leave me for a moment. We will join you when we have finished our work here."

The very Leontine bark that cleared the streets caused Kaylin to grimace in recognition. It wasn't a familiar voice, but the words were familiar words. The fact that they were obeyed more or less instantly—any crowd contained stupid people and stragglers—would have made Marcus green with envy. Or whatever color it was Leontines turned when envious.

But when they had gone, Sanabalis sat down heavily on the burned-out flooring. "That was unwise of me," he said. "And no doubt word will travel. It has been a very, very long time since I have attempted to speak the language. I'm surprised they recognized it."

"If they heard what I heard—"

"They heard only part of what you heard, if I'm any judge," he said. "And I *told you to wait in the carriage.*"

"Yes, Sanabalis."

"Meek doesn't work on me unless it's consistent."

"Yes, Sanabalis."

He frowned. "For what it's worth, I'm grateful that you handed me this difficulty."

"Because of the Leontines?"

"Yes, but not in the way you think." He ran his hands over his eyes again, after which his eyes were orange, but ringed with dark circles. She had never seen Sanabalis look so tired.

"Have you seen this done before?" he asked Kaylin as he pushed himself off the ground. Soot clung to the back side of his robes, but Kaylin didn't fancy her chances of surviving the simple act of brushing it off.

"About a hundred times."

"Good. Did you pay attention?"

She nodded briskly. "We needed the information."

"What did you see?"

It wasn't the question she was generally asked. "Me?" *I'm not a mage* started and died on her lips. "I don't think people generally see anything," she said, punting.

"I didn't ask you what other people saw—or did not see. I asked what *you* saw."

She hesitated, and then surrendered. "A sigil," she told him. "Like a mark or a thing made of fire—but it wasn't fire and it wasn't light."

"Was it always the same?"

"No. But if it did look the same, the magic was performed by the same person."

"Always?"

"Always."

"You neglected to mention this to your superiors."

"Hells no. I told the Hawklord," Kaylin said.

"Ah. I imagine he has that discussion in his personal records."

"He usually does."

"Very well. You've seen the magic performed."

She nodded.

"And you've seen the results," he asked.

She nodded again.

"Watch now," he told her quietly, "and tell me what you see."

"But you'll see it—you're the mage."

"Ah. No, Kaylin. What you saw on those occasions is *not* what the mages saw."

"But—"

"And what you saw today is not what I saw. Not what the Leontines saw."

She said, "It's the marks again, isn't it? The ones on my skin."

He didn't answer. Instead, he twisted one hand suddenly in the air. Since every mage of Kaylin's acquaintance worked differently—some in big ways and some in small—it didn't surprise her. But he nodded after a moment and began to walk farther into the wreckage. He touched nothing that he wasn't stepping on, and he made an effort to step on very little.

"Here," he said at last. She half recognized the room from the layout of the floor. It was the baby's room. She felt a twinge of unease, then, but said nothing.

He gestured again, and ran his fingers through his beard. The beard adopted black marks which he didn't seem to notice.

They waited. And waited. And waited.

Kaylin finally said, "I don't think this is the right spot—" She stopped. Because the black mess on the floor was not simply the charred remains of rug and broken wood. She hadn't seen it clearly at first because any symbol she had ever seen had emerged from thin air, as if it were a butterfly pulling itself out of a cocoon.

This…was different.

Strands of soot slowly began to rise from the floor, taking shape as they twisted upward in a billowing spire. She had thought it black, but black was a color her eyes could understand, and this suggested the absence of color. Nor did it take a form, a sigil she could clearly recognize or remember—it swayed as it rose, and it seemed to Kaylin that it tried and discarded many shapes, before any single shape was fully formed.

Moving, amorphous, it was fascinating. And it was hard to look at, hard to look away from. It could devour the attention. It could, she thought, devour more.

CHAPTER 12

"So," Sanabalis said quietly. She tore her gaze away from the growing sigil—to look at the Dragon Lord. His gaze was upon her, and only her, as if her reaction contained all the information his spell sought.

"I don't understand."

"No, I imagine you don't." He turned to Severn. "What did you see?"

Severn shrugged, but it was a brief, terse movement, shorn of his usual grace. "Kaylin?"

"Shadow," she told him. "It's not…it's not a sigil. Not the way they usually form. It's—it won't stick to a single shape, a set of lines. But…"

"You've seen it before."

"How do you know?"

"You recognized it." It wasn't much of an answer, but it was also true.

"Sanabalis," Kaylin said again. "I don't understand. Why did the shadows appear here?"

"At the height of day?"

She nodded, then shook her head. "No—at all."

"It is the source of the magic you saw," he replied evenly. "And it explains much."

"Not to me."

"No, but you are not aware of the history of the Leontines."

"And you are."

He nodded. "Come. We must speak with the castelord."

"And what are we going to tell him?"

"We are going to tell him to exhume a corpse. I believe that was what you intended."

She nodded. "Sanabalis—"

"I will tolerate only so many questions today, Kaylin. I am weary. The telling was taxing, and the spell, more so."

"It wasn't a normal spell."

"Astute."

"Could anyone else have cast it?"

"Perhaps. Among the Barrani, and the Dragon Court. But it is an old spell, and it is not much in favor at the moment."

She hesitated again, and he marked it; he was watching her like—like a Hawk. "The stories the Leontines tell—"

"Yes?"

"Well. One of Marcus's wives has red fur."

Sanabalis raised a brow. "A bold marriage. I am surprised that the Elders allowed it."

"They allowed it because—"

"Because they live in a city in which the old tales and the old laws are not valued. Pardon the interruption."

"He had to promise that he would kill any sons she bore him."

"Yes."

"But she's only had daughters."

"Then he is singularly blessed. And their fur?"

"Not red."

"Good." He began to walk away from the ruins.

"What if she'd had sons?"

"They would be killed."

"But they're *babies*."

"Yes. But the Leontine you met, Kaylin, was one such child. I am certain of it. You saw the shadows," he added.

"Sanabalis, you can't be *serious*. You don't expect me to believe that you can know—by the color of the *mother's fur*, that a baby is somehow evil!"

"Very well. I can't expect that." He stepped into streets that were now deserted. "But in this case, what you believe is not my concern." He turned to look over his shoulder, and his eyes were a dark shade of orange. "Please," he said, in a tone of voice that took all cordiality out of the word, "tell me that it is not my concern."

"It's not your concern."

He stared at her for a moment, and then the lower membranes of his eyes went up, hiding some of the fire of his gaze. "I believe I will also visit with Sergeant Kassan's Pridlea."

"You can't."

"Can't?"

"You're male."

He raised a pale brow. "And the significance of this?"

"Men aren't allowed in—"

"I am allowed to enter the domicile of any Pridlea that offers its hospitality."

She thought about the Leontine mob in the streets, captivated by the sound of his voice. "Maybe."

"We will visit," he said. "But we must speak first with the First Son." He looked at the sky. "And I believe you have less than two hours before Mr. Rennick is awake."

The truth of the matter was simple: Marcus had *never* shown this kind of awestruck respect to a Dragon. Seven years she'd dogged Ironjaw's steps, and admittedly for most of those seven there was a comforting lack of Dragons—but still. He'd been actively *hostile* to Tiamaris.

How was she expected to *know* the Dragons were somehow venerated by the *rest* of the Leontines? But clearly, they were. Although the mere presence of Sanabalis didn't invoke the same silent wonder that his words had, it invoked almost obsequious manners from males who were used to knocking each other over in the streets. This made the trip to the coliseum seem a lot shorter than it had the first time she'd made it.

And the guards who had gotten into a fight with Severn to establish a pecking order? Suspiciously absent. Sanabalis walked, with gravity and in silence, down the steps to where Adar was standing in just as grave a silence, his arms by his sides.

She glanced at him, and then looked at the cages. Marcus was still on the wrong damn side of a closed set of bars. He was watching Sanabalis, and his expression was unreadable.

Sanabalis made his way to Adar; Kaylin veered off as they reached flat ground.

"Kitling," Marcus said, his voice a weary growl. "Why is Lord Sanabalis here?"

Something about his voice... "Marcus, did you know what would happen if he came here?"

"He's Eldest," Marcus replied after a long pause. He glanced over her shoulder briefly, but she had his attention.

"What are they doing?"

"Bowing," he replied drily. "You probably have about ten minutes before actual conversation starts. Why is he here?"

"We had a small problem," she began.

"If he's here, it couldn't have been that small. Did you file an incident report?"

"With Mallory? I'd burn in the hells first."

"Kaylin. He is your commanding officer."

"He's *acting* Sergeant."

"And therefore deserves the respect due his rank."

"He wants more than the respect due his rank."

Marcus closed his eyes and ran his hands over them. She could almost hear him counting to ten, which would have been worse if he'd been on the same side of the cage as she was.

"Why is Sanabalis here? You can use small words if it helps."

"We had a small problem in the Quarter."

"And this caused the intervention of the Dragon Court."

"He's not technically here as a member of the Dragon Court."

"It doesn't matter why he came. He is what he is. The why, however, is of interest. To me."

"There was magery in the Quarter."

She saw the hair on his face stand on end. She saw his eyes shade into red. "Continue."

She wondered, idly, how long the cage could hold him if he didn't want to *be* in the cage, and decided not to press her luck. "A Leontine used magic. He tried to kill Severn and me."

"He didn't try very hard."

Kaylin grimaced. The implied threat was a familiar one and she lifted her throat, exposing it to the claws that were flexing just out of reach.

"I thought—" she said.

"You didn't think."

"I *thought* that if we examined the traces of magic around the area in which it was used, we could find the signature of the mage."

"You knew who the mage was."

"Yes, but—"

"Kaylin, please, tell me Sanabalis is not here to exhume a body."

She knelt by the cage and pressed her face as far as it would fit between the bars. "Marcus, we know magic must have been used on your friend—on the Leontine you killed. I wanted to prove that the source of that magic was the same as the magic used in an attempt to kill us. It makes sense. It's *what you taught me to do.*"

His eyes lost some of the red, but by no means all. "I asked you," he said, "to stay out of it."

"Marcus—they were going to try you and find you guilty of murder. I don't know what Leontine penalties for murder are, but you're *not* guilty. Not of that. I'm a *Hawk*. You're an innocent man. You can't ask that of me. Ever.

"I don't know why you're staying behind these bars. I don't know why you didn't speak up. But Kayala, the rest of your wives—"

"It is *because* of my wives that I did *not* speak." The snarl in his voice had so much edge Kaylin was half-surprised she wasn't bleeding. "Tell me," he said when his voice was under his control again. "What did Sanabalis do when he entered the Quarter?"

"Nothing until his carriage got stuck in foot traffic."

"And when it did?"

"He…he got out and…he spoke. In a Dragon voice, but not in Dragon. I think…he was telling the crowd a story. But I didn't understand his words," she added. "Severn couldn't place the language either."

He looked at her. The red receded further, but gold didn't take its place, not entirely; there was a gray to the eyes that she had glimpsed once or twice before. She didn't understand what it meant.

Anger was easy.

"You don't understand, kitling."

"No, I don't."

"They will kill Sarabe. They will kill Sarabe and her sister. They will kill any Leontines who had the misfortune to be born with the taint. Sarabe is *my* wife. If you had for once in your life obeyed me, I would die. But Kayala is canny.

"I cannot surrender my wife to the Elders. I cannot surrender her to the First Son. I will die anyway, but now, so will she."

"Marcus—"

"And so will the child," he said.

"No."

"Kaylin—"

"No. I promised his mother that I would protect him. I invoked that right."

"You invoked?"

"The right of the Pridlea."

"Kaylin, you are not her wife."

"No—but I birthed him. I licked his lids clean of birth fluid. I held him. If it weren't for me—" She swallowed, remembered the salty tang, the texture of fine hair against her tongue. "By Leontine custom, I *am* one of his mothers. And I won't let anyone kill him. Marcus, he's a *baby*."

"Even if it were in my hands," he said, "I do not think I could grant what you would demand."

"It's in your hands."

"No, Kaylin, it's not. It is now, in its entirety, in the hands of Lord Sanabalis."

"He won't kill a baby."

Marcus was silent.

"Marcus, I won't *let* him kill a baby."

"It is a caste matter."

"Not if it's in his hands, it's not."

At that, large brows rose slightly, and then Marcus chuckled. It was bitter, but there was genuine amusement in it. "You don't understand what he did," Marcus said. "You don't understand *why* he did it."

"You mean the story?"

"I mean the story."

"Does it matter?"

"It matters, Kaylin. Ask him."

"I will. He means to visit the Pridlea after we finish here."

"Ah."

She hesitated and then said, "The baby is there, Marcus."

His eyes widened. "What?"

"When whoever it was…attacked us…he burned his house down. We escaped—but we had nowhere else to go."

"We?"

"I took Marai there," she told him. "It seemed like the sanest place she could be."

"You…took…Marai…" He growled. "You had best hope that they keep me in this cage, kitling."

"Yes, sir." She rose from her crouch. "Marcus—you don't believe—"

"What I believe is not at issue here," he replied.

Kaylin nodded, squared her shoulders and turned toward Sanabalis and Adar. She took a step, and Severn was by her side in that instant.

"Be careful, Kaylin," he whispered. But he didn't touch her and he didn't stand in her way.

"Lord Sanabalis," she said, tendering him a very respectful bow.

He turned his head in her direction, and one of his silver brows rose. She'd managed to surprise him by being careful. She had also, judging from the sudden shift in his expression, made him suspicious.

She was truly tired of being careful in this particular way. Being careful seemed to mean—be something other than yourself. It was hard to do that for Mallory, but the alternative—losing the Hawk—was worse. Just.

It was harder to do that with Sanabalis.

But again, the possible alternative was worse.

She wondered if everyone who was polite and deferential and well mannered had to struggle so hard to be all those things, or if it came naturally to them. If it did, she envied them.

And if it didn't, she respected them now more than she would have thought possible when she'd first been allowed to tag along after the Hawks.

"Kaylin?"

"I want you to explain something to me."

"Ah. And that would be?"

"The story. The story you told the Leontines."

"Why?"

"Because I don't understand what's happening here, and I don't understand what *might* happen here. I need to know," she said.

Adar stood, his hands by his sides, his eyes slightly orange. He said nothing, however.

"Adar?"

"She is yours," Adar replied. "And what you feel it wise for her to know, I will not gainsay." Formal words. It took Kaylin a moment to realize that he was speaking in High Barrani.

"It is a caste matter," Sanabalis told Adar.

Adar nodded.

"And it is acceptable to you?"

"If you feel it wise, Eldest."

"Wisdom and Kaylin are seldom in the same court, and if they are, they are never on the same side."

Adar's albino brows rose.

"But I thank you for your indulgence. She is my student, and if no other students before her are remembered, I am *certain* she will be. But as are all students, she is troublesome.

"Very well, Kaylin. I told them a story, yes—but it is not like the stories you heard as a child. There are no stories in your language that come close.

"It is the story of their birth," he continued, his fingers playing with his beard. "No, it is more than that. It *is* their birth in the Old Tongue."

"I don't understand. Kayala told me—"

"The Leontines were created by the Old Ones," he told her. "As we were, but they were created later."

"But they're mortal."

"Yes."

"And the Aerians?"

"Kaylin."

"Sorry."

"They were not created in the same way that the Barrani or the Dragons were. We came, it is said, from the bones of the earth. We were carved, and we were given words."

"Names."

"Yes."

"But the Leontines—"

"They need no names to live," he replied. "They are as you see them. But they were not always as you see them now. Life is not…stone. It is not clay. I am not young," he added softly. "And I remember, although it is dim and distant, the stories of the Old Ones.

"Not all among them sought to create life, or to wake

it. Living creatures, living things—they are not one thing or another—they are shaped by forces that are outside of the words that the Old Ones spoke. There is, in them, some element of the darkness—some element of chaos."

"Sanabalis—" she said. Severn stepped on her foot. "Lord Sanabalis. I've seen the darkness. I've seen what it created. Some of it," she added. "They are *not* that."

"No. But without some touch of *that,* as you call it, they would not live at all. It is what makes living unpredictable, fascinating and yes, dangerous.

"The Leontines are cousins to the great cats that prowl the plains. The Old Ones—no, just one of them— spoke to them. He told them the story you heard, but it was longer and vastly more complicated. I cannot tell the whole of it if I were to take a year. I could not sustain that effort," he said. "But their creator desired new life, and companions, and he chose, instead of stone, to sculpt things that were already alive. To take their forms and change them. To waken in them some of his own intelligence.

"He did this," Sanabalis said, "and the Leontines woke into the world. And he was pleased with his effort. But it was not a stable effort, not in the way the Dragons or the Barrani were when they first woke. What he had touched and shaped was not entirely a thing of his own making."

"Sanabalis—"

"He understood the risk. And of course, in time, the cost of it became clear. The Leontines were susceptible, in ways that the Dragons and the Barrani will never be, to other words, other stories, and the shaping of other hands. They will never be wholly one thing or another. Mortal time is brief," Sanabalis added. "To the Old Ones. Even to the first born, the Dragons and the Barrani and the others that I will never name."

"He came back and found them changed."

"It was not so simple as that," Sanabalis replied, "although that is the legend that the Leontines tell each other. No, they came at the side of the Dark Host, and they carried the power of the shadows. Had they remained mere animals, they would have been changed, but they would always be lesser creatures, capable of cunning in the way that lesser creatures are.

"But they *were* transformed. They were not mere animals—they were vessels, and the power they could contain was vast."

"Vaster than Dragon power?"

He raised a brow and frowned at the same time. You had to love Dragon arrogance. "Sorry," she said.

"Had the entire race been susceptible to the power and the change," Sanabalis continued, when he seemed certain this particular interruption was over, "there would be no Leontines now."

"So only some of them."

"Yes, only some."

"And those would be the ones who are born to the red-furred Leontines."

He raised a brow. "Yes."

"Why?"

"Kaylin, it's *life.* There is no clear or logical reason for it."

"And why not the women?"

"Pardon?"

"Why not the women? Why only the males?"

He shrugged. "I don't know. Please do not use this as an excuse to expound upon the virtues of your gender," he added drily.

Something he'd said tugged at her for a moment before she paid attention. "You said they were susceptible."

He nodded.

"But that means they aren't dangerous in and of themselves, right? They have to be exposed or changed somehow?"

He nodded. "But it is more subtle than that, and less. I told them the heart of their story," he said quietly, "to remind them."

"I think they remember the stories well enough."

"They remember the way you remember," he replied. "And I wanted to speak those words in that place because it reminds them of what they *are*." He paused, and then added, "It cleanses them, if they have been touched by the wildness."

"You thought they might."

"I thought, indeed, that they might require it."

"Did you find anything?"

"Kaylin, it was not an investigative spell. It was not, in any true sense of the word, a spell at all."

"Could you tell that story again?"

"If it were necessary, yes."

Her silence grew thoughtful, inasmuch as Kaylin was ever silent and thoughtful at the same time. "Could someone else tell them a different story?"

His silence was distant and his expression remote, as if he looked down at her now from a long way away.

Well, above, if she was being technical. But give him this much: He answered the question. "Yes."

"And that would affect them in a different way?"

"Yes."

"Could this—this rogue mage—tell that other story?"

"That is the fear," he replied. He turned to Adar. "And we will, with your permission, exhume the corpse."

"Sanabalis—" She caught herself, as usual, just a second after her mouth had opened and dropped the wrong word. "Lord Sanabalis."

Adar, however, bowed. "Will the rites of preservation interfere, Eldest?"

"No."

"Then I will accede to your request. I will be a matter of hours," he added, with genuine regret. "But it would explain much, and I admit I did not relish the idea of the trial."

"Will you allow Marcus Kassan his freedom?"

"If you demand it."

"No. I will not interfere further in your law." Sanabalis bowed. "We do not have the hours at present to wait," he added. "But we will return when our duties to the Emperor are complete."

Adar bowed again.

"Lord Sanabalis," Kaylin began.

"We will require our coach," Sanabalis continued.

"Eldest."

"Kaylin, take Severn and wait in the coach. You can manage that?"

She grimaced. "Yes, Sanabalis."

"Good. Mr. Rennick, from all accounts, worked late and terrorized the kitchen staff for some three hours.

As even my appearance does not have this effect on the kitchen staff, I am both curious and reluctant to further antagonize him by your absence."

"The thing I don't understand is how someone can create an entire race of people from telling a single story."

Severn, his face in profile, said nothing. He'd said a lot of nothing while the coach made its way through the Leontine streets. Sanabalis didn't see fit to disembark and clear a path, but someone must have at least said something, because the crowds were sparse, and Kaylin recognized the Leontine equivalent of merchants on either side.

"It is not necessary to understand it," Sanabalis replied. "It is necessary to understand that it is true. The Old Language was almost a living thing, some part of the Old Ones that could interact with the world. It was not simply hello and good day," he said. "You don't understand the nature of Barrani names, but you accept the truth of their existence."

She nodded.

"Why is this different?"

"I don't know." She hesitated. "Marcus, the mage, his magic—you think he's—"

"Yes. Tainted."

"Could you tell him your story? Would he even hear it?"

"I could begin," he said gravely, "but I highly doubt that he would stand and listen. For better or worse, he has chosen. And no, it is not a simple story. It is a living one. Living things are complicated."

The other hundred questions Kaylin needed answers to she couldn't ask—not without exposing Marai and her cub. She fell into the silence that Severn had made his own. She was almost happy to see the Imperial Palace as it bobbed into distant view.

"I will allow you to return to the Quarter with me, when Mr. Rennick no longer requires your supervision."

"Are you going to tell the Emperor?"

"What do you think, Kaylin?"

It had been a stupid question. "You're going to tell him." She hesitated again, and then said, "One of Marcus's wives is red-furred."

"Yes."

"What are you going to do about it?"

"Nothing, Kaylin."

"What are they going to do about it?"

"That is an entirely different question. If I were you, I would not interfere."

"If you were me, you wouldn't be able to just stand by."

"True. It has been a long time since I suffered from the affliction known as youth." His eyes were orange-tinted gold, and they met her gaze, without blinking, for a very long time.

As if she were a story in progress, and he could read her, and he wasn't certain what the ending would be, or if he would like it.

CHAPTER 13

Richard Rennick met them at the door. Which is to say he flung it open, glared out into the hall and disappeared with a snort. He didn't, however, slam the door in their faces, which Kaylin took to be an encouragement to enter.

"I will leave you to your duties," Sanabalis said. "And I wish you joy of them."

"You've seen him like this before?"

"It has been my *privilege* to converse with the Imperial Playwright on many occasions."

"That would be a yes."

"It would indeed. This is far from the worst he's been, however. I imagine you might see the worst when he's finished."

"He gets worse when he's finished work?"

"Ah, you mistake me. At the moment, he has the company of his perfect genius, and all accruing doubts of said genius. When he is finished, he will turn his work over to the merely mortal."

"Pardon?"

"He'll have to cast actors to speak his lines. At that point, he is frequently unfriendly, unhelpful and deeply sarcastic. There is no other race that does sarcasm quite as well as humans."

"Oh, joy."

"My point," he replied. He offered her the slightest of bows. "I do not need to tell you to keep the morning's events to yourself."

"No."

"But as humans are often resourceful when attempting to find new ways to entangle themselves in difficulties, I offer the advice."

"Thanks."

The state of the dining room in which Rennick worked had initially reminded Kaylin of Marcus's desk. Now, it brought to mind the wreckage of a desk. As she was the Hawk responsible for bartering and haggling with carpenters for replacement desks, she was familiar with the disaster. It seemed to have grown in magnitude from the previous day's mess, and at this rate, in two days they wouldn't have to worry about Rennick—he'd never be able to find the door.

Not that this would save them from Mallory's ire.

She did find the chairs, although they weren't immediately obvious—piles of teetering papers did that. She picked up a sheaf and set it carefully to one side of the chair. Rennick, leaning back in his chair as if, at any minute, he intended to pass out, watched her.

She looked at what she'd moved. It was not only not in Rennick's writing, it wasn't Rennick's work. It also appeared to have nothing at all to do with the Tha'alani.

"What are you looking at?" Rennick barked. It really was a bark; his voice sounded like sandpaper would sound if it could speak.

"This isn't about your work."

"Not directly, no."

She considered asking him what it was, thought better of it and took her chair.

"Don't make yourself too comfortable," he said, in about the same tone of voice. "After we have breakfast, we're going out."

Food, when it came, arrived on small tables with wheels. It was brought by servants, five in all, each of them at least twice as old as Kaylin. It was left in silence. Clearly, there was a bit of friction between the serving staff and the playwright.

But food seemed to help. It certainly helped Kaylin. As did the mess, the ordinariness of piles of discarded paper, even the unshaven, blearly-eyed face of a man pushing himself—and everyone around him—too hard. There was no magic here, no shadows, no death—and if Rennick did his job, if he was as *good* at his job as he had to be, there wouldn't be mobs in the city streets on either side of the Tha'alani gates.

He ate for a while, idly flipping pages. "You haven't asked me where we're going," he said, without looking up.

She shrugged. "Does it matter? We're assigned to you for the day. We go where you go."

"Having discarded the admittedly cheap and easy love story, and clearly not wishing to offend the Tha'alani with a lack of truth as they perceive it, I was at a bit of a loss. But something you said suggested a possible way out."

"Something I said?"

"People do occasionally pay attention to the words that fall out of your mouth," he replied. "Don't look so surprised."

"It's not surprise. It's suspicion."

He laughed. It was the first time he'd shown anything like humor this morning—well, technically this afternoon, but Kaylin had a rather vague idea of morning as well—and she surprised herself by grinning in response.

"When we first talked about the Tha'alani, you mentioned that you'd taken orphans to the Quarter. Human orphans," he added, as if this was in any doubt.

She could see where this was going, and the grin dropped from her face as if it were weighted by anvils. "No."

Give Rennick this much: he wasn't an idiot. He didn't try to feign surprise, and he didn't bother with word games. "Why not?"

"They're children and I don't want them involved."

"In what? Talking to an unshaven Playwright?"

"That, too."

"I don't actually need your permission," he replied. "I can speak to Marrin on my own." He stood. "You're free to wander off wherever you like."

"You can't just—"

"It wouldn't be the first time I've been there," he

added. "And it certainly wouldn't be the first time I've interacted with the foundlings Marrin guards so ferociously. The fact that I got in once could be accident— but if I had crossed the lines she's carved in the floor, walls, and anything else in the Halls that's not bright enough to move out of the way, I would never be allowed back. I probably wouldn't be allowed to leave."

"Not in one piece, no."

"Kaylin, I don't like children all that much. I like the theory of children, but the practice is both noisy and tedious. I'm happy to have other people have them—I think of them as future customers.

"But children are universal. We all have them, doesn't matter which race or which religion. Well, okay, maybe strict adherence to some religions, but you get the general idea. The Tha'alani *like* children. And I think your orphans may well have liked the Tha'alani. I want to speak with them."

"Rennick."

"What are you afraid of?"

"I don't like to drag children into my work."

"Do you think they'll tell me anything you don't want me to know?"

She forced her hands out of the fists they'd become. "No."

"Do you think I'd injure them?"

"No. Not you."

He stopped before the next words left his mouth, and then grimaced. "You could play along with the script."

"What?"

"I think he expected you to say something else," Severn said drily.

"I answered his question. In spite of anything he's said or done, he doesn't seem like the type of person who would terrorize or harm the helpless."

"Thank you. I think. But if you don't think I'll harm them, what is your objection?"

She shrugged and gave up. "I don't know," she told him quietly. "But—they've had a hard enough life. They're never going to have easy lives. I just—" She shook her head. "Why children?"

"Because if children—and children without family and with few friends at all who aren't likewise destitute and dependent on the charity of a fanged and intemperate Leontine—aren't afraid of the Tha'alani, grown men and women might pause to feel a bit ashamed of their own fear." He lifted a hand as she opened her mouth. "And yes, if they understand that the Tha'alani treat even the least of us with kindness, it will also give them something to think about."

"What did you have in mind?"

"I told you, I just want to talk to them."

"I meant for the play."

"Ah. That. I'll explain it as we go."

Amos was in the garden at the front of the Halls. This meant he was weeding and trimming the hedges, and watering the occasional flowers; as gardens went, it was not a very fine one. Had he been in the back garden, he would have been tending vegetable patches and fruit trees with a number of the older foundlings at his disposal. While Marrin did manage to get money out of the city's more wealthy inhabitants, she liked to be as self-sufficient as possible.

"Kaylin," he said, wiping his gloves on an apron that was at least as dirty.

She smiled.

"This is your...friend?"

"Yes. I promise not to try to kill him in the Halls again."

"Good. Once was more than enough." He removed a glove and offered Severn a hand; Severn took it without hesitation.

"Kaylin's got a bit of the Leontine in her," Amos told Severn. "At least where her temper's concerned. But Marrin seems to have forgiven her the incident." He smiled. "And she approves of you."

"I'm happy to hear it. It means I'll survive crossing her threshold."

Amos laughed. "And this young man?"

All men were young to Amos. Rennick smiled. "Richard Rennick," he said, taking the outstretched hand. "I've been here before with the Festival troupe. I spent most of the time dressed as a tree."

"Oh, the talking tree with the creaky voice?"

"That one."

"The kids liked it," Amos replied, as if that were all that were necessary. Or important. Kaylin had often wondered why Amos worked at the Foundling Halls, but she had never asked. And probably never would.

"Is Marrin busy?"

"Not more than usual. Go on in. One of the kids will know where she is."

Marrin was with the youngest of her foundlings, so her claws were completely sheathed, and her lips were pulled over her fangs. It made her look older, but definitely safer to be around.

Holding a baby of maybe seven months—it was often hard to tell, because they appeared on the Foundling Halls' steps in various states of health—she turned to smile at Kaylin and Severn. She also smiled at Rennick, so his guess that she'd let him in was accurate.

"What brings you to the Halls?" she asked.

"Mr. Rennick," Kaylin replied. "He wants to speak to the kids that we took to visit the Tha'alani Quarter."

"Why?"

Rennick rolled his eyes. "Is *everybody* this suspicious all of the time?"

Marrin snorted. "It's my job."

"Fine. That doesn't explain the Private's attitude."

Leontine chuckling was very much like Leontine growling if you didn't know them. But the baby apparently understood the difference, in the way that babies do; it was looking around, blue-eyed and alert. "She knows me fairly well," Marrin told Rennick. "And inasmuch as I'd trust anyone else with my foundlings—" and her tone of voice made clear that that wasn't much "—I'd trust Kaylin. But if you're here, she couldn't find a good reason to keep you out."

"Does that mean I can skip the explanations?"

"What do you think?"

He sighed, but he didn't offer her attitude. Instead, he told her more or less what he'd told Kaylin.

"Well, kitling, it seems harmless enough. How much time do you have?"

"All day."

"Given how much they like to talk," Marrin replied,

"you'll need it. Find Dock and tell him to gather the others. Not that you'll be able to stop him."

Kaylin laughed. "Where is he?"

"He is, in theory, on laundry duty, so he should be out back."

The children were not as small as they had been when Kaylin had first gone to the Foundling Halls. It always surprised her, how fast they grew. Some of the older children from those early years were no longer in the Foundling Halls, although Marrin checked in on them all.

The children who remained were, as usual, more than willing to talk to an attentive adult. They were also willing to talk to a bored adult, or an adult with glazed eyes and a fixed expression; people who expressed boredom in more obvious ways were not usually allowed to visit a second time, although exceptions were made for emergency visitors like doctors, officers of the Law and—once—firefighters.

Rennick was attentive. He also took a seat on the ground, forcing them to sit closer if they wanted to be heard first. Or at all. He didn't have paper with him; he wasn't trying to record their words. Or perhaps he was; he had seldom offered anyone else this kind of complete attention.

Marrin came into the room, and stood beside Kaylin for a while. "You don't like him?" she asked.

"I didn't," Kaylin confessed. "I'm really not sure what to make of him. But…I can imagine that he really does write plays for children, watching him now. He doesn't like children."

"No?"

"Well, he said he doesn't."

Marrin shrugged. "Humans are like that." After pausing, she added, "You don't look like you've been sleeping enough."

"I'm not one of your foundlings, Marrin."

"No. But you should have been."

There wasn't much to be said to that. Kaylin didn't try. But she stood a while in the comfortable presence of the only Leontine in the Foundling Halls. Possibly the only Leontine in the city who *wasn't* confusing or surprising her at the moment. "You couldn't have found us all," she said at last. "And if you had, you'd have had to turn half the fiefs into your Halls just to accommodate us."

"That would be worse than what's there?"

Kaylin shook her head. "It would be so much better than what's there." She shifted slightly, turning away from the conversation they were having. "Rennick is really good with them."

"Yes. He is not, unfortunately, as well mannered around adults, but that doesn't cause me problems." The Leontine's gaze swiveled back to Kaylin and stayed there for a little longer than was comfortable.

"Did you eat?"

"Rennick fed us."

"Did you eat yesterday?"

"When Rennick fed us."

"Kaylin."

Kaylin looked away from Rennick. And then looked back. Marrin's eyes were golden.

"We've had some trouble at the office," she said at last. "Marcus has...taken a leave of absence."

"Ah. I had heard something to that effect."

"How much to that effect?"

Marrin raised a brow. Her whiskers and the edges of her fur had grayed, but the gold that she must have been in her prime was still visible. It made her look almost silver in the light. "Come to the kitchen," she said. It wasn't exactly a request. It wasn't exactly a command.

Kaylin waited a moment and then nodded.

"Corporal Handred may join us, if he likes."

"You understand, dear," Marrin said, as she opened cupboards looking for a kettle, "that Marcus is a bit unusual."

Marrin and Caitlin were the only two people on the planet who were allowed to call Kaylin "dear." Something about the way they said it took the edge off it; there wasn't any condescension in their tone.

"I thought I knew that," Kaylin replied, leaning into one of the long, clean counters.

"And now?"

She shook her head. "I didn't. I'm not sure what I know now."

"What is happening in the Quarter?"

"How much have you heard?"

"Only a little. I don't visit often. This is my home."

"Marrin, what do you know about Dragons?"

The Leontine busied herself with bread and cheese, neither of which she ate in any great quantities. "Why do you ask?"

"I accompanied one to the Quarter," Kaylin replied.

"Ah." The chopping motion never stopped; it was a rhythmic, staccato beat. "That must have been interesting. Did he fly?"

"Hells no. It's sixteen different kinds of illegal, for one, and the only thing that polices the Dragons is the Emperor. This particular Dragon just…walked. And talked a lot."

"Talked?"

"Have you heard a Dragon talk?"

"No."

"But…"

"I wish I'd been there," Marrin said. Something in her voice had changed, but it was subtle in a way that Leontines usually weren't; Kaylin didn't know what it meant.

Kaylin hesitated again, and then said, "He was telling them a story."

The chopping stopped entirely. "A story?"

"About their creation."

The older Leontine turned slowly away from the countertop. "Why, Kaylin?"

"He thought it was necessary." As answers went, it wasn't a good one; she could see that in the expression Marrin gave her.

"Why?" The tone was sharper, but Marrin's claws were still sheathed, and her eyes had shaded into an odd color, not red, not gold, but not—quite—the orange that was a storm warning where Leontine temper was concerned.

"I'm sorry, Marrin, I shouldn't have mentioned it. I'm not really supposed to be talking about it. As in, big angry Dragon will rip off my legs if I do."

Marrin turned away, then. She was utterly silent, and completely still—if she hadn't been standing, Kaylin would have rushed to her side to see if she was still breathing. But after a moment, the old Leontine—and she looked old, suddenly—said, "I thought I had escaped all of this," and bowed her head.

After a moment, she began to speak.

"When I was younger," she said, "I lived on the plains. We knew of the city, of course, but it was no part of our lives. I was married."

Kaylin wanted to see her eyes, but they were hidden by her posture, which clearly said "keep your distance," even without evident fangs or claws.

"I was my husband's first wife and we were young. I was also his only wife, although I had some thoughts on who we might make offers for in the future. I was planning my Pridlea," she said. Her voice was so shorn of its regular growl it sounded almost human. "I became pregnant quickly—I think we both wanted that." She turned, without lifting her head, and reached for the counter, for the knife she had momentarily set aside. Slowly and methodically, she returned to the task at hand—as if feeding Kaylin was somehow important. Or as if it were an anchor.

"I had one cub, in the fall. She was healthy. Even though a litter of one is unusual, we would have been happy, but the child was—even at birth, and almost hairless—marked."

Kaylin's breath was sharper than the knife.

"Yes, kitling. She had red fur."

Kaylin closed her eyes.

"It had been many, many years since a cub had been born with the marks. I was exhausted, and weakened. The birth, as first births often are, was hard. I had no wives, then, but our mothers and their wives had come, and they saw, of course.

"My husband's mother summoned the Elders. She took my daughter from me before we could lick her fur clean. The cub was so peaceful, so quiet. She opened her eyes without the touch of tongues on her lids, and she looked at the world. The world looked back," she added. Her voice was neutral.

"Marrin, you don't have to tell me this if you don't want."

A graying brow rose as Marrin looked across the counter at Kaylin. "You've never asked," she said mildly.

"We all have secrets," Kaylin replied. "We all have a past."

Marrin nodded. Kaylin was certain she would have kept cutting if there had been anything left to cut. Instead, she reached into a cupboard, took out two plates, and began to arrange the food on them. As arrangements went, it was pure Leontine—it was food, not art, and as it was going to be destroyed instantly by people who were meant to *eat* it, there wasn't much point in prettiness. But it still took a while.

And while she worked, she talked.

"My husband's mother was angry," she said. "My mother was afraid. The Elders took my daughter." She examined plates as if they needed something she couldn't give them. "I was so tired, Kaylin. I was in some pain. I wasn't thinking clearly—and they understood that.

"But I left the birthing den, and I headed straight for the Elders. I think I injured two of them. I remember the blood." She carried the plates to the small table at which she habitually ate with guests, if she cared enough to feed them. And "ate with" in this case was entirely wrong; mostly, she hovered and made sure *they* ate, but didn't touch the food herself.

"They were not angry with me. They understood my panic, my fury, my fear—she was my daughter, and they had taken her from me. I would not have been held accountable for what occurred there. And had I desired it, when I regained my strength, I might have stayed."

Severn was a ghost in this conversation; she looked through him, as if he didn't exist at all as she set the plate in front of his chair.

"But my husband stood by. He did nothing. And when I had recovered, I was…angry. I knew the stories," she said, her voice so level she might have been telling the story of a stranger in front of a classroom of bored students. "I understood why the Elders had my child killed. But…I was not strong enough to accept it, in the end.

"And in the end, I left my husband. I released him from our marriage. I told him who I thought would make good wives from among our tribe. He tried to tell me that he was willing to try again, to have other children. He wanted my children," she said, "and he understood the pain that I felt, and the pain that he had caused.

"But I could not bring myself to trust him. And I couldn't bring myself to *try again*. I had failed my child, and she had died. I had no guarantee that any child born of my body would not likewise be marked."

Kaylin was definitely not hungry. But as Marrin had

gone through the motions of feeding them, Kaylin now went through the motions of eating.

"I came to Elantra."

Kaylin nodded.

"It was hard to live in this strange city. It was hard to wake up in the morning, in a small, cramped room, with none of my kin in running distance. There was no tall grass, there were no hunters. There were these small, cramped *streets*. I lived for some time in the Leontine Quarter, because I was homesick. That is the right word?"

"Yes."

"I made friends here, among the women. I avoided the men. But in the end, it was difficult. I had no family here. When my new friends married, when they began to bear children—it was more than *I* could bear. I left the Quarter."

"Did you know Sarabe and Marai?"

"I knew their mother," Marrin replied. "She was younger than I. I think they all were. But Sarabe's father protected his daughters. And in the end, Sarabe *married*." The word was spoken with such heat, it was almost impossible to hear it as anything but angry.

But Kaylin knew Marrin; she said nothing.

"And I wondered if things would have gone differently if my husband had been like Sarabe's father. I can't say. Sarabe's parents were consumed by fear for their daughters, and it devoured them. I do not know if they had much joy, parents or children.

"But two weeks after I left the Quarter, I was walking through the streets of this crowded city, and I saw a young child. He was begging. He was *also* stealing."

Her voice took on its familiar growl. "But I couldn't be angry with him. He was so scrawny, Kaylin. I asked him where his parents were, and he shrugged and said 'wherever the dead go.'

"I fed him. And in the end, I took him in. He had a place to stay, but I did not feel it was suitable for a child. The Foundling Halls came, in the end, out of that meeting. I couldn't believe that these children were left to fend for themselves when they were clearly still cubs—and I wanted to help them.

"I wanted children," she said softly. "And I gathered them. This is my home, this is my den. I knew they were not my daughter," she added, as if it needed saying.

"Sarabe had daughters."

"Yes. And none of them were marked."

"No. Marrin—"

"I understand why the Elders made the choice they made. I try not to hate them for it. But…this talk, today, this Dragon, the story of our beginning—it makes me feel young again. Young and helpless."

"If…there were…some proof that it *is* as big a danger as the Elders fear, would that help at all?"

"What do you think? She was my *child.* Even knowing that she might be a danger, even knowing that she *would* be, that the Elders were somehow right—could you have killed her?"

It was not the question that Kaylin had thought to hear. Not *here,* not in this place of safety, where the unwanted were loved and fed and taught. Her throat closed over any words she might have said—which was fine, because words had completely deserted her.

She realized in that moment that no matter how much

she thought she had accepted the past, her dead would always come back to haunt her, biting and cutting at totally unexpected times. The children she had rescued from the streets—the children who had trusted her. Her hands became fists on the table to either side of her plate. *Jade. Steffi.*

It was Severn who answered the question, and as he did, he covered one of those fists with a hand that was larger in all ways—but just as unsteady, when it came to that.

"No," he told Marrin. "If the world demanded their deaths in return for safety, she would have watched it burn."

CHAPTER 14

Marrin fell silent, watching them both. At length, she said, "What has happened in the Quarter?"

"The son of one of the marked," Kaylin replied quietly. "He—he's been living in the Quarter."

"Undetected." It was not a question.

Kaylin nodded. "He wasn't born here. He came, it was thought, from the plains."

"Then I know why your Dragon spoke."

"He's not *my* Dragon."

The older Leontine lifted a brow. "As you say." She shook her head. "You and I—we are not from the same race. No one knows where your race began," she added, "or why. But we are not so very different under the skin. Come, Kaylin. Tell me instead why you brought Rennick to my Halls."

"Rennick?" For a moment, she had forgotten he existed. She had the grace to flush. "It's work," she told Marrin. "What he told you—it's all true. We're assigned to stop him from botching his attempt at a play. He's got the tougher job—he has to write *something* that will somehow make the Tha'alani seem more like us. There are near-riots in the streets right now. It's ugly. We want them to stop."

"And you can't arrest the people in question."

"I'd like to," Kaylin replied. "But the Swords don't think that'll help, and they're the ones on riot duty. People are just stupid when they're afraid."

"People of any race," Marrin replied. "Are you going to eat, kitling?"

"I'm not really hungry," she said. It was true, for a change.

Marrin accepted the truth. She came and joined them at the table. "What is being done in the Leontine Quarter?"

"I don't know," was the miserable reply. "Marcus—he's in what passes for a Leontine jail, accused of murdering one of his oldest friends. I want to get him out of there. I *know* Marcus. There's no way—" She shook her head. "He's not very happy with me right now."

"You have the means of proving his innocence."

Kaylin nodded. "The Dragon does. It was my fault the Dragon was in the Quarter at all. I needed a mage I didn't have to go through the department's budget to get. With Marcus gone, someone else is in charge, and that someone else would be extremely happy to see me without the Hawk."

Marrin growled.

"I'm fine, Marrin. I can take care of myself," Kaylin said quickly, raising one hand to stem the flow of harsh Leontine. "But the Caste Court—the Leontine Caste

Court—claimed jurisdiction over Marcus. I was given a direct order not to interfere."

"And they expected you to obey?"

"Everyone else will."

"The Dragon is not under this stranger's jurisdiction." It wasn't a question.

"No. He answers to the Emperor. I think he'll prove that the man Marcus killed in self-defense was enspelled."

"By a Leontine."

Kaylin nodded. "By a Leontine."

"And your Sergeant Kassan is concerned that this will affect his wife."

Kaylin nodded again. "He thinks they'll kill her. And that he'll die trying to stop them."

Marrin's gaze was gold now, but it wasn't exactly peaceful. "There is more."

"Yes—there always is. But I can't talk about it, Marrin. I shouldn't even be telling you this much. The Dragon will reduce me to ash if he finds out."

"Kitling, do you understand what they fear?"

"Yes."

"Tell me what you think you understand."

"I think the Outcaste Leontine is a mage, but the power he uses is wild and dark."

"That could be said of all magic."

Kaylin, never the biggest fan of magic, nodded. Not much there to argue with, really.

"They're afraid," Marrin said quietly, "that he *is* the power. He is less than an agent, now. Whatever he was before he accepted the change is gone. They are afraid that he is like the Ferals of your childhood, in the heart of the fiefs beyond the Ablayne—but more cunning, more capable of hiding the truth of his nature. You saw him. What do you fear?"

I'm afraid that they'll kill the baby. But she couldn't say it. Instead, she said, "He's dangerous."

"So am I."

"Yes, but I understand why and when you could kill." There was no question at all in either of their minds that Marrin could, if provoked. No question that Kaylin could. "I know there are things that you would never do."

"Ah. And this man?"

She shook her head. "I don't have that certainty. He would have killed Marai and—" She bit back the rest of the sentence. "I don't think he cares a lot about any life that isn't his own."

"And that is the gift of the darkness?"

"I don't know. I haven't thought about it much because it doesn't matter. He has to be found, and he has to be stopped."

"Think about it," Marrin said, pushing herself up from the chair she had only just taken. "And while you think—and eat, if you can find your appetite—I will rescue Mr. Rennick."

"It doesn't sound like—oh. That's Dock."

"Yes. And Cassie. I believe they're about to embarrass me by starting a fight."

Rennick did not appear to be in need of rescue to Kaylin's admittedly jaundiced eye. He was, of course, the center of attention, and if the children kept trying to grab some of that attention for themselves, he obviously considered it natural.

But he rose when Marrin approached, and he offered her a tired but genuinely friendly smile. "I don't know where you get the energy," he said. "I should come here more often."

"Oh?"

"It'll remind me of what real work is like."

The low, throaty growl of a chuckle escaped Marrin. For that, if nothing else, Rennick rose a notch in Kaylin's estimation.

"Speaking of which, Dock—and I want the story about that name one of these days—and Cassie have expressed a very *serious* interest in my current work. I've half a mind to let them help."

"You'll lose the other half by the end of it," Marrin replied, but she was genuinely pleased.

"Oh, believe that your children are a positive joy compared with what's in my future." He offered her a hand, and she took it firmly. She was used to humans. "If it's not too much trouble, I'd like to visit again in a day or two."

"So you *are* capable of being charming," Kaylin said, as they settled into the carriage that had, like a miracle, appeared down the block.

"I won't deny it. Generally, it's too much work."

"And Marrin is worth the work?"

"I may complain about my work, but in general, I'm attached to my life."

She laughed. "And you got something useful out of your discussion?"

He nodded. "They weren't afraid at all," he said, dangling an arm out the window, as if to catch a breeze. "They wandered around the Tha'alani Quarter watched by every Tha'alani adult in range, and they didn't really care."

"The Tha'alani are used to curiosity in children."

"It's not the Tha'alani reaction, it's the children's reaction. As far as I can tell, Ari practically mashed foreheads with any adult fool enough not to get out of her way."

"Which would have been all of them. She's only five."

"My point." He lifted the dangling arm and traced the upper edge of the carriage window. "Whatever stories exist about the Tha'alani, they don't seem to touch Marrin's kids."

"Her kids are used to Marrin. They don't see the world in quite the same way."

"You're used to Marrin. You hated the Tha'alani."

"I had some experience with what they actually do for the Emperor."

"Ah. I don't suppose—"

"No. I don't want to talk about it."

He shrugged. "But before you met the Tha'alani?"

"There were stories."

"Yes, but from whom?"

"What?"

"Who told you those stories?"

"Does it matter?"

"Yes."

"I was afraid you'd say that."

"You can't answer."

"Not off the top of my head, no. Severn?"

"Street stories," he supplied. "But vague ones—most of our stories concerned Ferals and the fieflord, either of which were more likely to kill us than the Tha'alani."

"Do Tha'alani live in the fiefs?"

"What do you think?"

"That would be a no." Rennick turned to look at Kaylin.

"Pull that arm in or you'll lose it," she told him.

"My arm, my risk."

"That's the one you write with. You lose that arm on our watch, it won't be your head they'll remove."

He laughed at that, and dragged his sleeve back across the window edge. "You heard stories. The people with crossbows and clubs that look like table legs heard stories. But Marrin's kids didn't."

"Marrin's not big on stories that encourage fear of anything but her."

"Good point."

"She doesn't encourage gossip. The kids do it anyway, but they're hampered by the fact that she hates to let them out of her sight for a minute. And they know that fur, fangs and claws *don't* make her an animal. They've probably asked at one point or another why they weren't born Leontine, and she's probably told them that they were meant to be human. But being human, for Marrin, isn't the same as being human for children whose parents haven't died and abandoned them.

"I think she wants them to fit in here. To understand that this city isn't just human—or Leontine, or Tha'alani or Aerian or Dragon."

"You forgot the Barrani."

"Sue me. She's afraid that if they're too caught up

in the external differences, they'll—I don't know. Be afraid. They've got enough to be afraid of."

"You admire her."

"Who wouldn't?"

"Fair enough. I admit a sneaking admiration for her myself, and not just because she can keep a few dozen children in line. I'd pay a lot to know why she bothers."

"Is there *anyone's* life story you don't want to know?"

"Not really." His expression was unexpectedly serious. "Because people make a story of their lives. Gains, losses, tragedy and triumph—you can tell a lot about someone simply by what they put into each category. You can learn a lot about what *you* put into each category by your reaction to them. They teach you about yourself without ever intending to do it—and they teach you a lot about life. Put ten people in the streets at a crime scene, and ask them what they saw after. If they can't talk to each other at all during the interrogation, you'll probably have ten different versions of events. They edit what they remember. They try to make sense of it as they go.

"And I'll stop with the lecture now. I don't *like* people much—they irritate and annoy me. But I'm fascinated by them anyway."

She looked at him for a minute and then snorted. "You just like being the center of their attention."

"That, too."

When they returned Rennick to his quarters in the Imperial Palace, he opened the door, took one look at the mess he had made over the course of his work, and snorted. That said, he began to move piles of paper onto other piles of paper, in what seemed a completely random bustle. Kaylin, having had years to observe both Caitlin and Marcus, did the smart thing; she stood as close to the wall as possible and touched nothing.

"I hope you don't mind," he said, as it became clear he was trying to make some space on the table to do actual work, "but I'm thinking of using your foundlings."

"I mind." Pause. "For what?"

"Do you *always* say no before your brain catches up with your mouth?"

"Pretty much. It's safer that way—usually people who are asking me to do something aren't volunteering to shower me with gold, land or favors."

"You remind me of myself when I was younger."

"Thanks. I think. That was supposed to be a compliment?"

"It was an observation," he said, and if his voice had been any drier, it would have caught fire. "What I had in mind, as usual, is my current assignment."

"What about your current assignment?"

"The Tha'alani like children, and clearly the children—yours at any rate—aren't afraid of the Tha'alani. I'd like to use your little excursion in multiculturalism to present that aspect of their culture."

"Say that again with smaller words."

He glared. "You're doing that on purpose."

"Maybe."

"I would like to open the play with children—ours—in the Tha'alani Quarter. I'll probably add an older child, who can be naturally suspicious of the Tha'alani, having heard all the stories about the Tha'alani's abilities. This has the advantage of not offending the Tha'alani sense of truth."

"Go on."

"If we set the visit *before* the tidal wave, we can have the children in the Quarter when the Tha'alani become aware of the danger. The entire play will of course be set during that time."

"Rennick—"

"I understand that we're taking liberty with dates and facts," he continued. "Welcome to the world of fiction. I will be as true as I can be to the Tha'alani sense of themselves, but I *don't know* how they knew about the tidal wave. I'll have to make that up on the fly."

"If you're not damn careful, it won't matter what else the play says about them—you'll be adding to their problems."

"Believe that I'm aware of the danger, Private. But this has the best shot of accomplishing what the play is intended to accomplish. I hate messages," he added, with a genuine grimace of distaste. "And it can't *be* about the message, in the end, or people will fall asleep before it's delivered."

"What message?"

"Brotherly love, that sort of crap."

In spite of herself, she laughed. "If you'd known this was in your future would you have accepted the position?"

"Free room and board and the food's good. But yes, I don't completely approve of the job at hand, although I *do* understand the necessity. I'm basically trying to get a bunch of people to sort out their difficulties with their own inner thugs, but on a large scale. The type of people who *have* inner thugs are not generally the type of people I'd waste time on, and certainly not a lot of thought."

"They're just afraid. Everyone's afraid of something, Rennick."

"True. But if everyone tried to burn down an entire Quarter because they were afraid, I think the Emperor would turn the whole lot of us into small piles of ash."

"Not really," Severn said, reminding them both that there was a third person present. "The Emperor is something that is more terrifying than the Tha'alani—on a normal day. Or week. Fear can also be helpful when governing."

"I'm not particularly afraid of the Emperor," Rennick replied.

"You're not particularly afraid of Dragons, probably because you've never seen one in its native form," Kaylin retorted.

"And you have?"

Severn's gaze was mild as he looked at her. There was hardly a hint of glare in it. But the little that was there spoke volumes. Kaylin wanted to smack herself.

"Yes," she said curtly. "And since I *am* afraid of Dragons, I'm going to shut my mouth now."

Rennick raised one brow. "I highly doubt that."

At the end of the next four hours, during which time Rennick had crosshatched a number of pristine pieces of expensive paper, Kaylin was grudgingly impressed. "I think we can get the little historical lies past the Tha'alani," she told him. "With some difficulty."

"We being you?"

"Pretty much. Ybelline has worked in the Imperial Court for years, and she'll understand why we need to take the liberties we're taking. She might even be able to point out the dangers that we can't see that could arise out of our version of events."

"Good. I'll just go over and irritate all of the servants now, shall I?"

"You could try polite. I hear it works."

"Must be hearsay—I can't imagine you've got a lot of experience with it."

She grimaced. "I have a lot of experience with it," she told him firmly. "Severn's my partner."

Rennick laughed. Severn smiled. It was one of those rare perfect moments in which Kaylin felt she'd done something right. Or at least that it was possible to achieve something good.

But before Rennick could irritate the servants on their behalf there was a knock at the door.

Rennick, frowning, answered.

"It's for you," he said, stepping out of the way.

Sanabalis stood in the hall, unattended by anything that wasn't a wall sconce. "I believe you've finished your work for the day," he said, directing the comment toward Kaylin.

The moment of satisfaction burst, like the fragile and illusory bubble it was. "Yes, we've finished," she said.

"Good. I believe you have other duties to attend. Mr. Rennick." He offered a brief—and apparently sincere—bow. With Dragons, it was hard to tell. "I have taken the liberty of seconding your services for the evening," he told Kaylin as she approached the door.

"What?"

"I informed Sergeant Mallory that you will be excused from your verbal debriefing for the evening."

"I'm not sure you're allowed to do that."

"If he wishes to argue, he is free to pursue the argument through the customary channels."

She looked at Sanabalis's eyes. In the light from the hall—none of it bright, given that night was on the other side of the many windows—they were orange.

"The customary channels," she said, almost morosely, "are me." It was all the argument she was willing to offer.

Sanabalis wasn't without mercy; he'd arranged food, although he insisted they eat it on the inside of a moving Imperial Carriage.

"I've already eaten," he told Kaylin, eyeing the work of the Imperial kitchens with mild distaste when she offered him some of it.

"Does the Emperor know where you're going?"

He lifted one silver brow.

"I'll take that as a yes."

"I don't think you understand the magnitude of the difficulty," he replied, "although in this case, your ignorance is to our advantage. There are some things you would avoid, if you had any wisdom." He lifted a hand before she could speak in her own defense—and to be fair, she was about to embark on just such a speech. "I am doing you the courtesy of assuming that *if* you understood, I would not now be here."

"Why is that, exactly?"

"You would have been unlikely to enter the Quarter

on your own, and were that the case, you would have had no use for an unaffiliated mage."

"Is—is this going to get back to Mallory?"

"It is not a matter for the Halls of Law," Sanabalis said. "Not at present. The Emperor has taken a personal interest in the case, and the Caste Courts have not yet abandoned their resolve to keep the matter within their jurisdiction."

"They intend to let you examine the body."

"Yes."

"But that makes it a case for the Imperial Courts."

"No."

"Sanabalis—"

"The Emperor makes law, Kaylin. I do not completely understand your reaction to this case. I do not *want* to understand it. Is that clear?"

She considered the options. Nodded.

"Good. You have another five minutes to finish eating. I'd suggest you take it."

"I won't bring the meat to the Castelord."

"Very good. Don't bring anything else either."

"Yes, Sanabalis."

Adar was waiting. There were no lamps. The moonlight was clear and bright, and the air was heavy with humidity. Summer, in Elantra, was very slow to let go, and even the cool of night and sea breeze didn't drop the temperature enough.

But in the absence of lamps, there were torches on long poles that appeared to be stuck into the ground. Adar gleamed ivory and gold in the mixed light; he wore long, pale robes—they might have been gray or blue or white. He stood in the center of a semicircle comprised of Leontine men. They wore robes as well, but it was harder to see them; they were seated at Adar's feet.

Their whiskers twitched as Sanabalis approached, but nothing else moved. They didn't lift their heads; they didn't greet him. They rose only when Adar gestured, and they stepped away from him as he stepped forward, becoming part of the shadows that night was.

Sanabalis approached Adar and stopped a few yards from where the torches burned. He inclined his head but did not bow. His robes were the dark blue of the Imperial Court, the rich hue bleeding to black.

Kaylin and Severn wore working clothes. Tabards, chain shirts, regulation boots. They had not been required to leave their weapons behind—if there was a behind—because there were no guards to make that request. Guards of the type that they'd met the first time were not capable of this solemnity.

And, Kaylin thought, it's not as if the weapons made that much of a difference. Old or not—and these were, in her opinion, the Elders—the Leontines gathered here wouldn't have too much trouble with two humans if they felt the need to fight. They *would,* on the other hand, have a great deal of difficulty with a Dragon.

Adar did not kneel. He lowered his head gravely and spoke in Leontine. Kaylin understood almost nothing that he said, and she understood most Leontine.

Sanabalis, however, replied in High Barrani. "Yes. I will examine the body here. I trust Private Neya and Corporal Handred, and even if I did not trust them, I believe it necessary that they bear witness."

Adar didn't exactly jump for joy, but he didn't argue

either. "Eldest," he said, speaking in the growling cadence of a Leontine who in theory spoke Barrani. He gestured, and the Elders stepped forward.

They were carrying a stretcher.

From this distance, the smell was almost overwhelming. Severn moved toward Kaylin, and caught her arm. "They don't have mages," he told her, his voice quieter than a whisper, but clearer somehow. "They have no easy way of preserving the corpse."

"I'm surprised they didn't burn it." Or eat it.

"I believe they were waiting for the trial," he replied.

The scent of rotting flesh in the humidity of Elantran night made Kaylin really regret the meal she'd rushed through on the way.

But she'd seen worse. She tried to remember that. The Elders laid the stretcher with care at Sanabalis's feet and withdrew. Sanabalis bent, crouching just above the corpse's chest. His hand hovered over it.

Kaylin waited, watching him for signs of familiar magic. He lifted his head. "First Son," he said quietly, "step back, and tell the Elders to join you."

There was murmuring now, but it was low, too low to catch. The First Son hesitated for just a moment, and then he obeyed what was barely a request.

Sanabalis rose, and gestured. It was not, to Kaylin's eye, a familiar magic at all—but it was clearly magic. The ground absorbed the glow that emanated from Sanabalis's hands, swallowing it as if it were liquid. He began to speak, and when he did, he dispensed with the pretense of frail mortality: his voice was a Dragon's voice.

Kaylin glanced involuntarily over her shoulder.

Sanabalis was loud enough to wake every sleeping Leontine in the Quarter. He was loud enough, she thought, to wake the dead.

And, to her horror, he did.

CHAPTER 15

"Do not move," Sanabalis said, in harsh Leontine. He didn't turn to look at the Elders; his attention, as Kaylin's, was on the corpse.

She heard Severn's weapon leaving its sheath; heard the clear, soft sound of the chain at his waist being unwound. He backed toward Kaylin. She couldn't see what he was doing, and didn't look; he wasn't the danger here. Her daggers were in her hands, and her knees were slightly bent.

The corpse rose as if it were liquid falling upward. The jerky, stiff movements that were the delight of zombie stories everywhere were nowhere in evidence. The bloodless gashes across the dead Leontine's chest and throat—the wounds that had probably killed him—were gaping, wide, the only graceless thing about him. She knew his fur wasn't black, but in the night, with only the primitive torchlight at his back, he looked all of one color.

"So," Sanabalis said, in the thin voice that she thought of as "normal."

The dead Leontine leaped. He had been looking around, his body tensing—but the leap itself was in the wrong direction. He sailed *over* Sanabalis, and landed in front of the Leontines.

They were standing, tense, behind Adar, and Adar... folded his massive arms. From this distance it was hard to tell, but Kaylin thought his pale fur was standing on end. He did not move. He did not leap to the side; he stood and bore witness.

She wasn't sure that she could have done the same.

Sanabalis cursed and turned, but the dead Leontine was hampered by the magical barrier that Sanabalis had erected between the corpse and the Leontines. She knew this because he jumped toward Adar and *bounced.*

For a moment, the corpse staggered, awkward as it fell away, as if the force that animated it had been dislodged. But it was only a brief floundering. He turned to Sanabalis, and Severn swept in, his hands on chain pulled taut by the spinning movement. The Leontine corpse gestured, and lost his hand.

It didn't slow him down at all.

"You!" it said, its voice a hiss. *"Do you think you can stop us forever?"*

But if Sanabalis was not a Dragon in form, he *was* a Dragon. He opened his mouth and roared, and with the roar came a plume of flame that was wider and taller than he was.

Fire enfolded the corpse and the corpse burned. It wasn't the slow burning one would see on a pyre. It was sudden, hot. The flames, orange at the edges, had a white heart, a blue core.

The creature screamed in fury and, burning, it grabbed hold of Sanabalis, its jaws opened unnaturally wide to lodge themselves in the Dragon's chest. The handless arm flailed; the other did not.

The head rolled free as Severn leaped up behind the body, and shadow gouted, like blood, in the air.

Where it touched ground, where it touched the ground that Sanabalis now occupied, it sizzled, black flame, and only black.

Bodiless, the jaws still worried at Dragon flesh. This was the thing Kaylin most hated about the undead—nothing stopped them. They didn't need to be attached to their limbs.

Beneath her boots, she ground the hand Severn had cut off, and felt it struggle to get a grip on her heel. Cursing—in Leontine—she reached out and yanked a pole from its moorings and shoved the torch end into the hand, watching as flesh smoldered. She wasn't a dragon and she wasn't a mage—but the hand itself didn't seem to care much for burning. She held it in place, and black smoke—the greasy smoke of flesh charring—rose heavily in the still, humid air.

Sanabalis had pried the jaws from his chest. They were red with his blood, but the loss didn't seem to faze the Dragon. He grunted as he tore the bodiless head in half and tossed it aside. Then he reached down and pulled the claws from his chest; they were longer; there was more blood.

He shoved the body away and pointed one hand. Blue

light flew from his finger, enveloping what remained of the headless, handless corpse.

Sanabalis's robes were a mess.

"Corporal," he said heavily. "Private." He turned to Adar, whose arms were still folded across his chest. "So," he said quietly.

Adar nodded.

Kaylin turned to Sanabalis. "What the *hell* was that?"

"What you suspected, Private Neya."

"No. What *I* suspected was that the mage—the Leontine mage—had somehow possessed him. I've seen a possession in Records," she said, "and it bloody well wasn't like this." She added a few colorful Leontine phrases as the fingers that weren't charred struggled with the torch.

"Very well, allow me to be more specific. What you saw is what I expected to see."

"Sanabalis—"

He gestured her forward. She gave the corpse's hand another savage stomp and joined him. "Do not touch me," he said, quietly. "I am not in danger of expiring."

Since she hadn't intended to heal him—for one, she was wearing the damn bracer—she frowned. She would have added words to the frown, but he lifted a hand. It was red and glistening.

"Do you understand what you've seen?" he asked.

"No."

"Corporal?"

Severn said nothing.

"Very well. The story you first heard me tell," he said, looking at Kaylin, "was only one such story. There is another, and it was told to this Leontine."

"It killed him?"

"No. Your Sergeant did that—and were the death not intended, I think, to entrap him, he would have had much less success. We do not understand why some of the Leontines are more susceptible to...changes...than others. But they are all susceptible to it in some fashion. It is why the only race that was born in this fashion *is* the Leontines. The Old Ones did not choose to take that risk again.

"They were, creator and corrupter, *all* Old Ones. All Ancients. And what they did, for good or ill, no Dragon and no Barrani could hope to achieve."

"But *you* told them—"

"I told them what they *are*," he replied. "There are very, very few alive who could tell them that story."

"But—"

"This, too," he said, gesturing at the burning pieces that remained of the corpse, "is part of what they are. It is part of what all mortals are. This one could not contain *enough* of the chaos to tell the story to another. No more could the Elders who stand beyond you."

"Adar?"

"No." He paused. "But the Leontine you met—the one you called mage?"

"He could."

"So it appears. There is a reason why those marked are destroyed at birth," he said. "If, in the end, one is born who can contain enough of the shadows that lie beneath Elantra, the whole of the Leontine race cannot help but hear his voice, and know it. That Leontine, the one you mistook for a mage, had to hear the story—and it is *not* in any sense of the word what you mean when you say story—to come into the power he has shown.

"There is nowhere else in the Empire—to our knowledge or Barrani knowledge—where such a story could be told."

The child...

She swallowed. "The...corpse...recognized you," she said.

"Did he?"

"He said—"

"Enough. I have said before, and I hope not to have to repeat myself often, that there is a reason the Emperor chose to build his city in this place. You have seen the shadow's power and you recognize what you see. Believe that they are not less intelligent." He gestured with his hands and what remained of the corpse burned, blue and white, for just an instant.

There wasn't enough left to bury when the flames disappeared into that deadness of vision bright light causes.

He gestured again and nodded toward Adar. "First Son, I believe you have your answer."

Adar bowed. "Eldest," he said, his tone gravelly and grave at the same time. "We have much to deliberate this eve. Will you join us?"

"No. I have other business in the Quarter which will not wait. I will take my companions, with your permission, and we will adjourn. It is wearying, to speak the oldest of tongues. I was not born to it.

"But gather your people, First Son. Gather those you feel are at risk. I will speak with them all tomorrow."

"Eldest."

"Wait, what about Marcus?"

The First Son was slow to acknowledge Kaylin. "As I said, we have much to deliberate this eve." It was a dismissal.

Kaylin ground her teeth in frustration.

Sanabalis took a few moments to straighten out what remained of his robes. It didn't help, much. The robes themselves were scarred by claws and fangs, and the center portion hung in a loose drape of tatters that wouldn't have looked at home on a beggar. The Dragon Lord frowned. "Wait here," he told the Hawks. "I was prepared for difficulty." He left them and headed back up the stairs of graduated concentric ovals, in the direction of the carriage. Kaylin watched his back.

She was silent. Still. Severn touched her shoulder and the warmth of his hand was almost a shock. But she didn't look at him. She was calculating distance and time.

"He told you to wait," Severn said, correctly divining the direction her thoughts were heading in.

"Sarabe and Marai—" She stopped for a moment. "Marai," she whispered.

"She is not dead."

"Severn—he must have spoken to her. The same way he spoke to the Leontine who for all intents and purposes was dead when he tried to kill Marcus. *We have to*—"

"If she had been…possessed like that, you would have known."

"How?"

One dark brow disappeared behind his bangs.

She shrugged, restless.

"He wanted her to bear a child," Severn said, when it became clear that she would not speak. "How much could she change and still accomplish that goal?"

She nodded stiffly. "We don't know where he went."

"No."

"Maybe Sanabalis intends to find him." She held on to that thought as the Dragon Lord returned—in simpler and lighter robes. They were not as fine, and they were not as obviously official—but he didn't really need much in a culture where loincloths were often considered more than enough.

"Kaylin," he said, "I believe it is now time to visit the Pridlea of your Sergeant."

Hope withered.

They left the carriage. Sanabalis wanted to walk. He probably had good reasons for doing so; Kaylin didn't ask. She was a little too alert, a little too ready to fight or flee. He appeared to be watching the streets.

"We don't know where the—the mage went," she said.

"No."

It was like fishing with a club. She gave up. The night streets—and it was night, now—were as quiet and preternaturally silent as any jungle. The moonlight was bright and silver, reducing everything to shades of gray.

"They might be sleeping," she said, aware that she was trying too damn hard but unable to stop herself.

Sanabalis didn't dignify the words with a response. He walked as if he knew where he was going. She followed in his wake, because she *did* know, and even the hope that she could somehow get lost—and that had the advantage of being something she usually did a few times—left her.

She was miserable. Marcus would be found innocent—he'd better bloody well be or she'd raise hell—but he wouldn't be *home* when a Dragon came to visit his wives.

She stopped walking.

Sanabalis, a few steps ahead, stopped as well and turned. He looked older and wearier than she had ever seen him. "Private?"

"What do you intend to do?" she asked.

He could have pretended ignorance—not that it would have worked—but ignorance, apparently, was beneath the dignity of a Dragon Lord. "I intend to visit," he replied. "Just that."

"And Sarabe?" She couldn't bring herself to mention Marai, not yet.

"You refer to Marcus's youngest wife."

"Yes."

"Her fate is not in my hands," he replied. "Unless she chooses to attack me, which I think unlikely, I intend her no harm."

"You promise?"

A pale brow rose, was obvious even in the silvered light. "Kaylin, you are *not* a child."

She didn't even bridle.

"I spoke with the First Son while you spoke with the Sergeant," he said at last. "And I am aware that the ruins of the home we visited belonged to the…mage. I am *also* aware that Sarabe's sister lived there. There was no body," he added, "and you have failed to tell me what I need to know." His gaze was sharp. "I was only peripherally aware of Sarabe, but the fact that Marai lived with the mage has taken on new significance to the Elders. You will, of course, understand why."

"I—"

"You did not tell me why you chose to visit," he continued, when the sentence was abruptly truncated. "You did not tell me if the sister—Marai, I believe, is her name—was present. You failed to mention her at all.

"I can only assume that this oversight on your part was deliberate."

She said nothing. It wasn't the safest thing to do, but she was a miserable liar.

"Her sister, however, may be more forthcoming. Kaylin, this is *not* a game. There is a danger here, and it is profound. I will not ask you how you came to be at the mage's home. I am aware that were it not for that coincidence, we would not now be aware of the danger we face, and I am not unmindful of that debt to you.

"But it is not a danger that will affect only the Quarter. It is a danger that threatens the entire city. Marai was marked, and the wisdom of the Elders was overruled. She was not destroyed—at birth—as she would have been on the plains. And on the plains, it would have been far safer to allow her to live."

"She did nothing wrong—"

"Kaylin."

"No. I'm a *Hawk,* Sanabalis. There are *laws.* She did *nothing* wrong."

"And you are certain of this?"

She stopped, because she wasn't.

"I see," Sanabalis said.

"What of her sister?"

"Sarabe?"

Kaylin nodded.

"She has been closely watched," he replied. "And she is not connected—yet—with the stranger." He was silent for a long moment. "I would see her destroyed," he said at last, and heavily.

All of the hair on Kaylin's neck stood on end.

"But that decision is not in my hands."

"But it *is*. You can tell them what to do—and what *not* to do—and they'll listen to you. They'll listen to *you* in a way that they wouldn't even listen to their own. If you tell them that you don't think she's a danger—"

"You counsel me to lie?"

"She's *not* a danger. Sarabe has had her children, and she won't risk having more. All of hers were girls, and they survived. And why the *hell* is it just boys that are considered a danger?"

"We do not know," he replied. "It is perhaps because women *can* give birth, and the imperative to breed among mortals is physical, and requires some continuity and stability of form. It overrides much else, and on levels that simple magic cannot easily dislodge."

"She's Marcus's wife," Kaylin said. "She has a Pridlea, and children of her own. She's done nothing wrong. She's lived with the judgment of others all her life simply because she was born the wrong damn color. I don't care if you want her destroyed—you don't *know* her. I do. And you can't legally destroy her," she added. "It would be murder."

"It would be a matter for the Caste Court," he replied levelly.

"The hell it would."

"I think you'll find—"

"Marcus was willing to *die* to protect her—" Her brain caught up with her mouth and closed it down.

"I see. So he suspected."

Severn gave Kaylin a long, inscrutable stare.

"It doesn't matter," she said, her voice slightly thicker, the syllables a little too distinct. "I won't *let* it remain a matter for the Caste Courts. I was there and I'm not Leontine."

"You were forbidden to be there."

"No, I wasn't. I was forbidden to interfere in Marcus's case. This is entirely different. If Sarabe and Marai won't take the matter to the Imperial Courts, *I* will."

"No one is likely to thank you for it."

"I don't give a rat's ass. We have *laws,* and they're not written with specific exceptions for people you *think* might be dangerous. If we could kill everyone who *might* be a danger, there wouldn't be any bloody Arcanists."

"A fair point."

"Dragons," Severn said, joining the conversation quietly and unexpectedly, as he so often did, "are not known for their sense of fairness."

"No indeed, we are not. But I'm curious, Private Neya. The Hawk, of course, is yours to wear, but if you did not endanger it in pursuit of the truth about your Sergeant and his theoretical crime, what *did* bring you to the Quarter?" His eyes were amber, and seemed to glow faintly in the nightscape, as if lit from within by the fires that were legend.

The bastard *knew,* she thought. He *knew.*

Her hand fell to her dagger hilt; she had just enough sense of self-preservation not to draw it.

"This is not a game, Private," he said quietly. "It is not a lesson. I am not your teacher here—you are not my student. There is more at risk than you can imagine."

"Is there more at risk than there was when I developed my marks?"

He was silent for a long moment.

"Is there more at risk than there was when those children were taken by an *Outcaste* Dragon as sacrifices?"

She thought he might lie, and was prepared to tear through whatever reply he chose to make. But he lifted a hand, instead. "No."

"But I'm not dead."

"No. But in *your* case, Private Neya, there were mitigating circumstances. The danger you presented—and still present in your ignorance—could be weighed against the possibility that you might *also* do more good, and preserve more life, with the powers that none of us fully understand. There was the healing, for one." He paused and then added, "There was the freeing of the dead Dragon. There was also the disaster that you averted when Donalan Idis kidnapped the Tha'alani child, for another.

"In the case of the Leontines? There is no mitigating factor. The most—the very most—that we can hope for is that the marked will live quiet, unremarkable lives and die without giving birth."

She thought of Marcus. Of Kayala. Of Graylin and Reesa and Sarabe. All the lives touched by an unremarkable life. The happiness—and no doubt the tears—of living day to day, and loving. She straightened her shoulders and said, "But people like these Leontines are the *reason* we have laws, Sanabalis. They live their quiet lives, as you call them. They don't threaten other people—on purpose," she added quickly, when his mouth opened. "They love, they're loved, they have their work to do, and they do it. The farmers are all unremarkable—to people who don't know them and don't have a clue about their lives—but without them, the city would starve.

"I made my oaths when I accepted the Hawk. People like Sarabe—they don't *deserve* to be judged by people who think life can be reduced to—to math."

"She will be judged, not by me, but by her own people."

"I'm her own people," Kaylin said grimly. "I practically grew up in that Pridlea."

"I am aware of that," he replied coolly. "I will give you my word that I will not harm the Pridlea this eve. Will that suffice?"

She wanted more. But she had *also* lived in the fiefs, and she knew a final offer when she heard it. She indicated a grudging assent. After all, what he offered was in spirit what Kayala had offered when Roshan had been given over to her keeping. In either case, it was a courtesy; she couldn't stop Sanabalis from going to the Pridlea if she tried—although she was pretty certain she would at least live to regret the attempt.

They had walked at least another two blocks when Sanabalis stopped. He stopped so suddenly she ran into his back and bounced off it—it was like walking into a wall.

"Sanabalis?"

"I fear," he said, in a completely expressionless voice, "that we are late."

"What?"

He didn't answer; instead he began to move. Something that could be so inert shouldn't be able to move that quickly, but Kaylin had long since given up trying to make sense of Dragons. They were, in the end, magical creatures.

She ran after Sanabalis. Severn kept pace with her, although his stride was longer. Two more blocks, covered in seconds, and she could see what Sanabalis, with his strange Dragon sight, had seen: black smoke, rising into the midnight-blue of sky. Hazy, hot, very much like the air itself.

And she *knew* where the fire was coming from.

A block away from the Pridlea, the orange lap of flame could be seen; the flames were small compared to the shadow of smoke they cast into the windless sky. But the streets weren't empty, and for that, she was profoundly grateful, for in the light of the orange glow, she could see Kayala.

Kayala had her arms full, but she turned as they approached, her lips drawn over her fangs in a warning growl. It was the first time that Kaylin had ever seen naked aggression on the face of Marcus's oldest wife, and she missed a beat, stumbling in the darkness.

"Kayala, it's me!"

The growl ceased, but the ferocity of expression did not.

"What happened?"

"We had a visitor," she snarled. "And not a welcome

one." She turned and barked a command, and the other wives revealed themselves, coming from the sides of the buildings that faced other homes: Reesa, golden fur standing on end, Graylin, pale silvery hue darkened with soot, Tessa, black-furred, and very like the shadows.

"Where is Sarabe?" Kaylin said, a little too quickly.

"She's safe," Kayala replied in a more normal tone of voice. "She went to her children—they went out the back way."

"And Marai?"

Silence.

"Kayala—"

Sanabalis, so silent and still that he could, like Severn, be forgotten, stepped forward.

Kaylin waited for the Dragon effect to take hold. But if Dragons usually entranced the Leontines, the effect of Sanabalis's presence at this time was clearly not as primal as the defense of one's home and family; Kayala growled a warning note. Sanabalis actually took a step back.

"What did I tell you about bringing males here?"

"He's not in your home," Kaylin said, raising her empty hands so they could be clearly seen. "I wouldn't have brought him in without your permission."

"I see your Severn is wise enough to keep his distance."

"Severn's not a Dragon," she replied.

Kayala's brows rose at the same time. She actually looked at Sanabalis. Then she handed Kaylin the bundle in her arms without taking her eyes off the Dragon Lord. Kaylin knew what she carried, and she took the baby with the ease of long practice. But she didn't look at him, not carefully. If Sanabalis hadn't yet noticed, she didn't want to draw his attention.

"Eldest," Kayala said, in a growl. "Forgive the lack of hospitality. My Pridlea is not, at the moment, fit for visitors."

"No, it is not. But perhaps I can be of aid, if you permit it."

The fire had not gutted the building.

"We have attempted to put the fire out," Kayala replied, "but it burns as you see it."

Sanabalis frowned a moment, and then spoke—in Leontine. "You carry your home in your heart, and your heart is fierce." He cleared his throat. "Forgive my pronunciation. It is seldom I have reason to speak your tongue."

She nodded slowly. "Why have you come, Eldest?"

"You can ask me that while your home burns?"

She shrugged instead and turned to Kaylin. "Kitling," she said, and the weariness in her voice overwhelmed, for a moment, the threat. "We will not be able to stay here this eve, I think. Why is the Eldest here?"

Kaylin cringed and straightened her shoulders. "It's the—the Outcaste."

Kayala closed her eyes.

"If you will permit it," Sanabalis said quietly, "I will find other quarters for your family while we investigate the fire."

Kayala's hesitance was marked and it was cold. "*All* of my family?" she asked sharply.

"All," Sanabalis said.

She didn't trust him. That much was clear. But she also needed a place to stay in safety. "Where?"

"It would, alas, be outside of the Quarter. On short notice, I cannot navigate the complicated—"

Kayala raised a hand; it was almost as good as a "shut up." She raised her voice, spoke a few harsh words in Leontine.

From the alley came three Leontines. Two were golden, and one was gray-furred, although the gray was smeared; their eyes were wide and round as they approached Sanabalis; they were ten years old, shared a birthday and several mothers. Kaylin saw them, saw that they were both frightened and whole, and looked beyond them to the alley's mouth. There, standing with her arms tightly folded across her chest, stood their birth mother, bristling.

In the night sky, it was hard to tell that her fur was red. It was hard to tell anything much beyond the "approach with caution" that was Leontine panic.

"This," Kayala said, although Sarabe advanced no further, "is my youngest wife. It is my duty and my privilege to protect her with *my* life, Eldest."

"Her fate," Sanabalis replied, "is not in my hands. I am not Leontine, but I understand enough of the Pridlea to know that any offer I make will of course include all of your wives, and all of the children living with you."

Kayala tilted her head to one side for a moment, studying the Dragon Lord. Her breath came out in a hiss, but she hooded her fangs. "He is your friend, kitling?"

"He's my teacher," Kaylin replied. And then, after a moment, she continued, "But inasmuch as Dragons and humans *can* be friends, I consider him a friend."

"Then I will, on behalf of the Pridlea, gratefully accept your offer, Eldest."

Sanabalis nodded. Kaylin thought there would be questions, but he merely said, "Is this all of your Pridlea?"

Kayala nodded.

"Then follow. You will not all fit in the carriage, and at this time of night, it is safe to walk the city streets."

On this side of the Ablayne, Kaylin thought. She didn't say it.

"I will of course have questions," he added, "but they can wait the night." He bowed to her.

Kaylin kept her questions to herself, but it was hard. It would have been even more difficult if Severn weren't there, reminding her, with a silent glance, of the cost of words.

CHAPTER

16

The walk through the streets was long and silent. It wasn't until they approached the boundaries of the Quarter, harsh lines softened by the silver of moonlight, that Sarabe's children, huddled around her, began to speak amongst themselves. Kayala was silent, as were the wives, and the only words that Sarabe spoke were so muffled Kaylin couldn't hear them.

The streets outside of the Quarter were well lit but mercifully empty. How much of that emptiness had to do with a pack of Leontines, Kaylin wasn't certain—but she didn't really care. She wanted to get the Pridlea out of the streets. That much, she could do for Marcus. Better still, Sarabe wouldn't be in the Quarter, and whatever decision awaited her at the hands of the Elders wouldn't matter. In the parts of the city that were not subject to Caste Law, she would be safe.

Or as safe as she could be, when escorted by a Dragon Lord. Sanabalis had not spoken a word since he had begun to lead them to the palace. Words, apparently, weren't necessary. He'd made his offer, it had been accepted. Reluctantly accepted, but accepted nonetheless. Kaylin wanted to break the silence because it seemed so—so funereal. But Severn was by her side, and the one time she opened her mouth to speak, he caught her hand and gave it a gentle squeeze. She'd clung to silence as if it were a particularly difficult ledge. For her, it was.

The Palace never truly closed down. The lights were never dimmed, the torches never put out. People obviously slept, but the quiet and certain footsteps of patrolling guards, the rustle of servants' skirts, could be heard if one listened. Given the absolute silence of the Leontines—whose voices were very seldom called quiet— listening was easy.

Sanabalis was met at the front gates, and the guards took note of his guests, but they didn't question him, and they didn't speak to the Leontines. They nodded briskly to Kaylin and Severn—if there was any rivalry between the royal guards and the officers of the Halls, it was one grounded in grudging mutual respect. The fact that Kaylin and Severn looked as if they'd been in a messy fight, and the Leontines, in a bath of ash, didn't cause them to even raise a brow.

Then again, they were used to the whims of the Dragon Court. Kaylin wondered how often Sanabalis brought guests with him. She did not, of course, ask. Instead, she followed Sanabalis from the gates to the Palace proper without any obvious hesitation at all. Leontines could read body language the way sages could read dead ones. She didn't want to make them nervous. Or more nervous than they already were, at any rate.

The head of the household staff met them when they'd cleared the outer doors, the guards just beyond the doors, and the internal doors. What happened outside, this well-dressed and officious man's demeanor suggested, was not in any way a concern. Certainly not *his* concern.

And like the guards, he did not bat an eyelash or raise a brow, and the Palace lighting was good enough that he could easily see how grungy and bedraggled Sanabalis's guests were.

"I require the use of the east guest wing," Sanabalis said without preamble, and with no explanation at all. "My companions—the Leontines—will be housed there until further notice is given."

The man nodded. His head was faintly luminescent in the light of too much fire, even contained. "And there will be no other guests?"

"No. They will be Leontine quarters for the duration."

"Very good, Lord Sanabalis. I will inform the staff of the required levels of service. Do you desire me to show them their quarters?"

"No. Merely have them opened, and suitably furnished, and I will do the rest."

The man bowed again. It was a clean, clipped movement that was both respectful and entirely free from any sign of groveling obedience.

Sanabalis turned to Kayala when the man had disappeared from view. "There are doors," he told her, "and they are warded. We have no hangings and no keys. I apologize, but it is the one basic security precaution that is not overruled by cultural preferences. The ward will be set to recognize your Pridlea, and also Private Neya if you permit."

"And you?"

"No. If I wish to visit you, I will visit in the usual fashion. The Emperor, however, has access to any room in the Palace, from the highest tower to the lowest dungeon. It is unlikely that he will find cause to visit, but if he does not choose to follow the rules of courtesy…"

Kayala nodded and growled her assent.

"Food will also be brought to your chambers. It will be left outside the keyed doors. Unless you request it, the servants will not visit, and they will not clean or tidy without your permission.

"The wing contains a large bath chamber," he continued, his voice so blandly neutral it was a simple statement of fact. "The baths will not be drawn or filled unless you request it, and they do not adjoin the chambers in which you will otherwise live. While you occupy the rooms, they will not be used by anyone but your Pridlea.

"Should you wish to entertain visitors, there will be no interference while they are within your chambers. They will, however, be required to pass the same guards that we passed on the way in, and to answer any questions those guards pose. Again, it is a simple precaution, and the lack of hospitality is something that anyone who resides within the Palace accepts as the cost of their lodgings."

Kayala nodded again. No one else had spoken a word; even the girls were silent. Nor had Sanabalis addressed any of his comments or explanations to any of the other Leontines. Then again, they were all but cowering *behind* Kayala, so that probably made some sense. It was hard to talk rationally to someone who was cowering. Kaylin, as a Hawk, had some experience with this.

"Follow," Sanabalis said gravely. Kayala turned to the rest of her Pridlea, her glance encompassing Kaylin and neatly bypassing Severn before she strode down the hall after Lord Sanabalis. They took the hint and followed. Kaylin hesitated a moment, and Severn shook his head. "Pridlea rules," he said with a faint smile, "don't seem to extend to a Dragon Lord. I'll wait. If you're going to stay, let me know, and I'll meet you in the morning."

She nodded, and then trotted after the vanishing Leontine Pridlea.

Kayala, however, stopped for a moment and turned, causing a small pileup at her back. "Corporal Handred," she said, in formal Leontine, "we are not in our Quarter, and we are guests of the Dragon Emperor. As guests, some flexibility may be called for."

"The rooms are yours, Kayala," Kaylin began.

"Kitling," she said, waving a paw almost wearily, "shut up. Learn tactful silence from your Corporal. It's too much to be expected that you could learn it from our husband—since he also lacks the ability to use it."

The rooms were *big*. They made Rennick's rooms look small in comparison. There were, admittedly, more Leontines than there were Rennick's. There was also a hair rug on the floor in front of a fireplace that looked large enough to burn houses in. There was a low table, throws and pillows, and the table held fairly simple food: breads, cheeses, fruits—and a lot of meat.

There were two normal chairs, but they were larger than those in Rennick's room; large enough to comfortably contain a male Leontine.

Kayala's eyes widened slightly. "Eat," she told her wives and daughters. "Eldest, will you join us?"

"I will stay," he replied quietly. "But I do not require food. I require answers," he said. "What happened tonight?"

Kayala held out her arms, and Kaylin reluctantly handed her the sleeping baby. The Leontine then examined the chairs for a moment before deciding against them; she made herself at home on the floor by the table. Her wives and daughters were slow to move from her side, and their dignity—or Kayala's—would have suffered greatly if they'd been forced to huddle around a freestanding chair.

There was a long silence. Kayala glanced at Kaylin, and Kaylin nodded slightly.

"We were not yet asleep," she said—in Elantran. "My youngest wife was restless, and we were all concerned with the fate of our husband. We do not have your door wards," she continued. "And perhaps—just perhaps—there is wisdom in their existence. But we have what we were born with—our senses. Our instincts.

"We felt the intrusion of a stranger."

"And when you saw him, did you recognize him?"

Again, a hesitation. This time, however, Kayala did not look to Kaylin. "Yes, Eldest," she said at last, as if begrudging her words. Or sifting them. "We meet very few of the males, and never without the company of our husband. But this one, we have seen before. He frequents public areas. He was injured, and he did not speak coherently."

"This stranger," Sanabalis said, "can you describe him?"

"He was male. He is called Orogrim by my people. His fur is gray," she said, "although in the right light, it pales. He is taller than my husband, and slightly narrower of build.

"He came to our house to make demands of us," she continued, "and those demands were refused. When he understood that his presence was undesired and, further, that we were prepared to…enforce…his departure, he changed."

"Changed how?" Sanabalis asked quietly. The words, however, were dagger-blade sharp.

"I cannot describe it," Kayala replied after a pause. "It was not something seen, but something…smelled. Is that the right word?"

"It'll do," Kaylin said, in rough Leontine. And added, in the same language, "You're saying his *scent* changed?"

Kayala nodded. She closed her eyes a moment, and continued to speak, rocking back and forth without any conscious effort, child in her arms. "It was foul," she said. "And sweet. Like rotting meat.

"I knew there was a danger—" She shook her head. "One of us—I don't remember who—attacked him then." She opened her eyes suddenly, as if what she'd seen behind her lids might jump out of memory and become substantial.

"He called the fire," she continued, in a voice that had grown more subdued. "He called the fire and the hearth rug burned."

The silence was heavy with things unsaid. Kaylin, in particular, had to struggle to keep her lips firmly closed over the questions that she wanted so badly to ask. Severn's hand was over hers. His touch was light, but the fact of it helped to anchor her.

Sanabalis waited for a long moment, and then shook his head. "What happened to Marai?"

Kayala was good; she didn't so much as glance in Kaylin's direction. Her grip on the baby changed slightly as she straightened her shoulders, shifting her stance as if she were now accepting the weight of a heavy burden. She made no attempt to dissemble.

"Marai," she said quietly, "attacked the stranger. We were slow to react—she was not." Kayala hesitated and then said, "The fire burned her, but it did not stop her, and in the end, the stranger chose to retreat. She was injured, but she fought well. Our husband could not have bettered her." She took a steadying breath, and this time she did glance—at Sarabe. Sarabe's arms and lap were full of children who were too old to fit comfortably and too young—just—not to want to try.

Sarabe nodded, and her arms tightened almost imperceptibly.

Kayala continued. "We woke the children and we made our way out of the fire. It was not large, but it was not easily extinguished."

"It wouldn't be," Sanabalis said. "Go on."

"Marai—we tried to call her back. We tried to tell her

to stay with the Pridlea. But she was frantic. She left in pursuit."

Sanabalis lifted a hand to his eyes for a moment. "This is bad news," he said, wearily. "Did you see where they went?"

"No, Eldest. They followed the road that led out of the Quarter."

"But, Kayala—I don't understand—what was she *thinking?* We fought him the night before—she could have died then!"

"I cannot say. As you can guess, we had very little time in which to have a reasoned discussion."

Kaylin started to speak again, but Kayala caught her gaze. "Come, kitling," she said. She held the infant out and Kaylin accepted both the burden and the warning. With the baby came the certainty that she did, in fact, know what Marai was thinking: her child was safe, but his safety was tenuous. While his father lived, he could return, again and again. The Pridlea had been lucky, the stranger less so. But the Pridlea would have to *continue* to be lucky, and the stranger, Orogrim, would only have to be lucky *once.*

The baby stirred, and Kaylin stood. She began to pace in a little circle to one side of the low table. She had been with the Hawks for barely a few weeks when Marcus had taken her home and introduced her to Sarabe's daughters, cubs a few years older than the one she now carried.

"Out of the Quarter?" Sanabalis said, and his voice was almost a surprise. It was impossible to forget that Sanabalis was in a room, but...she'd almost forgotten anyway.

Kayala said, "I do not know if they will *leave* the Quarter, but if the stranger ran the road to its natural end, they would almost have had to do so." She hesitated once more.

Sanabalis was no fool; obviously, he had marked each hesitation.

"He left in the form of a panther," she told him. "He ran at a speed that none of us could equal." She turned to Kaylin. "If she returns, she must come to us. She must be *allowed* to come to us. Will you watch for her?"

Kaylin, holding Marai's son, nodded.

And Sanabalis looked at Kaylin. "I understand that you hope I am befuddled by the wealth of years I possess," he told her coolly. "And to my surprise, Private Neya, there has been some temptation to play at ignorance. But even old and distracted by concerns as I am, I cannot help but notice that you carry a baby.

"The babe is not Sarabe's. No pregnancy was registered with the Elders, and by Caste law, such registration *is* required. The baby could be Marcus's," he continued, "but none of the other wives have so much as touched the child. Only the Pridlea Matriarch—and you.

"Is the child Marai's?"

She saw the liquid orange of his eyes and knew that fire waited her answer. But she, as Kayala before her, straightened her shoulders. "Yes," she said evenly. "But by the common law of the Pridlea, he is also *mine*. I helped to birth him, Sanabalis. I licked him clean." This last was an exaggeration which she felt Marai would forgive. "And I promised Marai that I would protect him."

"It is unwise to give your word if your word cannot be kept."

"Or die trying."

"That," he added, with just a touch of dryness, "is more easily achieved." He rose. "This child of Marai's is the son of Orogrim." It wasn't a question.

"Yes."

"The Elders would not allow the child to live," Sanabalis told her evenly.

"No. But Marai was not married."

One brow rose.

"She wasn't married. Her pregnancy wasn't registered because in the mess of Leontine Caste laws, pregnancy doesn't seem to officially *happen* to women who aren't wives." Kaylin snorted.

"Do you understand the danger he presents?"

"Look at him, Sanabalis. From over there," she added. "How much of a danger can he *be?* He's been asleep the entire time. When he's awake, he's a *baby.*"

"He will not always *be* a baby. He will be his father's son—his father's and his mother's." Then he, too, rose. He was not, at his full height, a small man. Dragons never were. "And will you protect the city from such a child, grown to power?"

"Yes. With," she added quietly, "the same life I'd spend protecting him from you."

"And is there something else that you have neglected to mention?"

"Yes."

"Mention it now."

She opened her mouth, but she couldn't quite force the words out. Severn, as he so often did, came to her rescue from a silence that had almost made him invisible. "Marai was not entirely Leontine."

"What do you mean?"

"When we first encountered her…she was also, in form, entirely animal."

Sanabalis closed his eyes.

"No, Sanabalis," Kaylin said urgently. "She had the ability to shift her form, yes—but she wasn't somehow changed by shadow, I'd swear it. She was herself."

Marcus's oldest wife turned to Lord Sanabalis and said, "The child is as you see him. An infant, and scrawny at that. I understand the danger, Eldest—but my heart does not."

Kaylin felt some knot inside her suddenly unravel. She sat again.

"Would you risk your Pridlea by allowing the child to live?"

"You are speaking to the first wife of the only Leontine to labor in the Halls of Law," was the quiet reply.

Kaylin held the child calmly now, remembering something. Some small detail that she hadn't had time to pick at, she'd been so busy not dying. "Marai said— Marai said that he—that Orogrim had tried to sneak the baby out of their home. That she'd stopped him, and that she didn't trust him. She said he wanted to take the child somewhere."

A pale brow rose. "He didn't say where?"

"No, but I doubt she would have liked the answer, and he probably knew it." Kaylin turned to face Sanabalis. "The baby's not a danger yet."

Sanabalis was silent for just a little too long for comfort. "It goes against my better judgment," he said at last. "But I admit I have a mild reluctance to kill you all."

"Thank you," Kayala said, as if he were talking about a mild aversion to nasty weather. "We were not ourselves... entirely certain of the wisdom of Kaylin's decision. But, like you, we are fond of her. She is our only adopted daughter. It is hard to betray trust, even when it is unreasonably given."

He stood. "Kaylin, I would like to speak with you."

They left the rooms that the Pridlea was to occupy. Severn came with them, and followed where Sanabalis led; Sanabalis accepted his presence as if he were a natural extension of Kaylin, a shadow, something that couldn't be separated from her.

He led them to rooms that were familiar, and opened the door in silence, indicating the chairs he wished them to occupy. When they sat, he said, "Where has Orogrim gone?"

Kaylin opened her mouth to say *I don't know,* and closed it before the words could come out. She was tired and sore and dirty, and she wanted to go home to a bed, drop a trail of clothing from the door to the mattress, and fall over. But she looked at Sanabalis, whose eyes were a steady amber, and said, "The fiefs."

He nodded. "I think that must be the case. I will speak with the Elders in the morning, but I don't think they'll have much to say that will be of use to us. They don't track their own kin, and Orogrim, from all accounts, was respected in the community."

"Maybe by the men," she said with a snort. "The women think he treated Marai abominably."

"That would be my second question," Sanabalis continued. "Where has Marai gone?"

"If she was pursuing him, probably to the fiefs."

There was a long silence. Sanabalis looked out the window, turning his back upon them before he spoke again. "I have not been entirely forthcoming," he said at last.

"How not entirely do you mean?"

The silence was heavy. "Kaylin," Sanabalis said at last, turning toward her as if he had reached some decision. "You remember the Outcaste."

"The Outcaste? Oh, you mean the Dragon?"

Sanabalis nodded.

"It's hard to forget a ton of black Dragon who wanted to murder children in the city in order to somehow control me," she replied. Then, seeing the shift in his expression, she added, "Yes, Sanabalis," as meekly as she could. Given it was Kaylin, it wasn't very meek.

"He did not die when you encountered him. He retreated. He was injured," Sanabalis added, "and he left the field of battle. Lord Nightshade's men pursued him as carefully as they could, but they did not cross the boundary of their fief."

"That would cause a war," Severn said. "And a war in the fiefs is at best unpredictable."

"Indeed, so I have been led to believe."

Given the amount of ancient and little understood magic that lay fallow in the fiefs, *unpredictable* was a gross understatement. "There's no way he's in Nightshade," Kaylin said curtly.

"Ah. And you are certain of this how?"

"There's *no way* someone with that much power could

be in the fief of Nightshade without Nightshade knowing. He might have known of the existence of the black Dragon—he has one of the Dragonkillers in his weapon cache—but there's no way he's operating out of Nightshade."

"You found him in that fief the first time."

"You might recall that we didn't exactly welcome him with open arms."

"A point."

Severn raised a hand, as if he were in a classroom and Sanabalis was a teacher. "Lord Sanabalis."

"Yes?"

"When you spoke to the Leontines the first time, you spoke in a language that none of us recognized. Kaylin thought she *should* recognize it because it sounded familiar to her."

"Indeed."

"Can the Outcaste speak the same tongue?"

Sanabalis actually smiled. "Very good," he said to Severn, as if he had fallen into the teacher role that Severn's raised hand implied. The approval dimmed, but it had been offered. Kaylin couldn't decide whether or not she should feel insulted on Severn's behalf, it seemed so condescending. Sometimes she really didn't understand him.

Hells, most times. She looked at his profile as he watched Sanabalis like a...Hawk.

"There are forces and creatures older than Dragons who can speak the ancient tongue. They are not, in any sense that you understand it, alive. But they are not dead. Among the living, we are the last of its keepers," Sanabalis said. "For the most part, it is an antiquity that implies a great deal of power and offers relatively little in return. But the Leontines are special. They were the last race that the Old Ones awakened before their inexplicable departure from these lands. In them, the seeds of our power lie fallow. We can invoke what is there, if we know how to speak, for good or ill."

"Someone spoke to Orogrim," Severn said. It was not a question.

"Yes."

"Someone could have spoken to him in Elantran," Kaylin said sharply, "and it would probably still have been welcome. It's probably damn hard growing up a pariah. Knowing that at any time, anyone—any Leontine at all—considers it their sacred duty to kill you. Even if he wasn't inclined to, you know, destroy the whole world at birth, his life up until now would probably make it seem like a good idea."

Sanabalis frowned. "You are thinking about the child."

And she was. Of course she was. "It would be easy," she continued. "He'd be easy to manipulate. He wouldn't *have to hide* what he was, or who. He wouldn't feel that he owes any of his own kin *anything,* because, in the end, they're all death to him. His death. He has to know what his fate should have been, by Leontine Law. We *all* want to survive," she said, her tone shading into heated bitterness. "We do whatever we have to, just to survive. We might not be proud of it," she said, thinking back to her childhood, to the years of begging and stealing in the streets of Nightshade, "but we all feel we have the *right* to survive. And to protect our own."

"And would you spare him?"

She sensed a trap. "I wouldn't kill the baby," she said starkly. "I won't let you kill the child. I'm a Hawk. It would be murder. And do not even think of quoting Caste Law at me. It's *not* just about the Leontines anymore. I'm involved. I'm not Leontine. And I'll be damned to hell before I turn a blind eye.

"But…Orogrim…I wouldn't protect. I'm not trying to defend him," she said. "I understand that he *is* the danger you fear. I just think…he might not have been. If he had grown up in a Pridlea. If he had had a family, he would have something to lose—and when we have something to lose, we're careful. The only thing he has to lose is his life—but that's always been forfeit. He gains everything if he gains power. He gains freedom, and a sense of… purpose."

"Destiny?"

"Maybe. But if it's not a dog's fault that it's rabid, it doesn't make the dog less dangerous. I don't hate the dog," she said.

"You did, when you were bitten and you had to submit to Moran's ministrations," Severn pointed out.

"The stuff she made me drink and wear was *foul,* Severn."

"Just making a point."

"Stop making points or I'll start to keep score."

He laughed.

"The *point* I'm trying to make is that it wouldn't take huge amounts of power to convince Orogrim to join… whatever it is he's probably serving. It wouldn't take much at all. You could just point out all the ways in which the fear of the Leontines had prevented him from reaching his full potential—you could say a lot of anything. He'd want to believe it."

"True. It has been long since I was a youth, and driven by fears of that nature. Where is this point leading you?"

"I'm not sure." She held out her hands, palms up. "You think your Outcaste had a hand in making him whatever it is he's become."

Sanabalis nodded.

"I'm saying we all did, more or less. He's bound to be suspicious," Kaylin said. "But it's harder to hold on to your suspicions when you want to believe what you're hearing." She rose and stretched. "But I'll go."

"Go?"

"Isn't that what you wanted, from me?"

"It is," Sanabalis replied quietly. "Go with Tiamaris. Visit the Lord of Nightshade. Discover what you can, and return."

"I want two things in return."

"They are?"

"First—Sarabe," she replied. "I don't give a shit what the Elders say. I really, truly, don't. Marcus suspected what he was facing, and he was afraid that they would order her death. Don't let them."

"Had she and her sister died at birth..." he began.

"But they didn't. What ifs are not an issue here. I don't care about what *might* have happened. Maybe if she'd been a Dragon—if all this was just about Dragons—I would. I can't say. But Dragons and mortals are *not* the same. She's going to die anyway. The rest of us always do. I want her to die of old age a long time from now.

"I want Marcus *back.* I want him back, and whole,

and he will *never* serve again if they kill his wife. Because," she added, "he'll be dead first."

"Find Orogrim, Kaylin. Find him. If we can stop him from becoming more of a threat, an argument can be made. And I think I can guess what your second demand is," Sanabalis said.

"The baby. Roshan."

"I can argue for Sarabe's life," he replied. "But the child's? His existence is at the heart of the story I told the Leontines."

"Then tell a different damn story," she said, her voice rising. "Or damn it all, *I* will."

Sanabalis shifted his Dragon gaze to Severn. "Ah. I believe this is a game—what do humans call it? Chicken?"

Severn was silent.

"I will not promise that, Kaylin. If you choose not to visit the fieflord, all that follows from that decision will be in your hands. Hundreds—thousands—of children that you have never met or held may well face death if we do not find Orogrim. And some dozens of children whom you *have* held will face the same fate.

"He will retreat to where his power is strongest," Sanabalis said. "And he will summon it. What he does with it, I cannot yet determine—but in the past, a child born of the marked could destroy whole countries and feed every living thing in them to the Shadows. It is not a pleasant death, but, as you point out, all mortals are destined to die, one way or the other."

She swallowed bile. Her body was shaking, and she could not unclench the fists her hands had become. "I'll go," she said at last.

"I will summon Tiamaris. There are matters that the Dragon Court must discuss before you depart. It may be loud," he added, "and you may wish to sleep. If you can." There was no triumph, no smugness, in his voice or his expression. "Go home, I believe Tiamaris knows where you live, and he will meet you on the morrow."

"We still have Rennick."

"Yes. For the moment, he is still your problem." He rose and opened the door. "I play no game, Kaylin."

"It's not a game for me either," she said bitterly. "If it were, there might be some chance I could win it. But I want at least your word that you will not harm the child while I'm gone."

"It is not a practical word to ask for," he replied. "I do not wish to kill you, and the alternatives I see, should you be present, are all unpleasant. But if it will ease you at all, I can make that compromise. I will not harm him.

"I will visit him," he added. "I will speak to him in the Old Tongue. I will do what I can."

His tone of voice made clear that he didn't think he could do all that much.

But hope was stupid like that, and she took it anyway.

CHAPTER 17

Severn walked with Kaylin to the bridge that was a narrow avenue between the fiefs and the city that surrounded it. He was silent as he often was.

Severn had always been good at silences when Kaylin didn't have words. It hadn't happened often, but when it did, he knew when to stay and when to withdraw. He could somehow mute his presence and still *be* in the same room. Or on the same street. He simply ceased to take up space. There was no edge to his silence, no questions, no demands. No retreat, really. She didn't need to *be* alone to have privacy.

She didn't need to *be* anyone, to live up to anything. Whatever she was, he'd seen it all. They'd grown up together. Best and worst.

The city streets were likewise quiet as Kaylin and Severn proceeded through them. The magelights were burning, but they always were, and even this close to the river, no enterprising and desperate thief had managed to dislodge them from their high perches. People were afraid of magic, even magic that they saw every day.

That, and it was hard to carry a ladder furtively.

"It always comes back to the past," she said, listening to moving water against either bank.

"No." He leaned back on the bridge railing, while she leaned forward, staring at the water without really seeing it. "Had we never been born in the fiefs, we would still be called to them now."

"I thought I'd escaped them."

"They're part of you. Part of me. But they're not all of what either of us are."

"I thought if I left them, I'd leave it behind—the helplessness. The guilt." She shook her head angrily. "Does it ever get better? Does it ever get easier?"

"If it ever does, let me know. I'll start to worry, then."

She gave him a rueful grimace. "I thought it would be different. And it is—but at the moment it's almost worse. We were children," she said. "I never felt—the choices—they weren't all mine. But here? I *like* Sanabalis. I *love* Kayala and her wives. And it doesn't matter. It doesn't change their facts."

"No. But it doesn't change yours, either. It's not over, Kaylin. And until it is, nothing's decided. Go home," he urged.

She glanced at the side of his face. Just that, moonlight across his cheeks and the line of his nose, the white skin of old scars. "You're a mess," she said affectionately.

"I like to blend in with the company I keep," he replied with a lazy smile. The smile was slow to leave, but it did. "Tomorrow, the Elders will decide what is to be done with Sergeant Kassan. Sergeant Kassan will decide what is to be done with you—from his perspective." He stretched, leaned back, tilted his head toward the water so many feet below.

"But Sarabe will be safe for the moment. No matter what the Elders decide, she is now ensconced in the Palace. If I didn't know better—and Sanabalis is inscrutable—I would say his offer of hospitality was deliberate. They cannot harm her there. They can't even try—they wouldn't make it past the Palace Guard. No matter what happens, she's safe for now. As is the child."

"But—"

He lifted a hand, and caught hers in it. "'For now' is all we ever have. We have the illusion of forever. We have the illusion of stability. We have the illusion of safety—but that's all it's ever been. It's a story we tell ourselves."

"I want it to be a true story."

"Kaylin—you used to be good at *now*. Try to remember what it was like. We have now." He exhaled. "And we build on it. Come on. It's time to go home."

She nodded and led where he followed; it wasn't hard. He was still holding her hand. "I wanted to tell you something," she said, in a low voice. "Today. Yesterday. Whenever it was."

"The past?"

She nodded.

He stopped walking and turned to face her.

And she found she had no words. Saw, from his expression, that he hadn't really expected them. "Tomorrow," he said quietly, and she understood by that that he meant, simply, *not* now. He gave her that much when he wanted to hear what she had almost forced herself to say. And she couldn't be certain she could give him that much space or patience in return. It wasn't in her. And for this particular *now,* she felt humbled by the knowledge.

"You'll come?"

"No. I don't think it would be wise. We want information. And Tiamaris will be with you. I'll run interference at the office."

"There's no interference to run—"

"There will be."

"Sanabalis said—"

"That you were excused from reporting for the evening."

She nodded.

"Mallory will probably sleep at his desk tonight, waiting for an explanation of why."

"I won't be there."

"No. But I will."

"Severn—I didn't leave the fiefs." The words came out in a rush. "When I ran—I didn't leave them."

And he said, "I know."

"But I—"

"I don't care what you did."

She stopped.

"Do you understand that? I do *not* care what you did. I don't care where you were. You were gone for six months. You didn't stay there, and you're not there now. You're half killing yourself on behalf of the midwives. And the city. You find the time to teach the orphans, to take them places Marrin would never let them go otherwise. They have a little more than either of us ever did, and you don't resent them for it.

"If you need absolution, find a religion. What I care about is now."

"You waited for seven years."

"Yes."

She shook her head. "I don't understand you, sometimes."

"You don't have to work so hard at it. Come on. Home. Tomorrow is going to be a long day." He grimaced. "But if you could avoid getting into a fight that involves half the city until I've recovered from today, I'd appreciate it."

Sleep was a tense and restless affair, and Kaylin was awake in the morning. It wasn't a good kind of awake, but as it wasn't going away any time soon, she got out of bed, cleaned herself up—which involved a trip to the well with a bucket or two first—and ate. There wasn't a lot to eat; she'd been riding on the Rennick wagon. His food was, as he'd pointed out, good, and there was always an endless supply. Unfortunately, he wasn't here, and neither was his casual largesse.

When Tiamaris arrived at her door, she could hear the familiar creak of the floorboards as he approached. Dragons were heavy and there wasn't a good way for someone heavy to silence that particular creak. She liked the floors for that reason.

She answered the door after his first knock.

He wore a familiar surcoat, Hawk emblazoned on its chest. She'd chosen to forgo her uniform because she was awake enough to understand that it wasn't much protection where they were heading. Not that she didn't cling to her uniform when she was feeling particularly stubborn.

But this morning was not one of those times.

"The uniform?" he said, noting her expression.

"You could wear pink gauze and enough gold to buy a small village," she replied, as she fitted her belt, with care, and arranged her sheaths. "I'm not a Dragon."

"You travel in the company of one."

"Today." She grimaced as she twisted her hair up and pinned it in place with a straight stick. "But the trick to the fiefs is avoiding a fight. You can do it by raising or lowering your eyes' inner membranes.

"I do it by looking a little run-down and a lot like trouble," she said.

He looked at her face for a while. She realized—after he'd been doing it for some time—that his gaze rested on the small flower that adorned her cheek.

"I don't know if it helps," she said. "It certainly makes a difference to the thugs that serve him. But they're not the only danger."

"The Ferals are unlikely to care one way or the other."

"True." She motioned him into the hall and shut the door firmly behind her. "But it's the height of day. We're unlikely to meet Ferals where we're going."

The streets on either side of the Ablayne were open for business. Merchants or, more appropriately, the errand boys of merchants, were jostling their way from one end of the street to the other. It was hot and humid. At this time of year, sunlight burned away all trace of the evening's coolness before it cleared the horizon.

But the bridge across the Ablayne was, as usual, almost deserted. Kaylin took a deep breath before she set foot on it. Tiamaris never seemed to need to breathe.

"Why are you here, anyway?" she asked.

"Lord Sanabalis thought it would be safer."

"For me or for you?"

He actually smiled at that. He did not, however, answer.

"How much did he tell you?"

"As much as he thought I needed to know."

"Did he tell you about the Leontines?"

"Kaylin."

She grimaced.

"He understands why this is important to you. I don't believe you care why it's important to him—but he is, as he can, being careful for your sake. If we're finished on time, you can accompany him to the Leontine Quarter when he goes there."

"If we're not?"

"He will go anyway. He has made that commitment."

She nodded. "I don't know what he wants me to learn, in Nightshade."

"He's Sanabalis. He probably expects you to learn everything."

Kaylin laughed. "I keep forgetting you were one of his students."

"With luck and a few calm centuries, so will he."

Lord Nightshade's residence hulked against the skyline like a particularly graceful set of gallows. As they approached it the crowds in the streets thinned. Kaylin, who had stayed well away from the Castle for all of her life as one of Nightshade's citizens, understood why. There was only one law in Nightshade, and no recourse. The Halls of Law had many, many laws—she knew; she'd memorized all of them—and even when you broke them, there was the Court system, and the complicated brokering of cash as reparation. She didn't particularly care for that custom, but as it wasn't used for most of the cases she investigated, she tried to be pragmatic about it.

Besides, it made clear that there were *some* crimes you couldn't buy your way out of, and that discouraged people with a lot to lose. It didn't *stop* them entirely, but if it had, she'd be out of a job.

Still, in Nightshade, it didn't matter. There was only one Court here, and if you were seeing it up close, it probably meant that after a brief interval of pain and humiliation, it wouldn't matter much to you either.

They approached the gates, and the guards to either side of it. Both guards tendered Kaylin a careful bow. She returned a curt nod, hating what the bow meant. They didn't extend their politeness to Tiamaris, who would have probably appreciated it more.

"We're here to see Lord Nightshade," she said, with emphasis on the *we're*.

"He awaits you," one of the guards said. Neither of them were familiar to Kaylin. "I do not believe he has left word for your companion."

She waited. After a few minutes of that game had gone by, she said, "He's not leaving without me, and I'm not going in without him."

This earned her another perfect bow.

The guard passed through the gate. Since it wasn't, in

any practical sense, a real gate, she watched him shimmer out of existence. She particularly hated the gate and the way it moved you from the outside of the Castle to the inside. But having entered the Castle once in a less traditional fashion, she wasn't eager to repeat the experience and settled on the discomfort she knew.

The Barrani, on the other hand, never seemed to find the transition through the gate unsettling. The guard returned a handful of minutes later, and bowed *again*. "He will see you both."

These guards weren't Hawks or Swords or Wolves—although they probably had more in common with Wolves than was comfortable. They didn't ask her to leave her weapons behind, and while she wasn't exactly a walking armory, she certainly took no pains to hide them.

They didn't ask Tiamaris to surrender anything, either. In his case, on the other hand, they were just being smart. A Dragon Lord might carry a sword—and Tiamaris did—but it was the least of his weapons, and the only way to part him from the dangerous ones was to remove his head.

The Barrani and the Dragons had a history of war—a history that was murky to Kaylin, and something she was content to let lie. She had stories—most of them the kind that would set her Scholarly Master's considerable teeth on edge—and they had, in all probability, actual memories.

She gritted her teeth and made her way straight for the illusionary portcullis, grateful for the very meager breakfast she'd had.

* * *

If she had ever landed on her feet—and in truth, the passage from outside to inside was less like walking and more like being thrown—she might have hated the experience less. But it was *always* disorienting, and she was invariably failed by knees that had gone rubber in the passage.

Today was no different; she felt as if she'd been spun around a thousand times and finally spit out, and the world coalesced around her as she pushed herself to her knees. The marble in the front vestibule, with its veins of gold and blue, was particularly fine, and looked a lot like the last time she'd seen it this close.

Lord Nightshade simply waited to come into focus.

So did Tiamaris. Whoever had constructed this Castle had clearly had to deal with Dragons and Barrani before. Humans were, as usual, an afterthought or an inconvenience. Like rats, and anything else that *had* a life span.

She got to her feet unsteadily, supporting her weight by putting her hand against the nearest wall and leaning until the wall had stopped moving. But when it had, Lord Nightshade inclined his head.

"Kaylin," he said, the syllables wrapped in formal Barrani intonation. It made, of her name, a foreign thing.

"Lord Nightshade," she replied, striving for the same formality.

"Lord Tiamaris," the fieflord continued. "I did not expect you, but you are welcome in my home." There was a slight emphasis on *my,* but it didn't seem to faze Tiamaris. Then again, a rock slide probably wouldn't.

"I have taken the liberty of arranging refreshments,"

he told them both. "Let us repair to a more suitable set of rooms, where we may converse more freely."

The room was a familiar room. It was, as all rooms in the Castle, sparsely furnished. Or rather, it had a lot of furniture, but given its size, the furniture didn't make all that much of an impact. There were carpets, and Kaylin almost winced as she walked across them in her regulation boots.

She sat opposite Nightshade on a low couch. Lord Tiamaris took one of the heavier chairs. The Hawk on his chest caught the light like a reminder. They sat in silence while Nightshade poured wine into thin, clear glasses. He gestured at the bread, cheese, and fruit that were arranged on the table in front of them.

Kaylin's stomach made an unfortunate comment. She was hungry, but she wasn't certain she wanted to eat, because she had to leave the same way she arrived.

"Why have you come?" he asked them. He did drink the wine.

Kaylin didn't want to do the same on an empty stomach.

"We are currently investigating a minor difficulty," Tiamaris replied.

"Ah."

Kaylin bit back the urge to ask Tiamaris what he considered *major*. Dragons tended toward understatement.

"To be honest," the Dragon Lord added, "I am not entirely certain what brought Private Neya to Nightshade."

"Its Lord," Nightshade replied smoothly. "She has been absent for too long." His eyes were a shade of emerald that had blue cores. A warning, there, if you knew the Barrani. Then again, breathing could be considered a warning if you knew the Barrani.

Tiamaris didn't reply. Instead, he turned his gaze— his eyes a shade of amber that were the Dragon equivalent of Nightshade's—to Kaylin. He left it there a little too long.

Great.

She felt Nightshade's chuckle; it didn't leave his mouth.

You are seldom prepared, Kaylin. For anything. His voice—if you could call something that bypassed ears a voice at all—was softer than she remembered; the amusement was genuine.

"I came to ask for your help," she said quietly. She had meant to preface the words with some sort of casual preamble, but she knew that he knew she wasn't bargaining with a good hand. Or any hand at all, really.

"That is hardly the Barrani way," he replied.

She waited for the rest, but there wasn't any. Studying his face, the odd shade of his eyes, the careful neutrality of his expression, she thought he knew *exactly* why she was here. But he would, wouldn't he? She reached up, touched the mark on her cheek with the tips of her fingers. Felt them tingle a moment at the contact. Most days now, she forgot it was even there.

What did he want?

"What do you want?"

She grimaced. "You already know," she whispered. He said nothing.

Lord Tiamaris stirred in his chair but did not speak; she felt the weight of his gaze. So, apparently, did

Nightshade, who shifted his glance toward the Dragon Lord. "She does not understand, Lord Tiamarais."

"I am afraid, Lord Nightshade, that I am in her company."

"She is the *Erenne,*" Nightshade replied.

Tiamaris said nothing for a moment. Then he laid his arms against the chair rests, bent his elbows, and steepled wide hands beneath his chin. "Perhaps you will allow me," he said.

"Very well, Lord Tiamaris."

"We seek the Dragon Outcaste," Tiamaris said evenly.

Kaylin could feel Nightshade's surprise though she couldn't actually see it.

"That is not, in the end, what Kaylin Neya seeks."

"Perhaps not. Perhaps she is not aware of it. Kaylin's interest in the city has always been personal, and even when the city as she knows it is threatened, it will always *be* personal."

He glanced at Kaylin; she wondered how much he knew.

"They are connected, your request and her desire."

"They are indeed connected. Although I believe I was asked to accompany Kaylin as a precaution."

"Ah. The Dragon Emperor is concerned with her safety?"

"She is one of his citizens," Tiamaris replied. "And given the nature of her as yet unexplored abilities, she is valuable."

"I see."

"His interest in her, and your interest, Lord Nightshade, are perhaps not so different. But the fiefs are not part of his city."

"Continue."

"We believe the Outcaste has made another move, or several, outside of the confines of the city proper. What he did is now coming to fruition."

"And he will gain power from this?"

"He will gain power," Tiamaris replied quietly. "And in the process, we will lose a great deal. The effects of that loss will be felt first in the fiefs," he added. "It is in the fiefs that the ancient shades are strongest."

"And in the fiefs," Nightshade replied, with the hint of a wry smile, "that my power exists at all."

"That, I cannot say," Tiamaris replied smoothly. "But we feel it is in your interest, or we would not have come to you. Where is the Outcaste, Lord Nightshade?"

"It is not of me that you must ask that question," Nightshade replied.

"Then which of the fieflords—" He stopped.

"You begin to see," the fieflord replied. He turned to Kaylin. "You have seen the Outcaste," he said. "And more."

She stared at them both as if they were out of their minds, because she wasn't stupid. Of course she'd seen him. She'd seen him in the fief of Nightshade, surrounded by the undying Barrani and the children they had meant to sacrifice. Surrounded, as well, by dark flames, and bright, by the glowing remnants of old courtyard stone. By shadows and power.

His power. And hers. She had faced him, free of the confines of the ancient bracer that served to contain her power. She had fought, she had won; he had retreated. Had he been mortal, the retreat would have simply been called death. "You think *I* can answer that question?"

Lord Nightshade's expression did not change, but he raised a hand to his brow and massaged it a moment. "I begin to feel a certain sympathy for Lord Sanabalis," he told them both. He let his hand fall. "Kaylin," he said. "Look at me."

She did.

"What is the Outcaste's name?"

She started to say *how the hell should I know?* But her lips began to move, to stutter over something that felt as if it *should* be a word. Should be, but it was too vast, and too complicated for speech, for simple saying.

And she remembered. A word. So unlike the word that Nightshade had given her that she hadn't really recognized it. She stared at him. Then she turned to look at Tiamaris.

Tiamaris said. "It is as we suspected."

"You *suspected* that I knew his *true name* and you didn't *tell* me?"

"You cannot even say it," he replied. "We considered it safe."

"And if it hadn't been safe?"

"You are, thank your gods, Sanabalis's problem, not mine." He paused. "If you speak his name he will know. No matter where he is, Kaylin, he will know.

"If you try to speak it, he may not. We are not certain that he is aware. We were not certain that you were." He paused, and then added, "If it is helpful, I remain unconvinced. To see a name is not to know it."

She hesitated. She had seen the names of the Barrani, unencased by bodies, and she had no idea what they were and what they meant.

But Nightshade said, "You have not observed her for

long enough, Lord Tiamaris. I mean no criticism. But I believe that Kaylin can find him, if she uses what she knows. He will, however, certainly be able to find *her* if she tries."

"Will he dare the Castle?"

"Who can say for certain what an Outcaste Dragon Lord will dare? Were he Barrani, and Lord, he would storm it with hundreds, and he would not cease until she either took the reins of power, used his true name and ordered him to it, or she was dead.

"The name was not a gift. Not from the Outcaste. But I believe that, with the training and the knowledge, Kaylin Neya could see many things, if she made the attempt."

"Words," she said softly.

He raised a brow.

"When Sanabalis spoke I *saw* the words."

The brow rippled. "When Lord Sanabalis spoke?"

She nodded. "He spoke, and I could…see…what he was saying. I could see it as if it were light. No—that's the wrong word. All of the words I have are the wrong damn words.

"I could see them and feel them, as if they were more than simple speech. I mean, more than Elantran. More than Barrani, High or Low. Why is there a Low Barrani, anyway?"

"A great deal of sympathy for Lord Sanabalis," Lord Nightshade said. "If this is what he contends with. Kaylin, please, focus."

"I just wondered, that's all."

"Wonder another time. Tell me of this language."

She looked at Tiamaris. His shrug was slight but

clear; whatever it was she knew, he had no objections to Nightshade also knowing. Or, since he was a Dragon and Dragons were the epitome of practical in most things, he thought it unlikely that Nightshade wouldn't find out.

"He told a story," she said slowly. "But when he started to speak—I...I had to be there."

"A story."

She nodded.

"And the language?"

"I didn't know it. I didn't recognize it, but I felt that I should. That it was almost familiar."

"He told a story in this language. To the Leontines?"

"Good guess."

Nightshade ignored the sarcasm. He turned to Tiamaris. "The significance of this?"

"Uncertain. It is, however, certain that her companion did not see what she saw. We suspect that no one who cannot shape the tongue itself experiences it the way Kaylin did."

"Which implies that in time, she will be able to speak it."

There was a tense silence.

"Does it matter?" Kaylin asked.

"To the Dragon Emperor, almost certainly," Lord Nightshade replied. "And to the High Lord of the Barrani as well. It is, if I am not mistaken, the tongue of the Old Ones and it is not spoken. Until recently, I would not have said for certain that any of the Dragon Court could although, if I had to guess, I would have said the Arkon could. The great Dragon whose hoard is the Imperial Library and all it contains is ancient. And Sanabalis is old.

"Kaylin, the tongue can shape a race. When it is spoken with power and intent, it can change the very nature of its audience."

"I can't speak it," she said flatly.

"No. I didn't say that you could. I said merely that you have an affinity for it that only those who *can* speak it possess."

"The Outcaste can."

"No," Nightshade replied softly. "You are making assumptions."

"Sanabalis thinks he can."

"Sanabalis sees his hand in this, and that conjecture is more informed. But there are things that lie trapped in the fiefs that undoubtedly *can* speak the Old Tongue."

"If they're trapped here, they can't reach him."

"No?" Lord Nightshade rose slowly, abandoning his chair. "I will aid you, Lord Tiamaris. Follow."

Lord Tiamaris inclined his head and rose.

Kaylin stood last and trailed after them. The halls were both familiar and unfamiliar; the halls in the Castle had an unfortunate habit of shifting in place. But where Nightshade walked, she could also walk. He passed several closed doors, during which time Kaylin prayed fervently to nameless gods. There were some passages in this damn Castle that she'd walked before, and she had no desire to walk them again for any reason.

Nightshade did not approach the Long Hall, guarded by the sleepers. For that, if nothing else, she thought she should be grateful. But when he led them at last to their destination, she recognized the room: Mirrors adorned its walls. Only mirrors.

Nightshade glanced at Kaylin, and she remembered

that she had seen him walk *through* one of these shiny, spotless surfaces and vanish. She hadn't tried to follow.

"I would not," he warned, hearing the thoughts that she could never quite dampen. "Were I you, especially. Force of will is required to navigate these mirrors. They are part of the Castle, and they bend to the will of the Castle's Lord.

"You have had very little experience bending the will of others to your own purposes. You are afraid to force your will upon strangers. Such fear would be seen as weakness. And where these mirrors would take you then, even I cannot say.

"Come," he added. He gestured in front of the center mirror in the large room. It was rectangular, and if it had a frame, Kaylin couldn't see it. But she could see what shuddered into sight as the mirror accepted Lord Nightshade's silent command—as if it were Records. All of the fief of Nightshade, the streets so meticulously detailed she could see old wells, old horse paths, old carriage tracks. She could see the Four Corners and, with care, could make out the run-down building in which she'd spent so many years of her life.

But…it wasn't just Records. Because she could also see the people who traversed the morning streets. They stopped to talk to one another, or hurried out of sight, their furtive attempt at hiding made ridiculous by the merciless gaze of a mirror that seemed to watch them from above.

"If you desired it," Nightshade said, standing at her back as she stared, "you could master these mirrors."

"What would it cost?"

She felt his smile, even though she couldn't see it as

the mirror's surface was no longer reflective. "If you can ask that question, you are not yet ready."

"You can see the whole fief."

"Yes."

"At any time."

"Yes. It is perhaps not as interesting a pastime as you assume. But I watch these." He gestured and the image rippled, as if it were liquid. When the colors, muted and gray, reformed, she was looking at a different set of streets. Streets that were farther from the Ablayne than she had ever wanted to live. "These," he told her softly, "are the boundaries of my fief. You are familiar with the boundary marked by the Ablayne, but I believe you are less familiar with the others."

She nodded. "Can you see beyond them?"

"A curious question."

"I take it that's a no."

"You would not be entirely correct," he replied. "But it is…less reliable, and more difficult to look beyond my borders."

"Why?"

"Castle Nightshade exists as part of Nightshade." He waited. "Have you never wondered why there are seven fiefs?"

"I wondered. None of the fieflords seem like men who respect borders."

"Lord Tiamaris?" Nightshade said, acknowledging the silent Dragon.

"It is our supposition that the Castle in which we now stand is one of a handful of such buildings that exist in the fiefs. To rule the fief, the fieflord must be able to shape the building to his will. To some, such force of nature comes naturally," he said, lifting a brow as he glanced at Nightshade. "But there are some fiefs to which we have not traveled."

"You haven't?"

"It has been attempted," he replied.

Kaylin thought about this for a moment. "Any survivors?"

"Three. They were, to a man, mad. We could not clearly discern what they had seen, or what they had been seen by. It was not in your lifetime," he added, "but humans have no memory. What has been attempted—what has failed—is something they must try again in a generation or two."

Kaylin looked at the streets. "This is the boundary between Nightshade and Barren."

"Perceptive. It is."

"Barren isn't that much different."

"Perhaps. The fieflords are not a caste. They do not meet, and they do not interact. I do not know who—or what—rules Barren."

Kaylin said nothing for a long moment. Then she shook herself. "It's one of the outer fiefs," she said at last, and heavily. "It's a crescent—you can still see the city proper if you stand on the right street. But farther in?"

Nightshade said nothing. It was a pointed nothing.

"Lord Nightshade," she said, easing into the formality of High Barrani with a grimace. "The Outcaste—the Dragon Lord—could he *be* a fieflord?"

"Given his power and the scope of his ambition,"

Lord Nightshade replied, "I fail to see that he could be anything else."

There was a lot of silence then.

CHAPTER 18

She stared at Nightshade for about a minute too long, and then swiveled to stare—in the same fashion—at Tiamaris. "Do you suspect—I mean, did you—the same thing?"

Tiamaris shrugged.

"And you didn't *say anything?*"

"To you? No. But it wasn't necessary. It remains largely irrelevant, unless the Leontine has gone to the fief—the possible fief—that the Outcaste rules."

"He may well have," she began. Then she stopped. "No, you're probably right."

Tiamaris raised a brow.

"If he could do whatever he needed to do from the fief, we probably would never have seen him at all, until it was far too late. And I don't care where he was raised—no one with an ounce of sense goes into the heart of the fiefs for safety."

"That was our thought," Tiamaris said mildly.

"But he ran somewhere when he left the Quarter. I'm sure he didn't remain." She looked at Nightshade. "If he were in this fief, could you find him?"

Nightshade nodded.

"But not without looking."

"No. If I understand correctly what I'm hearing, his power is not great enough that I would sense it otherwise."

"There would be two," she told him.

"Two?"

"Two Leontines." She reconsidered her words. "Or two very large cats."

"And they are dangerous?"

"Have you ever fought a Leontine before?"

"Yes."

"Then you already know the answer."

Nightshade nodded, steepling his hands below his chin. "What is your interest in this, Kaylin?"

She stared at him as if he were speaking a language she couldn't understand.

And Tiamaris said, quietly, "There is a child."

She felt Nightshade's surprise. Wondered how surprised he would have to be to actually *show* it. "The Leontine you are seeking has a child?"

"Yes," she replied curtly.

"Excuse me, but I feel that I am not in possession of all of the facts."

Tiamaris smiled. It was a slight smile, and a subtle one; it was also completely unadorned by words.

Lord Nightshade gestured and the mirror went flat, its surface once again reflective. He turned to Tiamaris. "I am aware," he said, "as no doubt you suspect, of some of the events occurring in the city. I am not, however, privy to the Councils of the Wise for obvious reasons. I know some of what Kaylin knows, but not all. I understood that she was in the Leontine Quarter, but it would not be the first time she has gone there. If the Leontine that you seek can change his shape, he is dangerous."

Tiamaris nodded.

"Has Lord Sanabalis been to the Quarter?"

"Yes. With me," Kaylin said.

"Ah. He must have explained some of the difficulty you now face."

"He did. And you know about the difficulty how?"

"I believe you've seen it in the throne room. I have, in my time, counted Leontines among my guests. Seldom in the fiefs, but not never. The fiefs are a dangerous home to Leontines."

"To anyone."

"A different kind of danger," he replied coolly. "But the fate of the Leontines did not concern the Barrani over much. None of my kin can now speak the Old Tongue. Some very few can read what is written in it, but even then, the interpretation is not reliable. Lord Sanabalis is both wise and very old. Older, by far, than the Emperor."

"Older than the Arkon?"

"The Arkon does not leave his library. He is content to serve in the capacity of antiquarian. Lord Sanabalis has always been unusual for a Dragon. Dangerous, but unusual." He paused and added, "You distract me. I learned some part of Leontine history from Leontines— my understanding is filtered through their perspective.

"But I know of the marked, or the cursed or tainted as they are sometimes called. The Leontine you seek is one of them?"

She nodded.

"And the child of whom Tiamaris spoke is his?"

She nodded again.

"It is too much to hope that you are concerned with the Leontine's child because you wish to destroy it." He paused for breath but did not wait long enough for Kaylin's reply; clearly, he didn't need it. "I will search," he told them quietly. "Do not interrupt me."

Kaylin nodded.

But he hadn't quite finished yet. "The child is more of a danger than the father."

"The mother is marked as well," Tiamaris said.

Lord Nightshade looked at the Dragon Lord for a long moment, and then said, "Kaylin, Lord Tiamaris, please return to your duties in the city proper. When I have word, I will send for Kaylin, but a thorough search of the fief will take hours, and there are some aspects of these particular mirrors which, for reasons of security, I do not choose to reveal."

"But—"

"If they are within the fief, I will know. If they have passed through it, I will also know. But they are not the only things I am now looking for."

"The Outcaste?"

He nodded. "He is adept at cloaking his presence from those who rule. If it becomes necessary, you can attempt to attract his attention, but it is not the first option I am willing to consider."

Tiamaris walked briskly through the fief's crowded streets. The sun was still rising, which meant Rennick was still sleeping, and probably would be for another couple of hours. The Dragon Lord was silent, but it was the silence of preoccupation. He didn't break it until they'd crossed the bridge over the Ablayne.

"We will take a carriage to the Palace. Sanabalis will be waiting for you there."

"But I—"

"He is to return to the Leontine Quarter. He intends you to accompany him. If you are not to be derelict in your duties to the Hawks, you will arrive at the Palace as quickly as possible."

Mallory seemed a world away.

"Yes, I'd heard there was some organizational difficulty in the department. Inasmuch as he can, Sanabalis has lessened the consequences of your current tour of duty. I do not believe the current Sergeant is pleased with this departure from standard operating procedures, however."

"He wouldn't be. If it were up to him, I'd be without the Hawk so fast I wouldn't even hear the dismissal."

Tiamaris stepped into the street and held out a hand in the universal "I need a ride" gesture used by anyone familiar with the city. The only difference was that he was standing in the *path* of the moving carriage when it careened to a stop. Dragons.

Sanabalis was waiting for Kaylin as she stepped down from the carriage. It wasn't Imperial, and the driver was a little less suicidal than Teela—but in truth, not by much. Dragons apparently didn't ride horses. And horses, apparently, didn't like Dragons. Since her experience with horses and Dragons had all been Imperial, she found out the hard way how skittish horses could make the drive more challenging. She didn't intend to repeat the mistake anytime soon. As in: Not in this life.

She would have said as much—and loudly, with a smattering of anatomically impossible verbs in at least three official languages—but Severn was also waiting, and his very casual posture made it clear instantly that behavior—hers—could be an issue on this particular day. When he worked that hard to look casual, it usually meant trouble was in the offing.

Sanabalis issued her a curt greeting. To Tiamaris, he said, "Was Lord Nightshade helpful?"

"That remains to be seen. He was civil, however, and we encountered no difficulties in his domain."

"Ah. Very well, then. Kaylin? The Elders will be waiting."

She followed where he led, in this case, to a familiar carriage. Severn opened the door, and Sanabalis said, "I took the liberty of having food prepared."

"I—" She started to say *ate,* but managed to bite back the word. It was the only thing she'd really bitten today. Nightshade made her nervous enough that she hadn't wanted to eat while he was around. "Thank you."

"You may thank the Corporal," he replied. "It would not occur to me that any student of mine would be careless enough to go without necessary sustenance in a time of crisis. He, however, insisted that there was every probability you would do exactly that." The Dragon frowned a moment. "You are wearing your bracer?"

She was. When she gave it any thought, she hated the thing—but it had become easy, over time, to give it no thought whatsoever. "Yes."

"Good. Remove it. Give it to the Corporal for safe-keeping."

"Remove it? But—"

"I have been in discussions with the Imperial Dragon Court for the entirety of the morning—and the morning started when you left the Palace."

"That was the middle of the night."

"Indeed. Humans are often creatures of context, in my experience. I am therefore supplying you with necessary context. If you have some difficulty with a direct order, keep it to yourself."

"Yes, Sanabalis."

He sat heavily in the seat facing them and looked out the window. The carriage started to move, and Severn bent down and pulled a covered basket from beneath the bench they were sitting on side by side. He handed this to Kaylin.

"Eat," he told her.

She ran her hands over the studs on the bracer in a quick and almost natural pattern of successive moves. It clicked audibly. Severn took it from her wrist before she could remove it.

"This," Sanabalis said, still staring out the window, "is why I do not like to accept students. They are always a trial, and they complicate a life that is not, by any standard, simple to begin with."

She had bread with something in the middle in one hand, and she meant to move it to her mouth, but it got stuck halfway and stayed there. "What happened?"

"Nothing," he replied curtly. "And it was a great deal of work to ensure that that nothing happened."

"The baby?"

"I gave you my word, in the short term, Kaylin." His eyes, when he swiveled his neck to look at her, were the color of fire.

"The Emperor wants him dead," she said flatly. She had meant it to be a question.

"Kaylin, any thinking person wants him dead."

The urge to open the door and leap into the streets that were moving by at such a brisk pace was almost overwhelming. Severn caught her arm before she could move, and it steadied her. His presence steadied her. It always had.

But Severn, she knew, *could* kill the baby.

"The Emperor, however, has graciously agreed to allow me some meager sense of my own honor. While we deal with the matters at hand, he will not harm the child." He continued wearily, "No one will be allowed to harm the child while he is in residence. That much comfort, you may allow yourself. But that is as far as it goes, Kaylin.

"We will now speak with the Elders. The fate of your Sergeant will be decided today."

"But—but—he didn't murder a man! They can't indict him if—"

"He did worse, Kaylin. He suspected the truth—about the man, about the baby—and did *nothing*. Said nothing. It is not murder, no. But inasmuch as the concept exists among the Leontine enclave, it *is* treason."

She was silent for a moment. When she spoke, she could hardly hear herself. "Do they know about the child?"

Sanabalis turned to the window. He didn't answer.

* * *

The Elders were, as Sanabalis said, waiting. They were neatly attired for Leontines in summer heat, which is to say, they were wearing clothing. Mostly robes that stopped a few inches from their ankles. The robes were an undyed off-white, with loose sleeves or no sleeves.

The Elders stood in a group around the First Son, who was also robed in a similar way.

He bowed when Sanabalis approached, nodding, as he rose, to both Severn and Kaylin. It wasn't a particularly friendly gesture.

Kaylin had eaten what she could stomach in the carriage, but in truth, it wasn't a whole lot. She was restless, nervous, ready to fight. Her wrist felt naked. Her hands were empty, but they itched for daggers. Still, she managed to return the nod, not that the First Son seemed to notice.

"We welcome you, Eldest, to our Council." The First Son spoke in High Barrani. If he hadn't spoken the syllables so precisely, Kaylin wasn't certain she would have recognized them.

Sanabalis didn't seem to have that problem. He didn't bow, and he didn't kneel, but he did nod.

"We seek your counsel, Eldest," one of the older Leontines said. His High Barrani wasn't as clean or precise as Adar's, although it was spoken slowly. Clearly the Leontines weren't used to the language of the Imperial common law.

This did not surprise Sanabalis. It didn't really surprise Kaylin either. But her opinion didn't matter. Sanabalis inclined his head. "Speak," he told them. "And speak in the language of your kin, for if I am not mistaken, the counsel you seek concerns your kin."

The Leontine nodded and turned to Adar. "With your permission," he said.

Adar nodded slowly. "With your permission, Eldest, I will speak in the language of Law."

Sanabalis nodded.

"The first matter we wish your advice on concerns Marcus Kassan. He serves the outsiders," he added, using a Leontine word that there was no exact Elantran meaning for. Kaylin had heard it a handful of times in the Pridlea, usually spoken with scorn or apprehension.

"He serves the Emperor," Sanabalis said calmly. "The Emperor governs the City, and the Empire. I, as well, owe my allegiance to the Emperor."

The other Elders began to murmur among themselves, their low growls a contrast to the almost purring Leontine of the hearth.

"He was to be charged with murder?" Sanabalis asked, when the discussion had continued for that little bit too long.

"He was charged with kin-slaying," Adar replied. "And he accepted the charge. It was not to discuss charges that we were to convene, but consequences." Kaylin wondered, for just a moment, where he had been taught, and how long he had been away from his kind. In many ways, Adar was unique. Although he was unmistakably Leontine, there was something about his bearing that set him apart. That, and the deference he was granted. She wasn't sure how much of the latter depended on the former.

"However," Adar continued, raising his voice just a

touch. The slight increase in volume served to quell the discussion that was unfolding, in the Leontine version of whispers, all around him. "However, in light of your visit, and your investigation, those charges are withdrawn entirely. A man has the right to kill to preserve his own life."

"You accept the death as a result of self-defense?"

"We do."

"Very well. Continue."

"Marcus Kassan offered no defense of his actions when he was apprehended."

Sanabalis nodded.

"He has been unwilling to address the Elders," Adar continued. "It is a minor crime, among our kin, but it is not an unfamiliar one. It is, however, notable given the gravity of the situation and the possible nature of his attacker."

"Meaning that he will not speak to you."

"Meaning that, Eldest, yes."

"He will speak to me."

Adar nodded. "That is my suspicion. Will you speak to him on behalf of the Elders?"

"I will speak to him on behalf of the Emperor," Sanabalis replied coolly.

Adar turned to two of the Elders and spoke a quick, curt Leontine word that was so harsh Kaylin couldn't understand it.

They didn't have that difficulty. They bowed and turned toward the cage in which Marcus Kassan sat. He was out of the range of hearing, but not, Kaylin thought, of vision. He knew damn well they were there, and waiting on him.

But he took his bloody time gaining his feet when the cage door was opened and he was gestured out. It rankled. She wanted to snarl some choice Leontine phrases into the silence. But this was the one place it wasn't safe to do so. She held her tongue. Kept her hands by her sides. Waited.

Marcus was silent as he was led to Adar. He didn't snarl, didn't struggle—there wasn't much to struggle against. They hadn't bound or chained him, and inasmuch as a cage existed that could hold an angry Leontine, the one that he'd lived in for what felt like months—but was less than a handful of days—was purely decorative.

"Sergeant Kassan," Lord Sanabalis said.

Marcus looked at the Dragon Lord.

"You have been cleared of all charges of murder," Sanabalis announced.

Marcus's glance flickered off Sanabalis's face for an eye-blink. Kaylin saw him look at the ground. There, in dark, smudged ash, was what remained of his friend. But his head hadn't moved. And his lips didn't either.

Sanabalis frowned; it was the first familiar expression she'd seen on his face. "Sergeant," he said, his voice a shade more irritable. "We believe that you were called away from your place of work on urgent business."

Marcus nodded.

"What occurred when you met your friend?"

The silence was heavy.

"Marcus?" Kaylin said quietly.

He looked at her.

She took a breath and then another, deeper one. "The Pridlea was attacked last night."

His eyes widened, and his expression shed all neutrality in an instant.

Kaylin lifted her chin, exposing her throat. Given that she was wearing her standard beat kit, she didn't expose *much,* but it was the gesture that counted. She also held her hands out, palms facing him, but that was pure Elantran, pure human. Leontines, after all, didn't lift their hands to show they were unarmed. Why bother with handheld weapons when you already sported a better set?

"Tell me," he said curtly, bringing the full force of a Sergeant's voice to bear.

"Orogrim came to visit."

He closed his eyes and the Elders began to speak, some to each other, some to Adar. Adar lifted a pale hand. They fell silent slowly, because Leontines were generally never silent. They didn't *talk* a lot, but there was always a background growl—or purr if you were lucky—in any room that also contained Leontines.

"He was driven off," Kaylin said. "But the building sustained fire damage."

"And my wives? My children?"

"All safe," she answered quickly. "We didn't have anywhere to go—they didn't, I mean—so they're now in residence as guests at the Imperial Palace."

His eyes were a shade of orange that made him look almost draconic. He turned to Sanabalis, and everything about his stance was different. The Dragon Lord met his gaze and held it. Kaylin—at whom it was no longer directed—fought the urge to take a step back. Or several steps, all at speed.

Sanabalis now lifted a hand. "Kayala accepted the

offer of hospitality, and it is simply that. It was expedient to repair to the Palace. It is the one place in which their safety could be guaranteed. They are free to leave, and to wander at will. They are guilty of no crime.

"The same cannot necessarily be said of their husband, and that is why I am here. You did not speak when the charge of murder was laid at your feet. You will speak now."

Marcus was silent for a long time. Whatever deference other Leontines felt for Dragons Marcus clearly held in abeyance.

But he cleared his throat, breaking both silence and tension. "Gorran mirrored me. The mirror was keyed," he added, "and Gorran should not have been able to use it—but he spoke of some danger to my wives. He requested a meeting—"

"Gorran would not have dared—"

Adar growled at the Elder, who fell silent. Kaylin, on the other hand, said, "Was Gorran an Elder?"

"He was." It was Sanabalis who replied.

She looked at the men again. "I regret your loss," she said in perfect Leontine. It seemed to either surprise or offend them; given the slightly orange tinge to their eyes, she guessed it was the latter.

"Did it not strike you as unusual?" Adar asked, in his calm, deep voice.

"Yes, First Son. It did. But my first duty is to my Pridlea and Gorran was both friend and Elder. I agreed to meet him."

"And he suggested the location."

"Yes."

"You accepted it."

"Yes. I wanted to hear what he had to say. At the time, I didn't care where I heard it."

"Or you believed that Gorran did not wish to be overheard."

Marcus nodded slowly, and after a marked hesitation.

Kaylin would have bet money that the Elders would break out in another round of growls, but Adar's glare got to them before words left their mouths. They weren't happy, however.

Adar turned to Sanabalis. "Forgive my intrusion, Eldest." He bowed.

"You met Gorran."

"Yes."

"And nothing struck you as unusual?"

Again, silence. After a long pause—one unbroken by Sanabalis, who merely waited—Marcus said, "No. Something was unusual." He fell silent again, but this time, Sanabalis's posture changed. Clearly, he had tired of waiting.

"Sergeant Kassan, you have served the Emperor's Law for many years. You have made a name for yourself, and you have the Emperor's approval. It would cause some distress were you to be executed in this place, and it would also cause some unrest if you were to surrender your badge of office.

"We no longer have time for your hesitation and your personal life. If you cannot answer these questions to my satisfaction, I will call in the Tha'alani and they will extract the answers I require. The choice is entirely yours."

As if he had expected no less—or no more—Marcus Kassan seemed to wilt. It bothered Kaylin a lot more than she had thought it would. She'd seen him chew through solid wood in fury; she'd seen him bare his fangs when arguments about the duty roster had gone on for longer than his limited patience allowed; she'd seen him tired, and she'd even seen him hiding from his wives.

But this, this almost abject surrender? Never.

And she hated it.

She took two steps forward before anyone really noticed, and she inserted herself between Sanabalis and the Sergeant, turning her back to the Sergeant because she wanted to see Sanabalis's eyes. Her hands were near her dagger hilts, and although she otherwise stood in the posture that was called "at ease," she wasn't.

She even opened her mouth, but the hand that was placed on her shoulder wasn't the Dragon's. It was Marcus's. She turned, as he pulled her around, and met his gaze.

"Kitling," he said quietly, "you are not of the people. You are of my Pridlea, and you are loved and fiercely defended by my wives, but you do not understand what the Elders, what the Dragon, offer."

"I know damn well what they offer. I've *been* through a Tha'alani investigation before."

"Yes." His eyes were almost gold.

"Marcus, can't you just *tell* them what they need to know?"

"No, kitling. No."

Something in his tone of voice made her wince.

"Sit with Corporal Handred, if you can. Wait, if you must. Lord Sanabalis must have prepared for this eventuality, and it will not be long now." He turned to Adar for the first time. "First Son," he said gravely. "She is young and she is ferocious in her defence of kin." As if she were a child and he was making excuses for her poor behavior.

But Adar nodded, and the hint of a smile—with Leontines, it was only a hint, and frankly, given the lift of lip over canines that could rip a throat out, it was often hard to distinguish from, say, imminent death—transformed his features. He looked younger than he had at any other time she'd seen him. "The daughters worth having always are," he replied. "She would die for you, I think. Kill for you, certainly."

Marcus's expression was, however, impassive. "She would do both, if she were allowed."

Lord Sanabalis waited a moment, and then inclined his head in Marcus's direction. "Yes," he said softly, "I was prepared." He turned and walked away, climbing the steps of the vast coliseum as if they were flat and tiny. He didn't look like he moved quickly, but he covered a lot of distance anyway. Kaylin watched his back until it was out of sight.

"It was clever of you," Marcus said, when he had gone. "To mention my wives at a time like this."

"It was the only thing I could think of that would make you speak."

"Yes." He looked tired. "How has the operation in the Palace proceeded?"

She would have dropped her lower jaw if it hadn't been attached to her face. The aforementioned Corporal Handred, however, came to the rescue of her dignity. Or perhaps Marcus's. It was hard to tell.

"It has proved interesting," Severn now said. "And involved one visit to the Foundling Halls."

"The Halls?"

"Mr. Rennick wished to speak with children who had visited the Tha'alani Quarter before the unrest. He wanted their opinions and their impressions. They were, of course, happy to give him exactly what he asked for."

"Ah. And was it of use?"

"I believe so. The Tha'alani like children. As they did *not* like his first attempt at public communication, he is now attempting to give them a story they will at least have less cause to dislike."

"It's not finished yet."

"No. The Swords are out in full force around the Quarter. Some of the Wolves have been seconded for service there as well, although less visibly. The city has been in arms for the duration. There have been scuffles and some injuries—" he held up a hand in Kaylin's direction before she could ask a question "—but they all occurred outside of the Quarter, and were caused by either gross incompetence on the part of men who aren't actually accustomed to handling weapons, or by the Swords in their attempt to disperse the more mob-like crowds."

Severn lowered his hand. "I spoke at length to some of the Swords when I made my report to Mallory this morning."

Kaylin shook her head. "I should have expected as much," she said almost ruefully.

Severn nodded. "But you were otherwise occupied." He turned toward the outer height of the coliseum. "Sanabalis is returning."

Kaylin turned to look as well, and saw the Dragon Lord descending the steps far more slowly than he had climbed them. He had two companions. One was a Dragon; she recognized the build and the walk. She didn't recognize the face. She might have if she'd stopped to think, because she'd met the Dragon Lords of the Imperial Court before.

But by his side, in a gown the color of pale cedar, was a woman she recognized. Her hair was the color of honey, and her skin, bronze in the morning light.

Ybelline.

CHAPTER 19

Sanabalis, what the hell were you thinking? She shouldn't be walking around outside the Quarter at a time like this. It was her first thought. It was her second thought. The third thought, that the first two should remain behind closed lips, came quickly enough that she actually snapped her jaw shut. But she detached herself from the Elders and walked up the steps to greet Ybelline. The Tha'alani Castelord smiled and held out her arms. Kaylin walked into them and hugged her carefully, aware that the hilt of her daggers wouldn't be exactly comfortable.

Ybelline brushed Kaylin's forehead gently with her antennae, and Kaylin, instead of stiffening, leaned into them. So much had changed, and in so little time. *Why are you here? What was Sanabalis thinking?*

You will have to ask him, was the grave, but amused, reply. *We are never called upon to touch the thoughts or memories of the Dragons.*

But the Quarter—your home—

We are safe, Kaylin. And thanks to your intervention at a crucial time, we remain so. There is fear and worry, yes, and not a little anger—but it is held in check. The children watch, she added softly. As if the children were the keepers of all conscience.

And maybe, Kaylin thought, just maybe, they were a *good* keeper. To protect your children, you struggled with your anger, mastered it. You struggled to explain away your fear, or theirs. There probably wasn't all that much difference, in the end.

You worked hard to be worthy of the trust they so carelessly—and completely—placed in you.

Yes, Ybelline told her. *But the Leontines are waiting, now. What do you fear?*

I—I don't know. Marcus won't talk, Kaylin said. *He could, but he won't. I think he* wants *you to take the memories. He can't give them up. And I didn't want him to suffer*—she remembered, briefly, the first time she had met the Tha'alani. She shuddered, tried to pull away, and felt the soft curve of Ybelline's arms around her.

I'm sorry—I—

You have no secrets, came the soft reply, *because you don't need them. Not with me. Not from me.*

Kaylin felt the tension ebb from her shoulders, her legs, the fighting stance she had tried—while being held—to adopt.

Ybelline nodded. *You were afraid for him.*

I was.

And now?

Kaylin shook her head. *I trust you,* she told Ybelline.

She stepped back, almost overbalanced on the edge of a step, and cursed in Leontine as Ybelline pulled her back, laughing. It was warm, that laugh, and it was audible. The antennae no longer touched Kaylin's forehead, but it wasn't necessary; Kaylin could feel the amusement and affection rolling off Ybelline like ocean waves against sand.

Kaylin turned to the Elders. "Sorry," she said in Elantran. They said nothing—at all—and she escorted Ybelline down the rest of the stairs.

Marcus was waiting. He seemed slightly surprised at the choice of Tha'alani presented to him. "It's not often that you are called upon, Ybelline Rabon'alani."

"No," she replied serenely. "But I have visited the Halls of Law before."

"Ah, yes."

"It was thought that my ability would serve best when dealing with the memories of a child," she added.

Kaylin raised a brow. "That's why it was you who touched Catti?" She felt a chill in the heat of the unfettered sun. Catti was one of Marrin's foundlings, and she had been kidnapped—almost sacrificed—because she was part of Kaylin's life. She'd survived.

"Yes. She was young, and while it was absolutely essential that we understand exactly what had befallen her in her captivity, Lord Sanabalis suggested that I might be the most suitable of the Tha'alani seconded to Imperial Service to perform the task."

Kaylin turned to look at Sanabalis.

"It is hard," the Dragon Lord replied, with no expression whatsoever, "to fear Ybelline."

"Catti was only a year younger than I was when I—"

"Catti did not attempt what you attempted." If his face still looked like carved stone, his voice had dropped a few degrees.

It was true. Kaylin looked away.

"Lord Sanabalis," Ybelline began, but Kaylin lifted a hand.

"I deserved that," she said quietly.

"If it comforts you at all," Ybelline added, "your preoccupation with the welfare of the young was noted, and I was asked to attend as much for your peace of mind as for Catti's." She reached out and caught Kaylin's clenched hands in her own, as unselfconscious at the physical contact as any member of her race might be. "I am glad that I acceded to the request, Kaylin. We are very, very different women, but we share some of the same concerns and the same goals—and we have chosen to let what we love, instead of what we fear, define us." She let go of Kaylin's hands.

"Did you bring her because you thought it would make things easier on *me?*" Kaylin whispered to her teacher.

Lord Sanabalis frowned. "Ybelline is far too modest," he replied at last. "Marcus is stubborn and he surrenders nothing gracefully. What she takes from his thoughts, she will have to work for. Very few of the Tha'alani are as... adept...at such work."

A different and equally unwelcome thought occurred to Kaylin, and she looked at Marcus. Marcus was staring straight ahead, so it took a bit of work to catch his attention. When he gave it, it was with the tired resignation of a parent who hasn't been able to sleep for more than three hours at a stretch and is seriously reconsidering the wisdom of having offspring.

"Yes, Private?"

"I—nothing, Sir."

"Good. Shut up and sit down. Preferably at a distance." He growled. She had started to lift her chin, to expose her throat in the accepted posture of submission. "I will not hurt her," he told her. "If that was your concern. I will *also* endeavor *not* to be insulted."

"Yes, Marcus."

"Good. Corporal."

Severn nodded, and put an arm around Kaylin's shoulders, drawing her back.

She watched in silence as Ybelline approached her Sergeant, and watched as their faces grew closer together. The antennae weaved in the air so gracefully it was almost impossible not to be hypnotized by their movement.

But they stopped suddenly against the fur of Marcus's forehead, and the Sergeant stiffened at the contact. Kaylin had to look away. She loved Marcus, yes. But she also loved Ybelline.

And if Marcus would only talk—

"You wouldn't," said Severn quietly, divining her helpless anger.

"Wouldn't what?"

"You wouldn't give them the information."

"If I knew damn well they were going to get it anyway, I would."

"No," he said quietly, and certainly. "If it meant the death of your wife—or the death of your children—you wouldn't."

She didn't answer. Put like that, there wasn't much she could say.

"Ybelline has seen worse." He was aware of all Kaylin's fear. "Far worse."

"And you know that how?"

"I know who she's touched."

She started to ask him how, realized that it must have been when he was a Wolf, and fell silent. "We're going to be late," she said tonelessly.

"We still have two hours."

"It won't be enough."

It wasn't even close.

Ybelline and Marcus stood facing each other in silence, while Kaylin watched. Sweat beaded Ybelline's perfect skin as the sun climbed. Somewhere in the city, Richard Rennick would also be rising. But she couldn't leave. Not while the striking antennae that characterized all of the Tha'alani were still nestled in Leontine fur.

Marcus might have been sweating—with Leontines, it was hard to tell. But his expression was the expression that had earned him the nickname Old Ironjaw; it was grim and set, and it didn't falter. There was no widening of eyes, there was no cry of dismay—or worse, shame— and in her time, Kaylin had done and seen both.

There was just Marcus, accused of treason, and Ybelline, beholden by Imperial Law to do as she was doing: rifle through his memories, discarding those that weren't relevant to the investigation.

Two hours after noon, the antennae withdrew. For a long moment, that was the only change in the strange tableau of Leontine and Tha'alani. Ybelline moved first.

She took a step back, that was all. But Sanabalis was by her side instantly, his presence clearly—if silently—warning all others to keep their distance.

Not that they needed the warning.

Kaylin could see the Leontines clearly. They were all watching Ybelline with barely veiled hostility and fear. She would have hated them for it—she wanted to hate them for it. But she had been exactly where they now were: witness to something alien and terrifying. Like most mortals, they had secrets to guard.

But if she'd walked in their shoes, she had discarded them for a pair that suited her better, to stretch the analogy, and she stood quickly and walked to Ybelline's side.

Severn gave her a warning glance, but he did nothing to hinder her. In his own way, he cared for Ybelline and the Tha'alani as much as Kaylin did. Possibly more.

Kaylin held out both hands, and Ybelline took them gracefully; her own were trembling. But she smiled, and if the smile itself seemed less brilliant, less effusive, it was real. There couldn't possibly be another person in the world like Ybelline Rabon'alani, but there only *had* to be one.

Ybelline did not touch Kaylin's forehead with her antennae. She spoke instead. "You were wrong, to fear for me, to fear what I might see. I understand why you care for him," she added. "He is unusual. But the secrets he kept—those secrets, Kaylin, would be understood even by the Tha'alani. And that is true of very few mortal secrets. Come." She did not surrender both of Kaylin's hands, but did free one so that she could walk, and drag the Hawk with her.

By her other side, Sanabalis walked in silence. But when he reached the Elders, he said, "The meeting may now continue."

"And the accused?"

"If you feel it necessary to cage him, that is your prerogative. I see little chance of attempted escape," he said, making his own opinion clear.

They bowed to Sanabalis's intent.

"Ybelline, what occurred on the day Gorran was killed?"

"Sergeant Kassan received a message from an old friend. It was routed to the office, to a small mirror that is keyed for specific use. As he was not one of the people for whom it was keyed, Sergeant Kassan was surprised and somewhat suspicious."

"That agrees with what he has said to the Council," Adar replied.

"His friend suggested a meeting, at a public place near the borders of the Leontine Quarter—but not inside them. Again, Sergeant Kassan was suspicious, and he asked at this point, why such a location was necessary." She drew breath.

"His friend replied, 'I fear that the Council of Elders will, upon discovery of relevant information, order the surrender of your wife, Sarabe, to the Elders' judgment. It is likely that you will keep her children, for they are not marked.'"

A hiss—a literal hiss—broke the flow of her words. Adar lifted a hand and in the high sun the glint of flexed claws carried all the warning he needed to give. Silence resumed before Ybelline spoke again.

"At this point, the Sergeant was…upset. His

attachment to his wives is as strong as any Leontine's. But…he is also an Officer of the Law. He asked his friend about the 'relevant information' in question. His friend said, 'I cannot discuss it at this location. I do not wish to alert the Elders, and I do not wish to be considered guilty of offering you any warning at all. If we meet, I will reveal what I know, and you may—perhaps—take precautions.'"

"So he agreed to this meeting."

"Yes. But he was still suspicious. He disliked the suspicion, because the man was an old friend, and if asked, he would have said he trusted him with his life. But he took some basic precautions against possible magical interference, and other unlikely difficulties. He had confidence in his ability to handle a physical fight."

"And the nature of those precautions?"

"I am not at liberty to detail them, as it involves the internal affairs of the Halls of Law," she replied smoothly.

Adar glanced at Sanabalis, and Sanabalis nodded.

"He then waited until the appointed time, and he went to meet his friend."

"He took none of his Hawks with him?"

"No. He told no one. If the Elders had been invoked, it would have been considered a Caste matter, and even if danger did arise in some unforeseen fashion, it would *still be* a Caste matter unless his Hawks were involved."

Adar nodded. "Prudent."

"He is Leontine," she replied. "He is a Hawk, but he is Leontine." She said it with more force than she had yet used, although her expression seemed the same calm expression she always wore.

"He met his friend at a pub. It was midday, and therefore very sparsely occupied. His friend was seated and waiting for him. When he saw his friend, he knew something was wrong. He wasn't certain what, but he knew." She paused, and then added, "The closest Barrani word would be scent—he scented danger."

Adar nodded gravely, as if this made sense.

"He approached the table, took a chair, tried to relax."

Kaylin snorted. She could imagine just how much relaxation he achieved. She wondered how much of the tabletop he'd shredded while making the effort.

"The man asked after his wife and children, and in particular after Sarabe. The Sergeant's replies were terse and neutral. And then the Leontine said, 'We have reason to believe that Marai has borne a child.'"

There was a sudden, deafening silence from the Elders. Kaylin, braced for bad news, felt herself beginning to crouch, and straightened her legs, moving her hands away from her daggers.

"And the Sergeant's reaction?"

"He said 'Impossible. She is not even married.'"

"What was he thinking?"

Ybelline's frown was slight, but it clouded her face. She turned to Sanabalis and said, "I do not believe it is relevant."

"Overruled."

She hesitated, and then said, "Loosely translated? 'Damn.' He was, however, surprised."

Adar looked as if he would question her further, but he fell silent instead. He was thoughtful, watching her face, the slight curve of her lips, the obvious antennae.

"'We believe,' his friend said, 'that the child is a boy.'"

All of the Elders now looked at Sanabalis, some with dread, some with no expression at all. Sanabalis, however, looked at Ybelline.

"The Sergeant said nothing, and after a moment, the friend said, 'We expected you might have some information about this, Marcus. One of your Hawks was said to have attended the birth. Did she say nothing of it to you?'

"To which the Sergeant responded, truthfully, 'No.'"

"The friend was silent, and the Sergeant—moved."

"Moved?"

"He leaped off his chair and away from his table, grabbing the edge of the nearest table and flipping it sideways. He rolled behind it."

Kaylin smiled. She had rarely seen Marcus in action—but that had Marcus written all over it.

"Why?" Adar asked.

"Instinct," Ybelline replied serenely. "It saved his life. There wasn't much left of the table. The payment for damages to the pub is still outstanding, and he regrets that."

"What was he fighting?"

"A Leontine," she replied. Her expression grew remote, as if she had moved away from them all while standing in place. "To the eyes of the barman and the pub's owner, that was all he fought. To his own eyes, on one level. But on another, because he was prepared, he could see… shadow.

"And because he could see the shadows clearly, he understood what the Elders in tribes across the plains fear. He understood the significance of the marked, and understood why they were exterminated. And he understood, as well, that Sarabe, marked but nonetheless his wife, would be in danger.

"He called out to his friend," she continued, still at a remove. "He called out three names. Only one is the name you call him," she said, "and I did not think it germane to press for further knowledge."

Adar lifted a hand. "It was not germane," he replied, "and I thank you for your hesitance. But if he understood the nature of what he faced, why did he call out?"

"They were friends," she said starkly. "And he could not—not completely—believe that his friend was no longer there. Controlled, yes. Enspelled, yes. Possibly enslaved—but not absent. He took some injuries in the fight because of this," she added quietly.

"But he killed the—the abomination."

"Yes. In the end, he killed. But there were Leontine witnesses in the bar by the end of the fight. Witnesses who had not been there at its beginning. He understood, then, that the death was a sacrifice, and he was its intended victim."

"And he said nothing."

"No."

Adar was silent for a moment. "I see." He turned, then, and offered Sanabalis a deep bow. "Eldest," he said. "We will deliberate, now. We thank you for your intervention."

Sanabalis nodded in return. "How much time will these deliberations require?"

"I am not certain. There is much to discuss."

"There is much that is relevant to the Emperor," Sanabalis replied in turn. "We will wait." ·

"Rennick is going to kill us," Kaylin told Sanabalis as they stood together some distance from the Elders. Ybelline had taken a seat along one of the curved stone benches. She was silent.

"While I would like to see him make the attempt," the Dragon Lord replied, "I took some precautions before I left the Palace. He is aware that you will be somewhat tardy."

"Did you tell him why?"

"No. I'm certain you'll—what is the phrase among your kind? Ah, yes. Think of something."

Leontine growls punctuated the otherwise silent day; the sun began its march toward the horizon while they listened. Kaylin heard snatches of conversation, but never quite enough to make sense of; her Leontine belonged to the Pridlea's hearth. She did, however, pick up a few of the more familiar phrases she occasionally used.

She glanced at Marcus. He remained standing where he had stood while Ybelline examined him; he hadn't moved an inch. His hands were by his sides, and his eyes were closed, probably because he was listening. He had stood there for hours, and could probably stand there for several more. They hadn't insisted that he return to his cage; they hadn't really spoken to him at all.

He didn't draw their attention to this oversight.

But when the Elders were done, his eyes opened.

Adar approached him in silence. The Elders followed.

"Marcus son of Horus, you are called before the Council." He spoke in very slow High Barrani.

Marcus nodded.

"We have considered the circumstances with care," Adar said, "and it is our opinion that, in choosing silence, you have endangered the kin."

Marcus nodded again.

"But if you have sidestepped an ancient law, you have done so because you have chosen to follow laws equally ancient. The laws of the Pridlea," he added. "The blame is ours, and we accept it. We should have ordered the deaths of Sarabe and Marai when they were presented to Council at birth. We did not. And because we did not, you were left little choice in the matter. You are a man. A man does not abandon his wives.

"You understand the threat we face, Marcus. You are not an Elder, but we ask you now what you would do, were you to carry the weight and responsibility of the tribe."

"If I were in your position, and I had decided that Sarabe and Marai must die," Marcus replied, without expression, "I would kill me."

"And would you decide that their deaths are necessary?"

"No."

Adar stepped forward until he was within arm's reach of the Sergeant. "No?"

"No. We failed to protect Marai. The failure is *ours*."

"She had a son."

"Yes. But she was not married, and she was adopted by no Pridlea. She was left to fend for herself. She is not tainted by the Shadows. Or she was not. And Sarabe has borne girls, and their births were registered. None of them are marked. They have lived their lives by the whim and rules of the Elders, and they have lived them as well as they can. Were I you, Adar, I would hunt the shadow-spawn, and I would kill him. If it were possible. But I would not destroy two innocent women to appease the wrath of Dragons."

"Even though you have seen for yourself the truth of the ancient story, and the danger."

"Even so."

Adar was silent for a moment. "The tainted one must be stopped," he said at last. "And a Pridlea must be found for Marai—one that meets the Elders' approval. Sarabe is, as you say, without blame. Her existence is not without risk, but it is a risk that we are—for the sake of peace between the Emperor and our kin—willing to accept. If the Eldest accepts it," he added, glancing toward Sanabalis.

"The Dragon Court is not without its misgivings," he replied slowly. "But the continued existence of the only Leontine to serve the Halls of Law is marginally more valuable to the Emperor than the death of the marked. The tainted one was not born within the city. He might not have been born within the Empire. Some investigations are ongoing with regards to this, but they do not concern the Caste Court at present."

Kaylin could see the sudden sagging of Marcus's shoulders, could hear the breath that he had been holding as he slowly, slowly let go. But he kept something in reserve, for he nodded warily, as if waiting for the other shoe to drop.

"Very well. If it is acceptable to the Eldest, it is

acceptable to the Elders. In these things, we take their lead."

Marcus nodded again, still silent, still wary.

"But the child—his son—must die."

"No!"

As one man, they swiveled to look at Kaylin.

"The child has done *nothing wrong*. How can he? He's a *baby!*"

They stared at her for a long moment, and then a few of them glanced at Marcus. Marcus was massaging his temples and, yes, showing his fangs. It was the universal sign of frustration in Leontines.

"Private," he said, a warning growl underpinning the familiar word.

"No," she said. It was a different no; it didn't sound as if it had been torn out of a place so deep it had left a wound on exit.

"It is not your place—"

"It *is* my place. I helped deliver the baby. There was *no one else* there. I licked the birth fluids from him. His name is in part *my* name."

"He is not your child."

"No? And Sarabe's children are not Kayala's?"

"There is a difference."

"There is no difference. They didn't bear those daughters, but they were there to catch the babies when they were born. Even you weren't present," she added. "Marai asked for me. I was there.

"And I claim the right of Pridlea law. I won't just step aside and wait for his death."

"The Ancient Laws supersede—"

"You just told Marcus that primal law counts for

something. That it is as old, and as honorable, as—as anything else. I believe that," she said grimly. "I also believe that it's my duty to defend the helpless. I have the right of a mother. I have the responsibility of a Hawk." She folded her arms carefully. It kept her hands from her daggers.

"The tainted," Adar said almost gently, "are not recognized at birth as kin. They are kinless, and they are motherless."

She snorted. She stopped herself from using the choice Leontine phrase that was hovering on the edge of her tongue by dint of pure will.

And Lord Sanabalis spoke.

The hair on the back of Kaylin's neck rose and she felt an answering tingle from the skin beneath it. From the skin on her arms, her thighs, her back. She heard his voice, and *felt* it. He was not speaking Leontine. Or Elantran. Or any tongue she could recognize.

But she recognized it anyway. It had been the language that he had first spoken when he had disembarked from their carriage into the crowded Leontine streets what seemed half a lifetime ago.

She could not see the words the way she had that day. They were not the same words, she thought, although the sound of each syllable was resonant with strength, intent, power.

The Elders forgot her. They forgot Marcus. They fell, slowly, to their knees before the standing Dragon, with his flashing eyes and his trailing beard of frost that made a lie of the infirmity of age.

When he had finished, and it was a short speech in comparison with the telling of the long tale of their creation, he bowed to them all and rose. "Private, I believe you are late."

She shook herself, coming back to the present. "What did you tell them?"

"The truth," he replied wearily.

"Which one?"

"That anything that knows life—anything at all—can be corrupted or swayed from its purpose." He offered a hand to Ybelline, and she accepted it gracefully. "Sergeant Kassan is to remain with the Elders," he said, "until the tainted is either contained or destroyed."

"But—but why?"

"Because you would not scruple to hold the city hostage for the sake of your convictions. And because I do not think we will come to the tainted in time without your aid."

"The child—"

"I will not lie to you, Kaylin. The child is safe—for now. But his fate is yet to be determined, and when it is, it will be by the Emperor. Who cares nothing, in the end, for the Pridlea laws or your personal loyalties."

CHAPTER

20

Ybelline shared the carriage back to the Palace. Sanabalis was not, and had never been, small; Kaylin was wedged between his bulk and the door, while Ybelline and Severn sat opposite.

"Aren't we going the wrong way?" Kaylin asked Sanabalis.

"No."

"I think we missed the turnoff to the Tha'alani Quarter."

"There are severe restrictions on traffic in that Quarter," the Dragon Lord replied, "but even if there were not, that would not be our destination. Ybelline Rabon'alani is to accompany you to your meeting with Mr. Rennick."

"Oh." She had almost forgotten Rennick.

"Your time with Mr. Rennick will be severely curtailed over the next few days," Sanabalis continued. "But

Ybelline has graciously consented to oversee his work
in your absence."

"Is he aware of this?"

"Not yet."

"And we're already late."

"He is less likely to frown on that than your Sergeant. Your current Sergeant," he added. "And if he
does shout or throw things—for which he is famed in the
kitchens—he nevertheless dislikes overweening pride
in authority figures. He will, however, accept it from
the Emperor."

"He'd have to. He's still alive."

Rennick must have crawled his way to the door, he
took so long to open it. Kaylin had a suspicion that
he wouldn't have answered at all if Sanabalis had not
cleared his throat. In the lovely, cavernous heights of
the Palace halls, it sounded suspiciously like a roar.

She wasn't quite sure what to expect from Rennick,
because she and Severn were, at best estimate, almost
four hours late. While this was not entirely unheard-of
in the office, even Kaylin recognized that days this late
generally caused starvation due to lack of employment.

But Rennick stared into the hall, first at Sanabalis,
and then at the Tha'alani woman who stood at his side.
Sanabalis's brow lifted—it was a subtle motion—and
Rennick, whose mouth had opened slightly, bowed instead of speaking. He rose and said, "I'm sorry—it's a
bit messy. I wasn't expecting guests."

"Kaylin and Severn were expected, surely?" Ybelline
asked.

"Well, yes—but they're Hawks. They're not exactly guests. Speaking of which," he added, "you're late."

Kaylin nodded. "We were waiting for Ybelline."

"And you didn't think to inform me?"

"It would have been a good idea, but there were other things on our mind at the time. Can we come in?"

"Yes. There's not a lot of visible floor, but you don't have to worry about what you step on. Unless it squeals or snaps."

He fully opened the door, and Kaylin shrugged. As mess went, it was pretty clean. Granted, she couldn't see the carpet. But the only thing that covered it was paper and books.

Rennick had busied himself shoving similar crumpled pieces off the surface of the large dining table, and from there, off the seats of various chairs. He pulled one of these out and gestured to Ybelline, who took it gracefully. Kaylin and Severn found their own chairs.

"I will leave you all to the matters at hand," Sanabalis said, eyeing one of the slender chairs with some disdain. "Private, Corporal, I will send Lord Tiamaris to retrieve you should we receive word that your services are required elsewhere."

"Hey!" Rennick shouted, before Sanabalis could touch the large, gleaming handle on the door. "They just arrived. Late, I might add."

"Yes. If all goes well, you will have their full attention—their full, *respectful* attention—for the remainder of the day. If it does not, Ybelline has graciously agreed to aid you in their stead. Since she *is* the Castelord of the Tha'alani, and she is noted for her ability to tolerate other races, you should be able to obtain any information you require from her."

Rennick looked like he wanted to argue—but Rennick always looked like that. He did however manage to snap his jaw shut before anything unfortunate could fall out of his mouth. Lord Sanabalis apparently tolerated his frequent outbursts with equanimity, but you probably didn't want to rely on that forever. Not with Dragons.

"What have you been up to?" Rennick asked, when Sanabalis had opened the door and closed it from the other side.

"Oh, same old, same old," Kaylin replied.

"Which means you're not going to tell me."

"Pretty much. It was Hawk duty, if that helps."

Rennick had finished what he called a rough draft. It sat before him in as neat a pile as office paperwork usually sat in. He started to hand it to Kaylin, stopped himself, and almost sighed. "Ybelline?" he said.

She nodded.

"This is a second attempt at writing to order. Would you care to read it?"

She glanced at Kaylin, but it was a quick glance, and it didn't stay on Kaylin's face long enough for Kaylin to reply in kind.

"Yes. I'm curious. I understand that this has been difficult for you," she said, "and I understand why the Emperor thinks it necessary. I also understand that we are not its intended audience, and I will do my best to keep this in mind." She held out her hand, and he placed the night's work—the long night's work, by the look of his stubble and the gray circles under his eyes—into her hands. Then he sat back into his chair and stretched like a cat.

Ybelline read. She was meticulous in her handling of the pages—far more than Rennick himself. But her expression—or rather, the total lack of it—was making Rennick nervous. Kaylin guessed this because it was making *her* nervous, and she hadn't written the damn thing. It was almost torture to watch, and Kaylin alleviated this by standing and pacing between the small mounds of paper all over the floor.

But when Ybelline cleared her throat, Kaylin took her seat again. Severn, damn him, hadn't really moved.

Her first question surprised them.

"May I bring my people to see this play?"

Her first reaction—that this was a bad idea in a hundred different ways—didn't escape before Rennick spoke, possibly because she couldn't decide which of the hundred to start with.

"Of course," he replied. And he smiled. It was a tired smile, but for a moment, he looked genuinely pleased.

"I liked the orphans," Ybelline continued. "We are not without accidents or illnesses, and many of our young have faced life without parents. But not this way." There was compassion in the tone that didn't dip toward pity. "Some of my kin might understandably wonder why you placed the orphans in the Quarter, but I think that such a complaint would not be reasonable." She turned to Kaylin, then. "There is a note in the margins—your foundlings are to act?"

"Not all of them," he replied. "And, boy, is *that* going to cause trouble."

Ybelline nodded. "Is that all, then? Will this play be performed soon?" And now, into the smoothness of her voice, cracks appeared. She was weary. Or worried. Probably both.

"With some luck," Rennick replied. "I have actors in mind for some of the parts, but the rest?" He shrugged. "I'll have to have auditions. I have to find the right people—*exactly* the right people—to play the Tha'alani."

"I would suggest some of my kin, but I do not think they would be well-suited to what I understand of your acting."

"Lord, no. We want them to think humans can be sane," Rennick said cheerfully.

"She knows *us,*" Kaylin said with a snort. "I'd say Ybelline, at least, is a lost cause."

Rennick chuckled, but the chuckle lost steam. He looked at Ybelline for a long moment, and then held out his hand; she placed the play into it.

"Rennick," Kaylin said. "Don't even *think* it."

"Don't you have somewhere you have to be?" Rennick replied. He flipped through the first few pages. Stopped, splitting the stack as if it were a deck of flimsy cards, and set the smaller pile to one side.

"Not yet, we don't. Rennick—"

A knock interrupted her. Rennick grinned at her glare. "Providence," he said cheerfully, "is on my side. Go on, answer it."

"What I'd like to know," Kaylin said to Tiamaris, "is how you can even *receive* a message from Nightshade. He's a fieflord. He's not exactly an Imperial Subject, and

I always thought the Emperor frowned on people who lived in the boundaries of his Empire who weren't."

"If the Emperor could in safety clear out the fiefs," Tiamaris replied as they trudged along the emptying streets, "you would have grown up in a very different world. If the fieflords do not serve the Emperor's will or law, they also serve no others."

"That you know of."

"That we know of."

"Which still doesn't answer my question."

"No. There *are* ways of sending messages you might be familiar with. They involve no mirrors and no magic." Dragons were not as good as Barrani at sarcasm, but Tiamaris was cutting it close.

"And you knew it was genuine because?"

Tiamaris had stopped by the bridge that crossed the Ablayne. He pointed, and Kaylin saw a familiar, armed Barrani waiting on the other side. Andellen.

He bowed to Kaylin as she approached. It was a pure Barrani court gesture; it was graceful, and it was absolute. It was also a little too serious.

"Andellen, what's happened?"

"Lord Andellen," Tiamaris said, bowing in turn. It was not as low a bow, and it was not as perfect, but it held genuine respect.

Andellen's bow had been an obeisance. To make this clear, he offered a nod to Severn, who was silent.

"Lord Nightshade sends word," Andellen replied, nodding at Tiamaris yet somehow implying that Kaylin had the entirety of his attention. "He requests your presence in the Castle, but also requests that you be prepared to move. Corporal Handred," he added, "he requests your presence as well, if you are available."

"I'm here," Severn replied. "How bad is it?" he said, in a level voice.

Andellen shifted his gaze toward the falling sun. "Not yet as bad as it will become," he said gravely. "If there is anything you require, retrieve it. I will wait."

Severn glanced at Kaylin. It was a subtle glance, but she understood what he was asking. Quietly, she rolled up her sleeves and touched the luminescent gems that studded her bracer in such an ornate row.

In the silence the click was like distant thunder. She handed the bracer to Severn, and he accepted it wordlessly.

Andellen said, "Lord Tiamaris, did you ever study astrology?"

Tiamaris glanced at the sky. It was cloudless, although the heat-haze of the summer months smudged the air somehow. "The moons," he said.

"That is our suspicion."

"They will not be full this eve, but they are close."

"It is why my Lord feels this eve is critical."

"I concur. Private?"

Kaylin said, "Let's go."

She accepted the passage through the portcullis as if it were of no consequence. She didn't have space left in her thoughts for the luxury of complaint. She accepted being dumped more or less on all fours on the marble floor of the hallway, and accepted, with as much grace as she had ever managed, Severn's silent offer of help.

She took the hand he held out and levered herself to her feet.

Nightshade was waiting. He wore robes, not armor, and she thought this was a good sign. Until she saw the hilt of the sword that hung by his side. A shorter man would have trailed it across the polished floor. Even a taller man might have looked somehow encumbered by it. It was one of the three named Dragonkillers. Kaylin, who had never named an inanimate object in her life, couldn't remember what it was called—couldn't remember at this point if she had ever known.

Tiamaris, however, looked at the sword, and the inner membranes of his eyes rose, muting the shade of orange the bronze was quickly adopting. But he said nothing, did nothing.

"Kaylin," Lord Nightshade said. "Lord Tiamaris. Corporal. Accept my apologies for the lack of proper hospitality."

"You found them," Kaylin replied. It wasn't the Barrani thing to say, but the Barrani thing to say would probably take two hours of pointless, pretty verbiage.

He lifted a perfect brow, and a half smile formed on his lips. "As you say," he replied. The smile vanished, as if it had never existed at all. "I am not certain we've found *them*. We have, however, found at least the female Leontine."

"Marai," Kaylin whispered.

"Yes. But be cautious, Kaylin. I do not know if she would respond to that name should you attempt to use it."

"What do you mean?" she asked, in the sinking tone of voice that made the question rhetorical.

He didn't reply. After a pause to let the non-reply sink in, he said, "We must leave, now, and in some haste. Andellen will have gathered some of my guards; and they will accompany us. Attempt to remember that *I* am Lord here. Andellen owes you a debt that you cannot conceive of, and he will tolerate anything you say or do. This will be understood by those who serve—who must serve—me. But I owe you no such debt."

"And they'll understand that just as well."

"Indeed."

Kaylin nodded grimly. If she could file reports with Mallory, she was certain she could do anything.

"Be wary, Kaylin," he added in a softer voice. "Be aware that there are those you cannot save."

The men who served Nightshade *were* armored. Even Andellen. It made a stark contrast between the men who followed and the one who commanded. It was also interesting to observe their reactions. They were, as expected, silent and deferential to their Lord. They were wary of Tiamaris—not that she blamed them, although she silently lauded their good sense—and they were…wary of Kaylin. Not in the same way. Men who see walking death—which, for the purpose of this observation, was the Dragon—tended to be wary in the *I don't want to die* way. They weren't that kind of wary around Kaylin. But she spent whole days not remembering the mark Nightshade had placed on her cheek, and this wasn't going to be one of them.

Severn, on the other hand, seemed to be entirely beneath their notice. It's not a mistake that Nightshade would have made.

In turn, the guards seemed entirely beneath Tiamaris's notice, and they didn't seem to be insulted by the lack of attention.

Nightshade walked past the guards. Kaylin followed, but his stride was longer and she had to work to match it. "Wait," she said.

He turned. "Andellen."

Andellen bowed briskly and broke ranks to join them.

"Kaylin Neya is, for the duration of our excursion, your responsibility. Answer any questions she poses, if they do not compromise our security. She is, of course, human, and is abrupt and somewhat graceless. You will overlook these flaws."

"Lord," Andellen replied, bowing again. The fall of his hair framed his face like a cowl made of dark light. "Lord Kaylin," he said, and bowed to her.

She bit back the urge to refute the title. While it had become a running office joke, she understood that to these men, it meant far more than her squirming, annoyed embarrassment. To be embarrassed by it at all would be an insult.

"Lord Andellen," she replied in kind, accenting his name in the High Barrani fashion. As much as she hated the language—and given the volumes of legalese that were *all* written in High Barrani there was a lot to hate— it forced a certain form and structure on her speech. Oh, she'd never be *good* at it, and it would never come as easily as Leontine—but High Barrani didn't have a lot of unfortunate curse words.

"Lord Nightshade will be occupied for some time. His sense of the fief is not ours, and in this case, it *is* required. If you have questions you wish answered, I will attempt to answer them."

"Are we going to stay in this fief?"

One dark brow rose. Clearly, whatever question he'd been expecting to field, it wasn't this one.

His lips curved slightly. "You have a Hawk's instincts." He began to walk. She fell in beside him, and Severn joined them, walking to the other side of the Barrani Lord.

"Was she human?"

"I don't understand the question."

Kaylin frowned, and realized that the Barrani word she'd spoken was *mortal,* not *human.* They used it to refer to humans so often, it was an easy mistake to make. "Did she still look like a Leontine?"

His silence was telling; he clearly knew the answer and just as clearly was reluctant to give it.

"No," he said at last. "I did not see her in the flesh. I saw what the mirrors saw, no more. But to my eyes, no."

"How did he know it was her, then?"

"He is Nightshade," Andellen replied gravely.

It took a moment for the weight of the sentence to sink roots. When it did, she was silent for at least two blocks.

"What does he want me to do?" she asked at last.

"Have you ever ventured across the borders of Nightshade?"

"Yes." The single word was as flat and hard as a dungeon door, and just about as inviting.

"Not across the river," he began.

"No. It wasn't."

"It is not considered safe—or wise—to cross the boundaries," Andellen said softly. "And if you did indeed cross them, and you are here, you were either lucky or deaf."

She said nothing.

"Kaylin."

She looked across Andellen's carefully composed expression, and met Severn's gaze. She looked away. Took a breath. "We're going to the edge of the fief."

"Yes."

"What do you expect to find there?"

"If we are both very unlucky and correct, a Dragon," he replied. If Tiamaris, who kept an easy pace with Nightshade several yards ahead, heard the comment, he didn't respond.

"And if we're lucky?"

"We attract his attention when we are prepared for it."

Which, to Kaylin's mind, would be never.

"I'm supposed to catch his attention."

"If necessary, yes." There was a subtle hesitation before Andellen spoke again. "Lord Nightshade will not leave the fief."

"But we're going—"

"Yes. It is possible for him to leave, but at this time, it is not deemed safe. He is not a prisoner here," Andellen added. "But if our enemy is stirring, if it is as we suspect, he cannot afford to be so far away from the core of his power."

"So he's just going to stand on the edge of the fief while we do—whatever it is we're supposed to do?"

"Yes. You will be the bridge," he said. "If it is possible."

"Which fief are we headed toward?"

"It has no name that we speak," Andellen replied. "And in truth, very little of Nightshade borders it. We do not travel there. I think very few who live do."

Severn was tense. She could see it in the way he moved. His stride was graceful, but there was a deliberation about his movements that made the entire street seem like a battlefield.

Which, in an hour or two, it could well be; the sun was on the wrong side of noon, and setting fast. She shivered in the heat.

"You can hear them?" Severn asked.

She started to say no—and stopped. Because she *could* hear the rumbling howl of distant Ferals. And it was still daylight by anyone's definition, even if morning felt like it had happened three weeks ago.

"How much do you know about the fiefs?" he asked her as they continued to walk. The streets cleared like parting water around a moving, dark rock.

What did she know about the fiefs, now? There were seven—or so it was believed. Of the seven fieflords, three were rumored to be Barrani; she was certain of only one, and couldn't even be certain that the other two weren't, in the Barrani sense of the word, dead. The Law was the fieflord's will. Enforcing the Law was the privilege of power. Had the Emperor been different, though, would the rest of the city not be a richer, more populated version of the fiefs?

"We grew up there," she said. "All we ever wanted to

do was cross the river." But she was not across the river now. She was walking the streets of Nightshade, as terrifying to the people who had never managed to escape as any of Nightshade's men had been to her when she had been a child.

"I wanted to arrest them—the fieflords—when I was made a Hawk. It was the first thing I wanted to do."

"And did you research ways you might do this?"

"Not exactly."

"Not exactly?"

"I badgered Marcus about it for two or three weeks."

Severn almost laughed. She could see the brightness of the sound in the widening of his mouth, but it didn't escape.

"I stopped when he threatened to eat my liver, after removing it slowly first."

He did chuckle at that, and she joined in.

"But he said no. He asked me to drop it, and in truth, Severn, I think I wanted to. I wanted it to be someone else's problem. I wanted to live in Elantra, not Nightshade."

"There are seven fiefs that we know of," Severn said.

"That we know of. If that much of what we know can actually be classified as knowledge, not myth."

"The Wolves have investigated the fiefs before. Sometimes people realize they're being hunted. They don't have the time to flee the city, and they're smart enough not to trust the gates or the closer inns in any case. But they know the fiefs are outside of the Law."

"So are the Wolves, when they hunt."

"I won't get into philosophical arguments about the nature of the warrants the *Emperor* issues. We hunt, they run. Some have been smart enough to cross the river. Those, we almost inevitably lose." He hesitated. "The fiefs are not the same in size. One or two are quite small."

"And you know who the fieflords are?"

"No. Not in the same way I know Nightshade. I think you have to live in one to understand it fully." He paused again and said, "To our understanding, the fiefs may change lords—but they don't change boundaries. It's not like the Quarters in the city, where the merchant's quarter has spilled out and taken over streets that were once residential—fief boundaries are fixed. They don't move."

She nodded slowly. "It...it agrees with something Nightshade said. About the fief, and its boundaries. But the fiefs border each other, don't they?"

"Nearest the city, yes. The streets demark the boundaries the way they do in any other neighborhood. But Kaylin? We're not heading toward the city, or the fiefs that border the city. It's considered unsafe to cross the boundaries of a fief in any case. Some of that is superstition—it seems foolish and hysterical to those who live without hunting Ferals and other night creatures."

"Where are we going, Severn?"

"In," he replied. "Not far."

"The Wolves went in?"

"Yes. They traveled through Nightshade."

"The way we're traveling now."

"With fewer numbers, no armor, and much less obvious weaponry, but yes, they took this route. I knew this fief," he said. "And they captured as much as I knew in a Tha'alani memory crystal."

"You let them?"

"I volunteered. They chose to travel in Nightshade where possible. They crossed the border of Nightshade into Barren, to the west, and Liatt and Farlonne to the east and southeast."

"Liatt and Farlonne border the city, at least in some places."

He nodded. "Nightshade and Barren have the easiest access to the rest of the city, and the widest borders city-side."

"The fiefs are almost circular."

"Irregular, but yes. Opposite Nightshade, also border-ing some part of the city, are Durant and Candallar. It is Farlonne and Candallar that are ruled, or so it is said, by Barrani."

"So it's said?"

"Ask in the High Court," he replied. "But don't be surprised if you receive no answer. Nightshade is Out-caste, but in some fashion, acknowledged. They would ride to war on him, if they could—but they accept his existence as the insult it is. The others…are less clear."

"Are they even alive?"

"Our operatives were not given instructions to visit the fieflords," he replied. "Merely to map out what they could of the fiefs. Much of what the Halls knows comes from those surveillance missions."

"That's six," she told him.

"Yes. Six."

"But there are seven fiefs."

"The operatives who traveled in the six returned. The operatives who traveled to the seventh—and it's not clear to me that something as simple as a seventh fief even exists—following the path and the map taken from my memories, came this way. We don't know what they found," he said. "They never escaped to make their reports."

CHAPTER 21

The streets in this part of the fief were narrower than the streets that bordered the city proper. They were also unfamiliar to Kaylin. The houses that overhung the street—and that was the right word—looked as if they wouldn't comfortably support a family of mice or a colony of cockroaches. Humans, on the other hand, could find a way to wedge themselves into anything; she could see glimpses of faces peering down through broken shutters. Only glimpses, though. No one was stupid enough to throw the shutters open for a better view.

Kaylin wouldn't have been. It was obvious that Lord Nightshade was in the street below, and attracting Ferals seemed safer and smarter.

But the road itself, such as it was, wasn't in good repair, and it was clear that wagons didn't travel here. Horses probably wouldn't like it much either, although Kaylin didn't ride, and couldn't be certain. She distrusted horses on principle. They were larger and faster than she was, and she seriously doubted that without their consent she'd have much control over what they did.

The Halls of Law *did* own horses, of course. The Swords were all required to ride them. Or at least to learn *how.* The Hawks weren't, and it was a distinction she was grateful for. Among other things, she really didn't like the way horses smelled. That, and the first time she'd been introduced to one, it had tried to step on her foot. There'd been a lot of snickering about that, but thankfully, none of it around Marcus. If *he* was too close to the horses, they were skittish and spent most of the time with at least two of their hooves off the ground.

"Lord Kaylin," Andellen said. There was perhaps a touch less deference in the title than there had been. She had the grace to flush.

"Sorry. I was thinking about horses."

"You ride?"

"Only in carriages that Teela isn't driving."

His lips creased in a slightly strained smile. "What do you see, Lord Kaylin?" he asked, and lifted his arm.

She frowned, as if it were a trick question. "Ratty streets with what used to be cobbled stone. Dead weeds. Buildings that should have fallen down half a century ago."

He waited. When it was clear she'd said as much as she was going to, he turned to Severn. "Corporal?"

"I see what she sees, with perhaps less disdain."

"What do you see, Andellen?"

"What you see," he said softly. He lifted a hand in command, and the men, who were keeping pace, stilled instantly. They began to fan out across the width of the narrow street, for reasons that were unclear to Kaylin.

"Lord," Andellen said quietly. The emphasis on the single word made clear to whom he spoke.

Nightshade turned. He had walked farther down the road than any of his men; only Tiamaris accompanied him. But when he stopped, the Dragon stopped as well, facing out and down the street, where Nightshade turned, at last, to the Barrani guards.

Kaylin took the opportunity to approach Tiamaris; when she was five feet from his back, he lifted a hand, the gesture almost exactly the one that Andellen had used. She stopped walking. "Tiamaris?" she said.

"Kaylin."

"What do you see?"

His silence was almost tangible. It was his only answer.

"Kaylin," Nightshade said. "Leave him. His task here is subtle and it requires concentration."

She walked back to Nightshade. "What is his task?"

"He attempts to see beyond the boundaries of my fief," Nightshade replied. "And what he sees—or does not see—will tell us much."

"Will any of it be useful?"

"Perhaps. Information is useful in unpredictable ways. He seeks some sign of the Outcaste Dragon."

"And of Marai?"

"He will not be able to sense Marai unless she is very, very close."

"She isn't here."

"No. But she was, and she traveled this road. She did not travel it quickly, and she did not travel it unharmed."

Kaylin opened her mouth. Closed it again.

"But the injuries she took were less, by far, than those she caused. If it eases you at all, she met Ferals."

"It does," Kaylin said. "Thank you."

"What do you see, Kaylin?"

"Why does everyone keep asking me that? I see a street, and we're standing in the middle of it."

"A street."

She nodded. "You?"

"I see the boundary of the fief of Nightshade," he replied. "Lord Tiamaris is standing on its edge. Beyond it? There is a road. It continues. But it is flat and illusory to me. Where it goes, I cannot go."

"You've left your fief before."

"Indeed. But never in that direction. Beyond this border is the heart of the fiefs, Kaylin. The fiefs surround it, bordering both the Emperor's city and each other—but they do not penetrate it. I ask what you see because in the fiefs, ancient words have power, and you are wearing more of them across your body than I have seen in any one place that is not my Castle."

She hesitated.

"You see what you expect to see," he continued. "See, instead, what is there. If you have any hope of finding your Leontine, it lies beyond Tiamaris." He lifted a hand and brushed her cheek gently; she felt the mark on her face tingle and cool. "Go."

She nodded, wordless.

"Not you, Corporal, not yet. You will know when it is safe, and she will be standing beside Lord Tiamaris, who holds her in some regard. Trust him. If it is difficult, remind yourself that *I* am doing the same."

* * *

She took a breath, straightened her shoulders and walked toward Tiamaris. He heard her; she knew it. But he made no sign and no further gesture. She didn't speak to him, she didn't touch him, she didn't attempt to engage him. Instead, she looked at where he'd planted his feet. Cracked stones that were fringed by straggling weeds formed a line that she could almost see, and she placed her feet on one side of them, standing beside Tiamaris. It wasn't dark, not yet; dark was a little ways off. She didn't fear Ferals here, either; the Barrani were armed and armored. But the part of Kaylin that had grown up in the fiefs feared night's fall. She could silence the child, but the fear had to be deliberately ignored—there was no reasoning with it.

She looked down the stretch of road, as Tiamaris was now doing. There she saw stones, weeds, the continuation of a line of buildings that should have toppled long ago. Flakes of paint on a worn sign. People had lived here, once.

She frowned.

"Nightshade," she said, without thinking. Thought caught up with her, and she added, "Lord Nightshade."

"Yes." His voice carried a distance.

"How long has this city been here?"

"Since before the first Barrani-Dragon war," he replied. "Why?"

"These buildings—this street—they look like they were meant to house humans. My kin."

"Indeed."

"But the fiefs—"

"Yes," he replied. "The fiefs were not always as they

stand now. There was a city here. In the heart of the fiefs, there was a palace, or so it is rumored. There were gardens, and halls that make the High Court halls seem paltry and almost worthless by comparison. Or so it is said. It is also said that there was a library contained in the heart of the city that was larger by far on the inside than on the outside, and it contained every word ever written by any race who practiced the art."

"Art?"

"The written word. The keepers of the ancient lore lived there, practiced there," he continued. "And fell there."

"Why?"

"No one yet knows," he replied. "But the fiefs… formed. The Shadows grew out of the heart of the city and into its streets, destroying—or changing—almost everything that it touched. The Ferals came, and beasts more dangerous than Ferals. I believe you have some experience with these."

She nodded.

"Wars were fought. Although to human eyes, they may not have seemed like battles. Many of my kin entered the shadowed lands, and few emerged. Some, you have seen. Those you call dead.

"Some you have never met, and if you are lucky, you never will. But I think most simply perished. Lord Tiamaris?"

Although Tiamaris did not move at all, he began to speak. "The Dragons went as well. They did not suffer the same fate as the Barrani, but many fell. And some returned changed. It was not felt, at first. The change was subtle."

She stared at the side of his head, her brows folding as she thought. "The Outcaste."

"Indeed. Kin to the Emperor, and birthed in the same fire. Yes, that is figurative, and no, I will not explain it now. If ever. He was a founding member of what has since become the Imperial Order of Mages. He was both wise and knowledgeable."

"Like the Arkon."

"As unlike the Arkon as two beings could be who could share the same race. The Arkon's specialty is entirely knowledge; he had no interest in the Arcane. But it is interesting that you mention the Royal Librarian, for they were friends, inasmuch as that word has significance among our kin.

"The Outcaste dared the heart of the fiefs, and he returned to us. He brought knowledge, and artifacts, stories of vast buildings and empty spaces; of words in the ancient tongue which he could not read but could remember. In the end, the Arkon chose to accompany him when he went back. Understand that the city is not now what it was then," he said. "And the Arkon was younger, although by our standards, still ancient. He traveled with the Outcaste and a handful of Lords, and he found some part of what had been spoken of.

"But he saw more in the words, and understood the significance of what he had seen. He will not speak of it so do not ask him."

Kaylin, who considered it a minor miracle that she'd survived meeting the Arkon once, nodded.

"It is from this second foray into the heart of the Shadows that we understood the subtlety of the Outcaste's treachery. We were ill prepared for it," he added. "And we did not have the mastery of ancient lore that he had. The Arkon waited until they had left the fiefs—which is not what we called them, then—and he confronted the Outcaste."

"With what, exactly?"

"Knowledge. Words."

"What's in there, Tiamaris?"

"Power," the Dragon Lord replied quietly. "Lord Nightshade?"

"It is rumored," Lord Nightshade said, picking up smoothly where Tiamaris left off, "that the confrontation between the Emperor and his closest kin almost destroyed the Dragon Court. It almost destroyed the Emperor. And during that time, the Barrani Lords chose to press claims, seeing weakness. It was to be a costly weakness.

"But when the wars were done, even before the wars were finished, this became the heart of the Empire. This place," he said. "By this time, we understood what it might presage.

"Some of my kin, as I have said, ventured here. Some were lost. Some…remained."

"The fieflords," she whispered.

"Even so. It was a surprise to us."

"That they would become fieflords?"

"Ah, no. That they would, or could? No. But that *humans* could? It surprised us all, I think—Barrani and Dragon alike. Some were called to the fiefs, and some fled to them. It doesn't matter, in the end—these lands, you must fight to hold, and the fight is not simply a matter of arms. The fiefs are yours, or your successor's. They do not exist without a Lord."

"But Nightshade—"

"Was ruled before my arrival. You have seen the servants who guard the doors of the Long Hall."

She swallowed, and nodded, remembering how very like statues they had been until they had scented blood.

"Here, the land and the Lord are almost one. It is ancient, this binding, and it is twisted. But it holds. No one has been called to the heart of the fiefs. Or if they have, they have not survived it."

"But…if you know all this…why were the Wolves sent?"

"The fiefs as you know them now are not what they once were," Nightshade replied. "And in any case, I cannot speak for the Emperor, and I cannot speak to his motives."

"Severn, did you know this?"

"No," he said quietly. It was the wrong kind of quiet. She wondered who had died here. Who had been lost. What they had meant to him.

"The fiefs cannot be shaped to our will," Nightshade told her. "It is not as simple as that. But where there is life, there is a solidity that defies the darkness, that erodes it. We make of what is here something mean and mundane, and by slow degree, the boundaries across the river become simple geography. People live here. They are born here, they die here. They need light and food and shelter. They require the boundaries that will give them the hope of those things. But nothing has changed or taken what lies fallow in the heart. We called it *Ravellon,* once."

"Why?"

"It is not important. What is, and believe that it is, Kaylin, is what it is called *now*."

"Because the fiefs take the names of their Lords."

"Yes."

She swallowed. "But why the Leontines?"

"Pardon?"

"Why are the Leontines significant?"

"They were changed," he replied. "At the whim of beings for whom the entire world was like Castle Nightshade. They were living vessels. Some few are born now who retain that ability. Think of them as if they were part of my Castle—malleable, subject to the whim of power and will. But living, cunning.

"They have been called before," he added, "in story and legend both. And they make Ferals look like starving kittens. If the Outcaste Dragon has summoned them here, he is ready."

"For what?"

"That, we cannot say. Only the Dragons can." His tone of voice clearly implied that it was not a question that would ever be answered by anyone who didn't want to be lunch afterward. "But we can surmise."

"You think he wants to take the—the last fief."

"I think it likely. It was our concern that he had, in fact, done just that."

"And now?"

"I think Lord Tiamaris would know. I am not entirely confident of that," he added quietly. "Nor is Lord Tiamaris."

"And what would the Outcaste be then?"

"God," Nightshade replied.

She turned back to the road. She had run out of things

to say, and the rest of her remaining questions weren't ones she wanted answers to.

The shape of a road. The broken stones. The slanted slats and open patches on roofs distant enough to be visible. Unoccupied; no glimpse of faces, no sign of movement. She frowned. A breeze blew across her cheeks, shunting strands of her hair to either side of her face. It was cool. Night cool. A reminder of winter in the fiefs. Of starvation. Of hunger.

She saw the sun above the street, but its heat was distant now. Leaning slightly into the unpleasant breeze, she lifted a hand and touched the Hawk on her surcoat. It was a symbol of flight and freedom—but conversely, it was an anchor.

It belonged, in its entirety, to Kaylin Neya.

She took a breath and closed her eyes. The feel of the breeze was stronger, and the mundane sight of the street no longer distracted—or frustrated—her. Instead of looking, she listened.

She couldn't have said, at first, what she was listening to. She started by listening for voices, for some sense of communication or contact, but there were no voices on the breeze. Not at first. There was the sound of dry weeds brushing up against each other; the sound of pebbles too small to have ever been rocks; the sound of…movement. Not steps against stone—but something that suggested motion.

It was the sound snakes would make, coiling against rock, if they could be heard.

She listened more intently. The Barrani had fallen silent at her back; she could make out the faint sound of breathing, the slight clinks of armor that betrayed motion, no more.

But in the distance, she heard those movements echo, gain texture and resonance. Slowly, so slowly she was hardly aware of it, the muted susurrus of whispering voices, overlapped and indistinct, could be heard.

They spoke no language she recognized.

But they spoke a language she thought she *should* recognize. Her eyes still closed, she lifted her head. "Lord Tiamaris," she said softly. "Could the Outcaste speak the ancient tongue?"

"Ancient tongue?"

"The language of the Old Ones. Sanabalis can," she added.

"No. Not when he left us. Why do you ask?" The question was much sharper than the answer had been.

"Because someone is speaking it now. Possibly more than one voice. It's not distinct enough for me to tell."

Lord Tiamaris touched her shoulder, and she opened her eyes. Opened them and almost closed them again, because what she now saw made no sense.

But wasn't that what she was supposed to see?

The road of fief continued forward, but in a gray that was leached of color. The dust brown dirt of road, the yellow green of weeds, all shades that she was familiar with—they were gone. And the buildings themselves, which had looked so solid—for decrepit, empty hovels— now seemed almost translucent, like the ghosts of the homes they had once been.

And the gray was not light or pale, but dark, night gray.

Tiamaris caught her chin between two of his fingers

and turned her face, gently, toward him. "I cannot hear as clearly as you hear, but…the words are not a good sign. Lord Nightshade, with your leave."

"You are not beholden to me, Lord Tiamaris. I am well aware that only one Lord commands your obedience."

"A habit. You have offered both hospitality and aid, and I would not overstep myself."

Lord Nightshade nodded. "You have little time, I think."

"I concur. Kaylin, stand over there."

"Over there? Why?"

"I don't want to crush you."

She started to ask him what he meant, shut her mouth and moved.

For the third time in her life, she saw a Dragon unfold.

He was red-bronze, this time, although that might have been the effect of the setting sun. His wings unfurled from his back, and shot up and out like elegant eruptions. His hands became clawed, scaled, and much, much larger. She watched in silence as his tail grew back, and his jaws grew larger, widening and lengthening.

The Barrani were still, but they were clearly uneasy; only Nightshade seemed unmoved. Then again, only Nightshade was armed with a Dragonkiller.

Tiamaris grew in height as well as length, and the shadow he cast was long and menacing.

And wrong. It was entirely wrong. The sun should have cast it in a different direction—

She opened her mouth to shout a warning, but Severn's voice was there before hers, his cry distinct.

"Tiamaris!"

The Dragon's head swiveled.

And across the boundaries of Nightshade, dark to his brightness, almost a mirror of his shape, a second Dragon emerged from the shadows and the ghostly buildings. He was solid, and he was not alone.

"You are late, hatchling," the Outcaste said.

The Barrani were in motion; she could hear their metallic steps, their utter lack of words. Tiamaris drew back, lifting a neck almost as long as he was—in his human form—tall. But the Dragon that faced him merely waited, and after a moment it became apparent why. To either side of his jet scales, which glimmered with a light that was cast by neither sun nor moon, forms appeared, coming, as he had come, from the mists of the illusory street. They were dark, as he was dark, but the light that played off his scales—the light that seemed to come from beneath their surface—did not grace them.

They were as tall as Nightshade's Barrani, and their armor was both darker and more stylized, tines rising from the bridge of their masked faces, small thorns adorning their mailed hands, their mailed shoulders. They wore helms, of course, and those helms hid everything from vision. But they were, like the streets, shades of gray, leached of color.

And they waited.

"You haven't the strength to cross this border," Tiamaris said. Kaylin was surprised that she recognized his voice; it was heavier and fuller, but somehow…somehow still his own. "You were badly injured in your flight." He stressed the last syllable.

Dragon faces didn't take well to human expressions. It should have been hard to gauge his reaction to the comment, because he didn't reply. But his eyes were bloodred, the color livid in the ebony of his massive head.

She took a step back and then held her ground. Her movement, however, drew his attention. The inner membranes of his eyes fell—she would have bet they had already fallen, given the color of those eyes. She was wrong. The eyes were the essence of blood and fire, and she could see how small her reflection in their surface was.

He drew himself up to his full height. "Have you not come to stop me?" he said, sibilance trailing the single *s* in the sentence. "Will you cower behind an Outcaste Barrani Lord?"

"He carries *Meliannos*," Tiamaris replied evenly.

The Dragon turned, for the first time, to look at the fieflord. Nightshade, arms by his sides, offered a curt nod, no more. "Impossible."

"Can you not hear its cry?" Tiamaris asked. "Even now, it demands to lose its sheath and join battle. But he wields it. It does not wield him."

"It is not the greatest of the three," the Outcaste replied. "And I have faced the greatest and survived. I do not fear it."

"Then come. We are waiting," Tiamaris replied.

The Outcaste did not move.

The armored men were likewise still.

But Kaylin felt—for just a moment—that the ground

had been pulled out from beneath her feet, leaving nothing but a long fall in its wake. She cried out, stumbling, and Severn was at her side in an instant. He caught the hand she held out, and as he did, the world returned cobbled stones and dirt to the underside of her boots. "Be careful—he's—he's—"

Nightshade gestured, no more, and she fell silent, in part because she had *no idea* what the Outcaste was doing.

But when the world had stopped spinning and she could stand on her own feet again, she looked. The buildings were slowly, slowly unraveling, as if they were made of dust motes or dandelion seeds, and the wind was blowing them away. And as they went, these particles, these shadows, she saw that the wind swept them into whirling patterns just beyond the reach of the Dragon's tail. They danced in air, lighter gray than the ground or the men who occupied it, and as they did, Kaylin recognized the strokes and dots, the crossed bars, the swirls, of written language. They were there for only a second, no more, but they left the same impression that staring at the sun will—the glare, the after-burn.

She opened her mouth, and a single word fell from her lips and echoed in the sudden stillness. *"Ravellon."*

The Outcaste looked at her then.

She stared back. She could feel the hair on the back of her neck begin to rise, and worse, could feel the sudden ache that washed across every inch of her skin—every marked inch. Her neck, her back, her arms, the inside of her thighs.

The Outcaste laughed, a wild, roaring trumpet of a sound that in no way conveyed amusement. Madness, maybe; the madness that might see a whole city in ash and cinders for the brief pleasure of dancing in the flames that consumed it.

"Will you call *me?*" he roared. "Will you dare that much, in your mortal ignorance?"

It *hurt* to stand in his glare, it hurt to stand still. Her body had already entered the subtle fold that meant she was ready for action—fight or flight.

"Try. *Try.*"

Not for the first time in her life, she struggled to keep her mouth *shut.* Memories of those other times tried to wedge themselves between Kaylin and the eyes of a Dragon Lord in his full glory. Some splinter of them—mostly of Marcus at the very edge of his fraying temper—held fast, they were that deep.

The rest scattered. She *knew* his name. Knew it the way she knew how to breathe—it was a reflex, something beneath conscious thought. But she knew that she could not speak it. Not here. Probably not *ever.*

She felt her handful of years more keenly than she had ever felt them—twenty and counting. Maybe she'd never see twenty-one. And standing, rising, on the other side of a barrier that she didn't understand, centuries glared back. Centuries, the knowledge of each year strengthening and deepening power. He was an ocean; she was a puddle.

She was rigid now, staring; she couldn't have looked away had she wanted to. And she did.

She could see in his eyes the shape of many things that Sanabalis had tried to teach her. Fire. Wind. Even water. And she could see, growing brighter and clearer as she stared, the shape of something so complicated it made the marks on her skin look like smudges.

She knew what it was.

She might even have started to try to put it into something as simple as words—foreign, strange words, but words nonetheless, had Lord Nightshade not spoken her name.

Kaylin.

She felt it as a tug, as a demand, as a question. Felt its insistence, the subtle strength of its hold. Kaylin Neya. A name she had invented for herself on the spur of the moment, a way of hiding.

She'd been so good at hiding, it had become its own truth.

She tried to answer.

She tried to speak Nightshade's name, his true name.

She stopped, because she couldn't recall it. At this moment, it was too slight.

He said something short in Barrani that she didn't understand. But she understood what she heard next: the sound, the familiar sound, of a sword leaving its sheath.

Meliannos blazed in the evening sky.

And Kaylin understood then why someone would name their weapon.

CHAPTER 22

If fire could be a thing with tongues of ice, *Meliannos* burned. Seeing it drawn, seeing the naked blade, Kaylin wondered at the sheath that could contain it and remain intact—but it was a brief thought; the rest of her body was already in motion. She *ran* to intercept Nightshade, because he was already on the border of the fief he ruled.

She didn't understand what bound them, fief and man, but she knew that something essential would unravel if he left.

"He does not yet own the heartland," Nightshade said, divining the thought, replying to it as she grabbed his sword arm in both of her hands and tried to slow his stride.

"Neither do you!"

"No," he said softly. "But you, little one, I claim."

The Outcaste had not moved an inch since the sword had cleared its scabbard, but the pressure of his gaze was gone from Kaylin, lingering only in the ache of her skin, which felt both new and raw.

The Emperor will know that you've drawn that sword.

Yes, he replied, his internal voice so much closer, so much clearer, than his spoken words. *He will know. He has always known. This is not the first time that I have drawn it in this fief. It will not be the last. You have seen it blooded,* he added, *but you have never seen its fire before blood quenches it. He will hear it, even in the Palace. And he will know why.*

She held his arm as tightly as she could, sword or no. They hovered on the border, and in the end, Nightshade grudgingly gave way to her silent, insistent gesture.

Makuron the Black, as the Outcaste was once called, reared up and roared, and as his jaws widened, flame reached, like orange fingers, across the invisible divide. Nightshade his raised sword, and the flames parted to either side; Kaylin could feel the heat. The stones to either side of her feet grew orange; the weeds evaporated. Heat caused the air to ripple, and the great, black form of the Dragon's extended wings undulated, shifting in the haze.

All around him, the landscape whirled, dark shadows folding around colors that were iridescent, almost opaline. There was no street beneath him, and Kaylin could no longer even imagine something as mundane as a street existing. She heard the wind's roar, felt its ice.

Nightshade's smile was thin and sharp, something felt rather than seen.

"Clever, Lord Nightshade," the Dragon said.

"You are not dead, and you are not bound, not yet.

Come, Makuron. In the elder days, we never faced each other upon the field."

"I chose, and choose, the fields upon which I fight," the Dragon replied. "And you are not unprepared, this time. But neither am I."

"You do not yet rule the Shadows," Nightshade said, "and you must have been greatly injured since your last sojourn into Nightshade to stay your ground there."

The silence was cold.

"You call me weak, when you will not step across the border with *Meliannos* in your hands? You, who stand on the edge of power and skirt it like a mortal?"

"I prefer to control power, rather than be controlled by it," Nightshade replied evenly. It was clear, however, that the Dragon's challenge—and accusation—was not to his liking.

"Like the rest of your kin—and mine—you hide from power. I was a greater adept, and in my centuries of study, *nothing* prepared me for what I might find, and take, here. If I do not rule the Shadows, they do not rule *me*. They sustain me," he hissed. "Nor will I give up the advantage without cause. I have no need," he added, and the sibilance reminded Kaylin why Dragons were sometimes called winged serpents. He roared.

And this time, the earth shook beneath him, and all around him, the shadows rippled, as if they were the earth, the wind and his voice.

They parted, those shadows, like curtains.

And from their depths, across a field of black, two shapes ran. It was hard, at first, to discern what those shapes were—had she been asked, Kaylin would have said they were Ferals. But they were larger than Ferals, and as they ran—and they ran *fast*—the strange, silent soldiers who flanked the Dragon on either side pulled back.

She saw them clearly, then, as they approached the front line, running for the border as if it didn't exist. They were black, ebony with eyes. Sleek, trailing shadows as if they were of it, and not quite free, came two creatures that Kaylin knew had once been Leontine.

In the ripple of their fur, she saw some likeness; in the fact of fur, the likeness was marked. But the fangs that jutted prominently from their open mouths—visible even at a distance—were no Leontine fangs; there were just too damn many of them. The shapes of their heads, as they approached, were an echo of the panther that Marai had been on that first evening, but it was a dim echo; they were misshapen, unique. Even the eyes were wrong—they had more than two, to start. And they were colored, like gems, flashing in chaotic sequence.

They ran on four legs, but as they approached Makuron, they slowed and shifted to two legs, and the legs… were wrong. They were furred, but resembled nothing so much as the great, twisted knot-work of the roots of ancient trees. Trees that broke rock, and resisted all attempts to uproot them.

But the worst thing about them emerged only when the first spoke. "Lord Makuron," it said. Its voice was a rumble, like the stories of avalanches in a distant, winter country. Kaylin's hair stood on end. All of it; she felt like a cat caught in a lightning storm.

"Orogrim. Marai." The Dragon inclined his head.

"Your enemies have come, at last, to destroy you, to unmake you."

Two heads swiveled as one.

Kaylin's hands dropped to her daggers, and they came, scraping slightly, out of their sheaths.

"They do not know or trust the words of power," Makuron continued. "And they have destroyed your kin since the Eldest first woke you from the sleep of animals."

"Kaylin."

Severn's voice sounded so slight it was almost a whisper in comparison. But she heard it. She always would.

"It's them," she told him, her eyes never leaving the Leontines. It was hard—if she blinked, they shifted, their shape subtly changing. If she watched, she could see them almost as obsidian mist, shaped and reshaped in an instant.

"Yes," he replied. He was behind her, and he stayed there. "But, Kaylin, you understand what they're saying."

She nodded.

"I don't," he said.

"What?"

"I don't. I know you do. I can sense it."

He so rarely made mention of what he could sense, usually preferring to wait until she offered him what she knew. Even when he already knew it. As a child, she hadn't even been aware of it; as an adult, she was grateful. Grateful in an entirely different way when he set aside caution, and privacy.

"Nightshade?"

"I do not understand it," Nightshade said, "but I recognize the cadences."

Orogrim howled.

Kaylin felt as if she'd been slapped by the hand of a god. As usual, she wasn't picky about which one.

"Kill them," Makuron said. "Kill them all."

She knew that he'd spoken normally, because every Barrani present understood what he'd said.

She *moved.* She moved without thinking, without planning; her instincts took over and she let them. Thought was slow. Around her, the ranks of the Barrani thinned suddenly, changing shape. She was aware of where Nightshade stood, aware of the way his guards shadowed him. Aware, as well, of his sword. It was like a constellation in the night sky, and it was night, now. Somehow, sunset had escaped her notice.

She heard Tiamaris roar, and felt the fire crest her back as it left his open mouth. The Leontines had crossed the border that held the Dragon and his honor guard in check. They were met by armored men, two of whom fell back at the force of their leap.

The others were moving, as Kaylin was; she brought her daggers down at an angle, and connected, briefly, with flesh. Blood darkened the edge of her blade; she felt its warmth as she adjusted her grip, acknowledging, as she leaped away, that it was a shallow wound at best.

Orogrim did not kill the Barrani beneath his claws, not instantly. But the claws themselves had sundered armor as if it were thin cloth, and what Orogrim did not do, time probably would.

He howled like a maddened beast, leaping beneath the arc of a blade. He was fast—the Barrani were faster.

But when a blade bisected his arm, and his arm shuddered, changing shape and texture before reasserting itself, the fight changed.

It was almost like fighting the dead—injuring them didn't stop them. Tiamaris roared again, and this time his wings bent, and they came down upon Orogrim.

She heard the crack of bone. Heard the shifting, grinding sound that bodies were never supposed to make as Orogrim absorbed the damage, remaking his body around it. Becoming a parody of whole.

She opened her mouth to shout something—a warning, something useless—before she was swept off her feet to one side. She rolled along the ground, rolled cleanly, came up in a crouch, both daggers ready.

Standing between Kaylin and the other Leontine was Severn. He'd unhooked the chain that bound his blades, and he was weaving them in the air; they whistled and keened all the warning he would give.

Kaylin. Nightshade's voice. She could almost feel his name on her tongue as she opened her mouth, he felt suddenly that close, that present.

The other Leontine hissed and her body folded to ground in a crouch, shadows scraping weeds from their moorings. What those shadows touched, they consumed as certainly as if they were fire, black fire.

The Barrani undead had been stopped by flame.

But...these weren't undead.

Eyes opalescent with hidden fire, the Leontine stared at her as if Severn did not exist. She opened her jaws and the gap of exposed teeth just kept on growing, as if she were adding fangs as she went along. She leaped before Kaylin could move—and before Severn could, which was worse. Her forepaws took him in the chest, and he grunted at the weight that bore him back. She snarled in pain as his blade bit into her left shoulder.

Kaylin leaped as well, throwing her right foot out in a kick that connected with the corner of the parody of a jaw. It sheared the bottom of her boots off. Had they been anything less than the heavy-soled regulation wear her job demanded, she'd be missing the bottom of her foot as well.

But Kaylin hadn't dislodged her. And in the silver of moonlight, she could see where claws had pierced Severn's flesh by the spread of blood.

What Kaylin failed to do, Tiamaris did not. The battering of his wings sent the Leontine flying. But the creature landed like a cat lands, and tensed to leap again; fire grazed her, hissing its way through fur. It didn't stop her—how could it? She was changing as she fought, her paws taking on the semblance of—of hands, her face and form shifting until she could easily stand upright. Two of the Barrani guards fell on her, and fell away; her tail, like a slender arm, had literally knocked them off their feet.

And all around the Leontine, black and misty, shadows twisted, forming symbols that her movement swept aside. She was staring at Kaylin, and she didn't so much turn as…shift in place, her face emerging, always, in Kaylin's direction.

Orogrim had launched himself into—and almost through—Nightshade's guard. More than that, Kaylin couldn't risk watching. She understood what Night-shade's death here would mean: the fief would be without its Lord. And without its Lord, she very much doubted that the *other* Dragon would stay so obligingly out of the fight.

If he was. She could hear the rumble of his voice, the forced play of syllables muted by Tiamaris's roar. The Imperial Dragon's wings were edged in shadow— or blood—but he didn't take to the skies. That he could wasn't in question—that he didn't said something about the nature of boundaries.

But if he hadn't been here, they'd be dead. All of them. It made her wonder how there were enough Barrani left standing for *three* Draco-Barrani wars. She had taken two deep gouges—fast, clean cuts, like knife wounds. She was certain she'd done worse in return, but it didn't seem to matter. Nothing did. They couldn't carve their way through the two Leontines—it was like trying to cut water. They *flowed* back into shape, no matter what you hit them with.

This was what the Dragons feared. *This* was why Sanabalis was perfectly willing to kill an infant. She saw it clearly, understood it perfectly. The fear. The truth of the fear.

What had Sanabalis said, that day the Leontines had flocked to him as if they were obedient puppies? What had he told them?

She dodged, pivoting and lifting her arms as the Leontine sailed past, caught by gravity and momentum. She heard the heavy landing, saw it, was already off her feet and rolling along the ground. She felt the slice of claws cut her cheek, was grateful it wasn't her forehead. She wasn't wearing anything that could absorb the blood fast enough; it would fall right into her eyes, and she couldn't afford that. Not and survive.

Kaylin!

She couldn't look, couldn't take her eyes off the Leontine. But she could listen, and above the sound of blade against claw and flesh, louder than the forced grunt of breathing and exertion, she heard the howls on the wind.

Ferals.

But worse, far worse, was the answering howl that left two Leontine throats in unison. The Leontines were talking to the Ferals. And the Ferals, Kaylin knew, were listening.

She needed to *think*. But she also needed to be alive to do that. And the Leontines weren't tiring, or if they were, it didn't slow them at all. Kaylin, on the other hand, was human. She could keep this up for another ten minutes, twenty—but her movements would lose edge and speed, would eventually slow just enough that there wouldn't be any more movement.

How many, she thought. *How many Leontines will hear what you hear and be changed the way you're changed?*

How many more would it take? These two, she thought, were enough. Even the Swords would have trouble containing them; they'd cut their way through Elantra, riding on the fear their presence evoked.

Her whole body ached now.

She turned just a little bit too slowly, and a claw passed through her upper arm, skidding across bone. She bit back a cry as Severn's blade came down across the arm the Leontine had extended to cause the injury.

The massive jaws of Tiamaris snapped in the air as the Leontine melted away.

It would be back, and in the meantime, she was losing a lot of blood. She grimaced, standing as Severn glanced at her. He couldn't put up his blade to bind the wound.

But he didn't have to. Because the pain had cleared her mind, shutting down fear, panic, the possibilities of a future that might never arrive.

She dropped a dagger into its sheath and, clutching her arm, steadied herself.

What had she said to Sanabalis?

I'll tell them a different story.

She wanted to close her eyes or plug her ears; it was hard enough to tell a story without the certainty of an audience. She did neither; she needed to see. Because she could—the shadows that were both dense and diffuse around both Leontines had begun to make sense: They were words. Something, someone, was telling them a story, just as Sanabalis had done when he had visited the Leontine Quarter. It was a different story, and the words were harsher and more frightening—but in the end? Words.

Like the words that were written across half of her skin. She didn't understand them; she never had. But she owned them. And knowing this, she used them now.

"Marai!"

A name. Just a name, a mortal conceit given to a living, breathing infant. Not a name in the Barrani sense, or the Dragon sense; nothing that was required to *give* life, or to sustain it. A Leontine name was *not* a soul—if you believed in souls, and if you believed that Barrani and Dragonkind possessed them.

But it was something that you grew into, and in the end, it was part of what you chose to become.

"Marai, listen to me."

The great, dense shadow that was half Leontine, half beast, and a menagerie of things in between, stopped. Just—stopped. And then its—no, her—great head turned, and a growling started behind a row of teeth that looked like it belonged in a dozen animals at the same time.

The Ferals were on the border now, and then, just as the Leontines, across it. Tiamaris breathed on them. She heard their howls of pain and fury—more fury, really—before she let her attention shift. They were, for once, someone else's problem.

Marai's body was already angled toward Kaylin, and the arm that Severn had lopped off had already reasserted its existence. Her claws were as long as swords now, but they suited the cast of her hands, which were also grotesquely large.

What did she know about Marai?

Almost nothing. She faltered, and the Leontine crouched, gathering to leap. "Severn, no," she shouted, but it came out in a whisper, in a sound so thin she couldn't even be certain it was heard; she could hardly hear it herself.

She could hear, more clearly, the keening of *Meliannos,* and wondered how in the hells she'd missed it the first time she'd seen it in Nightshade's hand.

She could hear, much more clearly, the syllables of Nightshade's true name, and she knew damn well she hadn't tried to say *that.* Louder still, distinct and deadly, the syllables of Makuron's name, the name Nightshade had guessed that she knew. She did.

But it was so long, so complicated, so terrifyingly dense, she couldn't have spoken it had she tried—it would be like trying to read the whole of Rennick's play out loud in a single breath.

And blending with these things, the syllables, the tone, the texture of the name she had taken for herself in the halls of the High Court, where the Barrani were given life. She did not speak this, either.

She spoke Marai's name again, but the speaking felt wrong; she knew what she was trying to say. What she said she couldn't even hear.

But Marai did. Around her, like a shroud, the strokes and lines of something that might be language to gods, grew sharper and harsher. The misty quality, the smudged movement, was gone. Those words, Kaylin thought, were speaking. No, that wasn't right. But it would have to do.

She wished, briefly and uselessly, that she had asked Sanabalis what the story of the Leontine origin actually was. Not the gist of it, but the words. Because she had Marai's attention, and in the space of at least two minutes, that attention was not focused on ending her life as quickly as possible.

"Marai," she said again. And then, taking a breath, giving up any attempt to force her lips to conform to what she *thought* she was saying, she added, "You were loved." Because that felt right, to her.

"Loved?" Orogrim's harsh voice. What she had said to Marai, he had heard. It had stilled him in the same

fashion, but the eyes he turned on Kaylin—not Leontine eyes, not even close—were burning like Dragon fury.

She risked a glance at Nightshade. Saw that he was bleeding, that his perfect skin had taken gashes. But his expression was neutral, and he met Kaylin's glance and offered the slightest of nods.

"Yes," Kaylin replied.

"We were almost destroyed at birth," he snarled. "And we are *hunted* now by those who would destroy us. What love in that?"

But she shook her head. Her hair was matted and sticky, and the movement was graceless. She could feel the whole of her arms, her back, her thighs, throbbing as if the skin had been peeled back and everything beneath it lay exposed to air.

"When the Leontines were created," she said softly, "they were loved."

His snarl matched his eyes. He tensed to leap, and Marai lifted one of those misshapen hands in warning. Her eyes were the color of night—a quiet, cloudless night.

"They will kill us," she said, speaking for the first time. Sibilance in the phrase, hissing that cut the ear, as if hearing it were exposing a vulnerability.

Kaylin ignored the comment, but it was hard. It had always been hard to ignore the truth. "But the Old Ones didn't understand their creations. They had hopes for their future. Maybe plans—I don't know. I wasn't there." She hesitated and then said, "We birth children, and we love them, but we *don't* know them. We don't know who they are because they're almost not anything. They're helpless, and we protect them with everything—*everything*—we have. But we have to wait, to see who they are, who they'll become, what their choices will be."

"They feared us," Orogrim said coldly. He was inching closer to Marai, and his lips were moving. As they did, the Shadows tightened, and Marai's form shifted.

"Yes," Kaylin said quietly. Her voice stilled the shifting. The word felt Elantran—but wasn't. "They did. Look at yourselves. Tell me that they were wrong. Tell me that you don't intend to kill us. Tell me that you won't leave the fiefs and return to your people and kill those who will not follow you.

"We're mortal. We *know* death when we see it." Most of the time. "We fear it, and we kill before we can be killed. It's ugly, but it's what it is. The Leontines were loved," she continued.

"And we are not Leontine?" Marai asked.

"You were not killed," Kaylin replied softly. "You were not hunted."

"They would kill my son."

And those were the magic words, Kaylin thought. "No," she replied. "Not while I live, they won't. I gave you my word, Marai. Whether or not I now regret it doesn't *matter*. He is *not* what you now are. And I will do everything in my power to make sure he *never* becomes it.

"Is this what you wish for him?" Kaylin said. "Look at yourself. You're covered in blood—some of it mine, some of it—" she gestured widely "—theirs. Is this what you want for Roshan?"

"I want his survival," Marai said. Her voice changed

as she spoke, becoming almost familiar. "And I will do anything, as you said, anything at all, to ensure that."

"He will be powerful," Orogrim told her. "We will tell him the truth, and he will be free."

"To do what?" Kaylin countered. "To live in the Shadows? To kill his kin?"

"I...have...not...killed my kin," Marai replied. Her face was changing now, the fur paling, the fangs receding into the shrinking line of her mouth.

"Orogrim has," Kaylin said. And then she stopped because her brain had caught up with her mouth. And she understood, finally, what the tainted meant. What they could do. "Marcus's friend. You never met him—"

"I met him," Marai told her slowly.

"But he's—"

"I have no Pridlea. I met him."

"He's dead."

"Marcus killed him."

"No, Marai—he was dead before he met Marcus."

"He *was not dead*."

"What's life?" Kaylin said urgently. She felt Severn's restless movement. *Yes,* she snapped, along the invisible line that bound them, *I know this is not the time for a philosophical discussion. I have a point, and this is the only way to make it.*

She felt the odd shape of his smile, his half smile. It caught her by surprise, but...she clung to the feel of it anyway.

"Marai, what does *life* mean? Everything that the Elder knew or believed, everything he loved—all the stupid things, all the smart ones, all the ugly and beautiful moments—they were wiped away entirely by Orogrim's words. The words weren't strong; they weren't spoken here, at the heart of the oldest of the Shadows. But they were strong enough. His body still moved, his mouth still spoke—but everything that made him what he was, like or hate it—was destroyed."

"That will not happen to our son," Orogrim told Marai. "You know this to be true."

"No, it won't. That's what makes you special," Kaylin said. "It's not the taint. It's the fact that, in the end, with enough power behind him, Orogrim's son could remake the whole of your race. It wouldn't be Leontine anymore, but it *wasn't* Leontine to start with. Your people—your sister—would be as different from Leontines as the Leontines were from the animals out of which the Old Ones made them.

"And they wouldn't have much choice," Kaylin added. "But *you* do. Your son will. Orogrim does."

"They feared rivals."

"No," Kaylin said wearily. "They feared the loss of what they'd brought to life. Not more, not less. But life is unpredictable. There are those born who can not only hear the words, even if they don't understand them. They can *use* them."

Kaylin took a deep breath.

And as she did, Makuron the Outcaste cried out in fury, his wings expanding in the darkness. Black fire filled the sky, and even before it lifted, she saw that he had crossed the border.

Orogrim smiled. Nothing about him had changed. The prominent jut of too many fangs glistened. But

Marai hesitated. She stood in the light of the moons, one just shy of full, the other a perfect, silver circle.

This was important, somehow. One more night, Kaylin thought. It wasn't her thought, but it took her a moment to realize where it had come from: Nightshade. Bleeding but unperturbed, he raised his sword, shifting his stance. He held it two-handed, standing his ground. And it was *his* ground; she could almost feel the link between them, fief and Lord.

"Marai," Kaylin said, the word a quiet act of desperation.

The Leontine—and she was that—turned. "My only living kin are my sister and my son," she said. "But my sister has her Pridlea."

"I will not let them kill Sarabe. I will not let them harm our son." She emphasized the possessive. "But, Marai... understand that I cannot let you harm him, either."

Orogrim growled, tensed to leap.

Marai met him in mid-air. She had not taken the Shadows back; she was smaller, her fur paler, the reds silvered by moonlight so they were almost invisible. "Tell me," she shouted to Kaylin. "Tell me my story. *Tell me, Eldest.*"

Kaylin started to speak, and fire rained down upon her. It should have killed her. It didn't. Instead, it passed to either side of her, like rushing water against a standing stone.

Nightshade was there, as if he were Severn.

She held out her arms, as if in plea, and saw Orogrim's claws pierce Marai's shoulder. Marai snarled and staggered back, and her form shifted, and the words around her began to swirl again. But they were different, now. Kaylin could see them clearly: as clearly as she had Sanabalis's words what seemed like months ago.

"Give them choice," Kaylin said. Her throat hurt. It was like speaking in Dragon, which she had done only once, and only to the dead.

"Give them thought and will and volition. Give them dreams and the ability to see beyond the next meal, the need for shelter. Give them hope, and light, and a span of days greater than the span they now have.

"Give them—" She faltered. Orogrim's claws raked across Marai's chest, and blood flew in a black, beaded fan. "No, Marai—"

But Marai snarled, growling, the wounds closing as she struggled. The Barrani were thrown back by the wind of Dragon wings, and Tiamaris charged, roaring, into the side of Makuron the Black. The larger Dragon snapped his neck to the side, his jaws grazing Tiamaris's flank. Scales *snapped*.

And Marai grew darker, again, and her face lost the Leontine shape that Kaylin knew in her heart she loved best of all mortal faces. The Pridlea's face. The mother's.

"Kaylin," Marai said, her voice lower, deeper.

Kaylin swallowed. She couldn't move; Dragon breath had melted stone.

But she could speak.

"Give them song, and story, give them fire. Grace them, in all things with the choice to do and be." Gods, her throat hurt. Her eyes hurt. Her arms, her legs, her back—it was like the chorus of a very badly sung song.

Marai struggled, returning claw for claw, bite for bite. Hers was now the shorter reach, and she had a lot fewer teeth. But she was shining now. The moonlight alone did not illuminate her—something else did; something brought the red fur to light, and gave it the semblance of…flame.

"I choose," Marai said, and her voice was exactly the voice of the Leontine woman who had given birth, almost alone, to a single cub. "I *can* choose. Orogrim— the Shadows offer power, and we have taken power. But what have we given?" Her mouth was black with blood. His mouth, red with it.

"We chose *life,*" he snarled. And then, maddened, said, "I chose life. You—you have chosen to throw life away."

"This isn't life," Marai replied. "But she is the mother of my son. She was there. I will not let you kill her."

"You will not stop *me,*" Makuron roared. And rose. Tiamaris lifted wings, and Kaylin saw, by the way one trailed ground, that flight would be denied him.

"Kaylin," Nightshade said. She could hear his voice so clearly she thought he must be speaking in the silence of her very crowded thoughts. But she saw his lips move. And she saw the Dragon rise. She thought the whole city must be able to see him; he eclipsed the very moons.

And she stood, watching him rise, until the Shadows called her back. The story was unfinished, and she knew that she would see it through to its end; its end was written, somewhere, on her body; had been a part of her for all of her adult life.

"Give them the peace of death, when age descends. Give them the freedom of death. Let them leave these lands when life is burden and not joy. Let none of us stand in their way, who know no such peace."

And she understood, for just a moment, why the Old Ones had chosen to fashion life from things already living. Just a moment. *We all want things for our children that we could not or did not have. And we try, and we're not perfect, and we can't always get it right. But when we fail, what do we do?*

She spoke a single word. It wasn't Elantran. It couldn't be. She couldn't even think of it as Elantran, although the rest had seemed very like it to her.

No names. No words to bind them. No words to give them life. No eternity. A life beyond words, outside of them.

We keep trying. We love, and we try not to fail again in the same way. We find other ways to fail. But we have *to keep trying.*

She saw Marai in the moonlight. She saw Marai begin to speak, and the words that bound her, the words that gave her power, faltered. It would kill her. And, Kaylin saw, in a brief flash, Marai would let it.

"No!" Her own voice. Her own thin voice. "No! Marai! Marai, you have Roshan!"

"My choice," the Leontine said, and for the first time, the only time, she was entirely calm and free of fear or need. "You will let me make it, Eldest. You will not take it from me. You will tell my son—*our* son—this story, when he is old enough to understand it. You will tell him that he was loved. You will tell him that love, in the end, is not an excuse. You will tell him that what I want for him is what you want. He will choose. And he will face the consequences of that choice, as I face them. You will tell him that I pray to the ancestors that he makes a different choice and faces happier consequences." And she reached out with Leontine hands, and those hands brushed Orogrim's unrecognizable features, as if they could discern what lay beneath them.

Orogrim tore her chest apart with his claws. And then he lifted his face and stared directly at Kaylin, who stood too shocked to move.

Severn was there in an instant. Severn, blade drawn, bleeding. He would face Dragons for her, she knew. And the Shadows. And memories.

Orogrim leaped and Makuron descended, and two blades rose: Severn's and Nightshade's. One devoured flame. The other impaled shadow. But this time, *this* time, the Shadows were solid. One misshapen arm lay on the ground, shuddering into stillness at the force of the blow; the rest of the arm was still attached.

Wordless, Orogrim looked at the long stump, and then, eyes rounding, he looked at Kaylin. He looked at Marai's body. He looked at Severn, and he moved then, but he was slower, now. He was not recognizably Leontine; that much, he retained.

And it was a kindness, in its way.

As much of a kindness as angry gods allowed.

"They did not love *us*," he roared, and one-armed, hampered, he turned to Severn. He could still fight; he could *not* fight and ignore the weapons and the blows aimed at him.

"No, Orogrim," Kaylin said, uncertain that he would even hear. He had just killed Marai. "They feared you, and love can't exist when there's that much fear."

His long, long claws caught the rotating chain of Severn's weapon, but the momentum of that chain pulled him off his feet. He rolled along the ground, clumsier, tried to put a hand out, and misjudged; he had no hand on that arm.

"But Marai loved you, Orogrim."

And Marai, child of shadows, had graced him—with death. Kaylin looked away as Severn closed, hating Orogrim and pitying him, and wondering if the face of death and danger was always tinged by this pathos.

Never wondering if she could have killed him, had she been Severn. She watched, bore witness to his furious struggles. His blood was dark, but crimson where it splashed stone; it sizzled where it splattered against molten rock.

Severn leaped, and landed; his blade was dark and wet and it didn't reflect moonlight—or any light, really. She saw it strike, fall, saw at last the misshapen head roll away from its shoulders. Saw Severn fall to one knee. She started to move toward him, and stopped. The ground that she stood on was a small patch of solid rock, and to her front and sides, what had once been dirt or rock was now orange and glowing.

She heard Tiamaris roar, and she saw Makuron, haloed now by moonlight, as he roared his fury and his rage. Wordless, animal, very like Orogrim, he plummeted from the sky that was, for a moment, his fief, his empire.

Nightshade was there. Nightshade, the fief. Nightshade, the man. She thought she felt the ground rise just in front of her feet, before she was borne back by the glancing blow of a single talon.

Her arm broke beneath her and she lost the ability to breathe. But she felt the force of the Outcaste's ancient

name, and she struggled against it, the sharp pain of
bones fading into a throb.

He said, *I will kill you.*

She might have nodded. She was exhausted, and
even if her ribs hadn't been broken—and she knew they
were—she wouldn't have had the strength to stand or
flee.

Standing to fight didn't even occur to her as a possibility. But she could see moonlight glinting off Tiamaris,
could see him move, see the stretch of his long, beautiful neck. She could even see the fire that suddenly blos-
somed around him, and could hear, in the timbre of his
answering roar, pain. The fire began to fade to a haze
of light and around her, against that haze, the shapes
of the Barrani faded into shadow. She closed her eyes,
then; it was too much work to keep them open.

Makuron said, again, *I will kill you.*

*Yes. But not now. If I could, Dragon Lord, I would
tell you your story.*

And she felt just a glimmer of something that might
one day become fear. *What are you?*

Kaylin...Kaylin Neya.

And then he was gone. Or she was.

CHAPTER

23

She woke to the crowded yet austere room that served the Hawks as an infirmary. Bandages, scissors and small jars with open lids littered the counter, and she grimaced as she caught sight of the flecked wings of the infirmary's chief doctor. Those wings were folded, which was generally considered a good sign—but Kaylin had known Moran for far too many years to pay them much attention.

Moran had—Kaylin would have bet money on it—eyes in the back of her head. "You're finally awake." It was almost an accusation. "If you try to sit up, you won't be."

Kaylin grimaced. "Broken ribs?"

"And a broken arm. It was a clean break. Some lacerations, bruises and gashes. Blood loss, but not enough to slow you down. Note that I am not asking you what you were doing," she added, "because I'm tired of hearing excuses."

Kaylin let her head fall back on her pillow. "Why am I not home?"

"Think about what you just heard." Moran ran a hand through her hair, and Kaylin saw her eyes. They were dark, and sunken.

"Moran, how long was I out?"

"Long enough," was the brisk reply. "How many fingers am I holding up?"

"None."

Moran nodded. "There are a list of people who wish to speak with you. It is, oddly enough, only slightly longer than the list of people I've recently been forced to offend."

"Moran, it's important—how long have I been out?"

"Long enough," she replied. "You heal quickly. How does your skin feel?"

"My skin? Fine. Except for the bits under the wad of bandages. Why?"

"When you were brought here, every single tattoo on your body—and, yes, I know that's not the right word—was incandescent blue, and very hot to the touch."

"Oh."

"Consultation with Records, however, shows that they're more or less the same."

"More or less?"

"Yes."

"Tiamaris?"

"Lord Tiamaris was not brought here."

"But was he—"

"As such, he isn't my patient and isn't my problem. Corporal Handred, however, asked me to tell you that Lord Tiamaris will live. I, however, will likely face the prospect of unemployment—and believe me that sounds tempting at the moment—if the Sergeant isn't allowed to speak with you when you regain consciousness."

This, Kaylin understood. "And when will that be?"

"When you think you're ready," was the steady reply. "Until then, do me the favor of lying still and pretending to rest."

"Can I at least speak to Severn?"

"Not unless you're willing to speak to everyone else." Her expression gentled slightly. "We were worried, Kaylin. All of us. The Quartermaster would like to speak with you," she added, "but grudgingly gave me permission to say that the loss of the boots and the melting of one dagger would not be docked from your pay."

"Oh. I must have looked *terrible*."

"Yes. It would have been slightly more helpful if Severn had brought you in about two hours earlier. The office wasn't full at that time."

"I'll talk to him about his timing."

"Do that." Moran shook herself, and then bent over Kaylin and hugged her carefully. "Good work, Private," she said softly.

Kaylin's idea of recovery did not include Mallory, and as a result, it was a full two hours before she declared herself awake enough to speak with Severn. The words had hardly left her mouth before the door opened and he walked in.

Moran's infirmary didn't include mirrors, and given Severn's bruised face, and a new line of stitches near the left side of his jaw, this was probably a good thing. On the other hand, she couldn't see what she looked like, but given that she was the one metaphorically strapped to an infirmary bed—and Moran had real straps, which she wasn't afraid to use—it was probably just as well.

Severn pulled up a stool. He was in a clean uniform, his hair was brushed back, and his eyes were as darkly ringed as Moran's.

"Do I look as bad as you do?"

"Worse," he said, with the hint of a smile. "Tiamaris was certain you were dead when the Outcaste landed."

"Tiamaris was injured—"

"Yes. It was impressive. He was impressive," Severn said. "I'm not sure he would have returned to the accepted Empire norm for Dragons if Nightshade hadn't intervened."

"Intervened?" She thought, for a brief moment, of his sword.

Severn shook his head. "No, not that way. He told Tiamaris that you held his name, and that because of this he knew, for certain, you still lived. He also intimated that any attempt to prolong a losing fight while you were somewhere directly beneath it would possibly change your state."

"Change *my state?*"

"Those were more or less the words he used." His smile broadened. "High Barrani."

"Of course." She snorted. It hurt. "Did Moran tell you how many ribs I cracked?"

"No."

"You didn't ask?"

"I'm not stupid."

"What happened to the Outcaste?"

"He ran up against *Meliannos* in the hands of a fief-lord," Severn said, his smile dimming. "But if you mean is he dead, no."

"And Marai—"

He looked away, then. "I don't understand Leontine well enough to follow all that she said—but I understand it well enough to know what it must have been. We brought her body home," he added quietly. "It's in the morgue."

"And Orogrim?"

"Dead."

"Also in the morgue?"

"No."

She didn't ask. Instead, she risked the wrath of Moran. She caught his hands in hers and pulled herself upright.

"Kaylin, Moran is going to kill me," he whispered.

"The baby," she said, ignoring him. "How long have I been out? I promised, Severn—the baby—"

"The baby is alive," he said. "Or he was this morning."

"You saw him?"

"I saw him. I went to visit Kayala's Pridlea early this morning."

"She let you in?"

"In the circumstances—and as she explained, as a guest herself—she was willing to consider the meeting ground neutral *enough* not to ask me to leave any vital body parts at the door. The baby was alive."

She let go of his hands and slumped back into the bed. "I feel like crap."

He placed a palm against her forehead. Nodded.

"What was that for?"

"Fever. You're fine. Before you start complaining, you *weren't* fine when you were brought in."

"I need to get up."

He looked dubious about that.

"I need to go to the Palace," she said. "I need to be with the Pridlea."

"I believe that Lord Sanabalis attempted to explain this to Moran. He was probably about as successful as you'll be if you try."

"Sanabalis? He was here?"

"Yes. He was concerned."

"Did you ask about Tiamaris?"

"No. I was told he'll live. Lord Sanabalis wasn't in the best of moods."

"Dragons never are," a familiar voice said. "And if you sit up, Moran will break my arms."

She sat up anyway and regretted it almost instantly. *"Marcus!"*

He was wearing his uniform. He was wearing the Hawk. He was in the infirmary, and Moran was standing behind his right shoulder with an expression that brought to mind the wrath of a god.

"Yes, *Private.*"

"You're back."

He nodded. "I should probably thank whoever installed Mallory as acting Sergeant. I can actually see the surface of my desk."

She wanted to laugh. Until she did.

"Sergeant." Moran's tone of voice was at its most pinched.

"They—they let you go? I thought I had to go back."

"Sanabalis felt that, in the circumstances, it would be a goodwill gesture to the Emperor. He imparted this information very diplomatically, and merely waited until they agreed."

"And that took how long?"

"About an hour, give or take a few side arguments." His expression softened. "I swear, I'm going to put you on paperwork if you ever come back in this condition again."

"Kill me now. It'll be kinder."

"I'd consider it if Moran weren't here, but as Moran *is* here, my life span would be measured in seconds, and I would hate to see all your interference in my personal affairs go to waste." He saw her expression change again; she was too tired to keep it in check. His growl softened. "Yes, kitling, the arguments were about the baby. Marai is dead," he said quietly. "I claimed her body for the Pridlea, for Sarabe's sake, and there will be a burial. The baby's father is likewise dead. Tell me what happened."

She shook her head. "I don't know all of it. I saw him fall—Orogrim, I mean. And I saw what he did to Marai—but Marai chose her death. And I let her."

"Sometimes that's an act of mercy as well," he said. His claws were sheathed, and the pads of his paws felt dry and rough against her cheek. "Sanabalis is waiting for you at the Palace."

"Marcus—"

"You saw, I'm told, what they can become. The tainted. The cursed. You fought them. But...Lord Tiamaris said that you also spoke with them, and Marai, at least, heard your words. Lord Tiamaris was injured, and if Lord Sanabalis does not consider it an impediment to his recovery, you'll probably be allowed to visit him."

"Marcus—"

He lifted a hand. "It isn't up to me, Kaylin."

"And if it were?"

He could have pretended to misunderstand her. He didn't. "I didn't see what Marai or Orogrim became. I didn't see them fight, and I didn't see them kill. To me, for better or worse, the knowledge that the ancient tales are true is still theoretical. The child *is* a child to me."

"Sarabe will be safe?"

His growl was low and deep. She didn't ask again. He turned to Moran. "I'm sorry," he said, "but Lord Sanabalis *is* waiting. He's sent a carriage—it's been in the yard for the past eight hours."

"She's not fit to travel."

"Short of strapping her to the bed—and yes, I'm well aware it's possible—I don't see how you'll detain her."

Moran started to speak, and stopped before words left her mouth. She took a deep breath before she spoke again. "A child, you said?"

"A Leontine orphan," Marcus replied.

"Then, no," she replied, surrendering. "Short of drugging her, there's probably not much more I can do." She walked around Marcus and knelt against the bed, pressing her forehead into the hard mattress. "I've had two long, almost sleepless days, Private. I advise you against leaving the infirmary. If, however, you choose to ignore my advice, I've sent unguents and oils with Corporal Handred. You are to apply these to your wounds when you change their dressing. You are also forbidden to carry any heavy weight, and you will not, under any circumstances, involve yourself in any physical activities for at least two weeks. Is that clear?"

"Yes, Moran."

It wasn't painful to walk, although it *was* almost humiliatingly tiring. It wasn't painful to sit, but it *was* painful to sit in a moving carriage, because the roads weren't really designed for people with broken ribs. She would have complained, because for Kaylin, complaining was one of life's little luxuries, but the worry was worse than the pain.

Silence, on the other hand, obviously caused worry, because Severn opened his pouch, took some bitterroot out, and broke its barklike skin. "Chew it," he said.

"I'm fine."

"That wasn't a request."

She made a face, opened her mouth, and made a less voluntary face in response; bitterroot was a completely descriptive name that somehow failed to live up to the texture and the actual taste of the plant. But it did help with the pain.

Sanabalis met them in the Courtyard. He was dressed head to toe in blue robes, which made his beard look a lot whiter. He waved the guards away, and also walked quickly past the liveried attendants whose job it was to help passengers exit the carriage with their dignity intact. He opened the door on Kaylin's side of the carriage, and held out a hand above the small stool the attendants usually placed just beneath the carriage door.

Kaylin, in what passed for dress uniform given the time she'd had to get dressed, hesitated a moment before taking his hand. He failed to notice the hesitation, and she allowed him to help her reach the ground.

But when she had both feet on the ground and it was clear they were going to support her, he touched her chin gently, lifting her face. His eyes were lambent gold, and the lower membranes were nowhere in sight—it was almost *hard* to look at them. "You did well," he said softly.

She couldn't think of anything to say in response— but it was always that way. She was used to Marcus and the rest of the Hawks; open praise unsettled her, and because it was so rare, she felt she had to somehow say something that showed she deserved it. Instead she said, "Well enough? You know what I want, Sanabalis. You know why I came."

He nodded. "The Dragon Court is aware of your feelings in this matter. It has been in session for some time."

"And you're allowed to be absent?"

"Kaylin, I do not think you fully apprehend the nature of your actions in the fiefs. We are in your debt."

She started to reply, and he lifted a hand.

"And a wise person does not wish to carry the Emperor's debt with her wherever she goes. Owing a debt is not a comfortable position for a ruler."

She was tired. But barter of this nature, stripped of pretty words, had been life in the fiefs. "Can I ask for anything?"

"You can ask," he replied. "What you are granted, however, is another matter entirely."

"Do I have to see him?"

"The Emperor? No. Not yet, although that took some finessing on our part."

"Our?"

"Lord Tiamaris and myself."

"Oh." Pause. "What did you say?"

"That your lessons in etiquette—"

"I'm not taking lessons in etiquette—"

"—have been sorely inadequate, and that your utter failure to comport yourself with the dignity due the *Imperial* rank would likely force him to terminate your existence when it is, in fact, almost required."

"Thanks. I think."

"The Emperor has, however, decreed that your education will be more fully rounded in future. He wished to meet with you," Sanabalis said in a softer tone of voice. "And in the end, he is the Emperor. He *will* meet with you. But not, I think, today. Come. Tiamaris is waiting."

"I thought he was badly injured?"

"No more than you, and you are here."

"Wait, where are we going?"

"Into the Palace. In fact, into a wing of the Palace you have visited before."

"Rennick?"

"Mr. Rennick is not currently *in* the Palace. He is—in his own words—pinning down the last of the difficult roles. I believe he called this 'auditions.' Ybelline, however, is with him."

"She can't go—"

"As are representatives of the Palace Guard. Private Neya, the Emperor has allowed us a period of grace. Nothing more and nothing less. We have limited time, and much of it has dwindled while you recovered. He will not wait out the day."

"I want to see Kayala."

"You will. The others, unfortunately, will have to wait." He held out his arm and she stared at it. He closed his eyes for a moment, and then said, in a slightly thinner voice, "Corporal?"

"Lord Sanabalis."

"Please see that she manages to navigate the Halls without falling flat on her face. I am already in ill-favor with the Aerian the Hawks have set to guard the infirmary."

They walked to the Library, of all places, although until she saw the great doors, she didn't recognize the Halls. Sanabalis winced slightly as he glanced at the doorward, but he was silent. He touched the ward with his palm.

Severn walked calmly toward it and placed his palm in its center after Sanabalis had let his hand fall away. Kaylin looked at the ward—no, the whole damn door—suspiciously. She remembered what had happened the last time she'd been here.

But to her surprise, the doors began to roll on their hinges.

Standing at the edge of his vast Library, in robes as fine as Sanabalis's, stood the Arkon. He felt *old,* although he didn't look that much older than Sanabalis—today. She would have sworn that he had looked much older and feebler when she had first met him, at least until he had started roaring in Dragon.

He looked at her for a long moment, and then to her surprise, he bowed. His expression, however, was missing anything that resembled warmth or friendliness.

"Private Neya," he said as he rose. "Corporal Handred. I trust you are familiar with the rules of my Library?"

Severn nodded. Kaylin wanted a recap, but couldn't quite force herself to ask for one.

"We have been waiting, Lord Sanabalis."

Sanabalis nodded. "We will wait perhaps another two hours—the moons will be aligned at that time."

The Arkon nodded.

Kaylin turned to Sanabalis. "Two hours?" she said. She almost added, *I dragged my butt out of the infirmary, pissing off Moran, and we have to sit around waiting for another two hours?*

Severn stepped on her foot.

"In the meantime, I have asked the kitchen to prepare food suitable for your consumption," the Arkon told them both. "It will not, of course, be eaten in any of the rooms that house the collection." He began to walk away, and they followed, passing through the cavernous walls of books, books, small statues, glass cases and *more* books. Kaylin wondered exactly how it was that something that burned so damn easily could end up as the hoard of an ancient Dragon, but she managed not to ask. Instead, she concentrated on being quiet, because the Arkon's temper when his rules were broken was probably more than she could survive—Dragon voices had a way of shaking the ground you were standing on, and the carriage ride had jarred her ribs enough. Her left arm was in a sling, and she let the sling carry most of its weight.

But the Arkon didn't speak and didn't stop until he reached the room with multiple doors. They were blessedly free of doorwards. He took a key chain from his pockets and he opened the door to the left. "This way," he said. "It is not much farther, and I apologize for the length of the walk. I am told," he added, glancing at Sanabalis, "that you should not be walking at all."

He led them down a hall that had normal ceilings—it almost felt like she'd taken a wrong turn and ended up somewhere outside of the Palace—but the hall opened into a room that looked, from this distance, to be round. She could see the gray of stone and the hint of curvature.

She could also see two familiar figures, seated in what appeared to be practical, plain chairs, which were pulled a little back from a table that would be right at home in the mess hall. Kayala and Tiamaris.

Neither rose to greet her, and in Kayala's case that was probably a good thing—Leontines were physical creatures, and being hugged by one right now would probably really hurt.

"Kitling," Kayala said.

Kaylin felt her whole body shudder, then. She could see clearly why Kayala hadn't risen—a small bundle with a furry face at one end was perched in her lap. It was true: the baby was still alive.

"Kayala."

"I've been warned not to hug you," the Leontine told her.

"I have four broken ribs. They'd like them not to pierce my lungs."

Kayala chuckled; it sounded like a growl to humans who weren't used to Leontines. To Kaylin, it sounded like home. "You're to eat," she added, and nodded toward the food.

"I can't."

"You can."

"I want to hold him," Kaylin said. "I need to hold him."

Kayala's glance flickered briefly across Sanabalis's face. The Dragon Lord nodded. "Then come and take him. He's sleeping."

Kaylin crossed the room and held her arms out. One of her arms didn't follow, and she grimaced.

"Your arm, kitling—"

"Hell with my arm. He doesn't weigh that much. I don't *need* both of them." Babies didn't count as heavy lifting. She lifted him awkwardly, cradling him against her chest, and remembering the night he was born. He stirred in her arms, and she looked at him with faint concern. "Is he hungry?"

"He's a baby."

"Is that a yes?"

"Babies are hungry, dirty, or sleepy. That one, though," Kayala said, with the hint of a frown, "is too sleepy, in our opinion. It's hard to wake him, and it's hard to feed him. He really is scrawny." She stood then, and pulled out a chair for Kaylin. "We've been waking him up for feedings, but he doesn't eat enough, and he doesn't stay awake." And her tone of voice, the subtle inflection in it, made clear to Kaylin that Kayala wondered privately if this wouldn't be the best possible outcome. And wondering that, tried *anyway*.

She really wasn't hungry, but Kayala growled at her, and she knew that particular growl. She allowed Kayala to drop food into her mouth because she really didn't want to let go of the baby.

"Kaylin," Tiamaris said, "Kayala has protected the cub in your absence. She can be trusted to protect the cub in your presence."

"It's not about trust," Kaylin replied, around a mouthful of food. "I was just so *afraid* he'd be dead. I'm tired of dead children," she said starkly. "I'm tired of having my life defined by them."

"And living children are a better definition?"

"I can't think of a better one. Honestly, can you?"

"I'm not human. Or mortal. And I will never have children."

She nodded. "To the Tha'alani, it would be better. To the Aerians, certainly. But it doesn't matter—to *me* it's better." She brushed the baby's forehead with her lips. "Marai died because of him."

"Had Marai died at birth, as is the custom in the plains, we would not be in this position."

"Tiamaris—if we *all* died at birth, nothing bad would ever happen. Nothing would happen at *all.*"

He nodded, his expression carefully neutral. He looked exhausted, but he still had Dragon dignity keeping him from falling over on his face; Kaylin, lacking that dignity, held a baby in its place. Severn sat beside her in silence—he was always so damn silent. But he ate, and he did smile slightly when Kaylin attempted to tell Kayala that she'd eaten enough.

And then the Arkon returned to the room. "It is almost time."

"Where are we going?"

"We are not required to leave this room. The ceiling, however, will open."

"With our luck, it'll be raining."

The Arkon sniffed. "That," he said, as he touched a mark engraved in the wall, "is what mages are for."

She almost laughed, but the ceiling, as he had said, opened. It wasn't like the Hawklord's tower—it was something…magical. The plain and unadorned stone of the round room just faded out of existence, as if it were simply chalk and someone had rubbed a brush across its lines. The stars were bright, even given the dim lights of the city; the moons were brighter. Silver and full, they were untroubled by clouds.

"Kaylin," the Arkon said.

She held the baby just a little bit tighter as she turned to face the Dragon, and froze. His eyes…were silver. Not gold, not orange, and thank the gods, not red. But she had never seen silver Dragon eyes before.

"Lord Tiamaris has spoken at length in Court. I have listened, and Lord Sanabalis has listened, and we two are possibly the only two who could make full sense of what he said—because it should make no sense. The Emperor," he said, his voice shading into the dry, "was patient. He did not interrupt.

"Lord Sanabalis argued on your behalf. Tiamaris was silent throughout the discussion about the fate of the babe you now hold in your arms." He squared his shoulders. "I'm aware that you feel that we would have to kill you to kill the child. It is not, however, true."

She should have been afraid. Maybe she was just too tired.

"I abstained from the discussion as well. I do not understand your attachment to a stranger's child, but Lord Sanabalis said—eloquently—that children are, in some metaphorical way, your hoard. And I therefore allowed him to talk me into this."

Sanabalis said nothing. His eyes were the normal gold of a Dragon, but his inner membranes were up.

"You heard Lord Sanabalis when he first set foot in the Leontine Quarter a handful of your days ago. You did not understand what he was saying."

She nodded.

"But Lord Tiamaris insists that you were speaking in the same tongue in the fiefs. Lord Tiamaris is young, and undereducated, a fact that has caused some discussion at Court. Only two living Dragons in the Empire can claim to speak the ancient tongue, but almost all Dragons would recognize it. I am uncertain that Lord Tiamaris is one of them.

"Therefore, Kaylin, you will speak to the child you now hold."

"What?"

"You gave your word, in the oldest tongue we know, to the child's mother. You will fulfill your word, and we two—Lord Sanabalis and I—will listen. And we will judge the risk based on what we hear. Do you understand? Lord Sanabalis did not argue for the child's survival. Given that the child presents a danger to the Emperor's hoard, it would not be possible to do so. It would certainly be unwise. What Lord Sanabalis argued for was the *possibility* of his survival, and this was granted—barely.

"I have no interest in the child, but I confess I have little interest in the Empire, either. I am also not responsible for your life in any way. I am therefore considered an unbiased judge. And jury."

His eyes seemed to grow, or the light in them did, until his face was suffused with it; he was hard to look at. But she looked because, conversely, it was impossible *not* to look at him.

"As you are unfamiliar with the tongue, I will guide you some part of the way. But only part. What you did in the fiefs, *I* could not do. Nor could Lord Sanabalis. What you did in the fiefs should not be possible. But neither, in the end, should you."

He began to speak. Kaylin couldn't understand a word he was saying, and she felt the ground drop beneath her feet. The fear that she hadn't felt upon first seeing the odd color of his eyes came in a rush, like unwelcome gravity might return to someone clinging by their fingers to a cliff's edge.

She couldn't *understand* him. The syllables sounded familiar, and in the growing light that surrounded him, she could *see* them begin to dance in the air, as they had danced for Sanabalis on that single day.

She must have clutched the baby too tightly, because he woke and began to cry.

"I will take him, kitling," Kayala said softly. The hush in the words was the only sign of reverence she showed. But the fact that it was there was unsettling. Her husband, Marcus, didn't feel any of the Leontine racial reverence for Dragons, or their magic. Or maybe he did. He wasn't one to let personal feelings get in the way of his job.

But she shook her head mutely and turned again to look at the words before her. Legal High Barrani had seemed like that, at one time. No, not quite—the individual Barrani words made sense, it was just the whole sentences that were as torture. These were different.

She tried to slip out from under the fear. It didn't help her—it almost never did. Right *now* she held the baby. Right *now* he was alive. She began to walk toward the Arkon. If he saw her, it changed nothing. He continued to speak, and she continued to struggle with the familiar cadences of a completely unfamiliar tongue.

But as she approached, she became aware of the tingle that stretched up the length of her back. It was uncomfortable, but it was welcome. She drew closer to the Arkon, and the tingling increased until it was actively painful. Shifting the baby's weight, she perched him carefully on her hip—which, given his age and lack of coordination, took a great deal more care than it did with Marrin's foundlings—and then reached out to touch one of the moving sigils.

She thought her hand would pass through it. It didn't. The symbol stilled in the air, and grew denser and brighter, as if the contact gave it form and shape.

"Sanabalis," she said, in a hushed voice, "can you *see?*"

"Yes," he replied, and his voice was equally hushed. "Is this what you saw when I spoke?"

She nodded. "I can't read it."

"Arkon?" Sanabalis said.

It was the space of ten very loud heartbeats before the ancient Dragon answered. "Yes. I see what you see."

"Kaylin, touch the others."

She nodded, not really noticing that he hadn't used her rank. She wished she had given Kayala the baby now because he was fussing, and the fussing was growing louder, and she had nothing to feed him.

She began to awkwardly try to rock him while she walked. She was lucky it didn't cause her to fall over. But while he fussed, she touched the words she could see, and as she did, they coalesced in dense, bright shapes, the movement of lines and squiggles and dots stilled.

It was only then that she realized the Arkon had ceased his story, if that's what these words were. No wonder the baby sounded so loud; everything else was utterly silent.

"Severn?"

"We can all see them," he replied. "As clearly as we can see the marks on your skin."

"Arkon, can you read them?"

The Dragon Lord—if that was the right word for him, Librarian just seemed wrong somehow—was moving, in a slow circle, from symbol to symbol. He reached out once, and then drew his hand back before it could make contact.

"Arkon?" Sanabalis said.

But he continued to walk, to stare and, eventually, Sanabalis said to Kaylin, "Cover the child's ears if you can, not that it will do much good."

"Cover his ears? Why?"

"I believe it best that we have the Arkon's attention. Elantran is not his first language. It is probably not his last, but there are a great many, most dead, in between. When he is absorbed with something, he tends to fall back on Dragon thoughts, and in general, our language is the best way to retrieve him."

"Got it," she said. She tried to cover the child's ears, but understood why Sanabalis was certain it wouldn't do much good.

Sanabalis *roared*. That sound, coming from an incongruously person-shaped throat, shook the entire room. If that's what they did to catch your attention when you were daydreaming, she never, ever wanted to see them at war.

The Arkon raised a brow. His eyes were still silver, but she could see some hint of gold emerging in their depths. "My apologies," he said, in his perfectly modulated, almost human voice. "I have not seen anything like this since I was all but a hatchling."

"Not even in Ravellon?"

Sanabalis covered his face with his hands. But the Arkon merely stared at Kaylin, as if seeing her for the first time. "Not even there," he said quietly. "And I gather, from the reaction of Lord Sanabalis, that you have been instructed not to ask."

She swallowed, bounced the baby and started walking in a fast circle. The Dragon's roar had momentarily silenced him—if by silence one meant the long intake of breath that precedes all-out screaming.

"Not there," he said again. "But I have wandered. What you saw in my speech is not what I see in the speaking. But I see it now. Bring the child, Kaylin Neya. Follow the path I walk. The words are not…in sequence, and not all of the words are present."

"Those are the ones I could see."

"Yes, and for that reason, they must be significant. What you did for Marai, I cannot do."

"I didn't *do* anything for her but let her die," Kaylin replied starkly.

The Arkon shook his head. "You did. You let her choose her form, and the moment of her death, and she accepted the limitation of *that form* to its end. She heard you," he added softly. "And I think…she heard the first story, the story of their creation *as it was spoken at their birth.* And she understood it."

"And you don't think she would have heard you?"

"I think it a pity that Tiamaris is so reluctant to take up his studies," was the severe reply. "But…I have doubts. None of us were Chosen." He held out a hand. It had the normal five fingers, it lacked claws, and yet it seemed, to Kaylin, utterly alien for all its semblance of the familiar. The baby was crying. Kaylin almost wanted to join him.

Instead, she took the Arkon's hand. And when the Arkon led her to the first word, which was not the first one she'd touched, she stopped before it. Without thinking she lifted the crying child into the radius of shed light, and his crying stopped.

She would have been embarrassed to admit that the first thing she did was make sure it hadn't somehow killed him. But she was also embarrassed to admit that she went out drinking with Teela and Tain. The baby's eyes were round… and blue.

"Kayala, what does blue mean?"

"Kitling?"

"Eyes. Eye color. What does blue mean?"

"That," the Matriarch of the Pridlea growled, "is a *Barrani* color." Which pretty much answered the question. "If his eyes look blue, they could be reflecting the light."

"Or capturing it," the Arkon said.

The baby reached out, and Kaylin lifted him closer to the light, and the shape that cast it. Human babies didn't have this much coordination. From Kayala's sharp intake of breath, Leontine babies probably didn't either.

But when his downy paws touched the word, the light slowly dimmed. He began to cry again. Her side was sore, and she was certain that running around in circles wasn't going to help. So Kaylin began to speak softly to the child. Nonsense words. Baby words. Soothing words.

Words.

The Arkon said nothing very loudly, and Kaylin had the grace to flush. But he was old enough to take care of himself, and the baby was, in the end, more important and immediate than her dignity. Nor did he choose to criticize her; instead he led, and she followed. At each sigil, the child quieted for a moment, and at each, he was lifted to touch some element of the word—a line, a dot, a stroke. When the light dimmed, he would cry, and when he cried, Kaylin would whisper or hum or even sing—because it seemed to help, and it was better than doing nothing.

The light in the room slowly faded. The blue of his eyes slowly grew.

And when the last word had dimmed, the darkened shells slowly faded from sight.

The Arkon frowned; he was staring at Kaylin. She realized this when Sanabalis cleared his throat loudly.

Before she could speak—or think of something to

say that wasn't baby nonsense—she felt a warmth at the base of her neck. She closed her eyes, and when she opened them, one last word hovered in the air before her face. It was golden in color, and the light it cast was not as bright as the light of the Dragon's words, but it was still recognizably the same language.

Her lips moved as she spoke it.

The child reached out, and she smiled at him, and lifted him one last time into the light. His paws batted a dot out of the way, and it left a smear of golden light in the air. He clearly liked this better than screaming, and he did it again. And again.

Half an hour later, when his lids grew heavy, the word faded, as if it had existed only to amuse and entertain; as if it were nothing more than a very fancy child's toy.

And she held him, and looked at the Arkon.

The Arkon bowed to her. It was a long, slow fold, and she had no idea what to say in return. But before she could try, Sanabalis touched her elbow; she looked at him, and he shook his head.

"I will speak with the Emperor," the Arkon said, when he rose.

"But—but—what will you tell him?"

"What I have seen."

"Will it—can we—is the—"

The Arkon winced and lifted a hand. "I have heard that you share a dislike of formal education with Lord Tiamaris," he said, "and I believe it best that you choose—as Lord Tiamaris does—silence. I do not understand what I have seen," the Arkon said. "But it bears study. I will recommend that we take the risk."

"Arkon," Sanabalis said, and offered the Imperial Librarian a bow as perfect, and as low, as the Librarian had offered Kaylin.

"I cannot speak for the Emperor, and I cannot therefore tell you what his decision will be. If he chooses mercy—and its attendant risks—there will be conditions placed upon the child's life."

She nodded.

"You may return to the Pridlea, if you desire its company. I will meet you there when I have finished."

Sarabe was somber and red eyed. The weeping—and there had obviously been weeping—was done. The guilt and the certainty that she might have been able to *do something* earlier to save her sister would take longer, and it would leave marks. Because guilt did.

Tessa, Graylin and Reesa surrounded her; the four wives were one big pile of fur. Somewhere in that pile were Sarabe's daughters; Kaylin could see the gold and gray of their fur in flashes, and could make out which limbs were theirs.

She held the baby and sat at a distance, watching. Severn sat apart as well, and that half smile she had felt in the fiefs adorned his face. So did new stitches and a couple of livid bruises. He caught her glance and the smile deepened as one of Sarabe's daughters snarled— a muffled sound—and bit one of her sisters. How she could even find one of her sisters to bite, Kaylin didn't know.

She loved to watch the Pridlea converge like this, but she needed to breathe more than they apparently did.

Kayala sat apart as well. "Sarabe will be fine," she

said. "She has us. And our husband. You did well, Kaylin."

"Marai died."

Kayala nodded. "But her son did not."

"Not yet."

As if on cue, the Pridlea Matriarch rose. "The Arkon is waiting for you in the hall. Will you take the child, or will you trust me with him?"

"How do you know he's out in the hall? And yes, I trust you with him. I trust you with anything I value in my life," she added. "Even Marcus."

Kayala snorted. She reached out and took the baby. "Your color is terrible, even for a human. You need sleep, kitling. Corporal, make sure she sleeps. And eats."

Severn nodded gravely, the smile still hovering on his lips.

"And I know he is there," Kayala said, when she'd settled the babe in her arms, "because I can smell him."

"What does he smell like?"

"A Dragon."

The Arkon offered Kaylin the same bow he extended to her at the end of their walk. Kaylin endured it self-consciously. She was used to people looking down on her; she was definitely not used to *this*.

Sanabalis was there as well; they were both wearing the same deep blue robes. If blue were blood, that would be its color, she thought.

"The child," the Arkon said, "will be allowed to mature. The Emperor has chosen to spare him."

"That took four hours?"

Sanabalis raised both brows, which was as much expression as she'd ever seen on his face.

The Arkon looked decidedly less respectful. "It took *only* four hours, and at that, only because we received word from the Lord of Hawks that your presence is required."

"Oh."

"The matter of where he will live, however, is undecided."

"He can't live here," she said flatly.

"It would be best for him if he did," the Arkon replied. "Among his own people, his origins will be known, and he will grow in the shadow of their fear. Is that the life you would choose for him?"

"No. But the Pridlea—"

"He is not their son."

"Sarabe is his aunt," she said, "and his only living kin."

"By Pride Law, that is not true."

"But—oh. You mean me."

The Arkon nodded.

"I can't raise a Leontine baby!"

"Perhaps. Perhaps not. But he has no legal kin save you."

"I can talk to Marcus—" She stopped. She thought about Orogrim. Thought about the lives that Sarabe and Marai had led. Sarabe had been lucky. And this child?

Kaylin loved the Leontines. She also loved being human. But her kind were standing with pitchforks outside of the Tha'alani Quarter, made stupid and ugly by fear.

"No," she said softly. "He can't live in the Palace. But...I think I know where he might be able to live."

EPILOGUE

"Rennick," Kaylin said, when Rennick ran by, cursing under his breath.

"What?"

"It's a dress rehearsal. You said a dress rehearsal is the last chance to fix problems. Just relax."

"It's a dress rehearsal in the nominal sense of the word," he shot back. He was running his hands through his hair. Watching him these past three days had been a bit of a revelation for Kaylin. Not that she hadn't seen him shouting before, because it was impossible to spend more than an hour with Rennick and avoid that, but because he was almost frenzied in his worry about little details. Costumes. Makeup. Stage props. Even the mages, who were generally held in awe, got the short end of his temper for somehow setting up lights in entirely the wrong way. That they did not reduce him to ash probably had more to do with his title as the *Imperial* Playwright than their own forbearance. No one could believe that the Emperor would miss him, but on the other hand, no one was certain that the Emperor wouldn't frown on disrespect done to a title he offered.

"And going bald is going to change that how?"

"Bald? What are you talking about?"

"She is, I believe, referring to the way you're pulling your hair," Sanabalis said, his voice dry enough to catch fire in the wrong type of sunlight.

"Oh. Ha-ha. Jenn, *not* that shrub. That's clearly marked on the back of the board—it goes to the left of the *well.*" He practically sprinted in the direction of the offense, and Kaylin shook her head.

It was true that the audience for this dress rehearsal was slightly out of the ordinary, but the Emperor had chosen to attend the *actual* first night. In his stead, Ybelline waited in the small audience, with her peers and the students of the Tha'alanari. It was *this* audience that worried Rennick. Truth be told, while he was sane enough to fear the Emperor's wrath, he privately didn't believe the Emperor could tell a good line from a bad one, and he wasn't overly concerned about his reaction.

But the Tha'alani reception—that was important, to Rennick. And at least for the first few weeks of the run, this was the *only* showing at which the Tha'alani would be in attendance. There was some wild speculation about a change in cast at that time, but Kaylin had been very carefully ignorant when asked. She had seen the striking woman that Rennick had grudgingly given the role of Tha'alani Castelord, and while that woman and Ybelline were never going to be the same, Kaylin knew it didn't matter. All she had to be was *good*.

She hadn't expected to see Evanton as part of the

stage crew, and he looked mildly surprised to see her, but Rennick was a smart, resourceful man. *I want the antennae to look real. I want them to look exactly like Tha'alani antennae.*

Evanton, therefore, had been dragged in by someone to achieve that startling effect. He considered it a waste of time, at first, but by the end of a few hours with Rennick, he had set about the work with something like passion. And while she had never thought of the wizened enchanter as a…makeup artist, she had to admit that he was worth whatever they paid him. Given what *she* had to pay him for her meager enchantments, she was sure it was a *lot*.

He wasn't in the audience, but he was somewhere backstage.

As were Dock and Cassie. Rennick was very careful, when dealing with the foundlings, to keep his voice even and his words clear; he even kept the growing obscenities to a minimum, and given what he'd been like the past few days, that was the most anyone could ask for. On the other hand, Marrin had also visited frequently. To give Rennick his due, he'd allowed it without a word. He admired the Leontine who had turned a hall for unwanted orphans into a personal cause.

"All right, everyone nonessential clear the stage. We're up in half an hour."

Kaylin was considered nonessential. Severn had already vacated the arena some time before. "Sanabalis," Kaylin said, "I'm going to find Ybelline."

"She'll be in the outer hall. They've turned it into a parlor."

In the two weeks since she'd woken in the infirmary,

her side had stopped aching and her wounds had completely healed. She was allowed to patrol her beat, although Marcus's long-suffering look made clear just what Moran would do to him if there were any incidents.

"I need to get her out of the office. She's bored, and she's causing unrest."

"And it's only for the morning," Kaylin said, trying to keep the desperation out of her voice. Two weeks of office work had convinced her that Marcus was, at heart, an absolute *saint*. "I'm still Rennick-watching in the afternoons."

"The point of patrolling is to be present when and if there's trouble," Moran said curtly. But in the end, she relented, because, as she said, she couldn't stand to see a fledgling batting its wings against the ceiling.

The Council of Elders accepted the Emperor's decree. They weren't happy about it, that much any moron could see—but they were respectful. Then again, it was Sanabalis who delivered the news. They were satisfied, however, by news of Orogrim's death, and Marcus was fully exonerated. If that word could be applied to the very, very informal Caste Laws by which they governed.

Kayala and the Pridlea still remained in the Palace, however. In the morning, if all went well, they would return home—and there would be a home; Marcus had been busy. He had taken time off to see to the "state of his home," and in that time, he had only paused once: for Marai's funeral.

It was very, very sparsely attended.

Sarabe and her children were there, as were Marcus and the rest of the Pridlea. Lord Sanabalis came, and Lord Tiamaris joined him. Severn brought Kaylin by

Imperial Carriage; she was still in theory confined to bed, but Moran had not argued about the funeral.

And that was it.

But it was enough, Kaylin thought.

Sarabe was not mentioned by the Elders. Or by Marcus. Kaylin wanted their collective word—preferably signed in blood—that they would never attempt to harm her; Marcus, however, seemed to trust them enough to bring his youngest wife home.

She wandered out into the Hall. The first person she saw was Severn, which, given the press of guests, servants and palace guards, said something. He smiled, detached himself from three Tha'alani—all younger than he was, by the look of them—and joined her.

"Are you ready?" he asked.

She nodded. "I think if we don't do this soon, Marcus will rip my throat out and eat it for breakfast. He misses the Pridlea," she said.

"Who wouldn't?"

They both wore dress uniforms. The Quartermaster had handed them over with a very grim warning about their condition, and the condition he expected them to be returned in. Given that they were expensive, and given Kaylin's history with uniforms, she would have worn rags if she'd been given any choice in the matter. But the Quartermaster was in the mood to forgive and forget. Or at least forgive.

She saw Ybelline in the small crowd, but it *was* a small crowd, and she didn't feel up to wading through it just to stand and bask in the glow of the Tha'alani Castelord's presence. And in any case, it wasn't Ybelline she was looking for.

It was Marrin.

Marrin had been invited to attend. She hadn't wanted to leave the Foundling Halls, and Dock and Cassie had had to work on her for days before she replied with an acceptance. The rest of the children were put out, of course, but Dock and Cassie had promised that they would all get to see the play at the *same time* as the Emperor, and this had mollified them.

Kaylin wondered if Marrin had changed her mind; she couldn't see her anywhere—and given that she was Leontine, it shouldn't have been that easy to miss her.

But twenty minutes before they were to take their seats, Kayala appeared in the hall. She was carrying a familiar bundle. "Kitling," she said, when she was close enough that she didn't have to shout. "Lord Sanabalis found Marrin and asked our permission to bring her to the Pridlea. She's with Sarabe, now. Do you have time?"

Kaylin nodded. She turned to Severn and hugged him—carefully—before she held out her arms. The broken arm was encased in splints, but it was mobile now.

Kayala smiled and handed Roshan to her. His eyes were still blue, but they seemed enormous to Kaylin, surrounded as they were by the sheen of healthy fur. He had sharp little teeth, unlike human babies, and he mewled like a kitten when he was hungry. Which was, as Kayala had warned her, all the time.

The Pridlea had kept him safe for two weeks now. And Kaylin had spent most evenings in the Imperial Palace, watching him, walking with him or feeding him.

She followed Kayala down the brilliantly lit Hall, past tables of food and drinks. Her stomach didn't fail to try to embarrass her, but the sound of conversation was loud enough to spare her, this time.

But Kayala stopped before they reached the wing that still housed the Pridlea. "Have you spoken with Marrin?"

"Not yet," Kaylin replied.

"Kaylin!"

"I didn't want her to say no," Kaylin replied.

"Kitling, that's almost dishonest."

"No, not dishonest. Just cowardly. Dishonest would be me telling Sanabalis that everything had already been arranged." She had the grace to flush.

"Lying to a Dragon Lord? The word *dishonest* is eclipsed by the word *foolhardy.*"

"Or brave. I always like that one."

Kayala swatted the back of Kaylin's head affectionately. It still hurt, but it was a good kind of pain. They walked the rest of the way in silence, and when they reached the door, Kayala placed her palm in its center with a grimace. "I never understood the fuss you made about these wards until now," the Matriarch said with a frown. "I swear, it makes every hair on my body stand on end."

Kaylin laughed as the door swung open. Sounds of Leontine conversation immediately flooded the hall, and Kaylin stood on the threshold for a long moment, savoring them. And then she entered, carrying Roshan with her.

Marrin was surrounded—literally—by Sarabe's girls. They were old enough to know better, but Marrin didn't correct them; it wasn't her job, and she seemed to enjoy indulging them. But she looked up as Kaylin entered.

"Kaylin," she said, rising. This took some time, but the girls did manage to untangle themselves enough to let her take a step or two without tripping her.

"Marrin—I was looking for you in the guest hall."

"Yes, well. This is a little more comfortable for an old Leontine, and I'm less likely to terrify the youngsters."

"The—oh. You mean the Tha'alani?"

"They seemed slightly intimidated by me."

"The Lord of Swords would be slightly intimidated by you," Kaylin said with a smile. The smile faltered slightly.

But Marrin's eyes were gold, and bright. "Is there something you want to tell me?"

One of Sarabe's daughter's giggled. Kaylin thought it was Leeandra, but couldn't be certain; they sounded very, very similar, even if you knew them. At least, Kaylin thought wryly, if you'd been born with human ears. She glared in the general direction of the giggle, which caused another round, and this time, there was no point in trying to pick out who'd giggled, because they were all doing it.

"I don't know how much you were told," Kaylin said hesitantly. "But—this baby—"

"Is Marai's child. Sarabe's sister."

Kaylin nodded gravely.

"Yes. I was told that." She didn't volunteer by whom.

"The Emperor has—has asked—the Elders to spare the child's life," Kaylin said, stumbling slightly on the words.

Marrin nodded gravely. "He is your son, by Pride Law."

"Yes, but I don't have a Pridlea," Kaylin replied. "I

don't live by Pride Law. I used it, yes—but I've studied the law. I know how to use it when I have to."

"And you had to, here."

"Yes. I didn't want him to die."

Marrin was still waiting, and she was waiting in utter silence.

"I wanted—I want—him to be raised in a Pridlea," she said quietly, looking for a moment at the baby's wide, curious eyes. "But I don't think he can be raised in the Quarter. He'll suffer too much, I think. People are stupid when they're afraid."

"Especially when there *are* grounds for their fear."

Kaylin hesitated, and then nodded. "But I don't want him to grow up like Orogrim. He had to die. And now that he's dead, it's safe to think about what he *might* have been like, if he hadn't spent his whole life knowing that the truth would be both feared and loathed. It's so easy to get twisted out of shape, when you're growing. And we don't *know* what he'll be."

Marrin nodded. She was absolutely still, now. Even the children—well, the almost-children—noticed.

And then, after a long, awkward silence, Marrin sighed. "I will take him," she said gently. "If that's what you are trying—very badly—to ask me." She held out her arms.

Kaylin looked at her. Yes, her eyes were golden, but they were filmed, Kaylin thought. Tears, something else, made the eyes glow in the soft light. "I can't think of anyone else I would rather have raise him."

She placed Roshan into Marrin's open arms.

Marrin kissed his forehead, and hugged him.

"It's not because of what you lost," Kaylin said

quietly. "It's because of what you *built*. What you made for other children that no one wanted. What you're *still* building day in and day out.

"And I know it's a lot to ask, I know—"

"Oh, hush," Marrin said softly, and there was something in her eyes, something in the baby's, the blend of blue and gold so natural and so profound in its simplicity, that made Kaylin want to weep.

She hushed up instead.

* * * * *

Domino Riley hates zombies.

Bodies are hitting the pavement in L.A. as they always do, but this time they're getting right back up, death be damned. They may be strong, but even Domino's mobbed-up outfit of magicians isn't immune to the living dead.

If she doesn't team up with Adan Rashan, the boss's son, the pair could end up craving hearts and brains, as well as each other....

Pick up your copy today!

  | **H** HARLEQUIN®
LUNA™ | ™ www.Harlequin.com

MICHELLE SAGARA

80283	CAST IN SECRET	___ $6.99 U.S.	___ $6.99 CAN.
80282	CAST IN COURTLIGHT	___ $6.99 U.S.	___ $6.99 CAN.
80254	CAST IN SHADOW	___ $6.99 U.S.	___ $8.50 CAN.

(limited quantities available)

TOTAL AMOUNT	$ _____
POSTAGE & HANDLING	$ _____
($1.00 FOR 1 BOOK, 50¢ for each additional)	
APPLICABLE TAXES*	$ _____
TOTAL PAYABLE	$ _____

(check or money order—please do not send cash)

To order, complete this form and send it, along with a check or money order for the total above, payable to HQN Books, to: **In the U.S.:** 3010 Walden Avenue, P.O. Box 9077, Buffalo, NY 14269-9077; **In Canada:** P.O. Box 636, Fort Erie, Ontario, L2A 5X3.

Name: _____

Address: _____ City: _____

State/Prov.: _____ Zip/Postal Code: _____

Account Number (if applicable): _____

075 CSAS

*New York residents remit applicable sales taxes.
*Canadian residents remit applicable GST and provincial taxes.

LUNA™ | HARLEQUIN®
™ www.Harlequin.com

LMS0911BL